Crime Files Series

General Editor: **Clive Bloom**

Since its invention in the nineteenth century, detective fiction has never been more popular. In novels, short stories, films, radio, television and now in computer games, private detectives and psychopaths, prim poisoners and overworked cops, tommy gun gangsters and cocaine criminals are the very stuff of modern imagination, and their creators one mainstay of popular consciousness. *Crime Files* is a ground-breaking series offering scholars, students and discerning readers a comprehensive set of guides to the world of crime and detective fiction. Every aspect of crime writing, detective fiction, gangster movie, true-crime exposé, police procedural and post-colonial investigation is explored through clear and informative texts offering comprehensive coverage and theoretical sophistication.

Published titles include:

Hans Bertens and Theo D'haen
CONTEMPORARY AMERICAN CRIME FICTION

Anita Biressi
CRIME, FEAR AND THE LAW IN TRUE CRIME STORIES

Ed Christian (*editor*)
THE POST-COLONIAL DETECTIVE

Paul Cobley
THE AMERICAN THRILLER
Generic Innovation and Social Change in the 1970s

Lee Horsley
THE NOIR THRILLER

Fran Mason
AMERICAN GANGSTER CINEMA
From Little Caesar to Pulp Fiction

Susan Rowland
FROM AGATHA CHRISTIE TO RUTH RENDELL
British Women Writers in Detective and Crime Fiction

Adrian Schober
POSSESSED CHILD NARRATIVES IN LITERATURE AND FILM
Contrary States

Heather Worthington
THE RISE OF THE DETECTIVE IN EARLY NINETEENTH-CENTURY POPULAR FICTION

Crime Files
Series Standing Order ISBN 0–333–71471–7
(*outside North America only*)

You can receive future titles in this series as they are published by placing a standing order. Please contact your bookseller or, in case of difficulty, write to us at the address below with your name and address, the title of the series and the ISBN quoted above.

Customer Services Department, Macmillan Distribution Ltd, Houndmills, Basingstoke, Hampshire RG21 6XS, England

The Rise of the Detective in Early Nineteenth-Century Popular Fiction

Heather Worthington

Lecturer in English Literature
Cardiff University

First published 2005 by
PALGRAVE MACMILLAN
Houndmills, Basingstoke, Hampshire RG21 6XS and
175 Fifth Avenue, New York, N.Y. 10010
Companies and representatives throughout the world

PALGRAVE MACMILLAN is the global academic imprint of the Palgrave Macmillan division of St. Martin's Press, LLC and of Palgrave Macmillan Ltd. Macmillan® is a registered trademark in the United States, United Kingdom and other countries. Palgrave is a registered trademark in the European Union and other countries.

ISBN-13: 978–1–4039–4108–4
ISBN-10: 1–4039–4108–4

This book is printed on paper suitable for recycling and made from fully managed and sustained forest sources.

A catalogue record for this book is available from the British Library.

Library of Congress Cataloging-in-Publication Data
Worthington, Heather, 1953–
    The rise of the detective in early nineteenth-century popular fiction /
    Heather Worthington.
        p.   cm. — (Crime files series)
    Includes bibliographical references (p.) and index.
    ISBN 1–4039–4108–4
    1. Detective and mystery stories, English—History and criticism.
    2. Popular literature—Great Britain—History and criticism.   3. English
    fiction—19th century—History and criticism.   4. Detectives in
    literature.   I. Title.   II. Series.

    PR868.D4W67 2005
    823'.08720908—dc22

                                                                    2004059166

10   9   8   7   6   5   4   3   2
14   13   12   11   10   09   08   07   06

Printed and bound in Great Britain by
Antony Rowe Ltd, Chippenham and Eastbourne

For David

Contents

Acknowledgements   ix

Introduction   1

1 Criminal Narratives: Textualising Crime   6
  1.1 Commodified crime: Murder for the masses   6
  1.2 Murderous illegalities: Legalised murder   9
  1.3 Murder for the literary classes   20
  1.4 Connoisseur of crime: De Quincey's defence of the
      'Murd'rous Art'   21
  1.5 Sensational literature and literal sensation: *Blackwood's*
      'Tales of Terror'   30

2 Making the Case for the Professionals   46
  2.1 Literary professional: Professional literature   46
  2.2 Preventive medicine: 'Passages from the Diary
      of a Late Physician'   49
  2.3 Legal treatments: Evidence of necessity   69
  2.4 Legal treatments: Proving the case   74
  2.5 Agent of the law: A gent of the law   79
  2.6 Accessory after the fact   97

**3 A Conspicuous Constabulary: or, Why Policemen
   Wear Tall Helmets**   103
  3.1 Police in literature: Literary police   103
  3.2 Transitional text, textual transition: From
      delinquency to detection   104
  3.3 A life, partly regular, partly adventurous   107
  3.4 The New Police: Perception and reception   115
  3.5 Preventive police or personal threat?   121
  3.6 A common sight: A site of
      commonality   130
  3.7 The profession of policing   140
  3.8 Dickens's 'Detective' Police   159

Conclusion   **170**
A rich inheritance   170

Notes   174

Bibliography   187

Index   198

Acknowledgements

This book is the product of my long-term addiction to crime fiction. What started as a tendency to align myself with the naughty characters in my childhood reading developed into a full-blown crime-fiction habit in my maturity. But, unable to confine my habit to recreational usage, I have allowed it to invade my academic life as well. Increasingly over the years I became dissatisfied with the traditional accounts of the origins and evolution of the detective figure that is so essential to most crime fiction. It seemed to me that such narratives were too simplistic, too easy and too much predicated on an informed retrospective perspective. There must, I felt, be other figures, other texts, other literary locations— an 'other' narrative of crime fiction. And what about factual accounts of crime and detection? That the framework of crime fiction relies heavily for its material on factual developments in crime, policing and on the law is self-evident, but this socio-historical framework of fact is largely absent from traditional accounts. And so I embarked upon a detective adventure of my own, seeking those other figures and other narratives in other locations. I am, though, not entirely alone, either in my addiction or in my detective work. Others share the guilt.

Foremost among these is Stephen Knight, who not only colludes with my addiction but has positively encouraged its development. His advice and assistance have been invaluable, and without his friendship, encouragement, and, when necessary, criticism, this book would probably never have been started, let alone completed. Also, I wish to thank Clive Bloom, whose editorial comments and advice have proved most helpful, and who has patiently put up with my questions and anxieties. I owe a debt of gratitude to my colleagues at Cardiff University both in the English Literature Department and in the Centre for Critical and Cultural Theory. Over the years they have been supportive of my work, and their own research and commitment have been informative and inspirational: coffee-time conversations and post-seminar discussions have played an important role in my detective work.

I am especially grateful to Martin Kayman, whose knowledge of crime fiction and cultural studies has sharpened my own approach and whose module on Nineteenth-Century Crime Fiction has allowed me to practise what I preach. Martin Coyle, while not directly involved in my work, has been an unfailing source of editorial advice as well as a friend. I would like to thank Peter Drexler, who read much of the manuscript in its early stages and whose comments encouraged me to continue; and Maurizio Ascari, who was also kind enough to read the manuscript and comment favourably. Sean Purchase kept an eye on my use of critical theory and saved me from excess and *faux pas*, and Louise Harrington provided not only wonderful IT support but also critical commentary and comfort in equal quantity.

My detective work took me to many strange locations. I would like to thank the librarians at Kendal Public Library for allowing me access to old copies of the *Westmorland Gazette*; the librarians at the Arts and Social Studies Library of Cardiff University, at Cardiff Central Library, at the Senate House Library of University College, London, and at Bristol University Library for allowing me to use their periodical collections; the staff at Glasgow University Library Special Collection; and the British Library, whose collections of nineteenth-century broadsides proved both fascinating and a fruitful source of untouched material. Further valuable sources of information were the River Police Museum at Wapping and the Metropolitan Police Museum, whose curators Bob Jeffries and Ray Seal were generous with time and help.

But the lion's share of gratitude must go to my family, most particularly my husband, David, who has been totally supportive, morally, emotionally, intellectually, and financially and who has put up with tears and tantrums as well as celebrations. My daughters Vikki and Pru have also always been there to listen and encourage me, as have my parents. My mother's and father's pride in my achievements has been an enormous incentive, while they also share the blame for encouraging me in my addiction to fiction. And finally, thanks to Audrey, with whom I shared many glasses of wine and on whom I tried out ideas and theories, but who still speaks to me.

Introduction

> The vast majority of detective, and indeed crime, stories written in the nineteenth century did not appear in book form, but in the pages of the elusive magazines and regularly appearing newspapers. This is the sea in which the detectives are born and first swim.
>
> Stephen Knight, *The Art of Murder*, 1998

The traditional narrative of the development of crime fiction as a literary genre follows a well-trodden, not to say beaten, path from Vidocq through Poe and on to Conan Doyle in what is a retrospective reconstruction of events. Through the lens of the fully fashioned, archetypal detective figure of Sherlock Holmes, it is a relatively easy task to discover similarities in earlier fictional figures associated with crime and to construct an apparently clear and coherent account. But as in crime fiction itself, things are rarely as straightforward as they might superficially appear. The Dupin stories (1841–1845) of Poe and the *Memoirs* (1828–1829) of Vidocq did not exist in a vacuum, but are the survivors of a mass of literature that, in various shapes and forms, had concerned itself with crime. Criminal narratives have existed throughout history, but, judging by the proliferation of such material, they reached new heights of popularity at the end of the eighteenth and beginning of the nineteenth century. And it was in the popular literature of the first half of the nineteenth century that many of the patterns and themes of the later fully-fledged genre of crime fiction were first articulated.

In this book I analyse some of the criminal narratives, factual and fictional, discovered in a trawl through the sea of ephemeral and periodical literature produced in this period. The results challenge the usual evolutionary theory of genre history. This material, I argue, is where crime

1

fiction has its origins, as the broadsides and periodical stories vary and develop the patterns found in the *Accounts* of the Ordinary of Newgate and in the *Newgate Calendars*. In the eighteenth century, and well into the nineteenth century, narratives of crime offering details of the criminal, the crime, the confession, and the consequent punishment most commonly appeared in the broadsides: cheap, single sheets of paper printed on one side only and available to a wide and socially disparate audience. The Ordinary of Newgate's *Accounts* told stories similar to those found in the broadsides, but were written at a slightly higher intellectual level, were more lengthy and complex in their account, and were more expensive, a factor which reduced their audience concomitantly. Over time, the *Accounts* coalesced into what became known as the *Newgate Calendars*—book-length collections of this criminographic material.

This developing genre of literature precariously balanced monitory, consolatory, and policing functions with the entertainment factor demanded by commercial interest: the narratives were, after all, produced for profit. Originating at a time when the social structure was based on a concept of small communities, the texts served to warn of the consequences of crime and therefore discourage others from criminal activities, and to suggest that crime was not rampant but was contained and containable. But in an increasingly urban and mercantilised society, as the textual strains, gaps, and fissures in the early nineteenth-century *Newgate Calendars* show, this system of crime control was no longer effective. Accounts of crime became more complex, a complexity which responded to the increasingly complex society in which they were produced. Crime and criminality were no longer a simple matter of discovery, confession, and punishment, and the problems evident in the penal and judicial systems were increasingly articulated in various forms in the criminal narratives found in the contemporary periodicals. In the early nineteenth-century context of new ideas about identity and society, the interest in matters criminal began to focus on the perpetrator of the crime and his or her motive rather than on the crime and its punishment. The existing simplistic accounts of criminality were no longer sufficient, and in the periodicals that proliferated at this time a debate was developed about the contemporary criminographic material which explored and exploited the already textualised criminal and his or her crime.

This intellectual appropriation of crime is particularly noticeable in *Blackwood's Edinburgh Magazine*, which first appeared in 1817 and which introduced the miscellany format to the periodical market. In this new format, fact and fiction, poetry and politics, history and social analysis coexisted, supplemented by book reviews, philosophical discussion, and satirical debates. It was in this last category in *Blackwood's* that Thomas De Quincey's defence of the 'Murd'rous Art' appeared, in his essay 'On Murder Considered as One of the Fine Arts' (1827), a piece which exemplified the intellectual appropriation of the subject of crime. It was also in *Blackwood's* that what became known as the 'Tales of Terror' were first published, stories of sensation and horror which often incorporated crime into their narratives. While the *Newgate Calendars* and the Ordinary's *Accounts* have been subject to in-depth analysis and discussion elsewhere, the broadside material and the *Blackwood's* criminography have received little scholarly attention. In the first section of this book, I seek to rectify this omission, and equally to fill in a gap in the traditional account of the development of crime fiction. I consider the form and function of the broadsides and their connections with and differences from the periodical accounts of crime.

Central to the accepted developmental narrative of crime fiction is the figure of the detective, and almost equally important is the case structure that is familiar to readers of crime fiction from Sherlock Holmes to the present day. Both the detective and the case had their origins in the criminography of the first half of the nineteenth century. Somewhat simplistically, these essentials of crime fiction are generally attributed to or extrapolated from Poe's investigative creation, C. Auguste Dupin. But I contend that the perceived necessity for a detecting figure and prototypes of such a being are to be seen first in the pages of the popular periodicals between 1820 and 1850. Initially, these periodical articles, often, but not always, concerned with crime, stand alone and do not interconnect or have any constancy, but in the 1830s this changes. Samuel Warren's 'Passages from the Diary of a Late Physician' offers a serial investigative figure, albeit in the field of medicine rather than crime, and brings into textual being the case structure that the work of a doctor necessarily requires and which becomes a recurring feature in later detective fiction. There is little crime *per se* in Warren's pseudo-autobiographical narratives, but there is a strong moral theme: moral misdemeanour is indissolubly linked with mental or physical malaise. What had proved successful and popular with the public in the case of medicine was readily mapped onto other professions. These pseudo-autobiographies of professional men proliferated at this time, and in the second section of this book I consider not only Warren's medical anecdotes, but the subsequent legal anecdotes of a barrister and an attorney, narratives where the investigative figures are working in the field of crime and felony rather than immorality, decadence, and disease.

These accounts created the discursive space for the detective in fictional literature, but concomitantly the detective made his appearance in factual literature and in reality. This was not the private detective so beloved of later crime fiction: rather, it was the police detective. There is a clear division between the policing of public and private, or domestic, spheres in the development of crime fiction, at least in the early stages: the former was achieved through overt, state-induced methods, the latter by means of ideology. A police was created by the state in order to control crime, and crime was seen as a trait of the poor that made problems for the rich. Crime or disorder in the upper tiers of society required a different treatment, in fiction if not in fact. But a discussion of the development of crime fiction would be incomplete without reference to the inauguration of the New Metropolitan Police in 1829 and an analysis of their role and the reception accorded to their presence on the London streets, and that is the focus of the third section of this book. Maintaining the principle of looking to popular literature for evidence of early crime-fiction patterns, I consider the only early nineteenth-century major fictional account of the work of a Bow Street Runner, a member of the organisation that preceded the New Metropolitan Police. I also examine the reportage that surrounded the beginnings of the New Police, both favourable and oppositional, and discuss the New Police themselves; Charles Dickens's incorporation of the police into his London 'Sketches' and his factual police detective anecdotes; and William Russell's series of professional anecdotes 'Recollections of a Police Officer' which appeared in *Chambers's Edinburgh Journal* from 1849 to 1853. In these 'Recollections' the investigative policeman is brought firmly into the public domain and public popularity.

The popular fictional accounts do not stand alone. The fiction is discussed in the context of and is accompanied by factual narratives concerned with crime and its control, with the problems of circumstantial evidence, and with the problems and implications inherent in policing a society whether by the use of ideology or the imposition of a state police or both. In conjunction with this social and historical material, I have drawn on Michel Foucault's work on the development of modern modes of power, specifically the emergence and role of what he calls disciplinary power. The fictional detective and his predecessors and prototypes, I suggest, are disciplinary figures with a disciplinary function in ideological terms.

Again following Foucault, I have here chosen to focus on the deviant and the marginal, both in the format of the material I have selected and in its criminal content. These marginal narratives are what come to construct and define the normative crime-fiction canon. Their fragmentary and elusive nature have also resulted in a somewhat deviant form for their display: this book comes not in chapters, but in three distinct sections, with further signposting to guide the reader through the appropriately Victorian 'baggy monster'. Crime fiction being not only deviant but also non-conformist, I can offer no coherent time-line across the three sections; rather, as the plot of a crime-fiction novel is convoluted, so is the temporal structure of this book. The first section considers the early material from circa 1800 to the mid-century; the second section covers the period 1830–1850 approximately; the third section covers roughly the same period but with a different focus. Overall, I offer a theoretically informed scholarly investigation into representations of crime and detection in the popular press from 1820 to 1850. My text incorporates narrative description and cultural and historical analysis to suggest that from the textualisation of crime and criminality emerges a genre: crime fiction. This genre functions not only to entertain, but to police its readers through the discipline of ideology and the depiction of the disciplinary detective. I end at a beginning; the narratives discussed here lay the foundations for the later, fully established genre, but that is material for another time and another place.

1
Criminal Narratives: Textualising Crime

1.1 Commodified crime: Murder for the masses

A broadside is an unfolded sheet of paper with printed matter on one side only—a proclamation, poster, handbill, or ballad-sheet. The form had been in existence since the sixteenth century, when the new printing technology made possible the production of almost instantaneous accounts of matters of public interest, functioning as an early form of journalism. The main function of ballads was to act as proto-newspapers, informing primarily the literate and illiterate lower classes of public events such as earthquakes, wars, murders, freaks of nature, and supernatural happenings. In the sixteenth century ballads concerned with criminality were the most popular, and in the nineteenth century criminal narratives had maintained, indeed increased, this popularity. Henry Mayhew, in his exhaustive exploration of the condition and earnings of the population of the metropolis *London Labour and the London Poor* (1851), estimated that 'Street-sellers of Executions &c' earned on average '9s. weekly' each, making the sum 'expended yearly, on executions, fires, deaths &c., in London £3,276'. This sum is exceeded only by the sales of popular ballads intended for singing (£4680), and of books (£5733).[1] Mayhew was writing in 1851 when literacy in the population had increased, and when a proliferation of cheap literature in periodical, book, and newspaper forms was widely available, but broadsides, particularly those concerned with the crime of murder and its punishment by execution, appeared to suffer no ill-effects from the competition.

The only complaint from the street-sellers Mayhew interviewed was the lack of outstanding cases of murder, for as one patterer commented, '[t]here's nothing beats a stunning good murder, after all'.[2] That there was an awareness of the competition posed by the newspapers in the

6

1840s and 1850s is made clear by the patterer who told Mayhew, 'it was better for us when newspapers was high'.[3] He was speaking of the rise of the untaxed and sensational weeklies and the fall in the price of newspapers after the reduction of stamp duty from 4d. to 1d. a sheet in 1836. This concentration on pecuniary matters is indicative of the fact that by the nineteenth century the motivation of the producers of broadside accounts of crime was purely and simply profit.

The profit motive was not a new phenomenon. The Ordinaries of Newgate had produced their *Accounts* as a way of supplementing their income, obtaining their information from the criminals in their charge. The writers of nineteenth-century broadsides, motivated by the same desire for financial gain but denied this direct access to the criminal, took their material from the newspaper accounts of crimes and the subsequent trials of the criminals, from local informants or witnesses, and, to a large extent, from their own imagination. While the reader is given names and dates which are accurate and verifiable, and graphic, detailed descriptions of the executions, so absolutely convincing in personal detail and horror that they appear to have been written by someone present at the event, in fact many of these were written before the executions they describe. When written after the event, they were often composed from rumour and press reports and were as much creative as factual. In the nineteenth century street ballads were printed to make money, and offered entertainment with a rough edge. The key word here is entertainment; to sell well, the broadsides had to entertain their audience, and they did so in the case of the criminal narratives by including as much graphic detail of violent crime and equally violent punishment as possible. There was some pretence to a moral and religious tone, but the broadsides made their appeal to the voyeuristic interests of the masses, exposing the gory and sometimes salacious details of the crimes and making public what had been private.

In the execution broadsides, the demonstration of sovereign or state power was encapsulated in pictures and prose and the spectacle of public execution reached a wider audience than would have been possible in reality. These broadsides represented the intrusion of the public gaze into the more usually private moment of death: the theatricality inherent in the ritualisation of the actual event is duplicated in the affective writing of the textual version. Michael Hughes proposes that execution broadsides 'by permitting vicarious participation, made the horrific concrete and tolerable, even, by their stylised, ritualistic descriptions, giving it dignity and controlled passion', but this proposal is subverted by the relish with which the broadsides depicted the not infrequently botched executions.[4] For Thomas Laqueur, '[t]he hangings and beheadings of seventeenth-, eighteenth- and nineteenth-century England [...] were more risible than solemn as they lurched chaotically between death and laughter'.[5] Gatrell, although arguing that '[s]caffold ritual represented authority, with [...] execution crowds gathered to witness a statement made by sovereign power', admits that there was 'a carnival element [...] in the hubbub and movement of people and in the commercialization of the event'.[6] However serious the reality of crime and execution, the broadsides were written primarily as cheap entertainment, and any cathartic effect they may have had was secondary to their primary function as commodities within a specific social sphere.

That this literature remained in the domain of the lower orders is evident from Mayhew's account of the sellers of street literature, from its low cost, which placed it within the economic reach of the poor, and in its form and content. The criminal broadsides in particular relied heavily on dramatic presentation and sensational content to promote sales. The emphasis on saleability and hence profit, in keeping with the commercial developments of capitalism, constructs crime and criminality as a commodity. The broadside accounts of crime, while paying lip-service to the notion of functioning ideologically as monitory devices against the evils of crime, were in fact primarily written to sell in large numbers. They appealed directly to the lowest common social denominator and relied on the prurient and voyeuristic tendencies of the masses and their seemingly insatiable desire for vicarious terror and cheap thrills. These texts constituted much of the literature of the lower orders, and articulated their culture. An anonymous writer in the *National Review* said of street literature that it was 'almost all written by persons of the class to whom [it] is addressed', figuring it as the literature of the people and for the people.[7]

Increasing literacy among the lower classes increased the potential audience for the broadsides, while their content tended simultaneously to confine the readership to that specific market; but circulation does not appear to have been entirely limited to the lower orders. Richard Altick observed that

> although respectable London families would not themselves be seen buying broadsheets describing the most recent outrage, they would send a footman out to buy half a dozen copies from a street hawker. The passion for real-life murder [...] prevailed as well by the firesides of the middle class and [...] more covertly, in the stately halls of the aristocracy.[8]

Class distinctions aside, the appeal of criminal narratives found no boundaries of age or sex. One of Mayhew's informants stated that 'murders are bought by men, women and children'.[9] This socially undifferentiated audience corresponds to the crowd that attended executions, and hence the criminal broadsides were implicated in the structures of sovereign power, speaking to the mass of the people rather than the individual subject.

The social specificity of audience for the broadsides is evident in the texts themselves, apparent in the language, form, and content; unlike those other collected criminal narratives, the *Newgate Calendars*, which were written largely by educated men and contained much factual and unsensational material, the broadsides were written in a very different register. Using simple, emotive language, with illustration wherever possible, and verse to make the content more easily memorable, these texts worked directly to have an affective impact on the reader, creating vivid word-pictures to dramatise the reality they purported to represent. Hastily composed and carelessly printed, the broadsides exemplify form following content, doubly debased, with the shoddy workmanship of their construction reflecting the degenerate material of the text. But their effect with regard to the criminal remained constant. He or she becomes a text to be read, and, as a closer consideration of these texts will show, in the nineteenth-century broadsides the criminal's unmediated voice is rarely, if ever, heard. Within a system of sovereign power where crime is constituted as an attack on the sovereign and it is the crime, rather than the criminal, that is punished, the criminal in text and reality is reduced to functioning merely as the signifier of crime and punishment. The textualised loss of individuality is paralleled in economic terms: in a capitalist economy founded on profit, the criminal individual, objectified in the textual representation, is part of a monetary transaction which provides a momentary diversion in the purchaser's drab life and a small profit for the vendor.

1.2 Murderous illegalities: Legalised murder

Bearing print on only one side and relatively small in size, the physical structure of the broadside was instrumental in shaping the format of its text. Factual or fictional, this format was the same. The title, printed in heavy black type, dominated the sheet and trumpeted its contents, for example, 'HORRID MURDER, Committed by a young Man on a young Woman' or 'Execution of JAMES NESBETT for the Horrible Murder of Mr. Parker & his Housekeeper'. The majority of broadsides carried a woodcut or engraving usually, but not always, appropriate to the subject. Sheets relating to the actual crime would use, wherever possible, a woodcut which at the very least depicted a murder, even if the method did not always match the actuality. Broadsides relating to trials and executions, when illustrated, carried depictions of the execution scene or a likeness of the criminal, and sometimes both. The execution woodcuts were standardised, featuring either simply the hanged individual, face concealed and suspended from the scaffold, or using a widescreen perspective that included the crowd and the condemned. In the latter, the crowd is generally foregrounded, with Newgate Prison to one side, the church of St Sepulchre in the background, and a standard representation of the gallows, with the criminal or criminals hanging from it, superimposed on the whole.

This gallows image could be altered according to the number of prisoners being hanged at any one time, a device that had the beauty of simplicity and was cost-effective, allowing the same woodcut to be used many times. A similar device was used for the perpetrator of the crime and the same likeness appears for different criminals. As one of Mayhew's informants observed: ' "Here you have also an exact likeness" they say, "of the murderer, taken at the bar of the Old Bailey!" when all the time it is an old wood-cut that's been used for every criminal for the last forty years.'[10] In famous cases such as that of John Thurtell or the Mannings, the patterer goes on to say, likenesses were done expressly for the newspapers, but there was nothing to prevent those likenesses then being used in subsequent cases. The individual is essentially irrelevant in these depictions; all that matters is the added impact that illustration gave the broadside. Today, surrounded by pictorial imagery, it is hard to imagine the impact of pictures on early nineteenth-century readers, and the broadside illustrations may well have been among the few available to the poor.

Illustrations frequently dominate the broadside accounts of crime, but in tandem with, or sometimes replacing, these pictorial representations, there would often be a 'copy of verses'. Many criminal broadsides consisted entirely of prose, but the influence of their historical forebear, the ballad, lingers in those accounts of crime written in verse. Such verses told the story of the crime and its consequences, and were set to well-known tunes which enhanced their memorability and made them familiar. A typical example is 'The Outrage & Murder on a Little Child at Purfleet', the story of six-year-old Alice Boughen, who was raped and murdered by a soldier-schoolmaster. There is a terse prose account, but the greater part of the broadside is in verse, with the suggested tune of 'Just before the Battle Mother' as its heading, and the opening lines:

You parents dear that Love your children,
Just listen to this dreadful deed,
A little girl she has been murdered,
It will cause each mother's heart to bleed.[11]

The affective and emotive language of the verses invokes sympathy rather than empathy in the reader, and has a monitory function, warning against the criminal acts related and illustrating the potential results of parental negligence with regard to children. The whole offers a condensed, musical, and hence mnemonic account which appealed to illiterate or semi-literate individuals, who could memorise the verses read out to them, a process further assisted by the use of stock phrases in the rhymes.

Many of the verse accounts opened with a variation on 'Come all you wild and wicked youth', for example 'Come all you thoughtless young men' or 'Come all you feeling Christians'. Such opening lines positioned the verses as exemplary, or enlisted the sympathy of the reader/hearer on behalf of the victim or the mourning relatives. Occasionally the criminal voice seems to speak directly to the reader, in verses which claim to have been written by the condemned man or woman. These supposedly offer a remorseful account, in the criminal's own words, of the various crimes. This strategy is made problematic by the moment of execution, where the criminal voice is once more silenced, and of necessity replaced by a narrating and often admonitory voice. In fact, all the verses were composed by a select group of writers or 'penny-a-liners' commissioned to produce specific pieces by the broadside publishers. Where prose and verse appeared on the same sheet, there was a difference in register between the two. The prose account incorporated some legal and technical language in the description of the crime and the practical details of the trial and execution, while the more sensational material of the verses was in much simpler language, speaking directly to its intended audience.

The audience was not only necessary to the profitability of the broadsides, but also an important component in their composition. Dramatic imagery is central to the textual representations of that staging of the sovereign's power and retribution which is figured in the spectacle of execution, and drama presupposes an audience. The prose and verse accounts required the active participation of the reader or listener in visualising the sensationalised dramatic images contained in the text. In the illustrated broadsides, life mimics art, implicitly including the reader in the audience which it depicts, watching with it the melodrama of execution being played out on the stage of the scaffold. The often-detailed depiction of the crowd as opposed to the small and indistinct representation of the scaffold and its victims has led Laqueur to figure the crowd as the central character in the drama.[12] But, in the context of my argument, the symbolic function of the scaffold image as an iconic rather than representational signifier of sovereign power is enhanced and emphasised by the lack of detail, while the smallness of the image and the perspective draw the eye. As in a theatre, the gaze is guided to and focused on the stage, or in this case, the scaffold, and its occupants. Theatricality is not confined solely to the configuration of the broadside illustrations: there is an element of dramatic structure in their prose. The divisions of the criminal text function in a fashion similar to the acts of a play. In varying order, and not always represented, are 'the crime', 'the capture', 'the verdict', 'the sentence', 'the confession', and 'the execution'. Within the 'acts' of this criminal drama, moral tone is lent by the reported words of a chaplain or judge, by the narrator, or by the purported words of the repentant criminal. The phraseology and interchangeability of these confessions, last words, and 'letters', which claim to reproduce the voice of the criminal, figure them rather as dramatic scripts than as reports of reality. Their voices silenced and their speech rewritten, the criminal individuals become characters in the drama and pawns in the play of power, reduced to two-dimensional representations which efface individuality and subjected to a script which prescribes their speech.

For a penny the purchaser of the criminal broadside can, positioned by the broadside with the crowd, vicariously participate in a melodrama of crime and punishment made all the more sensational by its affective treatment of, and connection to, reality. But the criminal content of these sheets, and the sometimes graphic illustrations which match the equally graphic prose, implicate the reader in a voyeuristic framework which replicates the prurient interest of the crowd in attendance at an actual execution. The pornography inherent in the broadside depictions of violent, often sexual, crime arouses and exploits a similar prurience in the reader. Detailed accounts of rape, murder, infanticide, and other acts of violence are common to both fictional and factual broadsides, with the factual versions borrowing from the style of the fictions or becoming classed as 'cocks', that is, accounts which may have had their origins in fact, but which over time and with repeated publication came to be regarded as fictional. One such 'cock', offered by Catnach, is the 'Shocking Rape and Murder of Two Lovers, Showing how John Hodges, a farmer's son, committed a rape upon Jane Williams, and afterwards Murdered her and her lover, William Edwards, in a field near Paxton.' Jane Williams is accosted by Hodges in a field, where he makes 'vile proposals' to her. On her refusal, 'he threw her down, and accomplished his vile purpose'. When Jane's lover appears on the scene and attacks her assailant, Hodges uses the bill-hook with which he had been threatening the girl to 'cut the legs clean from [Edwards's] body', and then kills the girl.[13] Sex and violence go hand in hand, in an exercise guaranteed to shock and titillate its audience.

A further example of a 'cock' is 'The Committal of W. Thompson, for the Murder of His Wife and Three Children', which glosses over the sexual motivation of the murderer, instead playing on the sensibilities of the audience with its emphasis on child-murder. There is a succinct prose account of the murder, a brief confession, and then the gruesome details are recounted in the accompanying 'copy of verses':

> Soon as the house he entered, he straightway locked the door,
> Soon seized upon an iron bar, and threw her on the floor;
> With which he beat her on the head as she lay on the ground,
> Her brains most awful for to view, lay scattered all around.

> Oh then he seized those lovly [sic] twins, while sleeping
>   on the bed,
> Now with your mother you shall die, the wretched father said—
> He seized them by their little legs, and dashed them
>   on the floor,
> And soon their tender lives were gone, alas! to be no more.

The doggerel goes on to describe the vain pleas for mercy from the remaining child:

> Again for mercy he did plead, whilst pearly tears did fall,
> The cruel father's hardened heart, was deaf unto his call—
> Again took up the iron bar, and beat him on the head,
> And soon the blood of the dear boy, was spilt upon the bed.[14]

Maintaining the public appetite for broadside entertainment required a steady supply of material, and Mayhew's interviewees admitted to the sale of 'cocks' when there were no real crimes to tout around the streets. Some stories had been in circulation for so long that they became 'classics'. Examples of these are 'The Scarborough Tragedy': 'It's about a noble and rich young naval officer seducing a poor clergyman's daughter. She is confined in a ditch [i.e. gives birth], and destroys the child. She is taken up for it, tried, and executed. This has had a great run.'[15] The 'Liverpool Tragedy' is about a couple who fail to recognise that the man they are killing for his money is in fact their long-lost son. There are no distinguishing marks to differentiate these 'cocks' from the factual broadsides other than the absence of dates and often a vagueness about specific location. Fact and fiction blur together: the fictional broadsides laid claim to authenticity, and may often have had their origins in fact.

Conversely, the factual broadsides, while authenticated in their contemporaneity, simultaneously invented much of their content, embroidering the bare facts of the crime, attributing unsubstantiated motives for the criminal's actions, and imagining the condemned criminal's last words. Their use of factual material was selective, the most sensational details being extracted from the dry accounts of arrest, imprisonment, trial, and punishment. The purchaser of both factual and fictional broadsides was seeking diversion from everyday life, and read the criminal literature for prurient and voyeuristic, sometimes pornographic, pleasure rather than information or education. The reader of such material made no attempt to analyse the broadside content or question its authority. There is no need of explanation or translation as the text speaks directly to its reader in the simple language of the verses or the symbolic imagery of the illustrations. The broadsides function as sensational commodities: the crime is central to the account, the criminal merely the physical referent of the act. There is no investigation of the psychology of the perpetrator, no questioning of his or her guilt: these texts generate no necessity for a detecting figure.

The detailed content of the factual 'gallows literature' as opposed to the fictional 'cocks' is no less gruesome, but its relation to reality and the specifics of dates, places, witness statements, medical reports, and so on enhance its sensationalism and make it more shocking, at least to the modern reader. A direct factual comparison with the William Thompson child-murder 'cock' is the case of John Gleeson Wilson, tried and executed in 1849 for the murder of two women and two children. Headed by the standard execution illustration, with scaffold, crowd, Newgate Prison, and St Sepulchre, in spite of the hanging actually having taken place in Liverpool where the murder was committed, the prose account is short and factual, giving brief details of the crime, the trial, and the execution. It reveals the entertainment aspect of both the execution and its own representation of the case in its final line: 'Upwards of 100,000 persons were present, the railway running cheap trains from all available parts.'[16] The spectacle is doubly commodified, with railway owners making a profit from the extra sales of tickets generated by the event and the broadside sellers and publishers profiting from the increased audience and hence potential customers.

Following the prose section, as seen in the Thompson 'cock', there is then a 'copy of verses', which dwells on the injuries inflicted by the murderer, cloaking its relish in the authority of the surgeon who examined the bodies:

The surgeon thus describes the scene presented to his view,
A more appalling case than this he says he never knew,
Four human beings on the floor all weltering in their gore,
The sight was sickening to behold on entering the door.

The mother's wounds three inches deep upon her head and face,
And pools of blood as thick as mud, from all of them could trace,
None could identify the boy, his head was like a jelly;
This tragedy is worse by far than Greenacre or Kelly.[17]

The lilting, almost jolly, meter of the verse to some extent mitigates its grim content, and reiterates the entertainment aspect of the broadside. Simultaneously, the affective element of the purple prose and the overt violence it portrays creates a cathartic response in the reader, purging his or her emotions in its evocation of pity and fear.

Graphic violence always ensured good sales for the broadsides, but as the 'cock' about the rape and murder of Jane Williams illustrates, sex and violence were an irresistible combination. According to Gatrell, '[i]n the second quarter of the nineteenth century a good quota of murderers [...] dismembered their female victims as if there were a fashion that way', and the murderer Greenacre, mentioned in the 'verses' which accompany the John Gleeson Wilson account, is a case in point.[18] James Greenacre, deceived by his betrothed Hannah Brown about the size of her property and incited by drink, beat her savagely, and, according to popular myth, finally knocked her unconscious with a rolling pin.[19] He then killed her, and disposed of the body by dismembering it and depositing the (wrapped) pieces in different parts of London. This in itself is sensational enough, but the broadsides enlarged, expanded, and illustrated the case in pornographic and gory detail. The dismemberment of the victim permitted the depiction of the sexualised female body. In a broadside held in the British Library the central illustration is the victim, compartmentalised into stylistically feminised sections: torso, curvaceous and full-breasted; legs, shapely and still wearing stockings with bow-ornamented garters; and the severed head with cupid lips and surprised eyes. There is then a further illustration, purporting to represent the head 'as preserved in spirits in the Workhouse at Paddington' awaiting identification.[20]

In contrast, Catnach's account of the 'Life, Trial, Confession and Execution of James Greenacre' is on first impression more muted. It is headed by a suitably villainous portrait, supposedly of the murderer, and then offers a long prose section, without accompanying 'verses' or any further illustration. It is in the body of the text that the sensationalism lies, couched in the authoritative voices of the attending surgeons, Birtwhistle and Girdwood. The former 'deposed, that he had carefully examined the head; that the right eye had been knocked out by a blow inflicted while the person was living [...] the head had been separated by cutting, and the *bone sawed nearly through'*. Girdwood's contribution was to show 'incontestibly, that the head had been severed from the body *while the person was yet alive*; that this was proved by the retraction [...] of the muscles [...] where they were separated by the knife, and further, by the blood vessels being empty, the body was drained of blood'.[21] In both these accounts, the criminal takes second place to the victim and it is the victim's body which speaks. Catnach's version, although appropriating medical discourse in order to shock, is early evidence of forensic detection in its reading of the body to reveal the cause of death. The first account is overtly and sexually pornographic with its illustration of the dismembered female body, while the second, confining itself to prose, is more covert in its scientific intrusion into the hidden places of the physical body.

The sensational and entertaining presentation and content of the criminal broadsides, calculated to generate profit, may on the surface appear to subvert the function that I earlier suggested for them, that is, to disseminate the spectacle of sovereign power and reinforce its status. Certainly Laqueur considers that public executions in England, and thus implicitly their representations in the broadsides, 'were unpromising vehicles for the ceremonial display of power, if by this is meant the sovereign power of the state'.[22] I suggest that he is telescoping several hundred years of executions into an apparently short time frame and conflating rural and metropolitan practices; certainly the executions of the nineteenth century appear to have been carried out on the whole with a certain authority. Laqueur's work is further undermined by his statement that 'the imposing facade of Newgate itself [...] was also studiously ignored in most popular prints'.[23] My own research would suggest precisely the opposite: Newgate Prison is invariably represented in the broadside accounts of executions; not necessarily as central to the illustration, but present as a reminder of secular state authority, while the church of St Sepulchre represents a related and validating higher power.

These reminders of state power and the religious authority which supported that power meant that the execution broadsides functioned as the signifiers of sovereign power. But, although dissociated from the actuality of what they signified, the urban mediation of the broadsides contains an element of disciplinary power in its demonstration of control over the individual. Within the event of execution itself, the reality of the state's vengeance on the criminal individual is represented in a series of ritualised acts which reduce the participants to signifiers. The processional from the condemned cell in the company of the prison chaplain; the pinioning of the criminal; and the covering of the head which effaces his or her individuality: these prescribed and ritualistic stages of the execution process convert the criminal individual into a signifier of crime. The other participants in the scenario, hangman, chaplain, and sheriff, signify the power of the state, while the scaffold is the symbolic stage on which the drama is played out. There is no space for individuality in this system of signification: the identities of the criminals become synonymous with the crime they have committed, and the aberrant criminal individual is absorbed into the robotic citizen model required by sovereign power. In the broadside accounts, the crudity of the illustrations reiterates the iconic status of the spectacle of execution: sovereign power, faceless and nameless but visible in its signification, is articulated in the anonymous figure of the criminal.

Essential to this signification of power were anonymity and the displacement of individuality, whether in actuality or in its broadside representation. The disruption resulting from the intrusion of reality into the ritual figured in the reinstatement of the individual can be seen in the description of the execution of Charles Thomas White. The details of White's crime and execution are in an undated broadside from Catnach. White, accused of arson, is described as an 'unfortunate young man' who initially protested his innocence, arguing that 'what could have been his motive to commit so flagrant a crime, when his circumstances were not embarrassed, and his prospects flattering'.[24] He finally confessed his guilt, pleading temporary insanity, but to no avail. The broadside makes much of White's terror at the thought of his death—'the bare contemplation of the awful moment of execution unmanned him'—and dwells at length on the manner of his demise:

> White [. . .] raised his arms, and extended his chest, as if desirous of bursting the cords, and by the effort loosened his wrists. The cap was drawn over his eyes [. . .] he bent his head down, and pushed off the cap [. . .]. The action was made with so much strength and violence,

and his struggling appearing to increase, that a dreadful yell, and cries of the utmost horror burst from the crowd [...] he leaped upon the platform, and by sinking his head, was able to grasp that part of the cord which was affixed round his neck under his chin. It appeared to be a desperate effort to prolong that life which he so fondly clung to. At this moment, the spectacle was most horrifying— he was partly suspended, and partly standing on the platform. During the violence of his exertions, his tongue was forced out of his mouth, and the convulsions of his body and the contortions of his face were truly appalling [...]. The distortions of his countenance, in the agonies of death, could be seen by the crowd.[25]

This return of the real into public consciousness disrupts the barrier, figured in the edge of the stage in conventional theatre, which prevents the spectator entering into the 'reality' on the stage. Such a disruption brings the spectator into the scene and, in the spectacle of execution, forces the recognition of reality. The silenced criminal signifier is reconstructed as an individual, whose distorted face and contorted body speak for him, and in this sense he becomes a victim as the disruption of the symbolism and drama of execution reveals it to be the state's destruction of the individual. The recuperable identity of the criminal individual subverts the spectacle of sovereign power and is indicative of the gradual move towards ideologically disseminated disciplinary power and its focus on and internalisation by the individual subject.

The audience reacted strongly to the spectacle of White's agonising and protracted death, making its displeasure evident vocally and threatening to disrupt the proceedings. As the text states: 'The crowd were greatly affected by the horrid sight which they had witnessed.'[26] In contrast, White's companion on the scaffold, Amelia Roberts, who went calmly to her death, face covered and unresisting, aroused no such response. The reduction of the individual to a signifier, as well as increasing the symbolic effect of execution, to some extent protected the audience from the reality of what they witnessed. Gatrell suggests that for scaffold witnesses, 'what they watched was fearsome if experienced too closely', and the re-emergence of the individual from the ritual would certainly have closed the distance between the spectator and the focus of the spectacle, that is, the condemned man or woman.[27] In White's case, the broadside account textualised the event, converting it into a sensationalised and affective entertainment and commodifying it. The crowd's reaction becomes part of the affective construction of the broadside, the distance between viewer and victim is reopened, and the purchaser of the broadside can share the experience at second-hand without the direct horror of the reality. Further, the broadside account reinstates the function of execution in the maintenance of sovereign power in its closing words: 'we trust this example will have its due effect upon the minds of the thoughtless and wicked'.[28]

The inscription of the individual and his or her sensations into the text, while not permitting him or her a voice, nonetheless speaks directly to the reader of the account. The sensationalism inherent in vicariously sharing the individual's experience, criminal or otherwise, will be central to what came to be known as the 'Tales of Terror' in *Blackwood's Edinburgh Magazine*. The experience of the individual will characterise the criminal narratives of the middle and upper classes, and the crude sensationalism of the broadsides will be replaced by the more subtle psychological sensationalism derived from an empathic presentation of crime and criminality encapsulated in literary prose. No longer merely the signifier of crime, the criminal is reinstated at the centre of his or her narrative and performs a different function. The focus on the criminal and his or her fate locates the text as a warning to the individual reader: this is not so much a warning against committing crime, but against becoming a criminal. Rather than the overt statement of sovereign power embodied in the spectacle of execution, the reader internalises the covert warning against following the criminal example: he or she is subjected to what is in effect the discipline of ideology. This reinstatement of the criminal individual also permitted and encouraged an understanding of the criminal, which in the reformist climate of the time offered the possibility of the recuperation and reformation of the criminal individual as a productive subject.

As the old systems of discovering crime and punishing its perpetrators were seen to be failing in the urbanised, industrialised, and increasingly secular world, so the evidence of this failure and the search for a solution to the problem can be found in the criminography of the literary periodicals. With the focus on the individual, proximity and possibility are no longer sufficient proof of criminality; motive and method are required to give meaning to the criminal act. Circumstantial evidence is no longer perceived as wholly reliable, neither are the statements of witnesses to be accepted as the unvarnished truth. The perception of such instabilities in the system is evident in the proliferation of narratives concerned with the wrongful accusation of the innocent. The perceived necessity for protection of the innocent as much as for the prosecution of the guilty, in conjunction with the need to know the criminal's motives and methods are major factors in the generation of the detective figure.

1.3 Murder for the literary classes

The criminal narratives contained in the broadsides share with the *Newgate Calendar* the raw material of crime. But, while in the nineteenth-century editions of the *Calendar* there are indications of an unease with the existing system, a questioning of the quality of evidence and doubts about the justice of the penalties which suggest a recognition of the individual, the broadsides' textualisation of the criminal shows almost none of these concerns. The crime is central to the account; the criminal individual is subsumed into a signifying system constructed to generate profit, a system which relies on sensationalism, that is, on the incitement of physical and psychical effects in its audience. To achieve this end, the writers of the criminal broadsides appealed to the voyeuristic and prurient aspects of their audience, fulfilling the public's desire for sex and violence whether in the reportage of violent crime or in the accounts of its equally violent punishment. Martin J. Wiener refers to public execution as 'a pornographic invasion of the integrity of the body, carried out in public by the agents of the state', an invasion which, in the interests of sensationalism and the generation of profit, the broadsides promoted and disseminated.[29] Simultaneously, the broadsides were a vehicle for the dissemination of the statement of sovereign power inherent in such public spectacles.

The format and content of the criminal and execution broadsides were calculated to appeal to a particular social stratum, being the literature of the 'lower orders'. Yet public interest in crime and criminality was not confined to the poor and the emergent working class: the propertied middle and upper classes had a vested interest in the prevention of crime, as criminality was perceived to be a direct threat to property. The exemplary function of the spectacle of execution was unnecessary for the educated and wealthy, and in the increasingly reformist mood of the 1830s and 1840s many voices, including those of Dickens and Thackeray, were heard speaking out against public execution. The attendance at executions that prompted both authors to put pen to paper on the subject is indicative of the interest shown in crime and punishment by members of social classes other than the purchasers of broadsides.

As one of Mayhew's informants stated: 'Gentlefolks won't have anything to do with murders sold in the street; they've got other ways of seeing about it.'[30] 'Gentlefolks' had access to books—factual accounts of crime such as the *Newgate Calendars* and the fictional narratives of the Newgate novels—and periodicals.[31] Most newspapers carried factual reports of crime, although the gory details depicted in the broadsides could also be found in the cheaper weekly and Sunday papers which proliferated in the 1840s and 1850s and which borrowed heavily from the sensational presentation of the broadsides, using illustration and purple prose to entertain the reader and increase sales. But it was the literary periodicals, particularly the new miscellanies of the 1820s and 1830s exemplified by *Blackwood's Edinburgh Magazine* and imitators such as *Fraser's Magazine*, whose fictional offerings filled the gap in the market, providing an acceptable and respectable version of criminography in an intellectualised format. And it was in the pages of *Blackwood's* that Thomas De Quincey's spirited defence of the 'Murd'rous Art' was published in 1827.

1.4 Connoisseur of crime: De Quincey's defence of the 'Murd'rous Art'

That the prurient interest in violence and death, whether in illicit acts such as murder and rape or in the legalised murder of public execution, was not limited to the lower orders in both the intellectual and social sense is evidenced in the work of Thomas De Quincey. Highly intelligent and from a well-to-do middle-class family, De Quincey was to make his living from journalism, writing for periodicals such as the *London Magazine*, *Tait's Magazine*, and later, *Blackwood's Edinburgh Magazine*. De Quincey's acquaintance with Coleridge and Wordsworth, who were central to the group that later came to be known as the Lake Poets, was instrumental in his decision to locate himself in the Lake District, specifically Dove Cottage in Grasmere, a property occupied by Wordsworth before his removal to Rydal Mount. Already practised in the pursuit of journalism as he was, De Quincey's residence in what was then the county of Westmorland made it possible for him to take up, on 18 July 1818, the post of editor with the *Westmorland Gazette*, a weekly journal published in Kendal. It was in this periodical that De Quincey's fascination with violent crime was first made apparent. The *Gazette* was a local publication with Tory leanings that reflected the politics of its owners. Its contents were concerned mainly with the reportage of items of local interest, interspersed with the latest London, and occasionally world, news. Within weeks of De Quincey's appointment as editor, however, the tenor of the *Gazette* changed.

The local news, including political activity and comment, which had previously held place of honour on the front pages of the publication, was quickly relegated to the back pages or even entirely omitted in favour of crime reports. These took the form of accounts taken from the assizes; descriptions of violent murder and rape which had been perpetrated locally, nationally, and even upon occasion, in Europe and America; reports of the crime-solving activities of the Bow Street Runners; and details of executions and the crimes of the executed. The content of such articles is indicated by their titles: 'Dreadful Murder at Newington' (31 October 1818), 'Mysterious Case: Murder of Margaret Flood' (4 December 1818), 'Dissection and Exposure of the Criminals, Chennel and Calcraft' (22 August 1818), or 'Most Interesting Charges of Child Murder' (22 August 1818). When there were no sensational criminal activities to be reported, articles such as 'Asiatic Superstitions' (10 October 1818) or 'An Account of a Family Predisposition to Haemorrhage' (27 December 1818) appeared in their stead. The former piece was an account of the rituals undertaken by a Hindu man 'for the purpose of gaining greater bodily strength and vigour', and a woman 'that she might obtain an offspring'. After the presiding 'priest' has sacrificed a live kid by ripping out its throat with his teeth and sucking its blood, both the supplicants voluntarily undergo graphically described torture. In the latter piece, an apparently scientific examination of a medical condition permits the inclusion of the results of human dissection. The superior intellectual register in which these articles were written notwithstanding, the sensationalism of the material represented would have been familiar to the reader of the broadsides.

The altered content did not escape notice. Regular contributors to the *Gazette*, their essays and articles ousted by De Quincey's inclusion of crime narratives, wrote letters of complaint both to De Quincey, in his capacity as editor, and to the proprietors of the journal. While these letters do not appear in the records of the *Gazette*, proof of their existence can be seen in the frequent apologies made by De Quincey in the pages of the periodical. The ire of the proprietors centred rather on the displacement or exclusion of political news and items of local and national importance, exclusions which were instrumental in De Quincey's eventual dismissal from the *Gazette*. But in response to early criticism for his concentration on matters criminal, De Quincey formulated a robust defence:

This week it will be observed that our columns are occupied almost exclusively with Assize Reports. We have thought it right to allow them precedency of all other news, whether domestic or foreign, for the three following reasons:

First, Because to all ranks alike they possess a powerful and commanding interest;

Secondly, Because to the more uneducated classes they yield a singular benefit, by teaching them their social duties in the most impressive shape; that is to say, not in a state of abstraction from all that may explain, illustrate, and enforce them (as in the naked terms of the Statute); but exemplified (and, as the logicians say, *concreted*) in the actual circumstances of an interesting case, and with the penalties that accompany their neglect or their violation;

Thirdly, Because they present the best indications of the moral condition of society: taken for twenty-five years together, there is no doubt that from these Reports, better than from any other source, may the statesman and the moralist appraise the true state of this country; and determine the problem which, in respect to its vital interests, is of leading concern—whether, in what relates to morals and respect for the written law, it be in a progressive state, (or, as some allege), in a state of declension.[32]

The second point of this defence equates to the function I have attributed to the broadsides, that is, the dissemination of the spectacle of sovereign power, while the third point can be read as a movement towards modern power in its concern with crime and criminality as indicators 'of the moral condition of society'. That which is 'other', or marginal, to society, is what defines the (normative) centre; thus, the excesses of criminals, revealed to the masses, confirm those masses as the law-abiding norm. De Quincey's first point is, of course, that crime narratives appeal to all, regardless of social status or intelligence.

Although prevented by his dismissal from the *Gazette* from carrying out his oft-deferred 'Plan for improving and exalting the Paper into a philosophical Journal', nonetheless, De Quincey 'certainly raised the literary character of the paper'.[33] The responsibilities of an editor and the nature of a provincial periodical meant that, as Charles Pollit has suggested, 'De Quincey's contributions to the columns of the *Westmorland Gazette* were necessarily of a very miscellaneous character.'[34] This apprenticeship in miscellany made De Quincey an ideal contributor to *Blackwood's Edinburgh Magazine*, which was itself a journal of miscellany. A further connection between De Quincey and *Blackwood's* can be seen in his friendship with its editor, John Wilson. In his long association with the periodical, De Quincey's contributions to the 'Maga' ranged from discussions of German philosophy to participating in the regularly appearing and popular comic pseudo-debate 'Noctes Ambrosiae'. He also wrote short stories in the Gothic mode such as 'The Avenger' (August 1838) and 'The Household Wreck' (January 1838). While these tales are to some extent concerned with crime, De Quincey's interest in criminal matters reveals itself rather earlier in his satirical essay 'On Murder Considered as One of the Fine Arts', which appeared in the February 1827 issue of *Blackwood's*.[35] It is my contention that this essay exemplifies the intellectual appropriation of the sensational crime of the broadsides by the literary establishment.

The essay, as the title suggests, takes murder as its theme, satirically elevating it to a fine art to be compared to other great works of philosophy, literature, and art. As an example of this 'art', De Quincey used a contemporary and notorious murder case, the Ratcliffe Highway Murders of 1811.[36] This case comprised the apparently unmotivated murder of seven individuals in two unrelated families. On the night of 11 December 1811, a shopkeeper called Marr, his wife, their three-month-old son, and James Gowen, Marr's apprentice, were killed, their skulls being shattered and their throats slit; and on 19 December of the same year, Williamson, a publican, his wife, and their elderly serving woman suffered a similar fate. The murders all took place in the East End of London, in the vicinity of the Ratcliffe Highway, hence the name. De Quincey's interest in the case had first become apparent in his 1823 essay 'On the Knocking on the Gate in Macbeth', in which he relates the knocking of the title to the housemaid's knocking on the door of the Marr's shop when the murderer was still inside.[37] It is in this essay that De Quincey makes a first gesture towards an analysis of his own fascination, and, indeed, that of the general public, with violence and murder. His direct reference in 'On the Knocking on the Gate' to the Ratcliffe Highway Murders presages the content of his later work 'On Murder': 'At length, in 1812, Mr. Williams made his *début* on the stage of Ratcliffe Highway, and executed those murders which have procured for him such a brilliant and undying reputation.'[38] He goes on in this first essay to speak of 'the connoisseur in murder', a figure that is central to the later account, and to call Williams, the supposed murderer, a 'great artist [...] born with genius', positioning the act of murder within the framework of the fine arts.[39]

That the subject of the essay was problematic is evidenced by De Quincey's use of a framing device in its construction. Rather than the text speaking directly to the reader, De Quincey, writing anonymously as 'X.Y.Z', distances his fictional self from the content yet preserves its claim to authenticity by presenting it as a paper supposedly from the transactions of a club devoted to murder, a 'Society for the Encouragement of Murder [...] styled, the Society of Connoisseurs in Murder'.[40] The only way, the narrator claims, to defuse the potentially dangerous content of this paper, which has fallen into his hands by accident, and to disband the Society from which it originates, is to make its existence and purposes public knowledge: 'The publication of it will alarm them; and my purpose is that it should. For I would much rather put them down quietly, by an appeal to public opinion, than by such an exposure of names as would follow an appeal to Bow Street.'[41] The reference to 'exposure of names' implies that if such a club were to exist, then many famous and influential people would perhaps be involved: interest in murder is not confined to the lower classes, as the essay goes on to suggest. Wilson, the editor of *Blackwood's* writing under the alias 'Christopher North', also shows his concern about the reception of De Quincey's essay in the 'Note from the Editor' which followed De Quincey's framing introduction: 'We cannot suppose the lecturer to be in earnest, any more than Erasmus in his Praise of Folly, or Dean Swift in his Proposal for Eating Children. However, on his own view or on ours, it is equally fit that the lectures should be made public.'[42] Placing the article in the same context as Erasmus's and Swift's openly satirical essays ensures that the reader will not read it as a serious and factual account.[43]

In what De Quincey calls his 'Advertisement of a Man Morbidly Virtuous', that is, his preface to the paper 'On Murder', he quotes the fourth-century Christian writer Lactantius at length and in Latin, which he then translates for the benefit of those readers without a classical education. Lactantius was writing against the spectacle of the gladiators, concluding that 'merely to be present at a murder fastens on a man the character of an accomplice [...] to be a spectator involves us in one common guilt with the perpetrator'.[44] De Quincey, or the narrator, is not only ostensibly reading this account to the members of the 'Gentlemen Amateurs of London', that is, the connoisseurs in murder, but, I would argue, also implicating himself and the reader of his text in the accusation. To read of murder is, in a sense, to be a spectator at the event. In De Quincey's essay, the spectacle of murder makes the spectator/reader complicit with the act, necessitating a defence which will legitimate his or her interest, and in 'On Murder', De Quincey, however he cloaks his writing with satire and irony, is attempting just such a defence. To do this, it is necessary to elevate the topic of murder, to take it from the gutter press and refine it into an art. Considering De Quincey's previous spirited defence of his use of matters criminal in the pages of the *Westmorland Gazette*, in contrast, in the pages of *Blackwood's* he dismisses his earlier audience: 'As to old women, and the mob of newspaper readers, they are pleased with anything, provided it is bloody enough. But the mind of sensibility requires something more.'[45] And in 'On Murder', De Quincey is appealing to a different audience, constructing a witty and intellectual defence of the fascination which crime, especially murder, has for many people, and a defence which speaks to the man possessed of a mind of sensibility rather than to the man in and of the street.

Not content with the intellectual gloss given by the litter of Greek and Latin phrases and classical quotations with which his text abounds, De Quincey furthers his claim to intellectualism by structuring his article after the style of an academic paper, borrowing the discursive technique and linguistic register of academia. This is evident in the designation of the second part of the essay as a lecture and in the title allocated to it: 'the Williams Lecture on Murder Considered as One of the Fine Arts'.[46] He makes his appeal to the intellect, setting the subject of murder in the context of history, with an exhaustive account of murder dating back to Cain and Abel; setting it in the context of literature, referring to Chaucer's and Shakespeare's use of murder in their texts; and, most importantly, setting it in the context of philosophy. De Quincey differentiates between a moral and an aesthetic approach to murder: it 'may be laid hold of by its moral handle (as it generally is in the pulpit and at the Old Bailey) [...] or it may be also treated *aesthetically*, as the Germans call it—that is, in relation to good taste'.[47] There is, De Quincey suggests, 'more [...] to the composition of a fine murder than two blockheads to kill and be killed, a knife, a purse, and a dark lane'.[48] His appeal to the intellect is supported by anecdotes about Coleridge, a man of letters and poet; Aristotle, philosopher and critic; and by reference to the discourse of science, encapsulated in 'Mr. Howship, the surgeon' and his rhapsodic study of the perfect ulcer: 'in a work of his on Indigestion, he makes no scruple to talk with admiration of a certain ulcer [...] which he styles "a beautiful ulcer" '.[49] The beauty, or sublimity, of an object or act, suggests De Quincey, lies in the perfection of its being; hence, an ulcer that is by its nature an imperfection in the system, can yet be a perfect example of its kind. Similarly, a murder, especially one which appears motiveless, has its sensationalism increased by its tragic, preferably domestic setting; and one where the perpetrator escapes, that is, a murder in which 'the grand feature of mystery' is to be found, can also be construed as a perfect artefact which is therefore aesthetically pleasing.[50]

Despite its ironic disguise, in 'On Murder' De Quincey was producing an intellectual legitimisation of the sensational appeal of murder. In support of his argument, De Quincey turned to philosophy, and much of 'On Murder' concerns itself with the notion that all philosophers, or at least good ones, are subject to murder or attempted murder. While this idea is not intended to be taken seriously, nonetheless, its presence indicates, and concomitantly requires, a certain level of intelligence and knowledge to comprehend the ironic intent. The covert message of De Quincey's conceit is, I suggest, not that philosophers are prone to being murdered in reality, rather, it is a metaphor for the temporally serial displacement of philosophical thought. Each philosopher's opus is subsequently replaced/rewritten by later philosophy, a notion here embodied in the spurious accounts of the murders of the philosophers themselves. The apparently tenuous connection between murder as an art and the discourse of philosophical enquiry is made firm in De Quincey's assertion at the end of his 'excursion' into the subject: 'I have traced the connexion between Philosophy and our Art.'[51] This statement is further bolstered by his observation that 'the final purpose of murder, considered as a fine art, is precisely that of tragedy in Aristotle's account of it; viz. "to cleanse the heart by means of pity and terror" '.[52] Pity and terror are emotions and sensations which the broadsides also attempted to elicit in their readers, and De Quincey's essay is an intellectual appropriation and reworking of familiar themes.

I would further suggest that De Quincey's interest in crime, and especially murder, situates him as an authorial proto-detective. His enquiry into the mechanics of murder and the attempt to analyse the psychology of the perpetrator and the emotions of the victim, while prompted by a possibly unhealthy fascination with violence, locate him as an investigating agent. A. S. Plumtree suggests that 'De Quincey [...] puts himself at the same time in the soul of the murderer and of his victims and makes the crime first and foremost a psychological drama'; and the ability to identify with the criminal, and to some extent with the victim, in order to reconstruct the crime is essential in later depictions of the detective.[53] De Quincey wrote two further papers concerned with the Ratcliffe Highway Murders. The second paper with the title of 'Murder as One of the Fine Arts' (*Blackwood's*, November 1839) offers little of relevance or interest to my argument, concerning itself mainly with the drunken celebration that the 'Society of Connoisseurs in Murder' enjoy consequent upon the instance of the Williams murders.[54] There is less effort to distance the author from the content, although there is a very specific disclaimer made by the narrator: 'allow me to say what my real principles are upon the matter in question [murder] [...] I never committed one in my life. [...] "But" say you, "if no murderer, you may have encouraged, or even bespoken, a murder." No, upon my honour, no.'[55] While admitting the fascination of violent crime, the narrator refuses any responsibility for the possible consequences of writing about it for public consumption.

De Quincey's continued awareness of the difficult nature of his material is evident in the third paper on the subject of murder, 'Postscript', which was published 27 years after his first article, not in a periodical but as part of his *Collected Works* in 1854. Masson suggests that 'the Postscript may have been in manuscript shortly after the publication of the first paper',[56] but De Quincey's own statement within the text that 'forty-two years have elapsed since 1812 [the date he persisted in allocating to the Ratcliffe Highway Murders]' appears to contradict this suggestion.[57] Grevel Lindop, in *The Opium-Eater: A Life of Thomas De Quincey*, observes that:

> [t]here are enough factual errors in the story to suggest that it was written from memory, but it is just possible that it had been composed at some time between 1827 and 1839, for it refers to a previous 'paper'—not 'papers'—on murder. Perhaps it was a rejected effort for *Maga* and had lain, unused, in one of De Quincey's heaps of notes for fifteen or twenty years.[58]

If De Quincey had made some attempt immediately after the publication of the first article to write an account which would include the factual details of the murders and the apparent solution of the case, he had obviously revised, rewritten, or expanded any such account by 1854. This later essay differs in content and format from the earlier work, as it is both an explanation of and justification for the previous essays, and, most importantly, as it is also a close examination and analysis of the Ratcliffe Highway Murders. In this, it is closer in style and content to the sensational tales in *Blackwood's* that would become known as the 'Tales of Terror', which would support Lindop's suggestion that it may have been written for *Blackwood's* and been rejected. But in view of the difference in content and the alteration in context inherent in the temporal gap between the texts, an analysis of De Quincey's 'Postscript' is inappropriate here. As an unpublished narrative, it could have had no effect on the contemporary criminographic material being written before 1850.

De Quincey's 'extravaganza', as he called it, notwithstanding, in the contemporary climate of penal reform the public's growing concern with the efficiency and fairness of the judicial system is combined with an increasing interest in the criminal as an individual subject, as can be seen in the Newgate novels of the 1830s and 1840s. These narratives, written by such luminaries as Edward Bulwer-Lytton, William Harrison Ainsworth, and Charles Dickens, implicitly questioned the role of the judicial and social system in the making of a criminal. Bulwer-Lytton's *Paul Clifford* (1830) examined the effects of social circumstance on the individual, suggesting that society itself was as much responsible for criminality as any subjective psychological predisposition to crime. Pre-dating and contemporaneous with the Newgate novels, and yet exploring similar territory in their concentration on the criminal rather than the crime, were some of the short stories published in the pages of *Blackwood's Edinburgh Magazine* from its establishment in 1817. Although not accounts of real crime, or limited in subject to criminal matters, many of these short stories either attempted to portray the subjective experience of criminality, or used crime narratives to question the value and reliability of circumstantial evidence. Periodicals as much as broadsides function on a profit basis, and the *Blackwood's* stories reworked the techniques of the broadsides to elicit interest and excitement in their readers, replacing the crude illustrations with prose portraits and relying on sensationalism in their content, but a sensationalism calculated to appeal to their educated and intellectual readers.

De Quincey was not the only writer to concern himself with crime in the pages of *Blackwood's*. His intellectual appropriation of the emerging genre of criminography used the discourses of literature, philosophy, and history, but made only a passing reference to medical science. In much of the *Blackwood's* criminography, both factual and fictional, medicine and crime are associated and recurring tropes. In the periodical format, sensationalism, combined with the authority of science in a morally improving frame of crime and punishment, permitted the publication of images, in prose and picture, which in any other context would have been considered pornographic. The broadside depiction of criminal and sexual penetration into the (female) body finds its echo in the literature of a higher social class in two short stories written for *Blackwood's* by John Wilson. 'Extracts from Gosschen's Diary' (1818) and 'Expiation' (1830), both recount in some detail the physical injuries inflicted on the bodies of the female victims of murder. The medical intrusion into the integrity of the body and mind is expounded in Samuel Warren's 'Passages from the Diary of a Late Physician' (1830–1837), published serially in the same periodical. The sensational illustrations of the broadsides are translated into prose by Wilson, while Warren's supposed 'Diary' brings sensationalism and science together in directly associating mental and physical disease with social and moral misdemeanour. This juxtaposition of discourses permits the techniques of medical examination, that is, the search for the cause and cure of illness, to be applied to other symptoms of social disorder, for example, crime and criminality. The use of medical methodology and terminology in association with criminality was in accordance with the movement towards a reformist and disciplinary penal system which would recuperate the criminal and reinstate him or her as a productive cog in the capitalist machine rather than simply eliminating a potentially useful individual.

The *Blackwood's* stories, intended for the solitary reader rather than the communal audience of the broadsides, locate the criminal at the centre of their narratives. The individual, who is objectified in the broadsides, is here reconstituted as subject in the attempt to depict the subjective experience of the criminal. This focus on the individual generated a reciprocal requirement for individual specialists or professionals to facilitate that focus. The process of investigating the experience and hence causes of criminality in the individual is an early stage in the discursive development of the detective as a recognisable professional figure. Further, there are parallels to be drawn between the practices of medical science and detection: as the physician seeks out the agent of disease, so the detective will seek out the agent of crime; and the relationship between medicine and crime will develop into the discipline that came to be known as 'criminology' and produce that invaluable tool of detection, forensic medicine. Such questioning of the causality of crime or consideration of the emotions of its perpetrator is absent from the criminal broadsides, but their sensational format, which generated profit, was precisely what appealed to the editors of periodicals such as *Blackwood's Edinburgh Magazine*.

1.5 Sensational literature and literal sensation: *Blackwood's* 'Tales of Terror'

Maintaining the tradition of the 'newes/novel' in their unstable location between fact and fiction, many of the *Blackwood's* stories, following the broadsides, purport to be true accounts; a claim to authenticity which supports the relationship between the two narrative forms and which enhanced the sensational effect upon the reader.[59] As Robert Morrison and Chris Baldick suggest, 'the more direct realism of *Blackwood's* terror fiction seems to be derived partly from the sensational "true crime" narrative often found in broadsheet, chapbook, and newspaper publications'.[60] The moment of real terror generated by the reinstatement of the individual experience exemplified in the broadside account of White's death is appropriated and reworked in fiction. *Blackwood's* tales brought together the commodified crime of the broadsides with the reformist interest in the criminal individual and his or her motivation, a move which was instrumental in constructing a discursive space for the development of the detective figure. The writers of the *Blackwood's* short fictions appropriated and re-presented the sensational aspects of the criminal narratives of the broadsides. It was not a purely one-way route: Henry Thomson's 'Le Revenant' (1827), a story about a forger who is caught, condemned, and hanged, but who survives his execution, appeared in heavily abbreviated form as a 'cock', entitled 'The Life, Trial, Character and Confession: The Man that was Hanged in Front of Newgate, and Who is Now Alive! With Full Particulars of the Resuscitated'.[61]

The symbiotic and intertextual relationships between various criminal narratives notwithstanding, the concentration in *Blackwood's* short fictions on the criminal individual and his or her experience rather than on the crime responds to the shift in focus from the crime to the criminal that was central to the contemporary process of penal reform. *Blackwood's* readers were upper middle to upper class, of good education, and politically conservative, and the periodical was a site for the articulation of public opinion. This was the class and these were the types of readers who would have been in a position to influence the process of reform, albeit in their own interests rather than those of the socially deprived or criminal individual. The accounts of crime in the short fictions of *Blackwood's* share in the broadside commodification of crime, but are also indicative of a reconceptualisation of crime, an attempt to comprehend the criminal that will enable a more effective containment and control of crime.

While crime and its punishment in the context of government reform were hotly debated in the serious quality periodicals and newspapers, the concentration on the criminal individual was to be found in the realm of fiction rather than fact. What was required to bring the criminal to the attention of the middle- and upper-class reader was a literary format which combined information with entertainment, a new genre of periodical which would buy into the existing market for serious literature, but increase its market share by offering a leavening of lighter works for the less serious-minded reader. This gap in the market was filled by *Blackwood's Edinburgh Magazine*, or *Maga* as it came to be known, which was inaugurated in 1817 by the Edinburgh publisher William Blackwood. He was motivated by the desire to produce a Tory periodical with which to challenge the supremacy of the Whig *Edinburgh Review*, but in contrast to the serious, factual format of that and other contemporary Reviews, 'Blackwood wanted his periodical to be a magazine [...] that is, to offer humour, a variety of articles, and original creative works.'[62] It was a winning format that would be copied in the 1830s by publications such as *Fraser's Magazine* and the *New Monthly Magazine* among others. The cost and content of the new *Blackwood's* made it the literature of the middle and upper class, rather than of the lower orders.[63] In any single edition, erudite essays, philosophical discussions, and articles of contemporary interest might rub shoulders with poetry, literary reviews, satire, and sensational short stories. The latter were an innovative and important feature of *Blackwood's*, one which distinguished it from its predecessors and peers and which arguably had a lasting impact on the literary world.

Notable contributors to *Blackwood's* included Trollope, George Eliot, Conrad, and Bulwer-Lytton, all of whom practised their skills in the pages of the periodical. The short stories published in the early years of the magazine offered realistic accounts of individual experiences in a form which prefigured the practice of serialising novels peculiar to the Victorian period. Featuring fiction in a periodical was not exactly revolutionary: Robert D. Mayo suggests that 'fiction is found in about one-third of all periodicals [...] between 1770 and 1820, and for many of those with a popular appeal it represented a very important staple in their fare'.[64] But the short fiction in *Blackwood's* differed from the often formulaic format of many of the earlier narratives, moving beyond the popular Gothic romances of the late 1700s and away from the imagined terrors of the supernatural to the physical sensation of fear and horror engendered by terror represented in a realistic register. The frisson of horror incited by the mysterious events in far-off places offered by, for example Mrs Radcliffe, is, in the *Blackwood's* stories, produced by credible and realistic tales of the here and now or of the recent past, often presented in the guise of a criminal narrative. The relocation of terror in a recognisable recent reality prefigures Wilkie Collins's domestication of the Gothic in the sensation novels he produced in the second half of the nineteenth century.

William Blackwood's innovative and relaxed formula allowed the inclusion of lighter material for the less erudite reader, and this included short fiction, which was frequently the location of sensationalism. Targeted at the individual reader rather than at the plural audience of the broadsides, *Blackwood's* fiction nonetheless utilised the same macabre material of murder and retribution, but presented in such a way as to be acceptable to the socially or financially more elevated reader at whom it was aimed. This meant that a distinctive style of sensationalism took shape in the *Blackwood's* tales, a sensationalism which was founded on the personal experience of the narrator, either reported directly to the reader, or as told to or by a framing narrator, often a doctor or priest. Where the theme is criminality, in accounting for their crimes the criminals reveal something of their various motivations, a revelation central to the process of reform, where the shift of attention from the crime to the criminal was essential to the disciplining and reformation of the criminal individual. I do not wish to suggest that *Blackwood's* pages were filled with criminal narratives: on the contrary, many of the short stories relate to individuals placed in extreme, but not necessarily criminal, circumstances, for example Daniel Keyte Sandford's 'A Night in the Catacombs' (1818), William Maginn's 'The Man in the Bell' (1821), or the anonymous 'The Last Man' (1826).[65] The editors of *Blackwood's* were aware of the public's perception of the apparently increasing incidence of crime and were quick to capitalise upon it in factual and fictional form.

This awareness of the public concern with matters criminal can be seen in an article published in 1818: 'Cautionary Hints to Speculators on the Increase of Crimes', which opens with the statement '[o]ne strong feature of the times is the prevalence of atrocious crimes'.[66] The article goes on to suggest that 'present temper and condition is not the result of present causes merely, simple and prominent; it is the complex result of a multitude of causes, acting often with very obscure operation, and through long successive periods of time', requiring attention from 'that general philosophy which investigates the laws, the powers and the revolutions of human society'.[67] Such a statement implies that while the ordinary man may be interested in the subject, action is best left to those in authority. The text uses the metaphor of disease for the increase of crime, likening it to 'a contagion spreading over the lives of men', a metaphor which is extended into the notion of a body and mind of society which equates the body with the mass of the populace and the mind with the ruling minority: '[t]he mind of society turns to a consideration of its [the body's] disorders'.[68] Despite this insistence upon a reliance on the existing authorities, the article tacitly admits the need for 'some deliberate and earnest inquiry', returning to the metaphor of disease in suggesting that crime requires 'remedies, which are not to be attempted without intelligence of the disorder', and using a medical paradigm which in turn posits the necessity for an expert or professional figure.[69] The specialised knowledge that the physician possesses of the diseased body of the patient enables him to heal that body. This medical framework can be read as paradigmatic for the development of a knowing professional figure empowered to deal with crime and criminality, that is, a detective.

A further indication of *Blackwood's* interest in factual crime can be seen in 'Hints for Jurymen' (1823), an article which shows an awareness of the importance of understanding medical and technical evidence in criminal cases and an increasing concern with the apparent unreliability of circumstantial evidence within the judicial system.[70] This article makes a direct association between crime and the science of medicine: it is in essence a review of a legal textbook, *Medical Jurisprudence* by J. A. Paris MD and J. S. M. Fonblanque, Barrister at Law. The co-authorship and content of the text make clear the connection between medicine and the law in matters of crime in a literal as opposed to metaphorical fashion. While disclaiming the necessary authority to write a review of a scientific text, the writers of the article seek to justify their interest in the book, insisting that 'every juryman [...] ought to read Paris and Fonblanque. And certainly, if such reading were to become common, we do not think it could fail to have the most admirable effects, both directly upon the minds of the jurymen themselves, and indirectly upon the minds of [...] professional persons.'[71] But a more believable rationale for the article can be found in the comment that follows this rather sanctimonious statement, a comment in which the writers admit that 'it is a most amusing as well as an instructive and learned book'.[72]

The remaining 11 pages of the piece offer excerpts from a selection of sensational cases taken from Paris and Fonblanque's text. These include an analysis of the trials by ordeal of the 'Hindoos' reminiscent of De Quincey's article in the *Westmorland Gazette*; a gruesomely detailed account of a case of spontaneous combustion; various tests to expose feigned madness or handicap; cases of mistaken identity which result in the execution of the innocent; a long section on 'the frequency of living interment and the proof of the fallacy of those signs which are commonly received as signs of death'; and extracts from the chapter on the 'ever popular subject of "Hanging"' and the reported subsequent apparent 'resurrection' of the hanged individual.[73] These last items were represented in fictional form in two of *Blackwood's* 'Tales of Terror': John Galt's 'The Buried Alive' and Henry Thomson's 'Le Revenant'.[74] Such accounts, based on the verifiable cases offered by texts such as that of Paris and Fonblanque, illustrated the close connection between fact and fiction in matters of sensationalism and crime.

The final section of the article, and the subject which the writers found 'the most interesting', is devoted to 'the means of discovering whether such a person found dead has been murdered by another's hand, and by whom'.[75] There is no suggestion of a specialist figure to facilitate 'the means of discovery', and the first, and longest, extract selected by the writers of the article from this section of the text was chosen as much for its sensational aspect as for its relevance. The extract concerns a case of murder in which the victim is disinterred for anatomical investigation, a choice of case which permits a detailed description of the deceased: 'patches, arising from extravasated blood, were seen in different parts of the throat, and distinct abrasions corresponding with the nails were visible; the face presented the physiognomy of a strangled man'.[76] Such a description differs from a broadside account of murder only in its use of scientific terminology: the appeal to the voyeuristic nature of the reader is the same, although disguised by the complex and technical language of the *Blackwood's* version. The evidence in the case is, according to Paris and Fonblanque, 'wholly circumstantial', but there are elements of the methodology to be found in later detective fiction. As the text states:

> Who then committed the murder? From the circumstance of its having been perpetrated in a field containing several old mines, without any attempt on the part of the villain to avail himself of the advantage which these caverns would have afforded for the concealment of the dead body, the author was convinced that the perpetrator of the deed would be found in some stranger to the country, for such a one alone could be unacquainted with the mines to which we refer [. . .].
> Were there any suspicious strangers in Penzance or its neighbourhood? Had the deceased been seen in the society of any person unacquainted with the country?[77]

Such a logical train of thought might be found on the pages of a Sherlock Holmes story, or in the musings of Poe's Dupin. The requirement for a professional or specialist agent in matters of crime then, while not articulated in 'Hints for Jurymen', is nevertheless implicit in this extract, specifically in its reference to 'the means of discovering whether such a person found dead has been murdered by another's hand, and by whom'. The method is sketched out in the article and the means indicated in the actions of the author, who prefigures the detective in his methodical reconstruction of the crime and the profiling of a possible perpetrator.

Blackwood's was not an illustrated magazine, and had therefore to rely on the talents of its writers to bring to life in prose the events that the broadsides could encapsulate in pictures. The spectacle of execution, reduced in the illustrated street literature to a series of signifiers and symbols, is intelligently and yet graphically and sensationally recreated in prose by Robert MacNish in his *Blackwood's* article 'An Execution in Paris'.[78] It is an execution distanced from the reader both by the textual medium and by its geographical location: as MacNish admits, '[t]o my shame be it spoken, I wished to see an execution by the guillotine'.[79] He emphasises the association between the guillotine and the French Revolution, an association which enhances the sensationalism of the article to its readers who, had they been French in the revolutionary years, may well themselves have been victims of the guillotine. As in the broadside accounts, the scene of execution is depicted in detail, albeit entirely in prose: the crowd and its deposition and disposition is described; the cost of a window seat with a good view noted (MacNish himself has a ringside seat, obtained through friends in the military); the reception of the child-killer Papavoine and his response is reported, and finally, the mechanics of the execution itself are told in horrid detail, as are its physical effects: 'I saw his head slip from the body and tumble into a basket ready to receive it, while the blood spouted forth in little cataracts from the severed trunk.'[80] MacNish even gives an account of his subsequent visit to the *École de Médicine*, where he watches the phrenologist Dr Gall examine the severed head. The writer attempts to justify his own prurient interest in the proceedings, arguing that the guillotine is much more efficient and humane than the gallows and suggesting that his interest is purely scientific. His final disclaimer is at the end of the piece, where he states that 'I am not sure that I have done right in making such a scene as the above the subject of an article. There is something in the minute details of an execution at which the mind shudders', but it is of course precisely this physical and psychical sensation which MacNish wished to produce and the reader desired to experience.[81]

The spectacle of execution here is not a statement of sovereign power, disseminated in prose to reinforce its effect. As written for the *Blackwood's* British audience, socially neutral and subjectively focused, it is rather an exercise in sensationalism. Geographically distanced by its French location and intellectually removed by the difference between British and French law, the monitory effect it may have been expected to exert upon French citizens is here negated. Speaking of the few moments prior to Papavoine's execution, MacNish tells his readers that 'my respiration was almost totally suspended—my heart beat violently, and a feeling of intense anxiety and suffocation pervaded my frame'.[82] The physical manifestation of the response to terror is the very sensation the short fictions of *Blackwood's* attempted to elicit in their audience, and the case-histories of medical jurisprudence proved a fertile source of material. The facts of the criminal cases found in Paris and Fonblanque's text are re-presented in the fictional tales, drawing on the sensationalism inherent in the factual accounts and on an analysis of the sensations provoked by terror. In a later review of an American volume of medical jurisprudence, the writers state that 'we know of no romance half so interesting as the real "tales of terror" to be found scattered over these pages', tales which by dint of their location in a text that combines law and medicine are frequently connected to crime and violence.[83] The phrase 'tales of terror' is somewhat misleading, as not all tales in *Blackwood's* were of terror any more than they were all concerned with crime. The fiction in *Blackwood's* can be broadly categorised into three genres: the burlesque tale, which has no place in my argument; the social fable, that is a narrative set in idyllic rural surroundings, in which a working man refuses to be content and turns to criminality, which I will examine later; and the tale of sensation, which I propose to consider in its criminal aspect.

If MacNish's account of an execution re-presents the execution broadside, then John Wilson's 'Extracts from Gosschen's Diary' (1818) is a prose version of those broadsides which offered sexual sensationalism with their criminal narratives.[84] The tale is framed by the narrating voice of Gosschen, apparently a priest, but the bulk of the story is told in the voice of the criminal. Although his name is never given, the use of the criminal's voice, elided or appropriated in the broadsides, is here a reinstatement of the criminal individual in his or her own narrative. Locating the tale in a foreign country distances the narrative from reality, but the first-person narration reduces that distance, permitting the criminal to speak directly to the reader. There is a Gothic resonance to the story in the setting and in the tormented Byronic protagonist, and the overt references to the eroticised naked female body and the emphasis on the motive of sexual jealousy situate the narrative in the more sexually open climate of the Regency. The crime in question is the horrid murder of a beautiful young girl by her lover, a story that would be familiar to a reader of the broadsides. In Wilson's tale, the protagonist and his victim are of noble blood, with no suggestion of the drunkenness or deprivation that so often accompanied the murders of real life. The pornography implicit in the Greenacre broadside, where the dismembered female body is openly displayed in the illustration accompanying the text, here lies in the graphic account of the actual murder:

I slew her;—yes, with this blessed hand I stabbed her to the heart. Do you think there was no pleasure in murdering her? I grasped her by that radiant, that golden hair,—I bared those snow-white breasts,—I dragged her sweet body towards me, and, as God is my witness, I stabbed, and stabbed her with this very dagger, ten, twenty, forty times, through and through her heart.[85]

The erotic implication of the repeated penetration of the dagger is reinforced in the passage that follows:

I took her into my arms—madly as I did on that night when first I robbed her of what fools called her innocence [...] and there I lay with her bleeding breasts pressed to my heart, and many were the thousand kisses that I gave those breasts, cold and bloody as they were, which I had many million times kissed in all the warmth of their loving loveliness.[86]

The eroticised female body is exposed by the narrating murderer to the gaze of the reader. What differentiates this tale from the broadside is not merely the register in which it is told, but the centrality of the criminal who, although textualised, speaks his own story. The tale is a fiction, but the suggestion that it is taken from the diary of a priest lends it authenticity. The highly literate murderer offers not just a confession but also his motive for the murder and a detailed description of the sensations it aroused in him before, during and after the act. This early *Blackwood's* tale reinstates the criminal at the centre of the criminal narrative, constructing that narrative as quasi-biographical. In the later tales, this biographical trope becomes more pronounced, responding to a realignment of the function of the penal system which relocates punishment: no longer will it be the crime that is punished, but the criminal individual.

In 1827 *Blackwood's* published Henry Thomson's short fiction 'Le Revenant', which purports to be the autobiographical account of a forger and his fate. The story is firmly located in the recent past and in domestic as opposed to foreign space, stepping away from the Gothic and into a more realist register. There is an immediate claim to sensationalism in the opening statement: '[t]here are few men, perhaps, who have not [...] felt a curiosity to know what their sensations would be if they were compelled to lay life down'.[87] The narrator alludes to the attempts of poets and painters to depict the 'estate of a man condemned to die', but suggests that representations cannot equate to the reality, a reality he insists is portrayed in his autobiographical tale: 'I am in a situation to speak, from experience, upon that very interesting question—the sensations attendant upon a passage from life to death. I have been HANGED, and am ALIVE.'[88] Again, the emphasis is on sensation, that is, on his own feelings which will in turn affect the reader. The story offers proof of authenticity: while not giving his name, the narrator tells his audience that it can be found 'in the list of capital convictions in the Old Bailey Calendar for the Winter Session 1826'.[89] This not only authenticates his tale, but the proximity of the date of the trial to the date of the publication of the narrative lends it an immediacy that makes its contents even more sensational. There is a brief account of his circumstances prior to his offence and of the motives (poverty and love) which led him to commit it, but the bulk of the tale is concerned with his experiences and the sensations and emotions they invoke: the fear of certain discovery prior to his apprehension; the inhumanity of the machinery of the law and the indifference of its officials; the wait in the condemned cell; and the moment of execution. This is the criminal's voice as never heard before, and the story received widespread acclaim and incited much interest. Charles Lamb wrote that 'there is in Blackwood this month an article MOST AFFECTING indeed called Le Revenant, and would do more towards abolishing Capital Punishments than 400,000 Romillies or Montagues'.[90]

In 'Le Revenant', the discursive space for the criminal voice, socially contained but eroded and elided in the broadsides, is rediscovered. The ideological impetus which sought to contain criminality in the silencing of the real-life criminal and which put repentant words into the mouths of the human signifier of crime in the broadsides is redirected. The first-person narration of 'Le Revenant' invites the reader to identify with the speaker, increasing the sensational effect, but any criminal contamination is avoided, as the tale is, finally, moral. The repentant criminal escapes death on the scaffold, but faces the social death of exile. The mechanics of his escape are not clear; as the narrator himself states: 'of my actual execution and death, I have not the slightest atom of recollection [. . .] with the first view of the scaffold, all my recollection ceases'.[91] The story makes a neat reversal of the perspective from which an execution is more normally seen, making the crowd the object of the gaze in an implicit critique of public hangings. Thomson's tale of terror encapsulates a maximum of sensationalism, but simultaneously, in the narrator's account of his motives and the emotions which led him into criminality can be seen an attempt to understand the criminal individual. A comprehensive understanding and knowledge of the criminal is essential to the containment and correction of criminality. The danger of knowing the criminal is that the contact will criminalise the observer or reader, an anxiety which fuelled the Newgate novel controversy in the 1830s: fictions with a criminal protagonist were accused of heroising the criminal and making crime glamorous. The *Blackwood's* short fictions on the whole avoided this accusation, emphasising the restoration of the moral *status quo* in repentance and retribution; filtering their criminal narratives through the voice of a respectable, often religious or medical, narrator, and by resorting to a third-person narration.

These techniques can most clearly be seen in the 'social fable' narratives found in *Blackwood's*. Sensationalism remains a factor in their construction, but the stories are more obviously weighted with specific meanings and messages: later tales such as John Wilson's 'Expiation' (1830) were utilised to express the growing public concern about the reliability of circumstantial evidence, while early tales, for example 'The Forgers' (1821), carried a more moralistic and didactic message reminiscent of the eighteenth-century criminal *Calendars* and broadsides. 'The Forgers', as its name suggests, shares with 'Le Revenant' the crime of forgery, but the motivation and mode of discovery are very different. The story is told by a pastor, placing the narrative in a religious frame, and the hand of God and the workings of Providence are evident in the mechanics of the plot. The location is rural and the context historical, but within living memory, as evidenced by the continued existence of the widow of the forger, whose fleeting appearance sets the tale in motion. From the initial paragraph, a brooding atmosphere sets the scene for a tale of horror and terror: 'whenever I come into this glen, there is something rueful in its silence', and later: 'The sky was black and lowering, as it lay on the silent hills.'[92] In essence, the story is simple. A respectable family are forced into poverty by the dishonesty of a relation, and, embittered at becoming tenants on land which had been their own, the father and son forge the will of another wealthy relative. On his death, the forgers fraudulently inherit the property, but it does not restore them to happiness. Implicit in the pastor's account is the notion that guilt prevents contentment. This relates back to the early *Newgate Calendar* system of apprehending criminals: as Stephen Knight has it, in a Christian system, the Christian conscience ensures that 'the sense of guilt makes them act rashly [...] so drawing attention to themselves'.[93] Here, there are no 'rash' actions, but the gaze of the pastor, in an earthly representation of the all-seeing gaze of the Almighty, sees the difference in the father and son. The power of the eye in the detection of guilt will be central to the construction of the early detectives, most notably in Dickens's 'Detective

Anecdotes'. The admission of guilt in confession and the community-based observance patterns of early crime narratives are no longer sufficient or effective: surveillance, whether direct and visible or as a concept of the self as the object of an unseen gaze, is central to the structures of disciplinary power and in later narratives of detection.

The father, aware of his guilt, is unable to meet the gaze of, in this case, the pastor: 'when my eyes met his [...] they were suddenly averted in conscious guilt; or closed in hypocritical devotion'. Meanwhile, the son, previously 'stained by no vice', becomes 'dissolute and profligate'.[94] Discovery is inevitable. The cousin, whom their forgery had disinherited, returns, apparently from the dead, and dramatically exposes their guilt: 'but, lo! God, whom thou hast blasphemed, has sent me from the distant isles of the ocean, to bring thy white head into the hangman's noose!'[95] In this context, God, or Providence, following the model of early criminal narratives, is the agent of justice, bringing the criminals and the wronged man into contact in order to expose the crime. The father attempts to hang himself, the son tries to take the blame, and the returned sailor takes pity on the two and offers to let them escape. But in an early social model of community the society is so tightly woven that flight is impossible: in the narrative, news of the forgery and its discovery are disseminated through the social body by an unseen agency, so that 'it seemed as if a raven had croaked the direful secret all over the remotest places among the hills; for, in an hour, people came flocking [...] concealment or escape was no longer possible'.[96] The sensationalism in the story is centred on the last days of the two condemned men and their experiences prior to their eventual execution, and the article closes in a fashion reminiscent of the gallows literature of the broadsides: the two men, repentant of their sins, are hanged with the phrase '[t]heir souls were in eternity' echoing in their ears.[97] The narrative resembles detective fiction only in its retrospective reconstruction of the crime, being more in the mode of many early criminal narratives such as those in the *Newgate Calendars* or, indeed, the broadsides. But there is an implicit critique of the social and legal system in the contrast between the unpunished 'dishonesty of a kinsman [...] which robbed them of their few hereditary fields', and the forgers' own crime which effectively duplicates the original, but is seen to be against the law.[98]

'The Forgers' offers early evidence of the notion that the criminal is somehow marked as 'other' to the norm by visible signs, that crime leaves its traces written not only on the body of the victim but also in the mind and on the face or body of the criminal, a notion that is increasingly explored in the later tales in *Blackwood's*. In 'The Forgers', the father is psychically marked by the guilt that he feels: 'his [. . .] fine features so intelligent, had no longer the same solemn expression which they once possessed, and something dark and hidden seemed now to belong to them'.[99] His son is 'stained' by vice, his dissipation evident in his appearance. The point is not laboured in this narrative, but in Samuel Warren's 'Passages from the Diary of a Late Physician', which was serialised in the magazine between 1830 and 1837, the effects of crime and vice on the psyche, physique, and physiognomy of the perpetrator are a central and recurring theme. Textually and temporally located between 'The Forgers' and 'Passages', John Wilson's 'Expiation' (1830) shares with the former the siting of a crime within a rural community, fitting into the 'social fable' pattern; and with the latter, attempts an examination of the effects of crime on the criminal.[100] Further, it is an explicit critique of the system of circumstantial evidence, a theme that will be picked up and expanded upon by the penny magazines of the 1830s and 1840s.

'Expiation' is an exemplary conjunction of broadside material, sensationalist writing, and an elementary inductive procedure that illustrates the need for a detective figure. It has a third-person narrator who, in the clues and hints given by the text that suggest the horrors yet to come, approaches the omniscient narrator who will feature in later classic realist fiction. The orphan heroine, Margaret Burnside, is too good either to be true or to expect a long life, as the narrative intimates: 'her hour was not yet come—though by the inscrutable decrees of Providence doomed to be hideous'.[101] Much is made of her innocence and religious bent, even under dire circumstances, and she receives her reward for piety and patience in the form of patronage from the local Laird's daughters. A putative love interest is introduced, aligned with the possibility of criminality, in another local family, the Adamsons. A relative newcomer to the area, the father, Gilbert Adamson, is depicted as an alien and unpopular figure, lacking a known history and made foreign by his sojourns abroad as a soldier on active duty: 'evil rumours of his character had preceded his arrival there [. . .] suspicions, without any good reason perhaps, had attached themselves to [. . .] the man'.[102] The qualification of 'perhaps' with reference to the suspicions he arouses is the first of several clues that should alert the close reader to the possibility of Gilbert's criminality. The son, Ludovic, is also an ambiguous figure, 'somewhat wild and unsteady, and too much addicted to the fascinating pastimes of flood and field', and yet 'singularly handsome, with manners above his birth, Ludovic was welcome wherever he went'.[103] The ambiguities in the text and the clues with which it is seeded position the reader as a detecting figure: apparently offered all the same information as the characters within the text, the reader is invited to draw his or her own conclusions from the 'evidence'. This textual methodology will become familiar in later detective fiction, being exemplified in the work of Agatha Christie and other 'Golden Age' writers, but 'Expiation' offers an early and innovative use of the technique.

As the narrative has hinted, Margaret Burnside meets a dreadful end: her violated dead body is discovered on the moor. It is at this point that sensationalism enters the text. The corpse is found 'in a pool of blood', 'maimed, mangled, murdered, with a hundred gashes. The corpse seemed as if it had been baked in frost, and was embedded in coagulated blood.'[104] The explicit sexualisation of the female body, as in 'Extracts from Gosschen's Diary', is absent, reflecting the changing sexual mores of the times, and while rape is implicit in the account, it is concealed in circumlocution: the word 'violation' is coupled with the phrase 'the satiating of another lust' and emerges only within the legal context of the trial.[105] Similarities to and connections with the broadside accounts of murder are evident in the prurient and voyeuristic details of the description of the injuries inflicted on the victim.

As the details of Margaret's murder are written on her body, so the guilt of the perpetrator is considered to reveal itself in his demeanour. Suspicion is thrown upon young Ludovic by an anonymous voice, which draws attention to his absence from the community at the moment the murder is revealed: 'where is Ludovic Adamson?'[106] Following the model of the early crime narratives of the *Newgate Calendar*, his absence marks him as criminal; the community rereads Ludovic's past actions in a different light, and concludes 'that none other but he could be the murderer'.[107] The text illustrates how, once Ludovic's guilt has been assumed, the circumstantial 'facts' can be made to fit the crime. That the efficacy of circumstantial evidence is itself on trial is indicated in the text with the words 'circumstantial evidence, which—wisely or unwisely—lawyers and judges have said *cannot lie*' (emphasis in the text).[108] Superstition plays a part, and Ludovic is forced to touch the body in the popular belief that a victim will bleed if touched by his or her murderer, and indeed a few drops of blood escape from Margaret's nose and mouth, but the text offers a rational explanation: 'the mouth and the nostrils of my dear Margaret did indeed bleed, when *they pressed down my hand upon her cold bosom*' (my emphasis).[109] There is an overt alliance suggested in this text between circumstantial evidence and superstition, which, in keeping with the increasingly secular and scientific contemporary mindset, devalues the reliability of the former.

The trial is recounted in detail, opening with the statement 'the evidence was entirely circumstantial, and consisted of a few damning facts, and of many of the very slightest sort, which, taken singly, seemed to mean nothing, but which, when considered all together, seemed to mean something against him'.[110] The weapon is assumed to have been Ludovic's; his shoes almost fitted the marks left in the mud near the body, 'but not so perfectly as another pair which were found in the house'; there was no blood on him, but he had (suspiciously) washed his socks; and small valuables belonging to Margaret were found in his possession along with a letter apparently making an assignation.[111] There is a detective element in this account, but the evidence is presented in the text as flawed, with room for doubt, and it is in this space that a detective figure will come to function, considering the evidence and fitting, not forcing, it to match the facts. In this tale, it is the obvious suspect who is actually guilty. Gilbert Adamson, the father, who was marked from the very first as 'other' to the community, has raped and murdered the girl, little realising that his deeds have been witnessed by his son, Ludovic, who maintains silence in order to save his father. Gilbert eventually confesses as Ludovic is about to hang, and when Ludovic's heart stops at the moment of rescue, the father kills himself. The sensational tale is folded back into a normative religious frame by the closing words: 'and the Pastor, bending over the bodies, said, "This is Expiation!"'.[112] The secular code of justice is revealed as fallible, in contrast to divine justice, which has the final word and which appears to offer a 'fall-back' position, recuperating the failings of circumstantial evidence in order to ensure the containment of crime.

Religious belief and the reliance on an omniscient God to see that justice was done were social sanctions that were gradually being eroded in this period. The tension between the secular and the spiritual was evident throughout the nineteenth century with the rise of science and the concomitant provision of empirical evidence for what had been suppositions and superstitions. What had previously been considered to be unknowable mysteries become puzzles to be solved in the knowledge that there is a solution to be found. Central to this secularisation and featuring strongly in nineteenth-century mystery fiction are medicine and psychology. The metaphorical association of crime and disease seen in the *Blackwood's* article 'Cautionary Hints to Speculators on the Increase of Crimes' and the interest generated by the medical jurisprudence text of Paris and Fonblanque suggest that connections were already being made between medical science and the mysteries posed by crime and criminality. The anatomical examination of the diseased/deceased body by the doctor or the dissecting surgeon will find its parallel in the psychological examination of the criminal and the physical examination of the evidence of crime, requiring a similarly professional agent. Prefiguring this professional agent of criminal investigation, and an important component in its evolution, is the narrating physician at the centre of Samuel Warren's short stories, written between 1830 and 1837 and published serially in *Blackwood's*.

2
Making the Case for the Professionals

2.1 Literary professional: Professional literature

Samuel Warren was an important and popular literary figure in the nineteenth century, an author whose reputation as a fiction writer briefly rivalled that of Dickens. His popularity was short-lived: as C. R. B. Dunlop observes, 'Warren's reputation was at its height during the 1840s and 1850s, after which it began to decline.'[1] Dunlop goes on to suggest that Warren was regarded by his successors as a member of an earlier generation of writers whose work was no longer relevant. This attitude seems to have survived into the twentieth and twenty-first centuries, as Warren has received little attention from either literary critics or cultural historians. His name appears in passing in histories of the legal profession, reflecting his role as a barrister and Queen's Counsel and acknowledging his literary contributions to the development of the legal profession as it now exists, but the mass of his literary output lies disregarded on dusty library shelves.[2] The body of his work incorporates fact and fiction, short stories, articles, book reviews, novels, and legal texts, and the subject matter is varied, as Warren made clear in the title of his collected essays, *Miscellanies Critical, Imaginative, and Juridical*.[3] Much of his work focuses on legal, frequently criminal, matters and questions of evidence, but Warren has found no place in the canon of criminography. Yet I suggest that, in the context of the development of crime fiction and the emergence of the detective figure, Warren's writing plays a key role.

My contention is that Warren's fictional 'Passages from the Diary of a Late Physician' (serialised in *Blackwood's Edinburgh Magazine* from 1830 to 1837) inaugurate the case structure that will typify later detective fiction, and, in the figure of the observing and analytic physician, explore a discursive space that will later be occupied by the disciplinary detective in the private sphere.[4] Further, these narratives have a disciplinary function in ideological terms: they discipline the reader as an obedient subject by acting as a form of moral policing. There are two later works that draw upon the paradigm of the 'Passages', but which have at their centre members of the legal profession: 'The Experiences of a Barrister' (*Chambers's Edinburgh Journal* 1849–1850) and 'The Confessions of an Attorney' (*Chambers's* 1850–1852). These texts have been attributed to Warren, and while there is no consensus on their authorship, the fact that they develop and redefine Warren's concept of the professional's memoir, albeit in a different professional sphere, locates them within the same newly established sub-genre of fiction: the professional anecdote. The question of authorship, while of interest, is not relevant to my argument: rather, the importance of the texts lies in their form and function in the context of criminography. The 'Experiences' and the 'Confessions' have at their centres investigating figures who, within the framework of the law function as early detectives. These later narratives draw on the structure and form of their predecessor, but move away from the medical into the legal sphere. Warren's own medical training and legal qualifications meant that he embodied, in himself and in his writing, the connections between medicine and the law referred to in the previous section of this book, and they give some credence to his having written the later legal anecdotes. His fictional narratives, most notably the 'Passages', offer rudimentary psychological evaluations of character and motive. Such evaluations are instrumental in the detection of crime, and the detective skills of the physician, used to decipher the mysteries of disease, are readily mapped onto the detective agents of the 'Experiences' and the 'Confessions'. In these texts, the diseased individual and the criminal individual are equally the subject of professional investigation.

The concept of a professional investigating figure called in to diagnose and treat a specific problem is familiar in later crime fiction. Conan Doyle's Sherlock Holmes refers to himself as 'a consulting detective' in *A Study in Scarlet*, presenting himself as a professional who is called in to advise other detectives on difficult cases of crime, rather in the fashion of a consulting physician.[5] The protagonist of the 'Passages' introduces the figure of the professional whose expertise is available for hire: he is a paid, professional enquirer with training in a specialised field, in this context, medicine. Warren's selection of a physician as his hero/narrator is significant in a number of ways. Most obviously, it permits the opening up of the closed world of the sickroom to the curious, sometimes prurient, gaze of the public, but in an authorised and authentic fashion.

Further, the profession of physician lends the narratives respectability and locates them firmly in the middle strata of society. In the first half of the nineteenth century the market for medical services was dominated at the higher end by fellows of the Royal College of Physicians, typically recruited from among the younger sons of the gentry or the sons of clergy. The physician in the 'Passages' treats patients across the social spectrum, but his attention is focused mainly on the middle and upper classes. The professional is also a businessman; his profession is what earns him a living, and physicians exercised a virtual monopoly on medical care for the rich. The respectable social background and education of the physician not only renders him a suitable role model for his readers, but also ensures his entry into the houses of the wealthy and aristocratic. This in turn enables the narrative to offer a subtle social critique of upper-class morality and behaviour that must have appealed to a largely middle-class audience willing to believe that the aristocracy were inherently dissolute and decadent. And this decadence, often associated with sexual impropriety, sensationalises the narratives, as does the temporal location of the 'Passages' in the recent and recognisable past. While the tales in the 'Passages' are largely undated, the introductory narrative gives 1820 as the 'now' from which the physician is retrospectively relating episodes from his career.

But of most significance in the context of my argument are the introduction of the case structure, which follows naturally from the work-pattern of the physician, and the quasi-detective skills that his work required. This textual structure establishes a literary sub-genre in which a variety of events or characters are linked by a single narrating figure whose profession determines the nature and content of the narratives. This innovative approach differs from earlier narratives which were either complete in themselves, as in the 'Tales of Terror' from *Blackwood's*, or where the single narrating figure functioned as a link between otherwise unconnected adventures, as in the eighteenth-century picaresque mode of literature. The separate narratives exemplified in the 'Passages' that collectively produce the case-history structure are in fact generic: each may present differently, but they are codified by the discipline of the narrator. Whatever the professional field, each case presents a problem, or a combination of problems, specific to that profession. The skills of the physician are directly relevant to the construction of the detective figure. These skills drew upon the physician's medical knowledge, but in practice relied on the observational and analytical ability of the practitioner. The physician's gaze is central to the diagnosis and classification of disease. The physician is empowered by his specialist knowledge—which is indissolubly related to the gaze that enables decision and intervention in cases of illness. The relationship between physician and patient constructs the patient as the object of the physician's gaze and subject to the power inherent in that gaze. The gaze enables the physician's decision or diagnosis, and the intention of the physician's intervention is to discipline the subjected body of the sick individual in order to restore him or her to health by the administration of drugs and the imposition of a medical regime. The physician's gaze, then, has a disciplinary effect.

This model is equally applicable to the relationship between the detective and the criminal, where the techniques of observation or surveillance are central to the detective function. In the case of both the physician and the detective, close observation of the deviance from the norm presented by the diseased or the criminal individual permits a reading of the symptoms that signify illness or criminality. Reading in turn permits analysis, and by inductive reasoning, it is possible to arrive at what was previously unknown from that which is known. The skills and methodologies of the physician are paradigmatic for those of the detective, and the protagonist of Warren's 'Passages' defines and demonstrates these practices within the discipline of a profession contained in the literary discipline of the case structure. The physician is, then, a disciplined and disciplinary figure, and, as such, creates the discursive space for the later disciplinary detective.

2.2 Preventive medicine: 'Passages from the Diary of a Late Physician'

Warren, born near Wrexham in 1807, 'was for six years actively engaged in the study of physic' prior to 1827.[6] He subsequently attended Edinburgh University, studying various subjects including Greek and medicine, and won prizes in comparative jurisprudence and poetry. While in Edinburgh he met John Wilson, the editor of *Blackwood's*, a connection that would be invaluable in Warren's literary life, as most of his work was published in *Blackwood's Edinburgh Magazine* or by William Blackwood's publishing company. He also met Thomas De Quincey at this time. Warren did not pursue a medical career, but in 1828 was admitted to the Inner Temple in London as a student of law. He was called to the Bar in 1837, and from 1838 to 1851 was employed as a barrister on the Northern Circuit. In 1851 he was made a Queen's Counsel and in 1852 became Recorder in Hull. He was made an honorary Doctor of Civil Law (DCL) in 1853 at Oxford University. He served as a Conservative MP from 1856 to 1859, representing Midhurst, and in

1859 resigned his seat to take up the position of Master of Lunacy, a post he held until his death in 1877. His fiction, which included two novels, was largely written in the period between 1829 and 1851.[7] He was, as a *quondam* medical student and a practising barrister, a professional man, and his writing, although not strictly autobiographical, drew on his own experiences. While this format was not without precedent, professional men having, prior to Warren, written accounts of their careers, Peter Drexler suggests that Warren's *Passages* were paradigmatic for the 'numerous "Memoirs", "Diaries" and similar sketches, written by judges, lawyers, prison clergy, doctors etc. which appeared in the 1830s and found further circulation until the 1860s'.[8] Such accounts, found in the contemporary periodicals rather than in (expensive) books, served both to consolidate and to popularise the status of the emergent professional classes.

It seems that Warren's legal studies were not too demanding of his time. It was in the period in which he trained as a barrister that he wrote, among other works, the 'Passages', the last of which appeared in periodical format in August 1837, the year in which he was called to the Bar. The first chapter, 'Early Struggles', was written in 1830, and as Warren records, 'was offered by me successively to the conductors of three leading magazines in London, and rejected, as "unsuitable for their pages," and "not likely to interest the public"'.[9] Prompted perhaps by the periodical's earlier acceptance of his Gothic short story, 'The Bracelets', and taking advantage of his acquaintance with John Wilson, Warren submitted his manuscript to *Blackwood's*, awaiting the reply with no very great hopes.[10] But 'at the close of the month I received a letter from Mr. Blackwood, informing me that he had inserted the chapter, and begging me to make arrangements for immediately proceeding regularly with the series'.[11] That it was intended to be a series is evident in the use of the plural 'Passages' and in the title and content of the first narrative, 'Early Struggles', which recounts the problems confronting the young physician as he sets up business in London. Warren must have read *Blackwood's* prior to this date and was perhaps in part inspired by the short, and often sensational, fiction found in its pages. Certainly, as the *Passages* proceeded, they became increasingly sensationalised, dwelling on the details of deathbeds and lingering over long-drawn-out illnesses. The focus on the emotions and sensations of the sufferers in the narratives is reminiscent of the 'Tales of Terror' discussed earlier. Morrison and Baldick include three of Warren's 'Passages' in their collected edition of *Blackwood's* short fiction, *Tales of Terror from Blackwood's Magazine*. Their declared reason for the inclusion is the way in which Warren 'orchestrates his melodramatic and horrific material to startling effect', but they acknowledge the 'cloak of sermonizing instruction' which imparts a covert monitory and disciplinary function to the narratives.[12]

In selecting a pseudoautobiographical format and electing to make his protagonist-narrator a medical man in this early venture into literature, Warren was taking advantage of, and adding to, an existing tradition. In the nineteenth century the medical profession was increasingly biographised and in the Victorian age, with its tendency to idealism and hero-worship, the figure of the physician was treated reverently in fictions and essays. And, in his focus on disease, Warren was, as Edgar Allan Poe noted, also taking advantage of the fact that '[t]he bodily health is a point of absolutely universal interest'.[13] Earlier biographies of medical men had focused on themselves and their careers rather than on their patients, an omission which is noted in the Introduction to *Passages*:

> It is somewhat strange, that a class of men who can command such interesting, extensive, and instructive materials, as the experience of most of the medical profession teems with, should have hitherto made so few contributions to the stock of polite and popular literature. The Bar, the Church, the Army, the Navy, and the Stage, have all of them spread the volumes of their secret history before the prying gaze of the public; while that of the MEDICAL PROFESSION has remained, hitherto, a sealed book.[14]

It is this promise of revealing the secret history of the medical profession which hints at the sensational contents of Warren's text, and it is in the Preface and Introduction to *Passages* that the monitory and disciplinary functions of the narratives are most apparent. Bringing the secret world of the sick man or woman into the public domain appealed to the voyeuristic and perhaps prurient nature of the audience, as had the detailed accounts of murder and execution found in the broadsides. But it also suggested that even the most personal moments of an individual's life were open to scrutiny and might be made public knowledge. Warren's *Passages* are not simply sensational accounts of illness, madness, and death, but make direct connections between deviance from moral codes and disease. Misbehaviour is invariably followed by malaise, just as in earlier criminographic material crime is followed by punishment. Further, the *Passages* are at pains to illustrate the effect that moral misdemeanours have not only on the miscreant but also on those close to him or her. In representing the deviant and diseased, Warren's writing implicitly defines by negative example the norm to which his readers should aspire.

In the 'Introduction' to the 'Passages' in *Blackwood's* and in the Preface that Warren wrote for the 1838 collected edition, the role of the physician and the contents of his diaries are made clear. The editorial introduction to the series in *Blackwood's* suggests that the physician performs 'instances of noble, though unostentatious heroism' in the treatment of his patients, who show 'calm and patient fortitude under the most intolerable anguish which can wring and torture these poor bodies of ours'.[15] This seems to locate the narratives in a strictly medical frame. But the 'Introduction' strays away from the purely medical as it suggests other subjects that might be found in the diary of a physician: 'What appalling combinations of moral and physical wretchedness [...] diversified manifestations of character [...] passages of domestic history—must have come under the notice of the intelligent practitioner of physic?'[16] This 'rich mine of incident and sentiment', the 'Introduction' insists, must be 'calculated to furnish both instruction and amusement to the public'.[17] The 'Introduction' authenticates the 'Passages' by stating that 'all possible care will be taken to avoid undue disclosures. Names, dates, and places [...] will be generally omitted—except when they can be inserted with perfect safety.'[18] The 'Passages' are introduced as factual accounts by a real physician, a device that seems to have convinced the contemporary audience. The 'Preface by the Translator' affixed to the German edition of the 1838 *Passages* states that the narratives 'bear [...] the undoubted stamp of genuineness [...] are at least founded upon truth [...] though, undoubtedly, here and there the reality has been coloured and veiled by a fiction-like dress'.[19]

Warren's own Preface to the English edition of 1838, in which he admitted his authorship of the text, while skirting around the question of authenticity, endorses the exemplary function of the narratives suggested in the 'Introduction'. He declares that 'all I wished was to present some of the results of my own personal observation of life and character in their most striking exemplification—to illustrate, as it were, the real practical working of virtues and vices'.[20] There is no mention of the medical component of the 'Passages'. It is as if Warren is acknowledging the monitory and disciplinary function of the narratives. This function is reiterated in the lengthy citation from the laudatory 'Preface by the Translator' to the German edition, which Warren elected to include in his own Preface. Amidst the more general praise for Warren's *Passages*, the writer notes that 'a bright fountain of advice and warning springs from them all'.[21] The profession of physician comes to serve as the excuse for the narrator's involvement in sensational cases of vice and depravity of which disease is the symptom. This reconstruction of the *Passages* from a collection of medical anecdotes by a physician into a series of moral tales marks the transition from 'amusement', or entertainment, to 'instruction', or discipline, and the later 'Experiences of a Barrister' and 'Confessions of an Attorney' will take the instructional moral model and apply it to cases of crime rather than disease. The observant and detecting eye of the physician will reappear in the detecting figures of the legal narratives, and moral deviance will be associated with criminality rather than cancer, consumption, mental decay, or bodily corruption. Warren's physician is paradigmatic for the disciplinary detective.

It is possible that Warren initially fully intended his series of stories to be, as the title suggests, medical cases taken from the supposed diary of a physician. Certainly, in the first chapter, 'Early Struggles' (*Blackwood's* 28:170 [August 1830], pp. 322–339), there is no indication of the increasingly sensational material that will follow. This chapter introduces the physician, describes his personal, financial, and family circumstances, and sees him established as a practising doctor. It further serves to place him as firmly middle class, and, as a married man with a child, locates him in a suitably domestic situation. His probity and professionalism are made clear, constructing him as an appropriate and admirable figure, a role model to which his audience might aspire, and equally, lending his narratives authority and authenticity. Centring each chapter on a single case or a number of short cases responds to the demands of serial publication and simultaneously ensures that each chapter will present accounts complete in themselves, moving from event through complication to closure. This imposes a discipline upon the text that enhances its disciplinary effect upon the reader: the warning that the narrative carries is immediate and present, rather than being diffused as it would be in a lengthier novel format. In practice, Warren quickly strayed from the discipline of relatively short accounts focused on medical matters into much longer narratives that concerned themselves more with morals than with medicine, although the connection between disease, mental or physical, and the behaviour of the individual continues to feature strongly in the 'Passages'.

The increasing length and complexity of the narratives is apparent in the collected editions of *Passages*. The first edition was published in two volumes in 1832 and contained the first 12 chapters of the 'Passages'. But where the periodical publication had at times included two or three cases in each chapter, the collected edition allocated a chapter to each case. The original 12 chapters, ranging in length from as few as three pages ('The Dentist and the Comedian') to thirty-five pages ('Mother and Son'), were expanded in this way into 23. Reference to the original chapters as they appeared in *Blackwood's* demonstrates the tendency of the later stories to recount single cases that maintain or increase the length of the earlier plural case-histories. This tendency is more marked in the 1838 edition of *Passages*, which reproduced the 1832 edition in its entirety, but added chapters 12 to 17, which had appeared in *Blackwood's* between 1832 and 1837. These last five chapters were single cases that covered nearly as much textual space as had the previous 12, or in book form 23. The discipline of narrative and the disciplinary effect of the cases are somewhat dissipated by the increased length of the later material, which read more as novellas than as case-histories, and sensational novellas at that. The immediacy of the sensational and monitory effect present in the shorter narratives is lessened when it is diffused into longer stories. Nevertheless, the use of purported medical cases centred on an individual created a precedent for later professional anecdotes, and, more importantly, for the case structure essential to crime and, particularly, detective fiction.

Not all of Warren's 'Passages' were sensational in content or monitory in function. In 'The Dentist and the Comedian' (*Blackwood's* 28:172 [September 1830], with 'Cancer', 'A Scholar's Deathbed', 'Duelling', and 'Preparing for the House', pp. 474–495), the physician narrates a brief account of the effect comedy has on pain. It is a light-hearted narrative, although the psychology of overcoming pain with laughter has some medical value. 'The Turned Head' (*Blackwood's* 29:175 [January 1831], with 'The Wife', pp. 105–127) is similarly light and comedic in content, dealing with a case of hypochondria where the victim is convinced that his head is on back to front. The physician cures him with a sleight of hand, persuading the deluded man's Negro servant to dress his master with the clothes reversed. Again, the medical value here is in the psychology that the physician employs, and the story is more humorous than serious. There is a quasi-ghost story, 'The Spectral Dog—An Illusion' (*Blackwood's* 28:173 [November 1830], with 'Consumption' and 'The Forger', pp. 770–793), which, as the title suggests, is concerned with the supernatural and which offers no rational explanation, merely gesturing towards the possibility of optical illusion. Of the strictly medical accounts, the most sensational and horrifying is 'Cancer', the physician's second narrative. The account opens by suggesting that cancer is 'that terrible scourge of the female sex' and continues with his diagnosis of the disease in a respectable married woman.[22] The diagnosis which, although heavily veiled in circumlocution, appears to be breast cancer, requires the attentions of a surgeon, and the physician duly calls in an associate to perform an operation. The procedure, presumably a mastectomy, is carried out with the patient seated upright in a chair, fully conscious and without the benefit of anaesthetic. Her succour comes from clutching a letter from her husband, which gives her the strength to withstand the pain. The covert message here is the value of patriarchally constituted domesticity. The good, devoted wife survives the operation and is pronounced cured.

There are other chapters that deal with the purely medical, for example 'Consumption' and 'A Slight Cold' (*Blackwood's* 29:181 [June 1831], with 'Grave Doings' and 'Rich and Poor', pp. 946–967). 'A Slight Cold' is an exercise in medical authority: the patient, suffering from, as the title suggests, a simple cold, neglects to follow the physician's advice and the cold develops into a serious illness which ends in the death of the sufferer. 'Consumption' is an account of a case of tuberculosis in a beautiful young woman who falls victim to the family tendency to the disease. Her symptoms and suffering are described in graphic, and at times eroticised, detail, while her pale beauty, enhanced by the feverish flush of the illness, permits the introduction of a love interest that serves to increase the pathos of the tale. There is an exemplary element in this narrative as the heroine, described as 'too good—too beautiful for this world', endures without complaint the vicissitudes that beset her, thinking only of her lover and the better world to which she will go after death.[23] As in 'Cancer', this is an idealised and ideal portrayal of dutiful femininity. The female body is at the centre of 'Grave Doings', a narrative that takes advantage of the contemporary public interest in 'Resurrection Men', or grave robbers. It also affords Warren an opportunity to defend the practice of human dissection as essential to the efficient practice of medicine: addressing his reader, he declares '[y]ou expect us to cure you of disease, and yet deny us the only means of learning *how*?'[24] The physician describes his foray into a graveyard to recover the body of a young woman whose relatives had refused permission for an autopsy to ascertain the disputed cause of death. This is, in a sense, an early forensic investigation, although the victim had died from natural causes rather than as the result of crime. The tenacity of the diagnostic physician and his desire to know the truth, a desire which leads him to break the law, are attributes that the established detective will share. The narrative also draws on the Gothic associations evoked by graveyards and ghosts to further sensationalise the topic, and ends with the macabre revelation that the young woman's skeleton and skull are now medical exhibits.

But the majority of the narratives in *Passages* are concerned with the physical and mental consequences of sin, moral misdemeanour, and, occasionally, crime, in a largely middle-class *milieu*. The association of vice, immorality, and crime with disease, or specifically contagion, was, in the nineteenth century, accepted as an unpleasant fact of life in the middle-class perception of the poor. Medical and social reform focused as much on moral education as it did on hygiene; but where it was relatively easy for the state to impose regulation on, and institute measures for the control of, the lower orders of society, similar symptoms of 'dis-ease' in the body of middle-class society required a different, and ideological, approach. Warren's text functions as an ideological literary tool with which to discipline its audience, offering an exemplary role model of appropriate behaviour and equally performing an admonitory role in its representation of the consequences of inappropriate, dissolute, or immoral actions. And this 'tool' would work on both male and female readers, as the contents of the 'Passages' suggest: *Blackwood's* included articles by and for women, and would have been read by women as well as men. It is this ideological function of the 'Passages' on which I want to concentrate, and, to that end, I will focus on those narratives that best exemplify the disciplinary aspects of the text and into which, in some cases, crime and criminality intrude.

The figure of the physician provides a positive masculine role model throughout the *Passages*, but other representations of masculinity tend to be negative, fulfilling a monitory role in the depiction of dissolute and depraved behaviour and its consequences. The narratives that focus on women not only offer both exemplary role model and admonition, but also permit a covert introduction of sex and sexuality which sensationalises the stories while containing it within the respectability of a quasi-medical discourse. The practicalities of appropriate feminine behaviour could be learned from the factual contents of conduct books and books on etiquette that were available in the nineteenth century, but the representation of the patriarchally constructed 'Angel in the House', that ideological paragon of domestic femininity, was more easily located in the fiction of the period. 'Passages', then, in its depiction of women exerted a disciplinary influence over the behaviour of its female readers and reinforced the expectations of the male audience. There are both positive and negative representations of women in Warren's text, and women are often portrayed as victims of dissolute men. For Warren, as for his readers, women were the weaker sex, both morally and physically, and this is evident in 'Passages'.

An early example of feminine weakness and inappropriate behaviour is 'Death at the Toilet' (*Blackwood's* 28:174 [December 1830], with 'A "Man About Town" ', pp. 921–940). This short account is an overt warning against the sin of vanity, and the narrating physician makes no attempt to conceal his contempt and dislike for this patient. The narrative opens with a daughter defying her mother, insisting that she will attend a party that very night in spite of her precarious state of health. The immediate impression the reader receives is of a headstrong, flighty, and disobedient girl, and the narrator confirms this in the next paragraph: 'A weaker, more frivolous, and conceited creature never breathed—the torment of her amiable parent, the nuisance of her acquaintance.'[25] Her behaviour is in part explained by the absence of a father; the mother is a widow. The absent male figure is a recurring theme in those 'Passages' concerned with women, reinforcing the perceived necessity for masculine control within the domestic sphere. Miss J——'s conceit is, as the physician points out, unwarranted, as she is 'far from being even pretty-faced, or having any pretensions to a good figure—for she both stooped and was skinny—yet she believed herself handsome'.[26] The physician's eye observes her demeanour and implicitly condemns it, and the narrative immediately continues with an account of the health problems that had initiated his attendance on the girl. This implies a direct relationship between Miss J——'s appearance and actions and her physical well-being. The physician diagnoses a heart problem that may, he suggests, result in sudden death, especially if Miss J—— maintains her present lifestyle of dancing and late nights. His advice is ignored and the consequences are inevitable.

On the evening in question, the girl withdraws to her room to dress for the party, and her lengthy absence invokes no anxiety in her parent, as the daughter's 'toilet was usually a long and laborious business'.[27] It is only when the maid goes to inform her mistress of the passage of time that Miss J—— is discovered dead, seated in front of her mirror. The physician is called, and gives a graphic account of the scene:

> An arm-chair was drawn to this table, and in it sat Miss J——, stone dead. Her head rested on her right hand, [...] while her left hung down by her side, grasping a pair of curling irons. Each of her wrists was encircled by a showy gilt bracelet. She was dressed in a white muslin frock [...]. Her face was turned towards the glass which, by the light of the expiring candle, reflected with frightful fidelity the clammy fixed features, daubed over with rouge and carmine [...] and the eyes directed full into the glass, with a cold, dull stare [...].

On examining the countenance more narrowly, I thought I detected the traces of a smirk of conceit and self-complacency, which not even the paralysing touch of death could wholly obliterate [. . .]. The ghastly visage of death, thus leering through the tinselry of fashion—the 'vain show' of artificial joy—was a horrible mockery of the fooleries of life![28]

There is a sensationalised and voyeuristic element in the intrusion of the male gaze into the privacy of the bedchamber and the rituals of dressing, but this is superficially justified by the medical context in which it occurs. The medicalised masculine gaze of the physician detects traces of the dis-ease of mind which finds expression in the disease of the body. His detecting eye sees the cause of death in the face of his patient: the physical cause is heart failure, but the text suggests that death is rather the result of Miss J——'s behaviour. He makes clear the dual message of his narrative. Had the girl followed his advice and obeyed the injunctions of her mother, 'her life might have been protracted, possibly, for years', and had she not been so conceited and frivolous, she would not have 'been struck dead in the very act of sacrificing at the shrine of female vanity!'[29] By implication, Miss J——'s death is the consequence not only of her vanity, but also of her refusal of masculine control and parental authority. The narrative implicitly instructs, or disciplines, the female reader by negative example.

A later, and much longer 'Passage' that focuses on aberrant feminine behaviour is 'The Magdalen' (*Blackwood's* 32:202 [December 1832], pp. 878–911). As the title suggests, this case-history concerns itself with the story of a reformed prostitute. The narrative functions as a negative exemplar for the female audience of *Passages*, but is strongly condemnatory towards the men who are instrumental in the downfall of the heroine. The case is a retrospective reconstruction of the events in the 'Magdalen's' life, moving from her presentation as a patient back into an account of the circumstances that have led to her illness and current predicament, returning to the present of the narrative and closing with her death. But the sensational nature of the material, dealing as it does with sexual matters, and the moral tone the narrative seeks to convey are apparent in the introductory paragraphs. The story opens with a series of exclamatory phrases which covertly describe the heroine's degradation: 'Despised daughter of frailty! Outcast of outcasts! Poor wayward lamb, torn by the foulest wolf of the forest!'[30] The 'foulest wolf' becomes, in biblical metaphor, an adder, despoiling the virgin purity of the lilies of humanity, and the male reader is invited to imagine himself in that role. Having set the tone of the piece, the narrator slips into the more prosaic role of physician and proceeds with the story, beginning when he is called to the bedside of a sick woman.

In case the subject matter of his narrative should not have been made clear to the reader in the introduction, the physician declares that 'I do not see why I should mince matters by hesitating to state that the house in which I found myself [...] was one of ill-fame.'[31] To his horror, the patient is revealed as an old friend, Miss Eleanor B——, known to the physician and his wife in the past. He overcomes his initial revulsion and makes a medical examination, suspecting consumption. He then carries out what seems to be the only medical treatment that warrants much description in *Passages*: he bleeds her copiously until she faints, following which he prescribes a restorative medicine. The narrative subsequently establishes the circumstances in which the physician and his wife had first met 'Miss Edwards', then the daughter of a respectable widow. Eleanor's beauty had earned her the sobriquet 'Madonna', an ironic nickname in view of her later occupation. Her beauty had also ensured the attentions of several handsome young men, including a member of Royalty, and leads to her elopement with a *roué* who has falsely promised marriage. But her appearance, education, tastes, and inclinations resulted in her falling prey to the sin of pride, and, as the observant and prescient physician had noted, 'Pride, unless combined with the highest qualities, is apt to precipitate such a girl into the vortex.'[32] The bare bones of the narrative are fleshed out with much sensational description of Eleanor's physical and mental state and graphic descriptions of her squalid surroundings as she is passed from one man to another. Immorality is, in this 'Passage', linked with crime. Eleanor's fall into prostitution forces her to live among the criminalised poor of the city, and her co-inhabitants of the 'house of ill-fame' plot to rob her. Overhearing them, the physician, with the assistance of a police officer, prevents the robbery. Real crime, as opposed to moral fallibility, requires a specialised agency, and the poor are policed by a state force rather than by ideological discipline.

Eleanor's recuperation and reformation are well under way before she relates her tale to the physician. It is a classic account of pride and the desire for better social status leading a young, fatherless girl into circumstances that she cannot control. Deserted by her male protector, and prevented by pride and an increasing addiction to drink from returning to her country home, she moves back to London. Eventually, destitute, she discovers that her mother is dead, and turns to prostitution as her only means of survival. Throughout this section, as Eleanor tells her story, she reiterates her desire for death. The moral message is made very clear. Moral degradation is indissolubly connected to physical and mental degeneration, and although the 'Magdalen' reforms, she never entirely recovers. The physician's hope that he might ' "minister" successfully to "the MIND diseased" ' proves unfounded, and Eleanor eventually succumbs to the consumption whose presence the physician feared, and which is implicitly the result of her life of dissipation. The sensational aspects of the narrative are cloaked in the medical and religious discourse which explain and excuse the content, but as in 'Death at the Toilet' there is a disciplinary function. The absence of a controlling masculine figure in Eleanor's young life, and her pride and social aspirations, lay her open to the machinations of unscrupulous men. Female sexuality, the text suggests, must be contained within the parameters of a patriarchal domestic sphere. Equally, masculine desire requires to be constrained in secure domesticity, as exemplified in the happy family circumstances of the physician.

In producing anecdotes that depict negative or deviant social and moral behaviour and its effects, the text reinforces the values of the domestic and familial norm. While 'The Magdalen' fulfils this function, it is also of particular significance in respect of the paradigmatic case structure that *Passages* inaugurates. In terms of the later detective narrative, the pattern of the crime, followed by a retrospective reconstruction of the events which led to it, and concluding with the attribution of guilt and subsequent closure, are all present in 'The Magdalen', albeit couched in a rather different, medicalised discourse. It is the physician who diagnoses the disease, discovers the history, fathoms the cause, and turns the unknown into the known, just as the detective will detect the crime, uncover its method, work out the motive, and ascribe guilt to the appropriate person.

Not all the 'Passages' have negative female role models. In 'The Wife' (*Blackwood's* 29:175 [January 1931] with 'The Turned Head', pp. 105–127), the wife is very much the 'Angel in the House', performing her domestic duties and even attempting to support the family by carrying out the legal duties that her abusive, dissipated lawyer husband neglects. The immorality here is centred on the husband, who marries for money, spends it on wine, women, and gambling, supports a mistress, and resorts to physical abuse when his wife has the audacity to complain. Despite his actions, the wife struggles to retain her affection for him and to maintain domestic stability. A further exemplary female role model is found in 'The Merchant's Clerk' (*Blackwood's* 40:249 and 250 [July and August 1836], Pt 1 pp. 1–32, Pt 2 pp. 181–206), where the female protagonist is again presented very positively in contrast to the depiction of the masculine characters in the story. As these 'Passages' suggest, there is greater emphasis in *Passages* on portrayals of negative masculine behaviour than on that of the female: moral policing is not confined to the feminine sphere.

The dangers associated with an absent father figure are equally applicable to young men. In 'Mother and Son' (*Blackwood's* 30:186 [October 1831], pp. 565–599), it is the actions and behaviour of a young man that are the focus of the narrative. The 'Passage' opens with a diatribe against the evils of gambling, promising, as the physician has it, 'a touching and terrible disclosure of the misery, disgrace, and ruin consequent on GAMBLING'.[33] Mr Beauchamp has been brought up by his mother, who, in trying to substitute for the absent male parent, has subjected her son to restraints which 'served, alas! little other purpose than to whet his appetites for the pleasurable pursuits to which he considered himself entitled, and from which he had been so long and unnecessarily debarred'.[34] On coming into his fortune, and influenced by his college tutor and mentor, one Mr Eccles, Beauchamp initially enjoys, but later becomes addicted to, gambling. The physician is quick to note that the boy has none of the other vices associated with gaming, and lays the blame squarely on Eccles. A long and complicated plot ensues, with the introduction of a love interest, a revenge trope, and, in order to draw in the physician, an account of the mental and physical effects that his gambling addiction and subsequent accumulation of debts have on Beauchamp. His health suffers, as does his mother's when she discovers the extent of his losses, and both mother and son require the attentions of the narrating physician. The machinations of the plot culminate in a duel in which Beauchamp kills his opponent. He is arrested, charged with murder, and taken to Newgate.

A protracted prison stay ensues, enabling the physician to make much of the deleterious effects that confinement has on Beauchamp and that anxiety and stress have on his mother and fiancée. The subsequent trial is described in graphic detail, giving meticulous accounts of the prosecution and defence arguments which suggest Warren's familiarity with the law. Eventually, Beauchamp is acquitted. The judge rules that he is the victim of a conspiracy, and, as such, innocent of the murder with which he had been charged. But the son's relief and happiness is short-lived: the stress on his mother's heart has been too great, and on his return home she dies in his embrace. Beauchamp suffers a long illness, as does his fiancée. Both seem to recover, but Beauchamp's tentative steps towards normality end when, in a fevered state of mind, he commits suicide. The narrative ends with the physician's explicit connection between gambling and its potential disastrous consequences. The 'Passage' suggests that a young man deprived of a suitable role model by the lack of a father is easily corrupted and led into dissipation. This is directly connected with disease, physical and mental, and with crime, carrying a strong monitory and moral message, and functioning to discipline the young male reader. To drive this message home a letter is appended to the 'Passage', which purports to be from the *Morning Herald* of 19 October 1831. It is from 'a ruined gamester', and in it he declares,

> [I]f I had a hundred pounds to spare, I would spend it all in reprinting the 'Gambler' ['Mother and Son'] from *Blackwood's Magazine*, and distributing it among the frequenters of C——'s and F——'s, and other hells. I am sure its overwhelming truth and power would shock *some* into pausing on the brink of ruin![35]

The letter is from —— Prison, and is dated 'Oct. 17'. Questions of its authenticity aside, it advocates the use of 'Mother and Son' as a warning against gambling, endorsing and reiterating its monitory message in the convict status and prison location of its writer. The covert discipline of the 'Passage' is overtly authorised by the remorseful voice of reality, the voice of a man whose lack of self-discipline has resulted in his subjection to the discipline of the state.

The profession of the physician in 'Mother and Son' serves as the excuse for relating the narrative, and its content introduces a theme which will reappear in the legally framed professional anecdotes and in William Russell's *Recollections of a Detective Police-Officer*, which I discuss later. Gambling, with its attendant risk of cheating and fraud, strikes at the heart of a respectable middle class in an increasingly capitalist society where property, or money, is what confers social status and confirms that respectability. The uncontrolled and unguided actions of masculine youth lead inevitably to the destruction of the family. While the message of the narrative is explicitly a warning against gaming, at its heart is the incomplete family. In this negative exemplar the text implies that the presence of a father to guide the young Beauchamp would have prevented his foray into gambling and ruin. But in 'A "Man About Town"' (*Blackwood's* 28:174, with 'Death at the Toilet' [December 1830], pp. 921–940), there are no such mitigating circumstances. As becomes increasingly frequent in the 'Passages', the narrative opens with a short preface by the physician, in which he sets the parameters for the case-history he is about to relate. These prefaces prefigure the tone of the 'Preface' to the collected edition, steering the reader to a correct understanding of the message contained in the sensational, quasi-medical accounts that follow. The physician states that his intention in relating this 'Passage' is 'to shew, if it ever meet their eyes, your "men about town", as the *élite* of the rakish fools and flutterers of the day are significantly termed, that some portions of the page of profligacy are black—black with horror, and steeped in tears'.[36] The narrative is included, he insists, purely for its monitory function. To this end, he will describe 'the pains and agonies, *which these eyes witnessed*' despite the 'feelings little less than torture' it accords the writer.[37] The emphasis is the narrator's own, reasserting the importance of the knowing physician's gaze while simultaneously authenticating his tale.

The physician first meets Mr Effingstone at the scene of a fist fight, in which Effingstone comes off worst and requires medical treatment. This is the start of a long medical relationship, as Effingstone's dissipated lifestyle takes its toll. Possessed of a good income, university education, and with a landed gentry background, he spends his time and money gratifying his every desire. An aside purporting to be from the editor of the physician's diary declares that five pages of the 'Passage' have been omitted as '[t]hey are too revolting for the pages of this Magazine, and totally unfit for its miscellaneous readers', an omission that incites the audience to imagine the contents as being of the utmost depravity.[38] The physician recounts Effingstone's medical and life history, linking the two as medical treatment follows quickly upon excesses of dissipation. Eventually, after giving many examples of the 'man about town's' dissolute and depraved behaviour, the physician is called urgently to what proves to be Effingstone's deathbed, and the remainder of the narrative is an account of his prolonged and agonised demise. The diary form is used for this section, giving the dates of the physician's visits and an account of the events attendant on each. It is preceded by a disclaimer which makes clear that the diseases and their symptoms are too shocking for any but a professional's eyes: the opportunity to share the physician's gaze that marks the majority of the narratives is here closed down, excluding the reader from the reality and simultaneously invoking undisclosed sensational speculation. It is not stated, but implied, that Effingstone is suffering from the consequences of his immorality, and that his illness, probably syphilis, is the result of his sexual adventures. It takes three months for him to die, and the narrative revels in the sensational and gruesome details of his physical and mental agony as he descends into madness.

Effingstone's final fate is to be interred under a false name, as his family disowns him.

This 'Passage' is highly sensational, and its content is dignified only by the medical discourse in which it is couched. It is a clear warning against the dissipation and degeneration that result from an abuse of intellect and a refusal of the proper, respectable professional role and domestic circumstances appropriate for an intelligent man that is exemplified by the figure of the physician. Effingstone's implied social status makes the narrative a covert criticism of the idle rich. But its major functions are monitory and disciplinary. The deviant individual becomes the diseased individual, as the disobedient subject causes dis-ease in the body of society, and the medicine that must be administered is self-discipline and discipline of the self. In 'A "Man About Town"', the physician is less a medical practitioner than an observant moral policeman. This 'Passage' makes the most direct and clear connections between moral degeneration and physical and mental disintegration. But the physician's observational skills are not limited to the surveillance of immorality and disease. In the only one of Warren's 'Passages' that is concerned solely with criminal as opposed to moral deviance, the physician's gaze functions to detect crime, demonstrating the ease with which the skills applied to the diagnosis of disease can be relocated in a criminal framework. This is in 'The Forger' (*Blackwood's* 28:173 [November 1830], with 'Consumption' and 'The Spectral Dog', pp. 770–793), an early 'Passage' that is reminiscent of Henry Thomson's 'Le Revenant', which had appeared in *Blackwood's* in 1827. Thomson's narrative had focused on the mental and physical effects that crime, subsequent guilt, and imprisonment prior to hanging had on the forger at the centre of the account, and this may have been the inspiration for Warren to write a 'Passage' examining these effects supposedly from a medical perspective.

In 'The Forger', the physician is requested to attend a 'Mr Gloucester' of Regent Street. The narrative immediately instils doubt about this person in the mind of the reader by proffering the apparently irrelevant information that he is not listed in the physician's red book. The absence of 'Mr Gloucester' from this book leads the physician to dismiss him as 'a recent comer', a phrase evocative of social climbing. As the narrative proceeds, the scene set continues to suggest that some kind of fraud is about to be revealed. The patient's room is 'spacious [...] somewhat showily furnished', and only 'the mild retiring sunlight' mitigates 'the glare of the gilded picture-frames [...] round the walls'.[39] As the physician observes, 'the whole aspect of things indicated the residence of a person of some fashion and fortune', implying possibility rather than certainty.[40] And while the physician finds his prospective patient's countenance 'rather pleasing, fresh-coloured, with regular features, and very light auburn hair', his comments on the rest of 'Mr Gloucester' are positively Holmesian:

> I may perhaps be laughed at by some for noticing such an apparently insignificant circumstance; but the observant humour of my profession must sufficiently account for my detecting the fact that his *hands* were not those of a *born and bred* gentleman—of one who, as the phrase is 'has never *done any thing*' in his life; but they were coarse, large, and clumsy-looking [...] there was a constrained and over-anxious display of politeness—an assumption of fashionable ease and indifference, that sat ill on him, like a court dress fastened on a vulgar fellow.[41]

The physician deduces that 'Mr Gloucester' is not what he appears to be, and immediately takes a dislike to him, declaring that '[t]hese sort of people are a great nuisance to one, since there is no knowing exactly how to treat them'.[42] His patient's crime seems, at first, to be no more than concealing his true social status and assuming a higher station.

'Mr Gloucester' gives the physician an account of his symptoms, which are those of 'a disordered nervous system', a diagnosis that the doctor confirms by physical examination. He then enquires into the possible causes: unpleasant events in the family, disappointment in love, losses at gaming, or any other source of secret annoyance. 'Mr Gloucester' denies all these possibilities, claiming a familial constitutional nervousness and demanding 'physic', which the physician provides, along with advice to seek cheerful company and fresh air. By the end of this first visit, the physician has come to the conclusion that his patient is 'neither more nor less than a systematic London sharper—a gamester—a hanger-on about town'.[43] But a second visit finds 'Mr Gloucester' in worse condition, agitated, deeply depressed, and suicidal, leading the physician to suspect hereditary insanity. Again, the physician's observant and detecting eye finds further evidence of 'Mr Gloucester's' true employment. He notices a 'bill or promissory note' on a side table, but when he picks it up it is snatched from his hand and 'Mr Gloucester' gabbles excuses for its existence. This confirms the physician's suspicions: 'I was sitting familiarly with a swindler—a gambler—and the bill he was so anxious to conceal was evidently wrung from one of his ruined dupes.'[44] This proves not to be the case. A knock at the door interrupts the consultation, and two 'sullen Newgate myrmidons' enter with 'a warrant to arrest Mr Gloucester for FORGERY!'[45] The physician's detective skills are no longer required, and the remainder of the 'Passage' is an account of the forger's arrest and the subsequent trial, conviction and imprisonment of 'Mr Gloucester', which the physician follows in the newspapers.

He is called to attend 'Mr Gloucester' once more, in Newgate Prison, a visit that permits the description of the prison interior, which 'horror has appropriated [...] for her peculiar dwelling-place', redolent with 'the foul atmosphere of all the concentrated misery and guilt of the metropolis'.[46] The physician dwells upon the altered physical state of his erstwhile patient and on his forthcoming fate, which is to be hanged.[47] 'Mr Gloucester' has moral crime as well as felony on his conscience: now repentant and apparently resigned, he requests the physician to attend to the young girl he has seduced under an assumed name, to see her through her confinement and to pass on some money for her and her child. Moral deviance, the narrative suggests, is congruent with criminality. The visit ends with the young man enquiring piteously about the actuality of death by hanging, a question that the physician cannot bring himself to answer. Propelled by 'an irresistible and most morbid restlessness and curiosity', the physician attends the execution, watching until the noose is placed around the victim's neck, then turning away in horror. The description of the scene is strongly reminiscent of those found in the broadsides, with the rowdy and anticipatory crowd gathered around the gallows and with St Sepulchre and Newgate in the background.

There is an implicit critique of the penal system in the comments of the physician's fellow-watchers, who are speaking 'on the subject of execution', and who 'unanimously execrated the sanguinary severity of the laws which could deprive a young man [...] of his life, for an offence of merely civil criminality'.[48] The whole is sensationally depicted, performing a monitory role within the broader disciplinary function of the narrative, which works as a warning against the social crime of seeking a status which is not one's own. Part of the message contained in *Passages* is the definition of the boundaries between classes: the true crime of the forger lies in his desire to better his social position, a desire which leads him into crime. Implicitly, the narrative suggests that had 'Mr Gloucester' gone into the trade that his industrious father practised he would not have ended his life on the gallows. While it is permissible, admirable even, to rise in one's trade or profession, the social barriers are sacrosanct, essential to the structure and well-being of society. The disciplinary function of the narrative is to reiterate this message. Transgression of social boundaries is a feature associated with the middle-class, or 'white-collar', crime found in the later nineteenth-century legal anecdotes, the 'Experiences of a Barrister' and the 'Confessions of an Attorney', and is indicative of the gradual erosion of the class system and the anxieties attendant on that erosion. But in terms of criminography, Warren's 'The Forger' is important in three respects. It brings together medicine and crime in a single narrative; it relates the physician's observation skills directly to detective skills, and it combines a moral message with a warning against crime. Moral policing is here connected to criminal policing.

The narratives are directed at the individual reader of the text, implicitly inviting him or her into the recognisable and familiar world in which the physician practises his profession. The first-person narrative speaks directly to its audience, offering the opportunity to share the perspective of the physician, to participate in his gaze. But this participation also works in reverse, as the observant eye of the physician is in turn metaphorically permitted to gaze upon the domestic space of that reader, while the narrator exhorts him or her to examine themselves for signs of 'dis-ease' similar to that portrayed in the narrative. The reality that the 'Passages' appear to represent encourages the reader to identify with the various characters depicted and with the dilemmas that produce their mental and physical symptoms, an identification which enables the disciplinary aspects of the narratives to function. The 'Passages' offer positive role models, most notably the physician himself, while the consequences of deviant, degenerate, dissipated, immoral, or even criminal behaviour, observed, reported on, and implicitly condemned by the physician are both monitory and disciplinary in their negative exemplarity. The overt role of the physician is as a medical practitioner, but covertly his narratives suggest that behind the physical illnesses he diagnoses lie social and moral deviance, the germs of disorder that threaten the orderly body of society just as sickness threatens the body of the individual. His observant eye is also investigative, examining less the bodily symptoms of disease than seeking its cause in the psychology and personal history of the patient. If the 'Passages' are a form of moral policing, then the physician is a policeman of morality.

Warren's 'Passages' began serialisation in 1830, one year after the introduction of the New Metropolitan Police force in London; a police specifically formed to control and contain criminality. But crime was, for much of the nineteenth century, in the main associated with those at the bottom of the social scale, that is, the poor and unemployed.

Middle- and upper-class 'crimes' were perceived rather as social and moral transgressions, and required a different kind of policing, a system predicated not on the imposition of an external force but on the assimilation and internalisation of appropriate values and modes of behaviour. This ideological method of policing was disseminated, then as now, via a number of media: the newspapers, educational texts, religious tracts, and the periodical press. Literature of all kinds was, and is, an ideal locus for the transmission of ideology. The 'Passages' epitomise this function of literature, exemplifying and endorsing correct behaviour and standards in their condemnation of social and moral misdemeanour, while their location in *Blackwood's* ensured that the moral message reached the largely middle- and upper-class audience which the contemporary standards of literacy and the cost of the periodical demanded. The discipline of the individual essential to an orderly body of society is not imposed by an external force, but inserted into, and internalised by, the individual via the medium of literature.

But as the century progressed and the professional, business-oriented, and increasingly property-owning middle class grew, so did 'white-collar' crime: forgery, fraud, embezzlement, and other variations of theft. In part, this was controlled by the increasingly efficient police force, which found a literary representation in 'Waters', a fictional police officer whose 'Recollections' were published in *Chambers's* from 1849 to 1853. But the policing of white-collar crime was reactive rather than preventive, responding after the event in its search for the perpetrator. As crime infiltrated the middle classes, moral self-discipline was not an effective defence against its temptations and depredations. The 'preventive medicine' prescribed by Warren's physician was an ineffective remedy for this new social malady, and a different treatment was required that would not only combine monitory and exemplary functions, but that would also serve to forewarn and forearm the potential innocent victim of crime. A secondary effect of the intrusion of crime into the middle class was the possibility that innocent men and women could become implicated in, or wrongly accused of, criminal offences, and would consequently require professional legal advice and assistance. A substitute treatment, then, for the literary ideological 'preventive medicine' of Warren's physician became necessary, one that would not involve the state-controlled police, but that would treat the disorders of the middle- and upper-classes with a remedy more appropriate to their status and that would preserve the confidentiality inherent in the patient–physician relationship. This was to be found in a literary representation of the legal profession.

2.3 Legal treatments: Evidence of necessity

Warren's physician was a textual response to the contemporary anxieties of a society in flux, where social cohesion was failing and the class boundaries were becoming less fixed, and where moral values were often undermined by the demands of capitalism and the desires of the individual. The 'Passages' are also indicative of an increasingly secular society, where the certainties offered by religious belief were being eroded, and where systems of management were being inaugurated in order to control and contain individual deviance and social disorder. One such system of management was the New Police, and an appropriate substitute for the physician might logically have been a policeman, whose work centred on crime and criminals, but the policeman was perceived as the servant and protector of the propertied classes against the criminal, and implicitly lower, classes, and, as such, was unsuited and unsuitable for policing the bourgeoisie, even in fiction. A better vehicle to convey ideologically loaded narratives that would both reassure and covertly discipline their middle-class audience was to be found among those other professionals who were of the same social status as the audience, but who dealt with matters criminal.

The legal profession which, with the exception of barristers, had long been regarded as corrupt and parasitic to the extent that being an attorney practically disqualified a man from decent society in the seventeenth and much of the eighteenth century, gradually improved its image in the nineteenth century through self-regulation and increasing professionalism. The Law Society was founded in 1825 and introduced a more formal system of training attorneys, or solicitors. It also instituted a Law Library, inaugurated lectures on the law for articled clerks, and began to regularise legal practice across the country. The public need for legal practitioners assisted their rehabilitation and aroused interest in their work. As professional men, barristers and attorneys were suitable subjects for literary treatment in the fashion of 'Passages', and their association with crime and criminals enabled the inclusion of sensational material that would ensure the popularity of the legal anecdotes. And once again, Warren's writing was instrumental in the construction of this new literary sub-genre, although his legal narratives were factual rather than fictional.

Warren made his first contribution to legal literature and the professionalisation and regulation of the discipline in 1835. Using his own experiences, he wrote *A Popular and Practical Introduction to Law Studies*. The text was a handbook for new law students, and is one of the earliest of its kind. Warren returned to the law as a subject for his literary endeavours in 1838, when 'My First Circuit: Law and Facts from the North', his account of his first tour of duty as a practising barrister on the Northern Circuit, was published in *Blackwood's*.[49] The letter to the Editor, 'Christopher North', which introduces the article serves mainly to advertise and celebrate the fact that Warren, or 'XYZ', as he signs himself, has become a barrister, and the bulk of the narrative that follows is more a travelogue than a description of legal cases. But between the details of the horrors of coach travel and the excitement of an early rail journey, located securely in the respectable domestic framework of his leave-taking from, and return to, his family, are embedded Warren's observations on a number of trials he attended while in Liverpool. His role was purely that of an observer, and permitted the same intrusion into, and exposure of, the private life of the individual that had been afforded by the 'Passages', substituting the legal for the medical profession.

The trials Warren selected were presumably the most interesting, not to say sensational, from what would probably have been a largely mundane collection. As with the 'Passages', each trial offers an individual case-history to the reader and provides a format which, expanded and embellished, can be seen in the later 'Experiences of a Barrister' and 'Confessions of an Attorney'. The concept of reporting on a specific trial taken from the legal circuit is reproduced in the collected *Experiences*, which contains two stories, 'The Northern Circuit' and 'The March Assize', that follow Warren's example. In 'My First Circuit', Warren considers both civil and criminal cases. On the criminal side, there is an indictment for manslaughter caused by dangerous driving, and a case of bigamy, which allows Warren to indulge in a little light humour over the accused man's rationalisation of his actions. The civil court offers minor disputes over property and points of the law, with the exception of a case in which the waste products of a factory are polluting the surrounding atmosphere and blighting the residents' lives in an early example of green issues. But it is the criminal court on which Warren concentrates. As he notes, '[c]an an observer of human nature have a richer field laid before him than a Court of Criminal Justice?', a statement that echoes his declaration on the material presented by the work of a physician and which suggests a future and fertile source for literary treatment.[50] The first trial covered is that of 24-year-old Mr Hill for the robbery, rape, and murder of an elderly woman, and included are an account of the evidence offered against him, witness statements, the cases of the prosecution and defence counsels, and the judge's summing-up and sentencing of the prisoner, who is found guilty. The second case is that of a man accused of 'forgery on a grand scale', which follows a similar pattern to the first, also ending with a guilty verdict, but where the judge, apparently regretfully, cannot pass the death sentence he feels the offence deserves because of 'the alteration in the law lately effected by the lenient legislature'.[51]

Warren presents the most sensational case last, that of a man accused of the murder of his wife. It is alleged that in the course of a domestic argument, he had thrown his wife to the floor, severely damaging her head in the process, and had then repeatedly kicked and struck her unconscious body. Close examination of the witnesses, including the man's five-year-old daughter, elicits the fact that the wife was a drunken spendthrift, who had driven her hardworking and respectable husband beyond the bounds of reason. Warren dwells upon the appearance of the child and the evidence she offers in defence of her father, and the pathos, or possibly bathos, of his representation is similar in its style and content to the physician's 'Passages'. The accused is acquitted of murder, but convicted of manslaughter and sentenced to 18 months hard labour, a sentence that Warren finds 'under the circumstances, [...] somewhat severe'.[52] What emerges from Warren's literary foray into the courts draws on the form and content of the 'Passages' to some extent, and establishes the barrister's perspective on crime and criminality as a potential source of literary material. Simultaneously, his accounts draw attention to the evidence presented in court, which is largely taken from possibly unreliable witnesses or is simply circumstantial. The contemporary movement towards penal and legislative reform, which had driven the 'lenient legislature' to abolish the death penalty for forgery and other crimes, and the concomitant focus on the criminal as an individual rather than as the signifier of his or her crime roused concerns about the reliability of the evidence on which most prosecutions relied. The certainty afforded by a religious belief that had assumed an omnipotent and omniscient God would ensure justice and guarantee and legitimate retribution was no longer sufficient in an increasingly rational and secular society. The anxiety over circumstantial evidence which is apparent in the numerous articles and essays on the subject that appeared at this time indicates the perceived necessity for a better, more reliable, and preferably empirical system to establish guilt or innocence.

Warren himself wrote two long articles on questions of evidence. The first was 'Who is the Murderer? A Problem in the Law of Circumstantial Evidence', published in *Blackwood's* (May 1842), followed in 1850 by

'The Mystery of Murder, and its Defence', which appeared in the March edition of the *Law Review*.[53] The later article centred on the accusation that the defence counsel in the Courvoisier case of 1849 knew his client to be guilty while pleading his innocence in court. Warren made a meticulous analysis of the evidence, using his own knowledge of the law, witness statements, court records, and the newspaper reports of the trial, in a successful bid to clear the counsel's name. Warren's analysis of the evidence, while not implying that Courvoisier was innocent of the crime, strongly suggests that physical evidence was planted by the investigating police officers in order to support the otherwise wholly circumstantial evidence. Warren's work on this case constructs him as an armchair detective in the style of Edgar Allan Poe's Dupin in 'The Mystery of Marie Rogêt', in which Dupin attempts to solve the mystery of the murder using newspaper reports.[54] Warren's retrospective reconstruction of the Courvoisier case employs similar methods, although Warren did not have the same motivation. The earlier article, as its title suggests, was wholly engaged with the problems presented by a case in which all the evidence was circumstantial, and here also Warren has an investigative function as he sifts through the evidence given at the trial in an attempt to reconstruct the crime and attribute guilt.

'Who is the Murderer?' is a sensational title for what Warren claims in his introductory paragraph to be an examination of points of law that will 'exercise the understandings of all clear-headed persons, lay or professional, interested in the administration of justice'.[55] He then ensures the interest of his audience by declaring that 'there are in [the case] circumstances of mystery and horror [...], but I shall reveal no more of them than is necessary for my purpose', and makes a sideswipe at 'the degrading appetite for the loathsome details of crime, which certain late publications have engendered in persons of inferior capacity and education'.[56] He both promises sensationalism and yet reassures the reader that he or she is of a superior intellect and will read on for intellectual stimulation rather than for prurient interest. In the event, there is little evidence of horror, and any element of mystery is soon lost in the extensive and exact repetitions of witness statements. 'Who is the Murderer?' is an account of the trial of Robert Gouldsborough for the murder of William Huntley. The trial took place in York in 1842, but the murder of which Gouldsborough was accused had allegedly taken place in 1830, when Huntley had disappeared in mysterious circumstances. Gouldsborough was suspected at the time of being implicated in Huntley's disappearance, but in the absence of a body to prove murder, no action could be taken. In 1841, the skeleton of a man was discovered by workmen digging drains, and was tentatively identified as Huntley by a 'long projecting tooth on the left side of the jaw', a dental deformity that had given Huntley, when alive, 'a sort of twist of the mouth' immediately noticeable to an observer.[57] The case bears an uncanny resemblance to that of Eugene Aram in 1759, as Warren notes in his introduction, where the accidental discovery of a skeleton led to Aram's arrest and eventual conviction for murder.[58]

Warren's account of the Gouldsborough case, although strictly factual, reads more like a fiction. With the legalistic introduction removed, and the *verbatim* witness statements excised, the narrative would easily slot into place among the later 'Experiences of a Barrister'. Within the text, Warren takes on an investigative role, and furthermore, invites the reader to participate: 'I shall proceed to detail all the material facts of the case with scrupulous accuracy, and so enable the reader to form a judgement on this case for himself, just as if he had sat beside me in court during the trial.'[59] Warren, and the reader of his narrative, can examine the evidence, consider the witnesses and their statements, and reconstruct the probable train of events which led to the crime and the circumstances of the crime itself. And the object of this exercise is to detect the guilt or innocence of the accused man. Warren suggests that the project is to arrive at a judgement, locating himself and the reader within the legal framework of his profession as a barrister, but his actual function, and implicitly the reader's, is more closely allied to that of the detective figure. The skills that are required are those of the detective: close observation, interrogation of witnesses, the ascertaining of motive, and the deduction of facts from the evidence presented. In the Gouldsborough case, the lack of scientific or forensic methodology with which to identify the skeleton positively, the absence of any witness to the alleged crime, and the temporal gap between Huntley's disappearance and the discovery of the skeleton, which rendered the witness statements unreliable, led the jury to return a verdict of not guilty.

In this they were heavily influenced by the judge's summing-up, in which he made clear that the evidence presented to the court was wholly circumstantial, and that it was unsafe to convict on such evidence. In a postscript to the narrative, Warren quotes the opinion, based on his account of the trial, of 'a very eminent judicial personage', who states that 'the Scottish verdict of "Not proven" would have exactly met the case'.[60] In its examination of the unreliability of circumstantial evidence, and in its construction of Warren and the reader as proto-detectives, 'Who is the Murderer?' is a major contribution to the creation of a discursive space for the private detective. It demonstrates the necessity for a professional investigator to seek out reliable evidence, a specialist with the training and knowledge that could overcome the 'problem in the law of circumstantial evidence' and ensure safe convictions of the guilty while protecting the innocent. Finally, in its personalised and sensationalised descriptions of the participants in the trial, in the depiction of crime, its motivation and consequences, and in the moral perspective of the narrator, 'Who is the Murderer?' forms a link between the medico-moral narratives of the 'Passages from the Diary of a Late Physician' and the later legal narratives of the 'Experiences of a Barrister' and 'Confessions of an Attorney'.

2.4 Legal treatments: Proving the case

The 'Experiences of a Barrister' were published anonymously in *Chambers's Edinburgh Journal* between January 1849 and June 1850. There were 11 'Experiences' in all, at first appearing at approximately monthly intervals and then less frequently, with a six-month hiatus between the final two narratives. Their publication in *Chambers's*, a periodical with a socially broader target audience than that of literary magazines such as *Blackwood's*, makes it unlikely that Samuel Warren was their author, as his work was almost entirely published in *Blackwood's* or by Blackwood and Sons. Nonetheless, as I have suggested, his criminographic writing was paradigmatic for the later populist legal anecdotes: while it is not possible to state firmly that Warren was the author of the 'Experiences', his 'Passages from the Diary of a Late Physician' and later legal essays offered a model on which other writers could draw. *Chambers's* was a weekly journal, priced at a penny-halfpenny, published with the stated intention of having 'something of interest and value for everyone' as Richard Altick notes, covering education, science, society, trade, commerce, agriculture, hobbies and so on, and including some fiction.[61] By 1849, when the first of the 'Experiences' appeared, *Chambers's* had been in production for 17 years and enjoyed a wide circulation, although, contrary to William Chambers's expect-ations, it circulated mainly among the middle classes rather than appealing to the working class. But the term 'middle class' now incorpor-ated a wide spectrum of society, including prosperous shopkeepers, skilled artisans and clerks, as well as businessmen and professionals, and, of course, their families. Across this spectrum was a common interest in the acquisition and retention of money and property and the desire to maintain domestic stability and respectability. Equally held in common was the fear of, and interest in, crime and criminality. The

'Experiences' functioned to illustrate these common concerns and values and to suggest the problems that might accompany increased prosperity, while simultaneously working to reassure the reader that truth and justice would prevail and social order be maintained.

In this sense, the 'Experiences' appear to support and endorse the existing judicial and penal systems. But, as an analysis of the narratives will demonstrate, they also function as critiques of those systems and of the contemporary reliance on circumstantial evidence in criminal trials. Following the model of the 'Passages', the 'Experiences' offer exemplary models of patriarchally constituted domesticity and social order supported by negative, often criminal, examples which both define the desirable norm and have a monitory and disciplinary effect. The moral and social discipline exerted in the 'Passages' is extended to include legal discipline in the implicit message that crime does not pay and that criminality, no matter how cunning, will be found out. As in 'Passages', sensational material ensures the reader's interest, with murder, illicit sexual desire, brutish husbands, forbidden romance, and imprisoned young women, to say nothing of deathbed scenes. But this material serves as a backdrop to the main message conveyed by the narratives: in contrast to the 'Passages', the drive behind the 'Experiences' is the protection of the innocent rather than the punishment of the guilty. Disease, in the 'Passages', is consequent upon moral misdemeanour and confined to the individual. But as a contagious disease infects all indiscriminately, so the 'Experiences' imply that crime can affect anyone at any time, and, further, that the cure offered by the existing judicial system is imperfect. Crime in the 'Experiences' is not limited to the depredations of a criminal class upon the property-owning bourgeoisie: rather, the narratives suggest, crime and criminality can be found in the middle and upper classes, and even in the domestic sphere, and they demonstrate that the existing system does not always attribute guilt correctly but may implicate the innocent. This is a major and important shift in focus, from the ascertaining of guilt, moral or criminal, to the proof of innocence, and is central to the establishment of the later detective figure and his or her function in the private sphere. Proof of guilt becomes part of the process of protecting the innocent. And while the 'Experiences' criticise the law, they also demonstrate how the law can be used to the advantage of the individual by a skilled professional practitioner.

Of the eleven case-histories that comprise the 'Experiences', eight are concerned with criminal offences: murder figures in five of the narratives, theft in two, and forgery in one. The remaining three 'Experiences' are not strictly criminal, but deal with legal problems, focusing on questions of property, marriage, and inheritance. These issues are also shown to be the motive behind the criminal activities described in the other 'Experiences', which share the common theme of the protection of the innocent man or woman who has become entangled in a web of circumstantial evidence that appears to prove their guilt. The unnamed barrister-protagonist of the 'Experiences' reprises the observant and diagnostic role of the physician in the 'Passages', but his anecdotes incorporate investigative work, carried out either by the barrister himself or by the various attorneys that he employs or who have retained his services. The quasi-detective function of the physician is, in the 'Experiences', more fully realised. The narratives draw on the case-history paradigm of the 'Passages', and utilise, in fictional form, the examination of evidence found in Warren's 'Who is the Murderer?' and 'The Mystery of Murder'. The format of the 'Experiences' is closely allied to Warren's 'My First Circuit', most obviously in the first two tales, 'The March Assize' (*Chambers's Edinburgh Magazine* n.s., 11:263 [13 January 1849], pp. 24–28) and 'The Northern Circuit' (*Chambers's* n.s., 11:268 [17 February 1849], pp. 107–111). The 'Experiences', drawing on an established genre, do not offer the reader the detailed personal and domestic framework found in Warren's piece. The narratives rather assume that the reader will take the social and professional status of the barrister as read. Details of the barrister's domestic and professional circumstances function as signifiers of his progress through life, as an increased caseload brings the prosperity that permits him to marry and, in due time, produce two children. There is no clear temporal sequence in the 'Experiences' and continuity in these mostly unconnected cases is ensured by the voice and presence of the narrating barrister.

The professional status of the barrister locates him socially as upper-middle class: in the nineteenth century the student intake for the profession of barrister included the sons of successful professionals such as attorneys and physicians, and the progeny of politicians and the clergy. The reader is given no details of the barrister's past life, but his profess-ional status is immediately recognisable. The contemporary audience would have been familiar with barristers and their profession from their frequent appearance in the newspaper reports of trials. But the social elevation that might have seemed to distance the barrister from his audience is negated by the fact that as a legal representative, his profes-sion required him to mix with all classes of society. To some extent, the barrister was slightly distanced from client contact by the agency of attorneys, who usually retained the barrister to act as prosecution or defence counsel, and this is the case in some of the 'Experiences'. Others demonstrate the effective contact with clients which constructs the barrister as socially mobile, an important requisite of the later detective figure whose investigative activities might take him into the meanest streets or along the corridors of stately homes. In the 'Experiences', this social mobility enables the reader to enter the world of the nobility in the company of the barrister, as well as providing a perspective on their own recognisable and familiar middle-class *milieu* and a glance at the poorer elements of society. Geographically, the narratives responded to the nationwide audience of *Chambers's*. The barrister is domiciled in London, but the nature of his work takes him all over the country as he works on the various legal circuits. This lends a certain authenticity to the 'Experiences', as well as avoiding the narrowing of audience that might have followed upon a series of cases centred solely in the metropolis.

Authority and authenticity are also conferred on the 'Experiences' by their legal frame. The trappings of justice and the rituals of the courtroom shape the narratives and inform the reader, drawing and expanding upon newspaper reportage of trials. The incorporation of relatively recent historical events such as the French Revolution (in 'The Refugee') locates the 'Experiences' in a recognisable and authentic past. Place and street names ground the stories in geophysical reality, and the occasional reference to Mr S—— or Sir T—— suggests an authorial strategy to conceal the names of real people, while in 'Esther Mason' the name of Sir Samuel Romilly, the great advocate of penal reform, is enlisted to add veracity to the narrative. *Chambers's* rather hedged its bets on presenting the 'Experiences' as true accounts. In the journal's index they are listed under 'Tales and Other Narratives', a category which seems balanced between fact and fiction. In contrast to *Blackwood's* introduction to Warren's 'Passages' there is not in *Chambers's* any editorial claim to authenticity for the 'Experiences', although in the 1856 collected edition of *The Experiences of a Barrister* there is a Preface which declares that '[t]he following remarkable papers [are] faithful transcripts of striking passages in the daily life of an eminent barrister'.[62] The use of the word 'passages' suggests a link with the earlier physician's tales in terms of genre, and the tone similarly promises authenticity while implying sensationalism in the words 'remarkable' and 'striking'.

While the 'Experiences' draw on the format and example of Warren's 'Passages', and to some extent his legal anecdotes, they also develop themes that had been represented in fact and fiction in the pages of *Chambers's* in the years between 1832, when the final 'Passage' appeared in *Blackwood's* and *Chambers's* was founded, and 1849, when the 'Experiences' first appeared. Peter Drexler analyses these themes in terms of political change, arguing that the reformist interest in judicial and penal reform is represented in *Chambers's* by the 'circumstantial evidence narrative, which appears regularly from 1832–43'—narratives which function as a 'criticism of the judicial system'.[63] He posits a 'conservative change of opinion' in 1842, the 'year of the Chartist petitions and the strikes and political action that followed'.[64] Between 1842 and 1849, Drexler suggests that this change is evident in the number of articles that focus on questions of law and order, and which also advocate 'the propagation of middle-class values such as self-help, temperance, sobriety, frugality, economy and progressiveness'.[65] Such articles culminate, after 1848 and the defeat of Chartism, in the 'moral-professional' narratives of the 'Experiences' and 'Confessions' and in the 'Recollections of a Police Officer'.[66] These narratives, then, have an ideological and political function: they are part of the disciplinary process that encourages the internalisation of social order and socially acceptable values. But in the wake of the defeat of Chartism and the removal of the threat of revolution, the stories shift their focus from the prosecution of the guilty to the defence of the innocent, a shift evident both in the private, legal anecdotes and in the public, police narratives. In earlier narratives such as 'Expiation' the innocence of the accused is revealed providentially or by the confession of guilt, but the narrative drive is the discovery of guilt: the proving of innocence is secondary. In this respect, the 'Experiences' represent a new, and important, shift in emphasis that reflects the fallibility of circumstantial evidence. The 'Experiences' offer a discursive space in which the now-permissible criticism of the judicial system and its reliance on circumstantial evidence can be expounded.

The moral policing of society evident in the 'Passages' is present in the 'Experiences' and 'Confessions', which continue to propagate middle-class values, but less emphasis on this aspect of the narratives is required in a more stable society. An important development in the 'Experiences' is the way in which the investigative, quasi-detective function of the physician is expanded in the barrister's tales as they concentrate on questions of evidence. The observation of symptoms of disease and the enquiry into its causes is, in the 'Experiences', mapped onto the symptoms of social disorder represented by crime, but the physician's techniques of observation and diagnosis are not, on their own, effective. A sick person will gladly admit to the symptoms, if not to the cause, of an illness, and willingly submit to the discipline of a medical regime in the interests of health. But the criminal will seek to conceal the evidence of crime, and even to attribute the guilt to others in order to evade the discipline of the state. Different investigative techniques are required that actively seek out the solution to the mystery of crime in the face of individual resistance. The elementary psychological investigation that accompanied the physician's physical examination of his patients is more highly developed in the 'Experiences' as the barrister not only requires evidence of the crime but questions the motives of the criminal.

The accumulation of evidence and the analysis of motive by a professional seen in Warren's factual legal essays created the discursive space for a similarly qualified but more forensically focused fictional figure, an investigator into crime. This is not yet the private detective: the barrister does not, *per se*, detect crime or pursue criminals. Rather, he is a private figure whose professional skills appear to support the individual caught up in the legal process. The legal system is both representative of sovereign or state power and a guarantor of the rights of the individual, a dichotomy realised in the 'Experiences', which act simultaneously to uphold the law and to protect the individual against the law. The narratives are a critique of the system, yet the barrister utilises the law that the 'Experiences' criticise in the defence of the innocent. Disciplinary power works at the level of the individual, and the 'Experiences' insert a dual discipline into the reader: sovereign power, embodied in the law, will prosecute the guilty and protect the innocent. But it does this through the agency and disciplinary techniques of the individual practitioner of the law—the barrister, who works as the representative and on behalf of the individual as citizen or as wrongly suspected person.

2.5 Agent of the law: A gent of the law

The barrister's 'Experiences' are retrospective. He presents his anecdotes, as in a memoir or autobiography, from the perspective of the reader's present in 1849. The temporal frame of the 'Experiences' locates them in the early part of the nineteenth century. Where dates are given, they move from 17— to 1802, 1806, and 1814. These four 'Experiences' are concerned with miscarriages or near-miscarriages of justice in cases which at that time attracted the death penalty. The cases not only function as critiques of circumstantial evidence, but also retrospectively deplore the barbarity of the so-called Bloody Code from a comfortable and relatively enlightened mid-century perspective. The immediacy of the criticism is lessened by its temporal distance from the present of the contemporary reader, a distance which implicitly suggests that the system has been to some extent reformed and improved. The first of these dated 'Experiences', 'The March Assize' (*Chambers's* n.s., 11:263 [13 January 1849], pp. 24–28), bears some resemblance to Warren's 'My First Circuit' as it is one of the fictional barrister's early cases, which he undertakes when he is 'a young man going on [his] first circuits'.[67] Its format is similar to Warren's 'Who is the Murderer?' in that it presents the history of the case before introducing the barrister, who does not appear until nearly halfway through the narrative, when he is called to act in his professional capacity to defend the accused man.

The defendant, Mr Harvey, has been charged with the theft of a gold watch. The account of events leading to this charge inform the reader that Harvey is the victim of an ex-employee, Cartwright, dismissed for theft from his post in Harvey's haberdashery business. Cartwright's response to his dismissal is to manufacture Harvey's bankruptcy, forcing him to emigrate in order to start anew. Not satisfied with this, Cartwright follows Harvey and his family to Liverpool, the point of embarkation for the Americas, and seizes the opportunity to conceal in Harvey's luggage the watch he, Cartwright, has stolen. Harvey is represented as an essentially good and respectable self-made man, fallen on hard times by virtue of his good nature. The evidence of the watch in his luggage, in conjunction with his exit from the hotel by the back stairs as if to avoid being seen, seems incontrovertible. There is a rational explanation for his actions, but the circumstantial evidence outweighs his attempts to tell the truth. He is duly arrested and charged, and the barrister is involved when Harvey's distraught wife, left with three children, asks him for help. This theme of the unprotected woman in distress recurs throughout the 'Experiences', confirming the necessity for masculine protection and guidance, a role which, in the absence of husband or father, the barrister assumes. In positioning a barrister as the patriarchal protector of the innocent, the narratives implicitly suggest that the legal arm of the state should perform a similar function in society. In 'The March Assize', the barrister is convinced of Harvey's innocence but, lacking any knowledge of the vengeful Cartwright, is not optimistic over the probable outcome of the case. The judge who will try the case is known to be severe in his judgements, and as the barrister observes, '[t]he more we investigated [. . .], the more dark and mysterious—always supposing Harvey's innocence—did the whole case appear. There was not one redeeming trait in the affair, except Harvey's previous good character.'[68] And as the barrister points out, 'good character, by the law of England, goes for nothing in opposition to facts proved to the satisfaction of a jury'.[69]

The law takes its course, and in spite of the barrister's investigation of the case and interrogation of witnesses, undertaken in the company of the attorney who has retained his services, and who is 'a sharp enough person in his way', Harvey is found guilty.[70] The judge, who is 'a staunch stickler for the gallows as the only effectual reformer and safeguard of the social state', passes a sentence of death, and despite the barrister's attempts to procure a reprieve, enlisting the help of the Society of Friends to petition the Crown for a commutation of the sentence, Harvey is duly hanged.[71] His wife, left destitute with three children, commits suicide. The barrister is much affected by this case, declaring Harvey 'a victim of circumstantial evidence, and of a barbarous criminal code'. There is, however, a coda to the case. At the time of sentencing, the condemned man had addressed the judge in prophetic terms: 'My lord, before another month has passed away, you will appear at the bar of another world, to answer for the life [...] you have impiously cast away!'[72] The prophecy is fulfilled. Providence, or God, arranges for the arrest of Cartwright on a charge of theft in Ilfracombe. The barrister is present in court and the same judge presides. When Cartwright is found guilty and condemned to death, he admits to framing Harvey. As the barrister records, 'to the unutterable horror of the entire court he related the whole particulars of the transaction, the origin of his grudge against Harvey, and his delight on bringing him to the gallows'.[73] The judge, whom Cartwright declares to be a 'legal murderer', suffers a seizure as the import of Cartwright's confession strikes home, and dies a few days later.

In this 'Experience', where the law fails in spite of the investigations undertaken by the barrister, rather after the model of the *Blackwood's* tales a higher power ensures justice of a sort. As the 'Experiences' progress, although 'Providence' or chance continues to play a role, human investigation becomes more efficient, indicating the erosion of religious belief in the increasingly secular society. The tone of the narrative is reformist, condemning a Draconian penal system, and is critical of circumstantial evidence. This tone is present in all the 'Experiences' to a greater or lesser degree, and the criticism implicit in the narratives extends to the law itself. Moral policing is evident in the depiction of Harvey and the actions and attitude of the barrister, while Cartwright functions as a negative exemplar. The 'Experience', despite its critical stance, works to discipline the individual as an obedient subject, although it is God, not man, who dispenses justice. In this, the narrative is closer to its fictional time than to its actual date, and has some affinity with the early *Blackwood's* 'Tales of Terror'. 'The March Assize' serves to introduce the barrister to the audience, and to suggest the themes and content of the 'Experiences' that will follow. But in presenting the reader with all the facts of the case, privileging him or her over the barrister, who remains in ignorance of Cartwright's actions until the end of the narrative, the story offers no mystery or suspense. The barrister's investigative role is minimal; he is, rather, merely the observer and recorder of events. In the later narratives, the element of investigation will become more pronounced, and the reader will only be given the same information as the barrister, inviting reader participation and speculation over 'who dunnit': these 'Experiences' function as precursors to the later 'clue–puzzle' mysteries epitomised and popularised by Agatha Christie in the twentieth century.

There is no logic apparent in the sequence in which the 'Experiences' appeared in *Chambers's* and which was duplicated in the collected editions, but the narratives fall loosely into two non-sequential categories: stories that are direct critiques of the fallibility of the law and the unreliability of circumstantial evidence, and cases which focus on the use of the law and the role of investigation in accumulating evidence. 'The March Assize' sets the pattern for the majority of the 'Experiences' that fall into the first category: there is a crime, the barrister is called in to assist, and, with the exception of 'Esther Mason', a solution is achieved that is in effect a restoration of social order. The second of the barrister's 'Experiences' 'The Northern Circuit' (*Chambers's* n.s., 11:268 [17 February 1849], pp. 107–111) is a case of robbery and murder, in which the barrister is retained as counsel for the prosecution. Following closely the pattern of 'The March Assize', the narrative opens with a long and detailed account of the circumstances of the crime, but in this case the reader is not given any more information than the barrister. He is retained as the counsel for the prosecution, and he declares that 'I had satisfied myself, by a perusal of the depositions, that there was no doubt of the prisoners' guilt', despite the circumstantial nature of the evidence.[74] A farmer, Mr Armstrong, and his wife, are accused of murdering their lodger in order to steal the mortgage deed he holds on their farm. The murder weapon, the deed, and a large sum of money are found in the possession of the accused couple, and witnesses give evidence as to the guilty demeanour of Armstrong when the crime was discovered. A further witness is the maid, Mary Strugnell, who claims to have been present in the house when the murder took place.

Such evidence serves to convince the barrister, and he makes an impassioned address to the jury 'upon the henious [*sic*] nature of the crime', using a technique 'which I have seldom known to fail'.[75] This technique consists of 'fixing my eyes and addressing my language to each juror one after the other'.[76] The barrister is employing the methodology of disciplinary power in his attempt to convince the jury of his case, a methodology that is replicated in narrative form in the 'Experiences' themselves as they speak to the reader. Unfortunately for the barrister, his case is weakened by new evidence presented by the defence counsel, which reveals that other property has vanished, and that a sailor called Pearce had been seen in the maid's company, but had now disappeared. Close cross-examination of Mary Strugnell casts doubt on her evidence, but the jury returns a verdict of guilty with a recommendation to mercy which reveals an element of doubt in their minds. The judge refutes the recommendation and the prisoners are sentenced to hang. At this point, Armstrong confesses to having stolen the mortgage deed and the money, but from the lodger's already dead body. The barrister, by now convinced of the Armstrongs' innocence, is 'sick at heart; for I felt as if the blood of two fellow-creatures was on my hands'.[77] As he observes, 'I denounced capital punishment as a gross iniquity [...] my feelings of course being influenced by a recollection of that unhappy affair of Harvey', and he is sufficiently upset to half resolve 'to give up the bar [...] rather than run the risk of getting poor people hanged who did not deserve it'.[78] Providence, or chance, affords a reprieve. A local landlady sees Pearce's name in the newspaper account of the trial, and informs the police of a portmanteau left in her care by Pearce. This proves to contain the stolen goods, and the Armstrongs escape hanging. The case is not immediately solved, but several months later the dying Mary Strugnell calls the barrister in to hear her confession, which proves Pearce to be the murderer.

This 'Experience' is more sophisticated than 'The March Assize'. The facts given to the reader at the beginning of the narrative allow room for doubt as to the guilt of the Armstrongs, and the circumstantial evidence on which they are convicted is only superficially strong. The facts elicited by the defence counsel suggest that further enquiries might prove otherwise, indicating the need for a specialist investigating figure. This does not yet happen. It is only by chance that the evidence which will prove the Armstrongs innocent is found, and, as in many of the broadsides, it is confession that finally fixes guilt. However, this 'Experience' is what determines the barrister's future approach to his work. He is never again represented as counsel for the prosecution, instead working always in the interests of those he believes, often against the evidence, to be innocent. In both the 'The March Assize' and 'The Northern Circuit' the role of the criminal is made more complex. He or she is no longer simply the perpetrator, but is active in contriving to shift the blame for the crime onto others, Cartwright for reasons of revenge, Strugnell and Pearce to prevent discovery of their guilt. The increasingly resourceful criminal is a major factor in the construction of the detective figure: such resourcefulness demands an equally resourceful opponent. As many later crime fictions demonstrate, the criminal and the detective share many of the same skills and traits, only their motivation differs. Where earlier narratives had simplistically located the criminal as other to society, somehow branded by his or her criminal actions, in the 'Experiences', the criminal is often unrecognisable, of the same social class as his or her victim, and with equal or even greater intelligence or cunning.

'"The Accommodation Bill"' (*Chambers's* n.s., 13:317 [26 January 1850], pp. 53–56), is a further example of the criminal's manipulation of evidence for his own purposes. James Hornby, bested in love by Henry Burton, eventually comes into possession of the mortgage on Burton's farm. Burton, generous and profligate by nature, is having difficulty meeting the payments due, and Hornby delights in the prospect of evicting him. But Burton's desperation to obtain the necessary money suggests a better revenge to Hornby. Burton is driven to ask Hornby for a 'bill of accommodation', that is, a loan to tide him over his immediate financial problems. Hornby pretends to accommodate him, but seizes the opportunity to make the bill appear to be a forgery carried out by Burton. The case comes to court, and a death sentence seems inevitable. The barrister is retained to defend Burton, but the case against him appears watertight, until a witness to Hornby's actions, motivated by religion-induced guilt, comes forward. She had seen Hornby write and sign the bill, and had subsequently been bribed by him to say nothing. The 'Experience' emphasises the ease with which the law can be perverted and the fallibility of apparently irrefutable evidence, indicating the necessity for all aspects of a case to be investigated, including the backgrounds and possible motivations of the person bringing the charge. Equally, there is a moral message in '"The Accommodation Bill"': it is Burton's profligacy that laid him open to the criminal machinations of Hornby, and his 'Experience' teaches him the virtues of thrift and care in matters financial.

These three 'Experiences' draw attention to flaws in the legal system that can result in miscarriages of justice, and to the apparent ease with which the law can be manipulated in the interests of the criminal. In contrast, 'Esther Mason' (*Chambers's* n.s., 11:268 [23 June 1849], pp. 403–407) is a direct attack on the penal system. Set '[a]bout forty years ago', and culminating in 1814, 'Esther Mason' is the story of a young woman, foster sister to the barrister's wife. As the 'Experiences' continue, the barrister more frequently has a personal interest in the cases, constructing him less as a disinterested legal functionary than a concerned individual. The young woman of the title finds herself and her child, through no fault of her own, deserted by her sea-captain husband.[79] Left alone and penniless in London, she is driven to theft by desperation and the hunger of her child: 'a piece of rich lace, lying apparently unheeded on the counter met her eye, and a dreadful suggestion crossed her fevered brain'.[80] She succumbs to temptation, and is immediately discovered, arrested, and taken to Newgate.

The barrister becomes involved when he receives a letter from the chaplain of the prison. He cannot dispute Esther's guilt, but states that 'I have no moral doubt whatever [...] that at the time of the committal of the felonious act, the intellect of Esther Mason was disordered.'[81] This was not sufficient defence. The McNaughten rules did not come into play until 1843, and, even then, a person could only be shown not to be responsible for a crime if when she or he had committed the act, it was without the capacity or ability to know if it was illegal and wrong. Esther had known that her action was wrong, whatever her motivation. The law takes its course, urged on by the owner of the shop, who 'had suffered much [...] from such practices, and was "upon principle" determined to make an example of every offender'.[82] Esther is tried, found guilty, and sentenced to death. The judge, in passing sentence, declares that her crime, 'but for the stern repression of the law, would sap the foundations of the security of property'.[83] Despite every effort of the barrister, the Society of Friends, and the representations of Samuel Romilly, Esther is hanged. The 'Experience' is presented as an account of an actual case, suggesting that there were many people still living who would remember the tragedy, and that Romilly had been incited by the injustice to embark on his campaign for penal reform. True or not, the case is the barrister's most savage and direct attack on the penal system, and makes no attempt to present any moral or disciplinary message other than to deplore the legal murder that Esther's death represents.

Property, or the possession of property, is central to all the 'Experiences'. It provides the motive for the crimes that are committed, whether murder, forgery, or financial fraud. A recurring theme in the 'Experiences' is that of property and/or money which, by inheritance, comes, or will come, into the possession of a young, usually orphaned, woman. This allows the narratives to emphasise the necessity for masculine authority and protection, represented by the patriarchal figure of the barrister, and, further, provides a romantic, sometimes sensational, aspect to the 'Experiences'. As well as being critiques of the reliability of circumstantial evidence, these 'Experiences' focus on dysfunctional families, that is, families which do not conform to the desirable patriarchal norm: masculine control is either absent, weak, or criminal. In all these cases, women feature either as the victims of unscrupulous men or, in one case, as the perpetrator of crime. In depicting negative examples of domesticity, as in the 'Passages', the 'Experiences' suggest the desirability of adhering to the social norm by highlighting the effects of social deviance. The distortion of family values evident in these 'Experiences' is representative of wider social anxieties about class distinctions and social stability. The individual and the family work as a microcosm of society, and the barrister, in his restoration of the microcosmic order in the narratives, functions as a social manager. He restores order and supports the *status quo*, and in the process, his anecdotes serve a parallel disciplinary purpose, instilling the values and order inherent in the 'Experiences' into the individual reader.

In 'The Mother and Son' (*Chambers's* n.s., 11:282 [26 May 1849], pp. 324–327), a woman of property is murdered by her Spanish house-keeper in order to enable the housekeeper's son to marry the murdered woman's daughter, thus providing him with both the girl that he loves and access to her fortune. The crime is doubly shocking: the perpetrator is a woman, and in murdering her employer, she threatens to undermine social stability and order. The barrister, working with a physician, carries out a detailed and quite forensic investigation, involving a *post-mortem*, searches for evidence, and the interrogation of witnesses. His conclusions, however, are incorrect. Circumstance and evidence point to the son as the perpetrator, but at the last moment, the mother confesses to save her son from the gallows. 'The Second Marriage' (*Chambers's* n.s., 12:299 [22 September 1849], pp. 177–181), as its title suggests, depicts the problems consequent upon an ill-advised second marriage. A widow, whose deceased husband's will leaves his money and property to her, and in the event of her death, to their daughter, remarries. Her new husband, thwarted in his attempts to obtain her inheritance, murders his wife and forges a new will, leaving the daughter destitute. The barrister is retained to try and regain the daughter's property, and it is in the course of his investigations into what he suspects to be a forged will that the murder is revealed and the perpetrator discovered.

'The Refugee' (*Chambers's* n.s., 13:355 [1 June 1850], pp. 340–345) is also concerned with the question of unsuitable marriage, as Mrs Rushton attempts to prevent her son marrying the French refugee with whom he has fallen in love. Her attempts are motivated by her desire to regain, through her son's suitable marriage, the social status she herself had lost in marrying into trade. Her murder is accidental, as she drinks the poison intended for someone else. The plot is convoluted, and in fact no intentional crime takes place. The barrister's role is limited: it is an old 'Experience' that occurred before he had qualified in his profession, and he undertakes no real investigation. The solution to the mystery and the plot device that saves the beautiful French refugee who has been accused of the murder are provided by confession. In both these 'Experiences', the restoration of social order is signified by marriage, although in 'The Refugee', the deviance from the social norm implicit in the girl's nationality and Catholic religion necessitates that the newly married couple are relocated in Ireland.

In all these 'Experiences', the barrister comes to the defence of the accused, either literally, in court, or by offering his services and knowledge in an unofficial capacity. The 'Experience' which most fully examines questions of evidence, and which weaves together many of the themes present in other 'Experiences' is 'Circumstantial Evidence' (*Chambers's* n.s., 12:303 [20 October 1849], pp. 242–247). This 'Experience' is internally undated, but occurs early in the barrister's career, 'in the second year of [his] connection with the northern circuit'.[84] At the root of this 'Experience' is an unsuitable marriage; property is the motivation of the criminal; it features an investigative attorney, Mr Sharpe, and it demonstrates how circumstantial evidence can be manipulated in the interests of the criminal. The barrister is drawn into the case by Mr Sharpe, 'one of the most eminent of the race [of attorneys] practising in that part of the country'.[85] The brief he offers the barrister is to act as the defence in a much-publicised murder trial. It comes to the barrister by default when the more experienced 'silk' to which it had been offered refuses it. As the barrister peruses the paperwork, it becomes apparent that this is a case 'dark, intricate, compassed with fearful mystery', on which even Mr Sharpe's 'research, prescience and sagacity' can cast little light.[86] At its centre is Frederick Everett, accused of murdering his wealthy aunt, Mrs Fitzhugh, a lady whose family 'came in with the Conqueror'.[87] Frederick is the son of her sister, who had foolishly besmirched the family name by marrying into trade, a folly that resulted in Mrs Fitzhugh cutting her out of the family. News of her sister's early death in India induces remorse and regret in Mrs Fitzhugh, and to atone for her actions, she offers a home to Frederick and to his supposed father, Captain Everett, who had married Mrs Fitzhugh's sister after the death of her first, unsuitable, husband. Further, she alters her will, leaving all to Frederick, or in the event of his death, to Captain Everett.

The contents of the new will are made public. Frederick initially endears himself to his aunt, but threatens to repeat the alienating actions of his mother when he falls in love with Lucy Carrington, the daughter of a local businessman. Mrs Fitzhugh announces that she will disinherit Frederick if he marries beneath him, and shortly afterwards, she falls ill. 'Unusual and baffling symptoms show themselves', and within a week she dies.[88] In the course of her illness, Frederick appears to have forgotten their disagreement, nursing her, and 'with strange fierceness, taking the medicine with his own hand from the man who brought it; and after administering the prescribed quantity, locking up the remainder in a cabinet in his bed-room'.[89] An eminent physician is consulted, who orders powerful emetics to be administered, but to no avail. On the death of his aunt, Frederick becomes almost hysterical, accusing himself of having murdered her, behaviour which to the physician appears to confirm his suspicions that Mrs Fitzhugh had been poisoned. Dr Archer suggests a *post-mortem*, and until the results are known Frederick is placed under 'surveillance' to prevent him destroying any evidence or leaving the house. Frederick makes the case against him appear even more black in his attempt to forbid the *post-mortem* and in his claims to have seen similar deaths in India. Mrs Fitzhugh's death proves to have been caused by acetate of morphine, and a search of Frederick's room reveals a small quantity of the substance in a bottle, in an envelope with the name 'Everett' inscribed on it. Finally, 'as if to confirm beyond all doubt the soundness of the chain of circumstantial evidence in which he was enmeshed', the butler deposes that he had delivered to Frederick the package which proved to have contained the poison.[90]

To refute this mass of evidence, all the barrister appears to have are the protestations of Lucy Carrington, who swears that Frederick is incapable of such actions, and a reliance on physiognomy. Frederick is described as 'a fair-haired, blue-eyed young man, of amiable, caressing manners, gentle disposition, and ardent, poetic temperament', in contrast to his father, who is 'a dark-featured, cold, haughty, repulsive man'.[91] This is, of course, a clue to the identity of the real criminal. But before this can be revealed, the case goes to trial, and Frederick is found guilty. Fortunately, in the course of his investigations into the crime, Mr Sharpe had discovered a Sergeant Edwards, who is known to Captain Everett. From Edwards, Mr Sharpe hears that Captain Everett is not Frederick's father, but had married his mother when Frederick was an infant. Captain

Everett's decision to bring the child up as his own was based on the expectation of eventual inherited wealth. Everett had bound the Sergeant and his wife to silence by paying them an annuity. He had then made use of Edwards in procuring the poison which had killed Mrs Fitzhugh, asking Edwards to purchase a 'rare and very valuable powder, which the captain wanted for scientific purposes'.[92] When the barrister acquaints Frederick with the fact that Everett is not his father, Frederick, loosened from his perceived bond of filial duty, reveals that he had seen Everett administer the poison. Frederick is reprieved, but Everett escapes the punishment of the state. When the officers arrive to arrest him, he shoots himself. Again, the barrister, with the assistance of the attorney, has ensured not only that justice is done, but has engineered the restoration of order. Frederick inherits, and marries Lucy.

This 'Experience' functions to criticise circumstantial evidence, and to prove the positive value of active investigation into a seemingly hopeless case. It also works to illustrate the development of the intelligent criminal, who bends the evidence not only to evade punishment for his crime, but actively to implicate another in the furtherance of his own fraudulent plan to inherit. Intelligent criminals, who manipulate the law in their own interests, require equally intelligent and knowledgeable opponents who can 'ferret' out the truth. And the remaining three 'Experiences' provide just such a figure in the form of the attorney, Mr Ferret, who, I suggest, is a prototype detective. The nature of a barrister's work requires the presence of an attorney. Those seeking representation in court would, by custom and practice, first apply to an attorney, who would then offer the case to a barrister. The protagonist of the 'Experiences' recognises this in 'Circumstantial Evidence' as he muses upon 'the capricious mode in which those powerful personages the attorneys distributed their valuable favours'.[93] There is a clear distinction between barristers and attorneys: simplistically, the former are qualified to plead in courts, the latter deal with everyday legal business. In many of the 'Experiences', an attorney assists the barrister by carrying out enquiries which will support the case that the barrister will make in court, and these 'Experiences' have focused on criminal actions. In the 'Experiences' that feature Mr Ferret, it is civil law that is central. These cases are to some extent more 'real', in that they deal with problems that the contemporary audience might have experienced: questions of rightful inheritance, marriage settlement, and so forth. The sensational element provided by murders and miscarriages of justice that attracts and holds the reader's attention is not entirely lost, but refocused on the wickedness of men in their treatment of women.

Mr Ferret is introduced into the 'Experiences' in 'The Contested Marriage' (*Chambers's* n.s., 11:274 [31 March 1849], pp. 193–197). He reappears in '"The Writ of Habeas Corpus"' (*Chambers's* n.s., 11:284 [9 June 1849], pp. 354–359) and 'The Marriage Settlement' (*Chambers's* n.s., 12:297 [8 September 1849], pp. 147–151). These are respectively the third, fifth, and seventh stories in the sequence, and appeared at fairly regular three-monthly intervals. All are concerned with the rightful restitution of property, and property is vested in, and transmitted via, the body of a woman: all these 'Experiences' feature defenceless women who require masculine assistance and protection in order to ensure that property remains in the right hands. In this way, these 'Experiences' serve to support and defend the contemporary social values and locate the barrister and the attorney as legal agents who use the law in the interests of the individual in order to restore social order. They share with the other 'Experiences' and the 'Passages' a disciplinary function, encouraging the reader to internalise the ideology they present. But the investigative activities of Mr Ferret extend and make more clear the disciplinary function of the legal agent. His work in uncovering secrets and tracking down evidence suggests that crime can and will be detected and the criminal brought to justice: no one is above or beyond the reaches of the law. And his methodology is that of discipline: his main tool is surveillance. It is his observant eye that enables his detective work, an eye that in its concealment from those it watches implicitly watches all.

The barrister becomes involved in 'The Contested Marriage' when he receives a letter of introduction from his friend Sir Jasper Thornely. The letter requests the barrister to lend his every assistance to the lady it introduces, whose son, Sir Jasper asserts, is the rightful heir to the estate of Sir Harry Compton. The letter is disjointed, and does not offer a coherent narrative, inciting a desire to discover more in both the barrister and the reader. Sir Jasper's interest, it appears, is not wholly altruistic. There is a political element in this 'Experience'. The safe election of Sir Jasper's friend as MP for the borough of —— is threatened by the Emsdales, who are currently in possession of Sir Harry Compton's estate. It is not only the social order that is threatened in 'The Contested Marriage', but also political stability. Sir Jasper's letter indicates that proving the lady's case in law might prove difficult, and he advises the barrister 'to look out for a sharp, clever, persevering attorney, and set him on a hunt for evidence', promising such an attorney a payment of 'a thousand pounds over and above his legal costs'.[94] The implicit assumption that the barrister will use his professional skills for no charge in order to oblige a friend, while the attorney will work better for a large fee, illustrates the perceived class divide between the two professions. The attorney is available for hire, where the barrister responds to the requirements of social obligation. Accordingly, he interviews Violet Dalston, a woman of 'singular and touching loveliness' who 'completely realized the highest *Madonna* type of youthful, matronly beauty'.[95] Her story is simple. Harry Compton, posing as Henry Grainger, persuades Violet into a secret marriage. On claiming his inheritance after his father's death, he seeks to rid himself of an unsuitable wife, and persuades her, in his guise as Grainger, that his business affairs are so bad that emigration is the only solution to their problems. She is to go ahead, with Grainger promising to follow. But, the arrangements having been made, Violet hears nothing further from her husband. A series of coincidences, a plot mechanism that features strongly in the 'Experiences', lead to Violet's discovery of Grainger's real identity, but she has no proof of her standing as Sir Harry Compton's wife. His silence is explained by the revelation of his death, which means that Violet's son should, by right, inherit the title.

This is the problem that is presented to the barrister, and, moved by Violet's unhappiness and concern for her child, he agrees to take on what appears to be a hopeless case. He follows Sir Jasper's advice, and turns to Mr Ferret as the 'sharp, clever, persevering' attorney required. In contrast to the depiction of the attorneys in other 'Experiences', Ferret receives a full, and fulsome, description of his skills:

> Indefatigable, resolute, sharp-witted, and of a ceaseless, remorseless activity, a secret or a fact had need to be very profoundly hidden for him not to reach and fish it up. I have heard solemn doubts expressed by attorneys opposed to him as to whether he really and truly slept at all—that is, a genuine, Christian sleep, as distinguished from a merely canine one, with one eye always half open.[96]

Attention is again drawn to Mr Ferret's observational skills, when the barrister refers to 'his quick gray eye', which recognises Violet as a client and which speedily reads Sir Jasper's letter, seeming to extract more information from it than had the barrister. He agrees to undertake the investigation, for a fee, which seems to arouse suspicion as to his probity in Violet, but the barrister reassures her: 'Attorneys, madam, be assured, whatever nursery tales may teach, have, the very sharpest of them, their points of honour.'[97] This is a direct refutation of the long-standing and popular conception of attorneys as self-seeking and corrupt, a refutation which, coming from the barrister, recognises and reinforces the relatively new standing of attorneys as respectable professionals. Much of the remainder of the narrative is devoted to an account of Ferret's investigative activities: the barrister's role in this 'Experience' is reduced to that of observer and reporter. Ferret visits the sites he considers of importance to the investigation: the church in Leeds where the marriage took place; Sir Harry's estate; Cumberland, where 'Grainger' had bought a house for his wife; and Shropshire, in pursuit of a witness to the marriage. His methods are practical. He checks registers and documents, listens to local gossip, and interviews possible witnesses. In effect, he reconstructs the events which have resulted in Violet's predicament. The clue that breaks the case is the discovery of the initials 'Z. Z.' in a corner on the register of marriage. A combination of luck and the application of wine to one of Sir Harry's retainers allows Ferret to trace the owner of the initials, one Zachariah Zimmerman, the rector who had performed the marriage.

The production of Zimmerman as a witness when the case comes to court ensures that Violet is confirmed as Lady Compton, and her son is guaranteed his inheritance. The court case is heard in a town on the Compton estate, and the local populace, tenants of the Comptons, turn out in support of Violet and her son, a support which indicates that they too wish for the restoration of the rightful owner. Social stability and order, this 'Experience' suggests, are essential to the well-being of society, while change is threatening and unwelcome. In contrast to some of the other 'Experiences', 'The Contested Marriage' is not particularly sensational. There is no genuine crime; the deaths that occur are natural, and there is no romantic interest. Violet represents the damsel in distress, but her status as widow and mother negates the possibility of sexual love or desire. The legal fiction offers a recognisable, almost prosaic, reality to the reader. The major interest in this 'Experience' lies in the activities of Mr Ferret, as he goes about what is essentially his work of detection. He is a specialist, a professional figure who, in the private sphere, replicates the work of the publicly-funded police detective. Framing Ferret's story in the barrister's narrative acts to endorse his professional status as well as advertise his existence and his skills. As an investigator legitimised by the law, Ferret takes the law into the home and heart of the individual, both in the text, and by extrapolation, reality. The reader too, may be subjected to, and by, his 'sharp gray eyes', and it is in this sense that Ferret functions as a disciplinary figure.

That Mr Ferret is knowledgeable in the law is made evident in 'The Contested Marriage', as he uses legal language and demonstrates his understanding of the legal ramifications of the case in his discussions with the barrister. In ' "The Writ of Habeas Corpus" ', he manipulates the law to the advantage of his client. This manipulation is a legitimate parallel to the manipulation of evidence by the criminal seen in other 'Experiences', and marks a necessary similarity between detective figure and criminal that will develop further in later crime fiction. It is the contest between two equal minds that will come to constitute the essential form of the confrontation in detective fiction, and which is evident in the contest between Dupin and Minister D—— in Poe's 'The Purloined Letter' and in the characterisation of Sherlock Holmes's arch-enemy, Moriarty. Mr Ferret does not enter into any contest with a criminal in those 'Experiences' in which he features, but he represents an important stage in the development of the fictional detective. In ' "The Writ of Habeas Corpus" ' Ferret is very much in the foreground. The case is related back to 'The Contested Marriage' by the figure of Lady Compton who, remembering Ferret's skills, calls for his help on behalf of a defenceless and threatened young girl. The barrister's role is secondary, as he concedes when he tells Ferret 'it is your affair, not mine'.[98] The shift in their relationship can be seen as, rather than the barrister employing Ferret on his business, Ferret calls upon the barrister, almost as an equal, to ask for his opinion of the legal stratagem he plans to employ.

The case centres on a young girl, Clara Brandon, who has been left an orphan, possessed of a small fortune, in the care of her uncle and guardian, Major Brandon. Under the terms of her father's will, Clara will inherit unless she predeceases her uncle, in which case the money will go to him. Major Brandon has a wife, for whom it is a second marriage, and she has a son. Mrs Brandon seeks to marry her son to Clara in order to obtain her inheritance, but Clara refuses. As a result of the cruel treatment meted out to her consequent on her refusal, Clara appears to be suffering from a mental infirmity. This is in fact a rumour perpetrated by Mrs Brandon. Lady Compton rescues the fleeing Clara, who has escaped her confinement, and takes her into care. Mrs Brandon resorts to the law to regain custody of her husband's ward, and it is at this point that Ferret's assistance is called for. Clara's custody had previously been contested by a devoted servant, Susan Hopley, a name that pays homage to Catherine Crowe's novel *Susan Hopley; or, Circumstantial Evidence* (1841), in which the eponymous protagonist is also a devoted servant. Susan had spent all her savings on an attempt to 'procure "justice" for the ill-used orphan', applying to the Lord Chancellor to change the custody 'of the pretended lunatic'.[99] Her application had been in vain, and Susan had lost her savings. This apparent aside in the narrative is vital to the plot: Susan's actions had come to the attention of Lady Compton, who had employed her after her dismissal from the Brandon household, and Susan had told Lady Compton of Clara's mistreatment. And it is Susan's actions in law that form the focus of Ferret's cunning plan to save Clara.

According to the letter of the law, Clara is certain to be returned to her guardians. Ferret is moved by Lady Compton's account of Clara's plight, and by the girl herself, to feel 'that he would willingly exert a vigour even *beyond* the law to meet his client's wishes' (emphasis in the text).[100] Inspiration strikes, and he recruits Susan to his cause, taking her to London with him, and insisting that Lady Compton return Clara to her guardian. His plan, hatched out under the disapproving eye of the barrister, is to issue a 'writ of habeas corpus', which, as the barrister explains for the benefit of the reader, is a writ to demand the presence before the sovereign, or her representative in the law, of a body or person alleged to be suffering illegal constraint. The barrister points out to Ferret that such a case has no possibility of success, but Ferret obtains his writ from the court nonetheless and gives himself the pleasure of serving it personally on the Brandons. They are forced to bring Clara to London for the case to be heard, and, as the barrister, who acts on Clara's behalf, had foreseen, the judge refuses to interfere in the matter. Clara is returned to the custody of her guardian. But as they leave the court, she is approached by 'two men, whose vocation no accustomed eye could for an instant mistake', and arrested for debt.[101] Ferret's cunning legal mind had discerned a way of removing Clara at least temporarily from her guardians by placing her in the hands of the law. The money that Susan had spent on her abortive attempt to rescue Clara is reconstructed as an unpaid debt.

The barrister is 'almost suffocated with laughter at the success of Ferret's audacious *ruse*', but affects seriousness when he tells Ferret that 'yours is a very sharp practice; [...] that the arrest is [...] illegal; and [...] a judge would, upon motion, quash it with costs'.[102] Ferret has manipulated the letter of the law to serve his own, and his client's, interests. Clara is released from debtors' jail and left in the charge of a respectable curate and his wife for the 12 months that remain until she reaches her majority. The Brandons are led to believe that she has gone to a *maison de santé* in France, and that she dies there some months later. As soon as Clara is 21, Ferret has 'the pleasure of announcing to the relict of Major Brandon [...] and to her brutal son, that they must forthwith depart from the home in which they [...] thought themselves secure'.[103] Clara receives her inheritance and makes a good marriage: order is restored, but this time not by the barrister, but by the 'sharp practice' of the attorney. The law itself is used to protect the innocent and ensure justice for the individual, rather than, as has been more usual in the 'Experiences', the knowledge of the barrister being used to defeat the law in its prosecution. A clear demarcation between the law and justice is becoming apparent in the 'Experiences', a factor that will figure largely in the later, fully-formed genre of crime fiction.

' "The Writ of Habeas Corpus" ' relies on the sensationalism inherent in the depiction of a young girl driven to the edge of madness by brutal treatment to draw its reader in, but then the attention is engaged by the legal skills of the attorney. There is no detection, but equally, there is no crime. Clara's treatment is morally wrong, but legally permitted. There is, then, an element of criticism of the law in this 'Experience'. But the law is shown to be a two-edged sword in the hands of a skilled practitioner, and this duality is evident in the final narrative featuring Mr Ferret. This is 'The Marriage Settlement', the seventh 'Experience' in the series, and it returns the barrister to his pre-eminent role. It is the only 'Experience' in which both the barrister and his family feature largely in the narrative. It is firmly located in the domestic sphere, in context and in content. The subject, as the title suggests, is marriage, and the 'Experience' opens with a cameo representation of the barrister's happy state of matrimony. He is playing boisterously with his two daughters, an event that causes his wife to suggest that as the girls are growing up, they require the services of a governess. The scene allows the barrister to represent himself as completely ruled by his wife in domestic matters, reinforcing the patriarchal myth of the wife as mistress of the home, a myth which the 'Experience' will later deconstruct. His wife's desire for a governess is in part dictated by social status: employing a governess was a luxury available only to the upper-middle and upper classes, and it is a Lady Maldon who has planted the idea in his wife's mind. He accedes to his wife's request, and Edith Willoughby, the orphan daughter of a respectable Reverend, enters the barrister's household. As he notes, 'in a very short time I came to regard her as a daughter', and in 'The Marriage Settlement' he acts very much as a father figure.[104]

It is with the anxious eyes of a father that the barrister regards a prospective suitor for Edith's hand. On the surface, Mr Harlowe appears an excellent match for the penniless Edith. Recently widowed, he is a man of property and a gentleman of good standing. But the barrister instinctively dislikes him, although he admits 'I could assign no very positive motive for my antipathy.'[105] Edith disregards the barrister's fatherly advice, and marries Harlowe. All the barrister can do is arrange a marriage settlement that will protect her interests should the marriage be a disaster, and this he does. It is at this point that Mr Ferret enters the story. As the witnesses to the settlement, including Mr Harlowe, are leaving the barrister's office, Mr Ferret appears. He looks at Harlowe 'with an expression of angry surprise', which prompts the barrister to ask what he knows of the man. It is nothing good. Harlowe's first wife had, prior to her death, been driven by his behaviour to seek a deed of separation. As time passes, the barrister's premonitions are fulfilled. Edith, thin and pale, and accompanied by her child, seeks refuge with the barrister and his wife. She tells him that Harlowe, who has obviously been abusing her although the narrative never states this directly, has become tired of her. In an attempt to dispose of her, he is trying to make her sign a document which states that his first wife is still living, and that Edith knew this when she married him, making her an accessory to a bigamous marriage. Suspecting Harlowe's real motives, the barrister directs Ferret to undertake an investigation.

Shortly afterwards Harlowe, stricken by tetanus, sends urgently for the barrister, who, unable to go, asks Ferret to undertake the journey. When he arrives at his destination, Harlowe is already dead, but Ferret meets the woman who is posing as Harlowe's first wife. A little further investigation reveals her imposture—her strong Italian accent, when the first Mrs Harlowe was a native of Dorset offers a fairly strong clue—and it seems that Edith will be able to inherit her husband's estate. But there is a further complication. In a staged confrontation between the two women, accompanied by their legal advisors, it becomes apparent that Harlowe had made a will leaving the property to his Italian mistress. All seems lost, but Ferret, 'filled with an exuberant glee', plays out the 'farce' to the end. The will is legal, but the marriage settlement so carefully drawn up by the barrister ensures that Edith's claim supersedes that of the mistress.[106] The astute brain of the barrister, in conjunction with the practical and legal skills of the attorney, effects the restoration of social order.

The three 'Experiences' that feature Ferret are distinct from the other narratives in the series, marking a shift away from the sensational into the real. The importance and attraction of these 'Experiences' lie in the investigative work of Ferret and manipulation of the law in the interests of the individual. Ferret's methods of investigation function as a template for later detective figures in the private sphere, as do the cases themselves. In the absence of crime *per se*, that is, no murder, fraud, or forgery, it is not possible to call in the police and, in matters domestic and personal pertaining to the middle-class domestic sphere, the presence of the police is unwanted. Despite the fact that the Metropolitan Police were fully established when the 'Experiences' were published, the police are not part of the narratives. This is in part because the 'Experiences' are located in the pre-police past, but also because the respectable middle-class reader in the mid-nineteenth century considered the activities of the police should be confined to dealing with the criminal classes, those implicitly at the bottom of the social scale. And although the characters in the 'Experiences' commit crimes, their social status precludes the intervention of the police. Mr Ferret and the barrister, as lower-middle and middle-class professionals, police in fiction their social counterparts. Similarly, the 'Experiences' themselves work on the reader to police his or her behaviour. These are disciplinary narratives, functioning by ideology to insert social values and the virtues of self-discipline into the individual. The barrister and Mr Ferret are both agents of the law and instruments of discipline.

2.6 Accessory after the fact

The 'Experiences' offered a legal treatment for the criminal ills of specific strata of society. They fully established the case structure and associated it with criminality and crime, and in the figures of the barrister and particularly Mr Ferret, introduced the concept of a legally empowered investigative agent. They are proto-detective fictions and, as such, are an important element in the construction of the crime-fiction genre. The 'Experiences' ended their run in June 1850. Almost immediately, a new series of legal anecdotes began. In October of the same year, the first of 'The Confessions of an Attorney' appeared.[107] The title, the location in *Chambers's*, and the temporal proximity to the 'Experiences' suggest that these narratives would pick up and develop the structures and themes of the 'Experiences', but this proves not to be the case. Certainly, the seven 'Confessions' utilise the case-history structure, and have a legal figure or figures at their centre. But despite the promotion of the attorney to narrator and protagonist, the representation of Mr Sharp does not replicate or expand greatly on Mr Ferret or the barrister. The themes of the 'Experiences' reappear in the 'Confessions': problems of inheritance, unsuitable marriage and its consequences, fraud, and an attempt to frame a man for a crime he has not committed. There is also a case of an unjustly executed woman. But the sensationalism of the 'Experiences' is absent. There are no murders. The 'Confessions' self-avowedly place themselves in the realm of everyday life as lived by their readers.

This is in part because the profession of the attorney does not usually take him into the criminal courts; his is the daily routine of business and its problems. The choice of an attorney as protagonist is perhaps a response to the changing demands of the audience, as the social status of an attorney permitted the reader more closely to identify with him than with the more socially elevated barrister. In the first 'Confession', 'The Life Assurance' (*Chambers's* n.s., 14:355 [19 October 1850], pp. 240–244), Mr Sharp reminds his readers that 'the attorney is the only real, practical defender of the humble and needy against the illegal oppressions of the rich and powerful'.[108] This strong statement is not supported by the cases that Sharp recounts, but suggests a class bias towards the honest working man as opposed to the implicitly idle and dishonest aristocracy. In contrast to the barrister, who often undertakes cases for chivalrous reasons, or because he is personally involved in some way, the mercenary inducement that inspired Mr Ferret's assiduous work in 'The Contested Marriage' is openly declared by Mr Sharp: 'I cheerfully admit the extreme vulgarity of the motive; but its effect in protecting the legal rights of the humble is not [...] lessened because the reward of exertion and success is counted out in good, honest sovereigns.'[109] Business, commerce, and the acquisition and protection of property are central to the majority of the 'Confessions', and this mercenary focus responds to the contemporary social attitudes and anxieties of the bourgeoisie. By the mid-century, fear of fraud had apparently overtaken fear of murder or robbery, as a short-lived periodical *The Detective: A Journal of Social Evils* suggests. The editorial address of its opening number starts by denouncing '[t]he amount of fraud and crime prevalent in society [...]. Every kind of Institution [...] becomes more or less tainted and corrupted by fraud.'[110] Other crime is hardly mentioned; the address articulates the fear of fraud and the threat it presents to society. The promulgation of social values and stability so apparent in the 'Experiences' in the wake of the Chartist riots is less evident in the 'Confessions'; indeed, some of the cases depict the criminal escaping punishment for his crime.

But as in the Mr Ferret anecdotes, the crimes in the 'Confessions' are not necessarily those that would necessitate the intervention of the law. The critique of circumstantial evidence is also absent from the 'Confessions', although Sharp, or his colleague Mr Flint, occasionally seek evidence to enable a resolution of a client's problem. The 'Confessions' are, by and large, straightforward accounts of cases that the narrator considers may arouse the interest of the reader. The focus on civil cases involving fraud rather than criminal cases of murder makes these anecdotes less sensational, but more relevant, for the contemporary reader. I say that there is no sensationalism in these 'Confessions', but the narrator attempts to engender a little excitement in the reader by suggesting that they are being invited to share 'a few incidents revealed in the attorney's privileged confessional'.[111] As in the 'Passages', the reader is being made privy to the usually confidential material of the attorney's work, and the voice of the narratives is that of a confidant.

And in contrast to the 'Experiences', which were temporally located in the late eighteenth and early nineteenth centuries, the 'Confessions' are closer in time to the date of publication. They are either specifically dated, or give historical pointers that place them in the late 1820s and 1830s. Despite Sharp's claim to be 'a man not of fiction, but of fact', who relates events that occur in the 'prosaic, matter-of-fact, working-day world' of an attorney's office, the 'Confessions' include two cases involving apparently bigamous marriages; a harrowing execution scene; and what appears to be a case of arson. For the female reader, there is an element of love-interest in several of the anecdotes, often involving unrequited love or unsuitable marriages against a father's wishes. Unprotected women also feature strongly, and the 'Confessions' implicitly continue the promulgation of middle-class and patriarchal family values seen in the 'Experiences'.

Sharp's first case is 'The Life Assurance'.[112] It relates the story of a man who, in an attempt to make easy money in an unwise speculative business venture, fakes the death of his son in order to claim on the insurance policy he had previously taken out on his son's life. Unfortunately, he had not taken into account the inheritance from a distant relative that was dependent on the son's continued existence. In effect, on discovering the truth of the affair through his client's confession, Sharp takes the law into his own hands. He organises full restitution to the insurance company, saving his client from certain transportation. As Sharp notes, 'in strict, or poetical justice, his punishment ought unquestionably to have been much greater—more apparent, also [...] for example's sake' than the social opprobrium the client suffers as Sharp makes known his attempted fraud.[113] This manipulation of the law in the client's interests bears some resemblance to Mr Ferret's activities in ' "The Writ of Habeas Corpus" ', but the reader is not invited to feel any sympathy for Mr Sharp's client, and the 'sharp practice' of Mr Sharp does not appear entirely admirable. There is very little investigative action in this 'Confession'; Sharp does instigate an enquiry into the son's death in response to the initial refusal of the insurance company to pay the policy, but his discovery of the crime itself is reliant on confession. The moral message of the narrative is the demonstration of the way in which a greedy man can, when circumstances combine with desire, fall from the straight and narrow into crime. The attorney is working to assist the individual against the power represented by the insurance company, and to protect his client from the workings of the law, but the fact remains that the client is in truth guilty of fraud. This subverts the moral message, and the clarity of moral example and the disciplinary function seen in the 'Experiences' is lessened. The audience is rather being invited to admire the cleverness and legal abilities of Mr Sharp, and this theme is apparent in the other 'Confessions'.

'Bigamy or No Bigamy' (*Chambers's* n.s., 14:359 [16 November 1850], pp. 307–311) is the blunt and sensational title of the second 'Confession'. The narrative bears a strong resemblance to 'The Contested Marriage', as it concerns the status of a young woman's marriage to a man of property and title, a marriage which requires proof of its legality in order to ensure correct inheritance. In 'Bigamy or No Bigamy', the plot is complicated by a first marriage and an attempt at blackmail, but these problems are resolved by the active investigation instigated by Sharp, but actually carried out by his partner, Mr Flint. Documentary evidence and a witness prove the legality of the second marriage, and the blackmailer is tried and sentenced to transportation. The agent of the law has restored the social order, but Sharp's motives, although presented in the narrative as concern for the titled lady who requests his assistance, are revealed in the last line of the 'Confession': 'the "celebrated" firm of Flint and Sharp derived considerable lustre, and more profit, from this successful stroke of professional dexterity'.[114] The desire for justice and the need to protect the individual that motivated the barrister, and which can be seen to be developing in Mr Ferret, are reduced to the level of commerce. Mr Sharp is a man of business, and his use of the law is in his own interests as much as those of his clients. Again following the pattern of the 'Experiences', the third 'Confession', 'Jane Eccles' (*Chambers's* n.s., 15:373 [22 February 1851], pp. 118–122), focuses on the injustice of the law in executing a young, and in this case, entirely innocent woman. Jane Eccles innocently and unknowingly passes forged notes given to her by the man she loves, and whom she refuses to incriminate. The account is far more sensational than that of 'Esther Mason', dwelling on the trial and describing the execution and Jane's state of mind, but its intention is identical. It functions to criticise 'the old Draco code' and to praise 'the great and good men' who had worked to reform it.[115]

'Every Man His Own Lawyer' (*Chambers's* n.s., 15:377 [23 March 1851], pp. 178–181) is essentially an advertisement for the legal profession.[116]

It describes the difficulties and financial and familial ruin of a man who considers he can conduct his own house-purchase without the benefit of legal advice. Humbled, and reduced to relying on the good wishes of the son he disinherited and the attorney whose services he had declined to use, he presents to the attorney and the reader 'a salutary spectacle, of obdurate tyrant-power compelled to humble itself before those whom it had previously scorned'.[117] Attorneys, this 'Confession' suggests, are essential to the smooth running of business and personal life. At this point, the series title is altered to 'The Reminiscences of an Attorney', but the narratives continue to feature *Messrs* Sharp and Flint. The confessional tone is lessened, and the remaining anecdotes are, as the new series title suggests, accounts of interesting cases. 'The Chest of Drawers' (*Chambers's* n.s., 15:388 [7 June 1851], pp. 355–360) and 'The Puzzle' (*Chambers's* n.s., 16:401 [6 September 1851], pp. 146–151) are respectively the search for a will concealed in a chest of drawers and the untangling of what appears to be a bigamous marriage. In both, the attorney ensures the property which is at the centre of both cases is restored to the rightful owners, and, in the latter case, that social and domestic order is maintained. This second case also makes reference to circumstantial evidence, and involves some investigation by Mr Sharp, but in comparison to the 'Experiences' it is lacking in depth and meaning: it is confession that reveals the truth of the case, and the 'crime' of marrying under a false name goes unpunished.

The final 'Confession', or 'Reminiscence', 'The Incendiary' (*Chambers's* n.s., 17:446 [5 June 1852], pp. 355–360) is a late, and slightly more complex, narrative than its predecessors and was not included in the collected edition. It is a moral tale, conveying a warning against the dangers of educating women above their station, and depicts a bungled attempt to frame an unwanted son-in-law for the crime of arson. Mr Sharp tricks his friend and client into confessing his plot against the son-in-law, and no crime actually occurs. The style and content of the narrative, including a criticism of how easily circumstantial evidence can be manipulated to incriminate an innocent person, are closer to the 'Experiences' than the majority of the 'Confessions', and the attorney is motivated by friendship rather than pecuniary interest. The overall differences between the 'Experiences' and the 'Confessions' suggest not only that they were written by a different author, but that audience expectations had altered and that the necessity for social, moral, and legal discipline evident in the earlier accounts was not as apparent. Nonetheless, the 'Confessions', as an 'accessory after the fact', consolidated the case structure as a definitive literary form, the legal anecdote as a sub-genre of fiction, and the legal agent as an investigative figure.

This figure would continue to appear in the literature of the second half of the nineteenth century. These literary successors would more often play a minor rather than central role, drawing on aspects, not always favourable, of the barrister and Mr Ferret and Mr Sharp. Tulkinghorn, in Dickens's *Bleak House* (1852–1853), is an agent of the law who sets in motion investigations in his own interests rather than that of his clients; legal agents appear frequently in Dickens's fiction and in that of Wilkie Collins; and M. E. Braddon made a barrister the central investigative figure in *Lady Audley's Secret* (1862). But these legal investigators were more often concerned with matters of property and inheritance than with crime, which increasingly was dealt with by the police. Much as the police become an accepted and ever-present part of life in fiction as well as fact, the legal professional is also an actual, as well as a literary, established and establishment figure. What the 'Experiences', and to a lesser extent the 'Confessions', do is construct and introduce the paid, investigating professional individual who works in the private sphere to solve problems, sometimes criminal, sometimes somehow outside the law. The ideological disciplinary function of these short narratives is enhanced and endorsed by what is essentially the work of detection undertaken by a professional individual—the prototype private detective. But these disciplinary narratives did not arise in isolation. The ideological policing that they represent had its parallel in the real world, in the form of a state police inaugurated to prevent, and later detect, crime and criminality. And this too would incorporate the discipline of ideology in its construction, its practices, and in its wooing of public acceptance.

3
A Conspicuous Constabulary: or, Why Policemen Wear Tall Helmets

3.1 Police in literature: Literary police

The police are noticeably absent from the criminography of the 1820s and early 1830s. A conspicuous constabulary they certainly were in terms of their physical presence on the streets of London; but in the contemporary literature they were conspicuous rather by their absence, existing at best as marginal figures. This can in part be explained by the fact that a police force in the modern sense did not come into being until 1829, when the New Metropolitan Police Force was inaugurated. There had been representatives of policing before this time, most notably the Bow Street Runners, who were equally under-represented in literature. Where policing of any kind appeared in periodicals and books it was invariably denigrated, despised or dismissed. Yet, by 1850, not only the preventive police, but also the relatively new detective police force, were being written about and positively celebrated in fact and fiction by, among others, an author as well-known and respected as Charles Dickens. I intend here to analyse this reversal in public opinion from opprobrium to approbation of the police with reference to the popular literature of the time.

Material on the police, and particularly on their forebears, the Bow Street Runners, is relatively scarce in the first part of the nineteenth century. The *Newgate Calendar* might occasionally mention a constable or watchman involved in the arrest of a felon, as did some of the later broadsides. Novels, such as those of the Newgate school, which incorporated crime into their narratives might also make passing reference to the Runners or other officials of the law. While there is a plethora of printed matter on the New Metropolitan Police, this is in the domain of fact rather than fiction, either pertaining to the functions of the police themselves or to the public reception/perception of their activities. In contrast, the vast majority of documentation on the Bow Street Runners is, according to Patrick Pringle: 'lost forever [...] almost all the official records were destroyed—not by accident or policy, but simply because they were not thought worth keeping—when the Bow Street Police Office moved [...] in 1881'.[1] Still extant is John Wight's *Mornings at Bow Street*, a collected edition of the articles based on actual cases brought before the magistrate at Bow Street that he wrote for the *Morning Herald*. As Wight observed, these were selected for their humour: 'The chief quality of these little narratives is certainly *"pour faire rire"*.'[2] As such, they offer little information about the officers of Bow Street and their work. But, as the Bow Street force was the precursor of the New Police, existing in parallel with them for some ten years, and because the Bow Street Runners were a detective force where the New Police had, initially, a purely preventive function, their presence is necessary to my argument. It was only after the disbanding of the Bow Street patrols in 1839 that the New Police could and did officially recognise the need for a police detective department, and even then it was not until 1842 that this was established.

As George Sala noted in his 'Introduction' to the 1875 edition of Wight's text, 'the period covered by Mr. Wight's book, occupies what might be termed the border land between the end of an old and the commencement of a new system'.[3] Similarly, the Bow Street force occupies an interstitial space between the old, semi-feudal systems of policing, such as they were, and the new, professionalised and state-controlled Metropolitan Police. Elements of the Bow Street system of policing are visible in the structures and duties of the New Police and in the methodologies of its detecting agents. But Wight's text offers no account of the workings of the Bow Street officers, concentrating rather on the 'criminals' and their largely petty crimes. The nearest thing to a contemporaneous account of a Runner's work lies in the realm of fiction rather than fact.

3.2 Transitional text, textual transition: From delinquency to detection

Although populist material which concentrates solely on the Bow Street Runners is rare, there is one nineteenth-century fictional text on the subject. This is the anonymously authored *Richmond: Scenes in the Life of a Bow Street Runner, Drawn Up from His Private Memoranda* (1827), published in three volumes.[4] The editor of the twentieth-century edition of the novel, E. F. Bleiler, argues that 'it is the first conscious collection of detective stories in English' (*Richmond*, p. xiv), and credits the anonymous author with a 'clear perception of a new literary form' (*Richmond*, p. xiv). But Bleiler's argument is retrospective: from a modern perspective, *Richmond* appears to some extent to be an early exemplar of the genre of detective fiction, but this perspective is influenced by the work of later writers such as Poe, Collins, Gaboriau, and Doyle. At the time of *Richmond*'s publication, there was no concept of detectives *per se*, or of a genre of fiction concerned with their activities. As a contemporary review indicates, on publication *Richmond* was perceived as a motley collection 'of visits to race-courses—of inroads upon gipsy haunts—of the vicissitudes of a thief-hunt—of shop-lifting—of larcenies, great and small, all those little schemes, and ingenious as well as straightforward exercises, in which juvenile depredators are known to be brought up'.[5] Form follows content, and I suggest that the text of *Richmond* conforms to two key words from the above review, 'juvenile' and 'depredator', or in modern terminology, 'delinquent'.

Richmond is a juvenile text in its historical location, situated between the 'infancy' of policing in its semi-feudal form with parish constables and watchmen, and its 'coming of age' as the New Metropolitan Police. If, to extend the metaphor, the gap between youth and maturity are the teenage years, then *Richmond* is a teenaged text; the teenage years are, notoriously, a time of transition, and the novel fulfils that definition in a number of ways. Further, the text and its contents are delinquent in terms of literary form and subject matter: *Richmond* and its characters evade the disciplinary framework of both literary and social convention. The evasion of literary discipline is evident in the *mélange* of genres which comprise the narrative, while the eponymous protagonist's actions are motivated by his evasion of the disciplinary institutions of society such as school or employment. Escaping the discipline of genre and with an undisciplined hero, *Richmond* lacks the monitory function of the spectacle of sovereign power found in execution broadsides, nor does it afford the ideological discipline implicit in the exemplary role model of, for example, Warren's physician. Yet as the narrative moves from the fluidity of the 'Early Life' section towards the more structured episodes of the second section of the novel both text and hero become more disciplined and hence disciplinary. In this, as in other ways, *Richmond* is a transitional text.

Richmond occupies an interstitial discursive space parallel to the temporal and social location of the Bow Street Runners. Within the contemporary society, funded partly by the state and partly by private endeavour, the Runners functioned in the grey area between criminality and legality. Temporally, they were located between the infamous thief-takers of Jonathan Wild's time and the as yet unformed New Police. Similarly,

Richmond is located, in the literary sense, between the picaresque narratives of the eighteenth century and the later detective anecdotes such as 'Recollections of a Police Officer' (1849) by 'Waters'. Further, it relates the adventures of its eponymous hero, Tom Richmond, in his transition from a semi-criminal, delinquent life on the margins of society to an equally marginal position that is technically on the side of law and order. Tom's new position as a Bow Street Runner falls loosely within the framework of the law, but he is not subject to strict discipline, and neither, in the main, is the text. But I suggest that the beginnings of a disciplined and disciplinary case structure can be found in the second part of *Richmond*, albeit in gestational form. There is a gradual transition from episodic narrative to an approximation of the formal narrative division of the case seen in Warren's *Passages* and in both *The Experiences of a Barrister* and *The Confessions of an Attorney*, that is, an episode which is complete in itself, linked to the remainder of the narrative only by the voice and profession of the first-person narrator.

The language of the law intrudes into the anecdotal style of the narrative as *Richmond* seeks to authenticate itself as fact, and the word 'case', which recurs throughout the narrative, comes to be used in its legal rather than its general sense. 'Case' in *Richmond* usually refers to specific circumstances which construct the victim of crime as a client of the law. Each of Tom's enquiries is made in response to a separate perceived criminal act and the subsequent events follow a logical progression of proto-detective work leading towards closure with the capture of the criminal or the solving of the problem. Within the framework of police and detection the nascent case structure of *Richmond* attains its fully-fledged form in 'Recollections of a Police Officer' by 'Waters' in 1849, and Dickens's 'Detective Anecdotes' in the early 1850s. In terms of form, *Richmond* is a transitional text, borrowing from past structures and laying the foundations for later forms.

In the twenty-first century, *Richmond* has both cultural and historical significance as an early example of what will become detective fiction. But the nineteenth-century reception of the text illustrates the lack of discursive space for a detective hero and the attitude, particularly that of the novel-buying upper classes, towards the activity of policing and the social status of those who policed and those who were policed. The apparent contemporary unpopularity of *Richmond* is evidence of the public's rejection of an unrecognisable genre and of the distrust and the disdain that the text's subject matter aroused. Published in March 1827, it ran to only one edition, although unsold sheets of this edition were reissued in 1845 with a new title page. It was reviewed in the literary press, receiving a damning criticism from the *Monthly Review* of June 1827. This stated that *Richmond* was 'almost beneath contempt [...] a lethargic and lifeless affair', and remarked that it was doubtful that the subject matter could 'be made attractive in any shape'.[6] The *Literary Gazette* was more generous: 'This is at least a variety in our literature', commented its literary critic.[7] Such reactions to the novel may explain the author's decision to remain anonymous. *Richmond* has been ascribed to Thomas Skinner Surr, and more commonly to Thomas Gaspey, both of whom wrote novels concerned with crime, but there is no compelling evidence for either as the author of *Richmond*. E. F. Bleiler, in his 'Introduction' to the Dover edition, makes a strong case against both. It is unlikely that the text's claim to autobiographical status has any basis in truth. There had been, prior to the publication of the novel, a second clerk called Richmond at Bow Street, but he had nothing to do with the narrative: there is a disclaimer in the 'Notice' that serves as a preface to *Richmond* which states that 'Mr. JOHN RICHMOND, late a clerk in the Police Office, Bow Street, is not in any manner, directly or indirectly, connected with this work.' And surely a writer intimately connected with the Bow Street force would have been more punctilious and accurate in the depiction of a Runner than is the author of *Richmond*.[8] The fictional and amateur status of the text is noted in the *Monthly Review*: 'there is not a passage in the three volumes, which might not have been [...] produced by any, the most careless amateur visitor of our police offices'.[9] The amateur status of the author is paralleled by the amateur status of the text and its protagonist.

3.3 A life, partly regular, partly adventurous

This amateur approach is evident in the way Tom is recruited into the Runners. There is no mention of the administrative or official details of his induction: reality is glossed over and elided, subverting any textual claim to authenticity or authority. Tom's introduction to Bow Street is through the agency of his friend and ex-partner in the theatrical trade, Jem Bucks, now 'on the establishment at Bow Street' (*Richmond*, p. 87). Tom decides that a new career as a Bow Street officer 'was precisely what accorded with the views I had been forming of a life, partly regular and partly adventurous' (*Richmond*, p. 87). The phrase 'partly regular' can also be applied to the form of the narrative. As Tom comes to work within the loose disciplinary frame of the Runners, so the text begins to take on a more structured form. Tom's 'only objection [to the Bow Street establishment] was the scarlet waistcoat' (*Richmond*, p. 87), referring to the uniform worn by members of the various Patrols. For Tom, the uniform is not merely the visible signifier of his new employment, but is contaminated with connotations of the servant class. When considering his career options, he declares 'I could not degrade myself by wearing a badge of servitude in the form of a livery—death would be preferable' (*Richmond*, p. 87). The Runners' uniform, he decides, 'although not quite so bad and low as a livery, was still a badge I could have done without' (*Richmond*, p. 88). A uniform marks its wearer as a member of the serving class, a social position that would form a barrier between the text and its potential readers, who would have been of the class to employ rather than to be employed.

The contemporary public perception of the Runners is encapsulated in Tom's own feelings upon joining the force:

> At first, I had an indescribable notion that I was now degraded and shut out from all society, as everybody has a dislike and horror at the very sight of an officer—caused no doubt by the very general prevalence of private unfair dealing and villainy, and the secret dread of detection.
>
> (*Richmond*, p. 89)

Such a statement makes puzzling the author's choice of subject, but it is possible that the recounting of Tom's adventures is intended to rehabilitate the Runners in the eyes of the public. Within the narrative, Tom finds consolation in the company of his fellow officers, 'a jovial set of fellows,—free, careless, merry, and full of anecdotes of their various exploits' (*Richmond*, p. 89). And his fears about the uniform prove to be unfounded: in fact, only the Patrol members, not the Runners, wore the red waistcoat. The uniform of the Bow Street Patrols marked them as a conspicuous force for the protection of the respectable (implicitly propertied) classes from the threatened depredations of the poor (potentially criminal) class. A uniformed police is representative of sovereign power, an overt reminder of the presence of the law contained within a disciplinary institution. The Runner, indistinguishable in his lack of uniform, escapes the institution. In becoming a Runner, Tom is paying lip-service to the framework of the law, but in fact is continuing the evasion of discipline which he had begun as a boy. His 'Early Life' catalogues Tom's constant rejection of or escape from the discipline of family, school, and work in a series of small acts of delinquency and encounters with those on the margins of society who are implicitly, or sometimes explicitly, criminalised by their social location. In his later 'regular' life, Tom's delinquency, his implicitly criminal attributes and contacts, are utilised in the interests of the law. The skills of the criminal now become the techniques of detection: in *Richmond*, Tom's criminal contacts and questionable practices facilitate his detective work.

As the narrative itself eludes the disciplinary framework of a single genre, moving from the picaresque to a quasi-realism, from romance to adventure, from crime to comedy, so Tom refuses the discipline of institutions which will limit his freedom of movement and his individuality. The delinquency inherent in the textual subversion of novelistic convention is equally apparent in the delinquency of its protagonist. Even Tom's social status is undisciplined, or at least undefined, a factor that may have been a contributory cause of the novel's failure to sell. Although his 'Early Life' seems to indicate that he is from a reasonably well-off family, his refusal to undertake a respectable or conventional trade or profession appropriate to his status prevents his definition in social terms. The reading public of any era buys literary material that it can comprehend and to which it can relate; in the case of *Richmond*, the relation between subject matter and reader is made complex. The contemporary market for the novel was limited not only by literacy, but by income; the larger part of the population in 1827 would not have had the means to buy a three-volume novel priced on publication at £1/11/6. And the wealthy reader's subject of choice was more likely to be a novel of the silver-fork school, a novel of fashionable high-society life that could act as a valuable source of information for the *nouveaux riches* in fulfilling their social aspirations. Such a reader would have little, if any, interest in a text which, in the case of *Richmond*, concentrates on the lower echelons of society, or in a narrative that, where it does portray the upper or middle classes, depicts them as at best stupid and venal, or at worst, corrupt. The implied ideal reader of *Richmond* is of the class that could not have afforded the text: the actual reader, while possibly socially mobile himself or herself, would have preferred the lower classes not only to know their place, but to remain in it. Tom's evasion of the disciplinary institution of class blurs the social boundaries, an erosion of the hierarchical structure of society that would have proved unsettling for the reader. Similarly, the absence of discipline evident in the text's slippage between genres and the lack of discursive space for a narrative of detection at the time of *Richmond*'s publication offer no fixed point of reference for the reader, further alienating the contemporary audience of the novel.

Yet another reason for the poor reception of the novel can be seen in Tom's attitude towards his pursuit of criminals. While describing his employment as a means of fulfilling his desire for adventure, Tom in fact speaks in the register of economics. He refers to his cases as 'enterprises' or 'jobs', terms suggestive of a businesslike approach to the capturing of criminals whose arrest will entail a financial benefit. As Clive Emsley notes with reference to the Runners, 'these men continued to profit from what might be termed an entrepreneurial system of policing'.[10] This economic emphasis is apparent in the text. The crimes in *Richmond* are all, directly or indirectly, concerned with property, and the reward system which supplemented the income of a Runner constructs Tom as a mercenary, working within a commercial frame. Tom, despite his protestations to the contrary, repeatedly returns to the subject of payment for his services. On accepting a reward from a client he declares 'I took the purse [. . .] more from a wish not to offend her by refusal, than from a desire for the money. The fine feelings which I had been the happy means of eliciting [. . .] were an abundant reward to me' (*Richmond*, p. 120). Similar comments nearly always accompany any mention of financial transactions, as Tom disclaims the true and commercial motivation for his pursuit of criminals. Tom's concentration on matters pecuniary accords with the contemporary public perception of the Runners as potentially corrupt. Equally, receiving payment for his services locates him firmly in the serving class, an unsuitable location for the hero of a novel.

A further contribution to the unpopularity of the text is made by the detective methodologies employed by Tom, which realise the early nineteenth-century fears concerning policing. Public conceptions of policing systems were based on the continental, specifically the French, model, which was perceived to be a spy system heavily reliant on informers. Such a system was seen less as a protection for the propertied classes against criminal depredation than as an intrusion into the private lives of those of all classes, and, therefore, an erosion of civil liberties. Tom relies on the acting skills acquired in his 'Early Life' in his detecting activities, and uses the techniques of the confidence trickster, which he learned in his time with the gypsies, in eliciting information from the unwary. Other methodologies he employs are eavesdropping, covert observation, and the use of informers. Such techniques know no social boundaries: they can be applied not only to the criminal classes, but also to the propertied classes that Tom purports to serve and whose property he is employed to protect or retrieve. As he says, 'I had acquired some tact in getting into the good graces and confidence of all classes of people by talking as much as I could in their own way' (*Richmond*, p. 112). 'All classes of people' include those who see themselves as the employers of the machinery of law, not as subject to its authority, that is, the class from which the novel would have drawn its audience.

The dubious detecting methods used by Tom and his location in the serving classes work against his construction as a heroic figure. The contemporary literary conventions and the socially elevated reader of literature required certain qualities in its heroes, and Tom does not possess them. His employment and slippery social status are not the attributes of a gentleman and, at the time of the text's publication, heroes were required to be gentlemen, however disguised. Tom's lack of heroic qualifications was in all probability a significant contribution to *Richmond*'s unpopularity with the reading public. That Tom was not a 'gentleman' might imply that his attentions would be confined to the potentially criminal lower orders of society, but this is not the case. Tom's detective work is not limited to the criminal classes: an unfixed and therefore socially mobile figure, his investigations extend into the middle and upper echelons of society, and his characterisations and perceptions of the bourgeoisie and aristocracy in the text are not flattering to either. Representatives of the middle strata of society are portrayed as miserly, venal, and as social climbers. Manson, the father of the kidnapped boy in Tom's first case is less interested in the child's safe return than he is concerned with the financial implications: '"I suppose" said Mr. Manson to me, "I must give you something for your trouble [...]. Every thing—every body cries for money"' (*Richmond*, p. 119). In a commentary on the probity of the clergy, Tom's second case concerns the bogus and rapacious Reverend Cockspur, whose attempts to make money out of his parishioners rouses them to play tricks on him. Tom is employed to discover the origins of the apparently ghostly goings-on at the vicarage. The portrayal of Mr Daniel Cockspur contains some interesting social commentary. Cockspur's original employment is as an attorney, and his characterisation in *Richmond* panders to the contemporary negative public image of that profession. The fourth of Tom's clients is Mr Banbury, who is a member of the newly emergent wealthy bourgeoisie. His 'crime' is to treat his new wife after the fashion of Petruchio in Shakespeare's *The Taming of the Shrew*. There is no real felony in this section of the narrative, which is less detective fiction than comedy drama or burlesque tale. But it can also be read as a satirical commentary on the aspirations and stupidities of the *nouveaux riches* and their pretensions to nobility and intellectualism.

High society's implication in matters criminal is seen initially in Tom's third case, which brings him into contact with dissipated aristocracy in the form of 'those two notorious gamblers, Sir Byam Finch and Lord ——' (*Richmond*, p. 151). *Richmond* initially depicts aristocratic criminality in terms of moral or financial misdemeanours rather than felonious acts, as did other contemporary novelists such as Edward Bulwer-Lytton.

Aristocratic crime consists of cheating at cards, fixing horse races, deceiving their fellows, and seducing young women. Sir Byam Finch and Lord —— are connected to and implicated in the world of real criminality by their employment of Jones, the kidnapper, body-snatcher and smuggler who is the object of Tom's investigations for three of his cases. In Tom's final and longest case, the narrative breaks with convention, and felonious crime, not moral misdemeanour, is located firmly in the higher echelons of society. The criminal is here 'a lady [...] with that dignified and noble air which can only be inherited within the pale of rank' (*Richmond*, p. 215). In her representation, immorality and crime combine in the figure of a dissolute woman of high society, a combination of female sexuality and sin which goes beyond the conventional contemporary linking of the two in its inclusion of felony. She is involved with a gang of forgers, and the crime of forgery was then a capital offence.

Tom overtly criticises the social circles in which this female criminal moves: 'it did not appear that any thing had as yet transpired, flagrant enough to exile her from what is called good society, which, indeed, tolerates every vice, so that it be kept within strict limit of *concealment'* (*Richmond*, p. 214, emphasis in the text). This is a direct critique of the social class from which *Richmond* might expect to draw its readers. There is a further attack in the text's depiction of Percy, the young man of property, who, seduced and deceived by Mrs ——, is prevented by Tom from committing suicide and who becomes the main source of information in the case. Percy's social aspirations and sexual naivety construct him as a fool who can only be saved by the intervention of the socially inferior, but implicitly intellectually superior, Tom. Again, this is a perceived threat to the social *status quo*, reversing the conventional depiction of society which located criminality and low intelligence in the world of the lower class, not in the social sphere of the reader of the novel, who would have aspired to, or identified with, the status of the nobility in the text, if not with their actions. This last adventure of Tom is not client-driven, but a purely personal enterprise. It is instigated by Tom's chance observation of Mrs ——'s criminal actions, and his initial response is not to arrest her for passing forged notes, as might reasonably be expected of a police officer witnessing a crime, but to consider her recruitment as an informer:

> I thought it would be pity to sacrifice so fine a woman, how criminal soever [*sic*] she might prove, and allow others to escape; for it was not to be supposed that she was both the forger and the utterer. There must be others employed in a crime of this kind; probably a whole gang of delinquents.
>
> (*Richmond*, p. 216)

To recruit her would be a reprise of Tom's own recruitment; that is, to bring the delinquent within the framework of institutionalised law, where he or she becomes a mechanism in the machinery of policing power. But Tom foregoes his planned recruitment of Mrs ——, feeling 'a sort of shuddering repugnance at the thought of subjecting her to the lowest degradation into which a criminal can fall' (*Richmond*, p. 216), that is, the role of informer. This is an ironic observation in view of the fact that Tom employs such people and to some extent fulfils the same function himself. Equally, it recognises the distaste with which informers were regarded by the contemporary society at all levels, an opinion which, I suggest, is implicated in the novel's lack of popularity.

Tom's reluctance to fulfil his immediate duty, which would be to arrest Mrs ——, is contingent upon his desire to discover and arrest the whole gang, a desire which is inspired by the larger reward such an arrest would generate. Within the narrative, he justifies his chosen course of action by speaking at great length of his wish to save a woman from disgrace: 'I had [. . .] saved one deserving woman from ruin; and it would be a noble subject of self-gratulation if I could [save] [. . .] another from a fate no less disgraceful' (*Richmond*, p. 217). Tom's concept of 'self-gratulation' negates any aspect of altruistic motivation. That this text is not reformist in intent is evident in the recruitment of the delinquent as an aid to detection rather than an attempt to reform the criminal individual; delinquent characters are not reformed in the text, rather their delinquency is employed in the service of the law. In this final case, there is an overt statement of an anti-reformist stance. Speaking through Tom, the text argues that 'there is but very little chance of any delinquent reforming after having triumphed for a time in security, and this generally applies most strongly to females' (*Richmond*, p. 216). Such a statement constructs the female as inherently delinquent, a construction supported by the largely negative—and minimal—representation of women in the text. Although crime enters the world of high society in this final case, its members are not subjected to secular law; Mrs ——'s criminality is curtailed by her suicide and her husband and partner in crime is killed in a duel with her erstwhile victim, Percy. The text relies on the overriding justice of God to punish those who appear to escape the rule of law.

Tom's delinquency is legitimised and partly contained by its employment in the interests, at least partially, of the law. Further, his use of criminal figures such as Blore, and his occasional partnerships with the previously delinquent Jem Bucks and Thady, the comic but potentially delinquent Irishman, bring them also under the *aegis* of the law, where they are implicated in the structure and machinery of policing power.[11]

But *Richmond* as novel does not share this legitimacy and containment. The delinquency of the subject matter evident in the characters and their actions allied with the text's refusal or inability to conform to a single conventional genre construct the narrative as inherently criminal in terms of the contemporary literary and social conventions. Retrospectively, it is easy to read *Richmond* as a detective fiction; at the time of its publication, there was no such genre. The discursive space for the detective in either fact or fiction did not exist, and, lacking the discipline that a specific genre imposes on the novel, *Richmond*, like its eponymous hero, escapes the constraints of disciplinary or literary institutions.

The text, unlike its protagonist, is not recruited into the service of the law, nor does it have a reformatory or monitory function. Tom's closing words, and implicitly those of the text, are '[m]y purpose will be answered if what I have recorded in these volumes shall serve to beguile an idle hour, or show to those, who are inexperienced, the innumerable snares which beset the path of life' (*Richmond*, p. 266). This is entertainment and advice, not instruction and example. Crime in *Richmond* is not inevitably followed by punishment; indeed, Tom rarely reports the fate of the criminal in any detail, and he himself escapes any chastisement for his misdeeds. There is little mention of the law or its officials, other than occasional references to the magistrates who legitimate Tom's actions by issuing warrants for the arrest of criminals. While Tom makes occasional reference to his duty as an officer of the law, even in his criminal cases he makes decisions on a personal basis rather than by reference to his superiors or to the machinery of the state. This refusal of the disciplinary institution of the law prevents Tom from being perceived as representative of a repressive state apparatus and distances him from the disciplinary role of later detectives. The social instability inherent in the juxtaposition of criminality with respectability is paralleled by the textual instability evidenced in the *mélange* of literary genres and tropes that the narrative employs. With no fixed point of reference, and a hero whose characterisation and behaviour preclude readerly self-identification, the reader has no specific location within the text, but is continually in transition from one perspective to another. In terms of structure, content, protagonist, and reader, the text is unstable and hence transitional. As an early prototype of detective fiction, *Richmond* is temporally juvenile: consequently, lacking the discipline of an established genre, it is a delinquent text.

Viewed through the literary lens offered by the fully-fledged genre exemplified in Doyle's Sherlock Holmes stories, there is in *Richmond* evidence of those features that will become standard in later works of detection. There is a nascent case structure, an investigating companion, the infiltration of the criminal world, and the use of detecting techniques such as surveillance, disguise, and pursuit. But there is little evidence of what Doyle called 'deductive' thought, or of forensic methodology or analysis of motive. Tom's investigative work follows a simplistic pattern of crime, pursuit and capture of the criminal which is closer to the *Newgate Calendar* pattern of crime followed by the capture of the criminal than to the Holmesian pattern of the crime followed by the solution and finally the retrospective explanation. The recruitment of Tom's delinquency in the service of the law and his subsequent adventures in pursuit of criminals figure him as a prototype of the detective and *Richmond* as detective fiction in a juvenile state. Before the detective proper can emerge in fiction and fact, a disciplined and disciplinary framework, social and literary, is required, and the New Metropolitan Police will be instrumental in the establishment of such a framework. This force, whose duty initially will be the prevention rather than the detection of crime, will come to combine within a single institution the modes of sovereign and disciplinary power in a major contribution to the construction of a disciplined society, and, in the process, achieve the popularity of the policing agent that eluded *Richmond*.

3.4 The New Police: Perception and reception

Robert Peel introduced the 'Metropolitan Police Improvement Bill' to Parliament in 1829. There was very little Parliamentary opposition and it became law on 19 June 1829. The transition from theory to practice was remarkably swift. Peel had appointed and instructed Colonel Charles Rowan as Commissioner by 9 July 1829, and Rowan, with his fellow Commissioner Richard Mayne, had organised and instituted the New Metropolitan Police within 12 weeks. As Belton Cobb notes:

> By September 29th [...] Rowan had enlisted a force of 825 men; he had divided them into five divisions, each consisting of a super-intendent, four inspectors, sixteen sergeants and 144 constables; he had subdivided the divisions into companies and sections; he had organized the necessary police station-houses; he had instructed his men (with Mayne's assistance) in their duties; he had seen to it that they had learnt the rudiments of drill and at least the principles of discipline; he had supplied them with a certain amount of uniform; and he had put them to work on their carefully mapped beats.[12]

This highly structured, uniformed, and above all disciplined, force is in sharp contrast to the loose framework of the law within which Tom Richmond functioned. Here is no space for delinquency, either in actuality or in its textual representation. Yet early perceptions of the New Police, and the initially high turnover of recruits, suggest otherwise. Many were dismissed for drunkenness on duty, but there seemed to be no shortage of replacement recruits. The press followed with interest the inauguration of the force and chronicled both its activities and the response of the public to this new presence on the streets of London. Almost immediately, the association of delinquency and policing prevalent in the public mind was being voiced in the contemporary newspapers and journals.

This is made evident in an article from the *Morning Herald* that appeared barely two weeks after the first policemen commenced their duties, and which reported the attempted theft of a loin of mutton from a butcher's shop by a police constable:

> It is not a very pleasant thing for the citizens of London to reflect that any of the persons who are appointed to guard their property, and to exercise surveillance over themselves and their families, may be men, like the prisoner, who only watch that they may devour. If the dogs employed to protect the sheep should happen to have the appetites and habits of wolves, they could do much more mischief [...] than the ravenous animals, that never come forth from their dens but with those warning manifestations of violence which alarm in their natural prey the instinct of self-preservation. The treacherous policeman, like the wolfish shepherd-dog, made free with the mutton it was his duty to protect.[13]

In fairness, it was acknowledged further on in the piece that there was not at the time of writing any proof that the man was a policeman, but a strong argument was made in support of the allegation, centring on the police uniform allegedly found at the man's home. The social status and perceived potential corruptibility of the police is made clear in the canine metaphor used in the article: the word 'dogs' constructs the New Police constables as both bestial and servile, a construction elaborated in the subsequent expansion of 'dog' into 'wolfish shepherd-dog'. An implicit association is made between the police constable and the criminal he polices: they are shown to share a common origin, and the poacher turned gamekeeper is always open to suspicion. The knowledge of and contact with criminal, delinquent, or deviant others that Tom Richmond found essential to the success of his detective work feeds the public perception of the police, or in Tom's case, the Bow Street Runners, as contaminated by criminality, a contamination which constructs them as potentially corrupt. Further, many of the articles published on the police in the early days of their existence made mention of the methodologies which it was feared the New Police would employ. These were perceived to be based on the French model with its use of espionage and informers. The visibility of the New Police, ensured by their uniform and tall hats, offered little consolation to the public. Rather, it meant that they were seen as a repressive quasi-military force that would act on behalf of, and would be entirely controlled by, the political party in power.

The New Police, therefore, had not only to prove their efficacy in the prevention of crime, which was their *raison d'être*, but also to overcome the public perception of a government-controlled police force as both a threat to civil liberties and as contaminated by the criminals that they were instituted to police. There are many excellent, authoritative, and in-depth accounts of the history of policing and the police in England, which recount in detail the arguments for and against the creation of the Metropolitan Police, and I do not propose to add to their number. Rather, I want to examine the strategies and techniques that led to the public acceptance of, even affection for, what came to be known as 'the British Bobby'. As Peter Drexler notes, '[e]ven a satirical review such as *Punch*, which since its foundation in 1841 had made the police a target for its most biting comments, concedes in 1851: "It is evident that the police are beginning to take that place in the affections of the people [...] that soldiers and sailors used to occupy."'[14] My contention here is that the internal disciplinary structure of the New Police and their visible presence on the London streets, in conjunction with the apparent gradual decrease in crime, turned the policeman from the enemy of the public to its protector, and that this change is evident in the popular literature of the time.

Without a reiteration of the history of policing, there remains the necessity of providing a context for the formation of the New Police. What makes a police presence acceptable, or at least perceived as a necessary evil, is crime, and crime in the metropolis of London in the eighteenth and early nineteenth centuries appeared to be increasing at an alarming rate. The absence of statistics in this period makes any definitive analysis of the incidence of crime impossible, and historians are divided in opinion between an actual and a perceived increase. The population of London expanded during this period, with the supremacy of England as a mercantile nation and the concomitant rise of the industrialisation that fed the newly emergent consumer society and which resulted in the migration of rural folk into the towns. By 1800 about one million people lived in London, more than one Englishman in ten. A proliferation of crime is suggested by the ever-expanding number of felonies redesignated as capital crimes at the turn of the century, but many of these crimes were what would now be considered rather as misdemeanours. Nonetheless, a large aggregation of people in a relatively small geographical area juxtaposes the poor with the wealthy and incites and makes possible, and more visible, crime and criminality. The accretion of the poor and the unemployed in specific areas of the city such as the infamous 'rookeries' of St Giles and Seven Dials and the association of poverty with crime created what would come to be perceived as the 'dangerous' or criminal class. And the geography of London ensured that the location of this so-called criminal class was an integral part of the metropolis, placing the rich and the poor in close proximity in urban terms.

Action against this assumed increase in crime had been taken as early as 1749, when Henry Fielding recruited his first seven Bow Street Officers, but it took until 1757 before any government funding was made available to Henry's brother and successor, John Fielding, for the support of this proto-detective force. Further funding in 1763 enabled the formation of a Horse Patrol to police the approaches to the metropolis against the depredations of highwaymen, but this funding was withdrawn within 12 months, in spite of the Horse Patrol's successful preventive function. It would be nearly 20 years later and require the terror induced in the government by the mob in the Gordon Riots of June 1780 before some official action would be taken against crime. The absence of any unified policing force meant that the army had to be called in to put down the riot, at a cost of 250 deaths. Subsequent to this, the new incumbent at Bow Street, Sampson Wright, received the government's blessing and public funds to set up an official preventive policing force, the Bow Street Foot Patrol. By 1792, Bow Street was no longer the only 'police' office in London; there were a further seven offices, each under a different magistrate. The metropolis now had a police, but it was not a unified system. Resistance across the social strata to any suggestion of a unified, publicly-funded police was strong. Between 1770 and 1828, 11 Select Committees were convened to inquire into the state of the police in the Metropolis with a view to introducing, expanding, or altering the existing systems in an attempt to control crime. The only one which seems to have produced any result was that of 1828, the year preceding the inauguration of the Metropolitan Police, and the Select Committee's positive response was, to a great extent, the result of Robert Peel's earlier legislative reforms.

Peel, appointed Home Secretary in January 1822, had personal experience in setting up a police force. As Secretary for Ireland (1812–1818) he had introduced the Peace Preservation Act to Parliament (1814), an act which legislated for the establishment of an organised police force in Ireland to replace the existing inefficient system, which was very similar to that in England. That he was able to do this without the objections normally put forward against a police force is undoubtedly because it was a measure taken in Ireland; what would be construed as repressive in England was merely prudent, preventive, and protective in what was essentially a colonial possession. Peel had historical and literary sources on which to draw: John Fielding's *Plan for Preventing Robberies Within Twenty Miles of London* (1755); Saunders Welch's *Observations on the Office of Constable* (1754); the reports of 11 Select Committees; the example of Bow Street; innumerable periodical articles; and perhaps above all, the work of Patrick Colquhoun. In 1796, Colquhoun published (anonymously) the first edition of his *Treatise on the Police of the Metropolis*, which would go on into a further six editions in the following ten years. While not a blueprint for the Metropolitan Police as they would become, nonetheless, his *Treatise* assessed the numbers and types of crimes being committed, and suggested preventive measures that might be taken to decrease the incidence of crime.

Colquhoun's conception of crime was centred on pilferage and theft: 'It is supposed that property, purloined and pilfered in a little way, from almost every family, and from every *home, stable, shop, warehouse, workshop, foundry and other repository*, may amount [in London alone] to about 700,000 L in one year' (emphasis in the text).[15] This concept of theft as a major offence against society as a whole was shared by Peel, who in 1826 stated that he considered 'the crime of theft to constitute the most important class of crime'.[16] Property, in a society which increasingly functioned economically on the production and exchange of commodities, became the focus of concerns about crime and criminality, but equally, in a mercantilist society, the inegalitarian possession of property promotes theft. While Colquhoun was not directly involved with the formation of the New Police, in 1798 he put into practice some of the ideas he had posited in his *Treatise*. He inaugurated not a city-wide police, but a system for policing that area most immediately concerned with property in the form of the commodities brought into and out of the metropolis, and where workplace perks and pilferages were, he estimated, costing the merchants some £500,000 per annum.[17] This was the Port of London. Here, the labouring poor were brought into immediate contact with the property that created and supported the wealthy merchants of London and beyond, a juxtaposition of poverty and riches which, located as it was in a relatively small area, can be read as a microcosm of the wider world of the metropolis.

Those who suffered most from the depredations carried out in the course of transferring goods to and from the cargo ships anchored in the Port of London were the West India merchants, whose shipping business made up the larger part of the dockyard trade. Approximately half of the losses through theft were borne by these merchants: all types of person employed on or by the river, labourers (or lumpers as they were then called), lightermen, custom officers, tidewaiters, and even ratcatchers effectively stole from their employers.[18] A remedy for this was offered by two people: directly by Colquhoun, who approached the West India merchants with a proposal for a river police, which was approved by a committee of the merchants on 30 January 1798, and more indirectly by one John Harriott, ex-merchant adventurer and inventor, who had sent a proposal for a river police to the Secretary of State six months previously: it had been ignored. Colquhoun met with Harriott, was impressed with his scheme, and recommended it to the government.[19] The combined approval of the West India merchants and the government resulted in the institution of a Marine Police Establishment, to be funded in part by the government and in part by the merchants. Colquhoun was appointed as the superintending magistrate, and Harriott as the resident magistrate, in charge of what came to be called the Marine Police Institution. This comprised two parts: a police department, consisting of 50 constables under a chief constable, who were to act in the prevention and detection of crime under the orders of the magistrates, and a department for the organisation of the lumpers, who were to be registered and employed in rotation. Essentially, the constables policed the lumpers, while watchmen on the ships were directly under the control of the police department. As the police section of the Marine Institution was funded by the Treasury, it was the first wholly government-funded police force within the metropolis.

Public acceptance of the new force prefigured to some extent the reception accorded later to the New Police, with the difference that resistance came entirely from the poor and working class who were most directly affected. The question of civil liberties was not raised—those who would later be most concerned about the possible loss of civil liberties, that is, the property-owning class, here stood to benefit personally from this new system of policing. The Port of London, located on the margins of the city, functioned largely as a separate entity, with its own rules and regulations, and the establishment of the Marine Police probably aroused little interest among those not directly affected. But there certainly was resistance from the labourers on whom the scheme most directly impacted. In October 1798, just three months after the inauguration of the Marine Police, Irish coalheavers, angered by the prevention of the appropriation of coal that they saw as a perk of the job, attacked the magistrates' office in Wapping. Several hundred of them threatened violence to those within the office. They were successfully repulsed, with Harriott and Colquhoun reading the Riot Act against them, but one constable lost his life in the affray. After this initial display of resistance, the Marine Police seem to have been so effective that Colquhoun could boast in his *Treatise on the Commerce and Police of the River Thames* (1800) that, in its first nine months, the Institution had reduced the amount lost through criminal depredation by over £100,000.[20]

This success resulted from the discipline that Colquhoun and Harriott instituted in the structure of the Marine Police. As Colquhoun stated, '[t]he first step [...] was to discipline and instruct the subordinate officers in all their respective departments'.[21] There were written instructions for all departments, and each officer had to take a solemn oath of office. A system of checks was inaugurated to detect any corruption or misbehaviour among the officers and, at all levels, regular reports, either written or verbal, had to be made to a superior. Prefiguring the disciplined beats that the New Police would follow, Colquhoun's men prevented the commission of crime by 'the constant perambulation of Police Boats, both by night and by day', in a 'systematic and regular' pattern.[22] His Marine Police were 'so arranged, disciplined, and instructed, as to insure Fidelity in the discharge of the duty required', and they worked with 'the same attention and punctuality which prevails in a disciplined army'.[23] Largely un-uniformed (Watermen, the equivalent of police constables, were issued with greatcoats), nonetheless, the Marine Police constituted, in their discipline and regulation, a visible force of law whose purpose was the prevention of crime. While not the direct forebears of the New Police, the methodologies and function of the Marine Police within the microcosm of the London docklands can be seen as a model for the later policing of the metropolis. But what was relatively quickly accepted in the commercial world of the Port of London would take rather longer to find acceptance in the wider world.

3.5 Preventive police or personal threat?

Central to Colquhoun's concept of a police for the metropolis was that its function should be 'the PREVENTION AND DETECTION OF CRIMES', with the emphasis in practice on 'prevention'.[24] Prevention of crime was also central to the function of the New Metropolitan Police. In the *General Instruction Book* produced by Commissioners Rowan and Mayne for the guidance of police constables, Part I, written by Rowan, specifies that 'It should be understood at the outset, that the principal object to be attained is *"the Prevention of Crime"*. To this great end every effort of the Police is to be directed.'[25] It may seem reasonable that such a laudable aim would have been received with general acclaim; in fact, the public response across the social scale was generally unfavourable.

The middle- and upper-class perspective on the New Police is clearly articulated in an article by David Robinson, 'The Local Government of the Metropolis, and Other Populous Places', published in *Blackwood's Edinburgh Magazine* in January 1831.[26] *Blackwood's*, by dint of its cost and content, found its audience in the higher social classes of a Tory disposition, and Robinson's essay makes clear the fears of those groups. The propertied middle and upper classes, for whom the protection of property concomitant with the prevention of crime should have made the New Police an attractive proposition, cavilled about the cost of the new force and feared the erosion of civil liberties which, they argued, was inherent in a state-controlled police. A police that directed its attention to the criminal and his or her punishment, as had been the case with the Bow Street Runners, presented no threat to the law-abiding citizen. A police that, in the interests of the prevention of crime, watched everyone, regardless of social status, was felt to be too close to the French system of a spy police. The fact that the New Police were highly visible in their uniforms, and highly disciplined in their actions, made no difference: rather, it gave them a militaristic aspect that, with its connotations of state control, was also deeply unpopular.

Written only 18 months after the inauguration of the New Police, and therefore criticising the institution before it had become fully established and organised, Robinson's article opens with a direct attack:

> The new system of Police confessedly forms one of the greatest inroads on the principles and practice of the British Constitution that modern times have witnessed. An intense feeling of hostility to it prevails in the Metropolis, which actuates the middle classes, as well as the multitude, flows much less from party prejudice and misrepresentation, than fair experience, and forms, in a revolutionary period like this, an important source of discontent and disaffection.[27]

Robinson purports to speak for the middle class and what he terms 'the multitude', constructing the New Police as enemies of both. That the article is written in a register which would have rendered it relatively inaccessible even to a literate member of 'the multitude' emphasises the sense that he is addressing an audience of his peers and pandering to their fears, rather than addressing the concerns of the populace generally. Much of the article is concerned with the threat to civil liberties posed by the New Police, disregarding the fact that the lower classes were largely excluded from those liberties. A constant thread running through the essay is the potential erosion of the powers of the magistrates, who were invariably members of the propertied class. While placing 'the multitude' on the same level as the middle class, as hostile to the New Police, Robinson then raises the spectre of revolution issuing from that 'multitude' as a result of their 'discontent and disaffection'. This neatly leads him to his next point, where he makes a direct comparison of the New Police with the French system of policing.

The government, he asserts, is '[g]athering its theories in foreign parts [...] not only ravished with the Code Napoleon, it must have its Napoleon Police'.[28] The duties of the police constable make him 'a general spy [...] the menial of the Ministry [...] a political spy [...]. Such a spy must of course be a finished tool of corruption.'[29] That the English policeman is uniformed does not seem to prevent him from fulfilling this function. The uniform rather constructs him as 'a soldier in disguise [...]. What difference does it make [...] whether his coat be a blue or a red one; or whether he be armed with a staff or a firelock?'[30] This concept is reiterated throughout the article. The New Police are designated as the 'blue army, almost unlimited in numbers and powers [...] the servile instrument of the Executive'.[31] The question of police corruption is addressed: the policeman's powers 'enable him to be a general robber', who will accept bribes, who is 'surrounded with every thing that can destroy his morals', who 'no longer belongs to, or can mix with, society', and who is 'instructed to look for reward and extortion' as a means of increasing his inadequate official income.[32] The presence of a highly visible police is dismissed as 'idle officers [who] swarm through every street throughout the day' and can be seen 'conversing with prostitutes' rather than performing any preventive function against crime.[33] Ultimately, the writer concludes, '[t]here are misdemeanours, crimes, tumults, and riots, because there is a Police'.[34]

Perhaps cost was the most telling argument against the New Police from the perspective of the middle-class reader of *Blackwood's*. A state-funded Police must be paid for through taxation, and Robinson dwells on this aspect of the new system. The New Police, he suggests, can 'tax the community for its maintenance without [...] consent'.[35] It is 'infinitely more expensive than the old one, and operates as a grievous new tax'.[36] And, damningly, in spite of this increased expenditure in the fight against crime, the New Police, '[i]n its leading objects—the prevention of crime and the protection of property—[...] is not more efficient than the old one; on the contrary, it is alleged to be less so'.[37] A revision of the old system, Robinson argues, would have served the purpose better. Much of the remaining 20 pages of the article is devoted to a defence of the existing system of magistracy; an analysis of the causes of crime which lays the blame firmly at the feet of the lower orders with their tendency to idleness, drunkenness, and failure to observe the Sabbath; and suggestions for a form of social rather than purely criminal policing. Crime, for Robinson, is directly associated with social conditions: poor housing and hygiene, the falling-off of religious observances, the lack of education, and moral and sexual dissipation are all factors in the creation of criminality. As he declares:

> Our general objects in all this are—1. The suppression of the houses which form the schools and bulwarks of vice and crime. 2. The severe, incessant watching of the barbarous, demoralized houses and streets, for the purpose of improving the character of, and duly dispersing, their inhabitants. And, 3. The prohibition of drinking and working on the Sabbath, as a great means, amidst others, of promoting religion, morals, and order.[38]

Robinson was not alone in suggesting that policing should incorporate duties other than crime prevention and detection. Edwin Chadwick wrote an article in January 1829 that made a case for the establishment of a police force whose tasks would include a social policing which would enforce the new street act, and 'see that the streets are duly cleansed [...] apprehend vagrants; keep the public thoroughfares free from obstruction; and perform other duties'.[39] For both Chadwick and Robinson, policing is related more to the archaic sense of the word, that is, the regulation and control of a community, rather than being solely concerned with crime. And the New Police did in fact maintain order within the London community, incorporating many of Chadwick's suggestions into their daily routines: crime prevention is more easily achieved in an orderly and ordered society.

Robinson's polemic does not pursue this theme, but continues with an attack on lawyers and barristers which constructs them as abusers rather than defenders of the law, and makes reference to the power of the press and the rise of literacy in the lower classes. 'The immense increase of readers amongst the lower orders', the essay argues, has led to 'the London press [placing] itself under the control of the populace': dissociating itself from 'the London press', the article allies itself rather with the press available to 'the intelligent classes'.[40] This disparagement of the London press and its circulation through the 'gin, beer, and coffee-shops, and eating-houses' presumably patronised by the lower orders, is surprising.[41] To a great extent, the opinion of the New Police voiced in the nineteenth-century precursors of the tabloid press initially concurred with that of Robinson in his article, albeit in more simplistic and sensational terms.

A handbill issued on the 10 November 1830 sums up the attitude of the general public succinctly. It purports to offer the individual protection from the New Police in the form of staves, issued free on request, with which he or she can fight off the police constable who will be armed with a truncheon. An article in the *Morning Journal* of 12 October 1829 entitled 'The Gendarmerie' suggests that the New Police are in fact a military force, and makes a direct comparison with the French police system, as the title implies. A correspondent calling himself an 'Every-day Reader' writes to the *Morning Herald* (6 October 1829) to complain of the inefficacy of the New Police in preventing crime, pronouncing the New Police system to be 'a mere humbug'. In the same edition, an editorial article criticises the standard of men employed by the New Police as constables: 'Every night we receive a number of reports of cases from police-offices which place the new guardians of the peace and morals of society in no very favourable point of view [...] a great proportion of improper characters had been admitted into the "regenerated" police.'[42] *The Times*, more often the voice of the establishment, was not above printing anti-police material. A letter to the Editor, 'The New Police', signed 'Civis', was published in the newspaper on 7 October 1830. The writer concentrated his animus towards the New Police on their militaristic nature: 'the police system [...] military not merely in their aspect, but by their whole discipline and training [...] by their unlimited obedience to their own officers [...] by their seclusion [...] in a species of barracks, and by their isolated employment; apart from their family connections'.[43] His suggestion for a return to a revamped version of the old system of watchmen, or 'Charlies' in London, seems to have been ignored by the Home Office, hence his appeal to the public through the medium of *The Times*.

But not all the material published on the New Police during their first years was unfavourable. Sympathy and support for the force is clearly evident in an anonymous essay in the *New Monthly* magazine of

November 1829. This essay makes a reasoned argument in favour of the new system in conjunction with a critique of the old. The New Police, the writer states, has, 'like all beneficial innovations in our prejudice-ridden community [...] been violently attacked'.[44] Central to its argument in support of the New Police is the article's direct refutation of the association of policing with spying, or, in the French model, *espionnage*. A visible and regulated police is 'the open, manly, straightforward method of preventing and detecting crime; the only way worthy of an Englishman'.[45] The political bias of those most vociferous against the New Police draws the comment that 'curiously enough, these charges are principally brought by the ultra-Tory newspapers', and are motivated by 'hatred to Mr. Peel'.[46] The nickname 'Peelers' used in derogative descriptions of the police consolidates the connections made in the public mind between Peel and his New Police. Quite apart from its defence and praise for the New Police, the article raises a number of relevant points about the structure and function of the police. It comments on the visibility of Peel's 'new men', 'the activity and watchfulness of his agents, exerted openly in conscious power'.[47] It praises the role of the press in the policing of criminality: 'By publishing accurate police reports, the general mass is aroused to the offence and the offender, and every individual takes an interest in his detection.'[48] It makes a case for the institution of a plain-clothes police force, a detective department of sorts: 'whether it would not be useful to have some portion of the new police, at times, dressed as other individuals'.[49] And it makes reference to the discipline necessary for the functioning of a successful police: 'it is difficult to conceive how such an end can be obtained without something like discipline'.[50] Visibility, detection, and discipline are essential factors in the eventual success and popularity of the police, while the role of literature in policing will go beyond the mere reportage of police activities by the press.

The beginnings of this role can be seen in the press coverage of policing that I have considered so far. The press essentially polices the police, watching and analysing its behaviour and the public's response to a new police presence. Initial resistance to the New Police is voiced in the press, as is its gradual acceptance. In opposition, Robinson spoke for the 'ultra-Tory' echelon of society, and the London dailies appealed to and constructed the opinion of the lower classes. In support, the anonymous author of 'The New Police' wrote for a wider, less socially elevated and non-Tory audience. But the attitude of the general public began to change, and the press was instrumental in this, both leading and following public opinion. In the wake of an anti-police demonstration in November 1830, *The Times* editorial expressed its 'abhorrence of the unjust and cruel spirit which the mob are continually displaying against the new Police [...] the system may have its defects: let them be fairly stated and examined'. The piece further refers to the police as 'this useful branch of public service'.[51] The demonstration also incited an editorial in *John Bull* on 7 November 1830, which directly castigated the attackers. Calling them 'cowardly and stupid', the article went on to argue that the 'cockney mob [...] the most dolt-like, idiotic thing alive' had transferred its hatred of the army to the New Police. In attacking the police, the writer observes, the mob allies itself with the very criminals that the police have been inaugurated to control. While admitting that 'there may be objections to the New Police, and we have ourselves said there are', the article goes on to state that opposition to the force had been generated on grounds of expense, loss of privilege, and loss of contracts to supply the watchmen who had preceded the police.[52] Although not wholeheartedly on the side of the New Police, being rather against the stupidity of the mob, the article supports the principles of policing in its new form and is sympathetic towards the police constables and their work.

Within 12 months of its inauguration, the public is becoming accustomed to the presence of the New Police, and public opinion is no longer entirely against that presence. Police reports from the various police offices around London increasingly appear in the press: the New Police are not only visible on the streets as they go about their duties, but their activities are documented for public examination. These reports made popular reading: although many of the crimes reported were minor, there were some that dealt with murder, arson, or other sensational crimes. And the temporal and spatial proximity of the crimes reported must have given the London reader a *frisson* of excitement as well as the comfort of reading about the capture and conviction of the criminal. The sensational content of the crime and execution broadsides found its way into the periodicals of the 1830s and 1840s via the police reports. But it was not only the sensationalism of the police reports which led publishers to print them. It was also the respectability and legality that such reports implied. This is evident in the incorporation of the word 'police' in the title of the radical paper *Cleave's Weekly Police Gazette*, a comprehensive working-class newspaper with an estimated circulation of 30,000–40,000. It strongly agitated for factory reform, repeal of newspaper duty, and the repeal of the Poor Law Amendment Act of 1834, and ran from 1834 to 1836.[53] John Cleave chose to express his radical views under the cover, literally, of the police. The front page of the journal was devoted to reports from the police offices of London, apart from the cartoon which invariably took pride of place below the paper's title, and which was equally invariably anti-establishment. Enclosed within the arms of the law, so to speak, the inner pages advocated the reform of the government whose policing activities were advertised on the cover. The selfsame Cobbett who, in the editorial of *John Bull* had been accused of rousing the mob against the New Police, was here given space to publish his letters and advocate the sales of his books.[54] Between 1829 and the inauguration of the Metropolitan Police, and 1834, when a radical journal appropriated police reports to lend itself an aura of legality and respectability, attitudes towards the New Police softened and changed. Their visibility on the streets, and their proven efficacy, had, it seemed, earned them acceptance if not popularity.

I want to suggest that this efficiency and acceptance were achieved by discipline, the discipline which was central to the construction, institution, and function of policing. Unlike Tom Richmond's life, which was 'partly regular, partly adventurous', the life of a police constable was, rather, wholly regular and wholly regulated. The delinquency of text and tale which had alienated the reader of *Richmond*, is, in the police and the factual, and later in the fictional accounts of their activities, entirely disciplined. The police reports featured in the press and exemplified in *Cleave's Weekly Police Gazette* followed a set pattern: the police office, the officers or constables involved, the crime, and its conclusion were not always presented in the same order, but the same factors were invariably present. Each report would be the account of a case, or cases, which had been reported to the office in question. This case structure will become central to later fictional and factual accounts of both police and police and private detectives, a discipline of form which was barely present in *Richmond*, and which would play its part in the policing and disciplining of the reader. In reading such accounts, the individual internalises the discipline of the form, and further, the framework of the law inherent in such accounts locates the reader as subject to and of the law as figured in the police. The literary representation of the police played a major part in ensuring their acceptance by the public; equally, such representation becomes part of the policing process in an increasingly literate society.

In ideal, and ideological, terms, the policeman should be seen as a public servant, a protector and guardian rather than an inspector and prosecutor. This ideological concept of the police was one which Rowan and Mayne sought to promote in the newly formed Metropolitan Police. The police were to be seen as employees of the public, not of the state. To this end, the police were not only to be visible on the street, but open to inspection by the public, an inspection which was reported in and facilitated by the newspapers and periodical press. The surveillance inherent in policing was to be subject to a reverse surveillance by the objects of the police gaze: the man or woman in the streets of London was free to watch and pass comment on the New Police, and he or she took full advantage of the fact as the contemporary reportage shows. The policeman's conspicuous presence on the streets is a constant reminder of the power of the state and the possibility of its gaze. But equally, that visibility opens the police to permanent inspection by the public. The policeman is subject to the gaze of the inspecting eye of the public, and what this eye sees is articulated in the press.

The media, therefore, has a policing function in its turn. In the case of the New Police of 1829, the press reports on police activities fed upon, and were in turn fed by, public opinion. The new public servants were subjected to the often critical gaze of their masters and mistresses, and, where criticism was justified, the police took steps to correct the fault by disciplining or dismissing the culprit. And as the police became established, and were seen to be effective against crime, it was again the press that informed the public of their successes. The press was instrumental in the eventual acceptance of the police, not merely because it policed police actions, but because the medium also has an ideological function, making normal the police presence. The publicity given to the New Police ensured their regular presence in the public mind. Scarcely a day passed without some mention of the police in the newspapers or periodicals, reports which finally ceased to criticise and instead became factual accounts of the activities of the various police offices around London. Familiarity did not, however, breed contempt. Rather, it ensured that the police became part of normal everyday life, and the police constable a familiar figure on the streets and in the periodical and newspaper press. The media which had initially policed the police were later the location which facilitated and revealed their acceptance. While police activities in terms of real crime and its detection and prevention remained in the domain of the newspapers, the periodicals would become the site of an increasing and generally approving interest in policing as a profession and the methods of the professional policeman. This can be seen in the 'Recollections of a Police Officer' by 'Waters', actually the hack journalist William Russell, which were published serially in *Chambers's Edinburgh Journal* between 1849 and 1853. But prior to this, the police presence was, by 1834, an accepted part of the London scene, both in the physical actuality of the policeman on his beat and in the textual presentation of the police in the media. The textualisation of the police was not only instrumental in enabling their acceptance by the public, but also created the discursive space for the later narratives of detection. And the process of textualisation was not limited to the newspaper reportage. Textual representations of the police as part of the contemporary culture gradually infiltrated narratives other than the purely factual.

3.6 A common sight: A site of commonality

That the police had become a familiar sight on the streets of London is evident in the early writing of Charles Dickens. Before he wrote the novels for which he is best known, before even *The Pickwick Papers*, the serialised novel that brought his name to the attention of the public, Dickens was producing short articles for the periodical press. Duane DeVries has suggested that Dickens's early career as a journalist was inspired in part by the example of his father, John Dickens, who worked as a parliamentary reporter, and by an uncle who was on the staff of *The Times*.[55] By 1832, Dickens was writing for *The Mirror of Parliament*, founded in 1828 by his uncle, John Barrow, recording parliamentary debates. Dickens produced similar work for the *True Sun* in 1832, but remained with his uncle's paper until 1834. In August of that year, he was invited to join the *Morning Chronicle*, a paper that had carried anti-police articles at the time of the inauguration of the New Police. He was already writing short items for the *Monthly Magazine*, and his new employer suggested that Dickens should produce something along the same lines for the *Morning Chronicle*. The first five of these, written under the pseudonym 'Boz', and called 'Street Sketches', appeared in the paper in the last three months of 1834. When in 1835 an offshoot of the morning paper, the thrice-weekly *Evening Chronicle*, appeared, Dickens was asked to contribute further essays in a similar vein, which he did, this time entitled 'Sketches of London'. He continued to produce short accounts of London life and scenes, many of which were published in *Bell's Life in London*, and in 1836 and 1837 the collected stories were published in book form as *Sketches by Boz, Illustrative of Every-Day Life and Every-Day People*, Series 1 and 2.

As the sub-title suggests, these essays were about everyday London life in the 1830s, reporting normal, everyday occurrences in ordinary, recognisable places. In 11 out of the 25 essays in the collected edition that come under the heading of 'Scenes', the police are mentioned in passing: the police constable is an integral feature, as much a part of the scene as the weather or the street furniture. The opening chapter of 'Scenes' is 'The Streets—Morning' (first published in the *Evening Chronicle*, 21 July 1835). The time is early morning, and the third paragraph commences with the words '[a]n occasional policeman may alone be seen at the street corners, listlessly gazing on the deserted prospect before him'.[56] The second chapter is a parallel piece, 'The Streets—Night' (*Bell's Life*, 17 January 1836), and again the policeman is part of the scene: 'After a little prophetic conversation with the policeman at the street-corner; touching a probable change in the weather.'[57] Here, the lad who brings round beer to the door for those who want it, stays his journey back to the public house which employs him to chat to the policeman on his beat. The topic of the conversation and the casual nature of the encounter are not suggestive of the policeman as a repressive threat. Rather it is an encounter of equals, denizens of the London streets. The third chapter also makes a brief reference to the policeman. In 'Shops and Their Tenants' (*Morning Chronicle*, 10 October 1834), the uninterested gentleman walker through the streets is described as wandering 'listlessly past, looking as happy and animated as a policeman on duty'.[58] The novelty of a policeman on his beat has, by 1834, worn off for the policeman as much as for the observer.

In 'Scotland Yard' (*Morning Chronicle*, 4 October 1836), Dickens gives a brief history of the area, and in part uses the police to illustrate the changes to and social elevation of the neighbourhood, noting the disappearance of small businesses and the alterations in the uses of the buildings: 'the Police Commissioners established their office in Whitehall Place'.[59] In July 1829, No. 4 Whitehall Place, which backed onto Great Scotland Yard, had been acquired to house the New Metropolitan Police Office. The rear of the building was altered to accommodate a police station house, and the area, formerly consisting of Great, Middle and Little Scotland Yard, which were the adjoining courts, soon became known as Scotland Yard, the name by which the headquarters of the Metropolitan Police are still known despite their subsequent removal elsewhere in the metropolis. This suggests that by 1836 the police are sufficiently well established and accepted for their headquarters to be used as an illustration of the changing face of London. The fifth chapter of 'Scenes', 'Seven Dials' (*Bell's Life*, under the pseudonym 'Tibbs', 27 September 1835) is a commentary on that area of London which was notorious as a known abode of the criminalised poor. It was also where many of the broadsides were printed, as it was where the publishers 'Jemmy' Catnach and Johnny Pitts had their printing works. Dickens's knowledge of this is evident in the first lines of the chapter: 'Seven

Dials! the region of song and poetry—first effusions, and last dying speeches: hallowed by the names of Catnach and of Pitts.'[60] The reference suggests that not only Dickens, but also his readers would be familiar with the broadsides, many of which had a criminal content, produced by both publishers. Seven Dials is adjacent to St Giles, another notorious 'rookery' of London, and an area which Dickens would later visit in the company of Detective Inspector Field in search of material for his later articles on the Detective Police (1850).

In the 'Scene', the police are less part of the picture than the consequence of the behaviour of the inhabitants of the area: 'The scuffle became general, and terminates, in minor play-bill phraseology, with "arrival of the policeman, [and] interior of the station-house"', and the essay closes with the words 'an assault is the consequence, and a police-officer the result'.[61] The containment of crime by the police is implicit in the structure of the narrative: the closure of the article asserts the authority of the police in reality as the miscreant is removed and order is restored. The police are portrayed not as interfering with or attempting to control the populace of the rookeries, but rather as dealing with the consequences of poverty and drink. They act to prevent further injuries and assaults, essentially working in a preventive and also protective way. Dickens makes the police part of what must have been an everyday event in the rookeries of Seven Dials and St Giles, at once informing his readers about an area that may have been unfamiliar to them, and simultaneously offering critique of the social conditions that cause the disorder which necessitates the presence of the police. This element of criticism is also present in 'Meditation in Monmouth Street' (*Morning Chronicle*, 24 September 1836). Monmouth Street was known for its second-hand clothes shops, and the piece uses the garments on sale to illustrate the fall from respectability to poverty and crime: 'There was a man's whole life written as legibly on those clothes, as if we had his autobiography engrossed on parchment before us.'[62] Second-hand clothes suggest poverty, and Monmouth Street is depicted as standing on the edge of respectability. This is evident in the way that the narrator, and his middle-class readers, who are implicitly present in the 'we' of the narrative, are regarded by the usual occupants of the street, and more importantly, the police in the scene: 'we' are 'an object of astonishment to the good people of Monmouth Street, and of no slight suspicion to the policemen at the opposite street corner'.[63] The policemen notice and suspect those people or events that are out of the ordinary. This is an essential part of the police presence on the streets, to watch and mark potential problems that may have a criminal or disorderly significance. But their appearance in this sketch is once more as an accepted part of London life, and, suspicions notwithstanding, the police are not portrayed as threatening, but as protective in their preventive capacity.

The image of the policeman as 'street furniture' recurs in 'Early Coaches' (*Evening Chronicle*, 19 February 1835). This is an account of the miseries of having to catch the early-morning coach of the title, and uses the weather to accentuate the unpleasantness of early rising. In the chill, dark morning, with wind and sleet, the policemen on their beats look, in their dark uniforms, 'as if they had been sprinkled with powdered glass' as the sleet settles on their coats.[64] They are mentioned in the same paragraph as the 'milk-woman' and early-rising apprentices on their way to work as part of the usual early-morning occupants of the London streets. 'The Last Cab-Driver, and the First Omnibus Cad' (*Carlton Chronicle*, 11 and 17 September 1836) makes reference to the police as agents of the law. The 'last cab-driver', accused of over-charging by his fare, balances his meagre takings from cab-driving against the prospect of 'board, lodgin', and washin' [. . .] out of the county', that is, in prison, and assaults the indignant passenger. The driver then calls 'the police to take himself into custody'.[65] There is no evidence of antagonism towards, or fear of, the police. In a sense, the cab-driver is availing himself of their services, albeit, in Dickens's account, in a somewhat tongue-in-cheek fashion. The 'first omnibus cad' is an ex-waterman, who delights in misdirecting potential passengers for the omnibus. As a result of complaints laid against him by members of the public, he receives 'a summons to a Police office [which] was, on more than one occasion, followed by a committal to prison'.[66] The police are acting in direct response to a public request for protection against the disorder created by the 'cad'. While the disorder suffered by misdirected passengers is not great, and the assault on the cab-driver's fare is not serious, the principle of the police as servants of the public is implicit in this 'Scene'.

There is an element of regret for the necessity of a police presence in the city in 'The First of May' (*Library of Fiction*, 1:3, June 1836). In this article Dickens mourns the passing of May Day celebrations, where in the past large numbers of people had gathered to greet the summer in traditional fashion. By Dickens's time, such large public gatherings and the concomitant possibilities for unlicensed and riotous behaviour were no longer acceptable. In its nostalgia for past times, the narrative notes that 'romance can make no head against the riot act; and pastoral simplicity is not understood by the police'.[67] Simple country pleasures cannot survive the urban sprawl of London, with its vast population: unlicensed public gatherings now represent a threat to order and necessitate a police presence. The constabulary is here represented as part of the cityscape, oblivious to the 'pastoral simplicity' of May Day and conscious only of the possibility of riot. Dickens returns to social critique in 'Gin Shops' (*Evening Chronicle*, 7 February 1835). This is a direct attack on the poverty and deprivation in the metropolis which literally drive people to drink. The police are the public servants who restore order after the gin that alleviates the misery of the poor subsequently incites them to violence: 'the landlord hits everybody, and everybody hits the landlord; the barmaids scream; the police come in'.[68] The police function is the restoration of order and the protection of the innocent, not the punishment of the social inadequate. The sketch makes clear its social agenda in the closing paragraph:

> Gin-drinking is a great vice in England, but wretchedness and dirt are a greater; and until you improve the homes of the poor, or persuade a half-famished wretch not to seek relief in the temporary oblivion of his own misery [...] gin-shops will increase in number and splendour. If Temperance Societies would suggest an antidote against hunger, filth, and foul air [...] gin-palaces would be numbered amongst things that were.[69]

Crime is inextricably linked with social problems, and in these early pieces by Dickens there is already evidence of what Philip Collins refers to as Dickens's 'passion for dramatising and commenting upon the outstanding topical issues of his day'.[70]

Social deprivation and crime, or the potential for crime, is part and parcel of the London street 'Scenes' as much as the presence of the police. And Dickens's well-known and documented fascination with crime and criminals is becoming apparent in the 'Sketches' he produced between 1834 and 1836. Some of the material he would use later in his novels, most obviously 'A Visit to Newgate' (*Sketches by Boz*, First Series, 1836) which, substantially rewritten, appears as 'Fagin's Last Night Alive' in *Oliver Twist*.[71] 'A Visit to Newgate' makes no mention of the police, but the chapter which immediately precedes it, 'Criminal Courts' (first published as 'The Old Bailey' in the *Morning Chronicle*, 23 October 1835), offers a representation of the police from a juvenile offender's perspective. A young pickpocket, whose 'offence is about as clearly proved as an offence can be', defends himself with the accusation that 'all the witnesses have committed perjury [...] the police force generally have entered into a conspiracy "again" him'.[72] While this section of the 'Scene' is relatively light-hearted, it is nevertheless an indication of the feelings of the criminal for the police. Far from regarding them as public servants or protectors, the juvenile delinquent sees the police as an enemy who will stop at nothing to prevent the criminal from following his trade.

This viewpoint could, in all probability, be extended to many of those at the bottom of the social scale, for as well as preventing crime, the police also policed street activities which lay on the boundaries of respectability and honesty: street-hawkers, public houses, prostitutes, and much of the social interaction that of necessity took place in the streets in areas where crowded living conditions made home entertainment impossible. The question of to what extent the police played a role in enforcing moral and social mores as well as carrying out their crime prevention duties has been addressed by Stephen Inwood, who concludes that '[t]heir aim in general was to establish minimum standards of public order, but not to provoke social conflict [...] the Metropolitan Police developed a practical compromise between middle-class ideals and working-class realities'.[73] Dickens's *Sketches* suggest that by 1834 this practical compromise had been reached. Although many of the 'Scenes' of London life depict the lower orders for the entertainment of the middle classes, there is no evidence of antagonism towards the police except from the young criminal portrayed in 'Criminal Courts'. The reference to the police is of small moment in the context of the chapter, but the implication is that they are honest in their pursuit of criminals, and effective in their fight against crime.

Such an implication, located in the popular literature of the day, plays its part in the process of making the police acceptable. Ideology works through culture: the media are part of culture, and Dickens's *Sketches*, as much as the constant newspaper reports on police activities, worked to normalise and make unthreatening the police presence on the London streets. In the 'Scenes' it becomes apparent that, just five years after the inauguration of the New Police, they are part of London life. Dickens made occasional references to the police in other 'Sketches', but it is their presence in the depictions of the London streets that emphasises the normality of the policeman on the beat. The 'Scenes' represent the police as part of the contemporary street culture, not as a threat, but as a comfortable and comforting presence, the servants and protectors of the respectable and the innocent, and the restorers of order. And the realistic, carefully observed detail with which Dickens constructed the backdrops to his *Sketches* suggests that his depiction of the police was accurate. It is important to remember that Dickens was writing for a predominantly middle-class, literate audience, that is, those who would benefit most from a police presence. The socially deprived and potentially criminal poor who were more often the object of police surveillance and actions must have found the police somewhat less acceptable. The policeman, then, had become part of normal, everyday life, even if his presence and his profession were not yet universally popular. Their actual role as employees and agents of the state and the law had been successfully integrated into a conception of them as servants of the public, as much a part of the London scene as milk-women and apprentices, cab-drivers, and drunkards. The question remains as to how this was achieved. It was certainly not through repression, but rather by constructing a positive public image of the police through ideology. And while this image was to some extent conveyed by and promulgated in the press, it was based on a reality constructed by disciplinary means. The servants of the public whose preventive function itself worked by discipline and surveillance were themselves subjected to strict disciplines which created the orderly body of men that would equally, in preventing crime, keep the body of society orderly.

The process was not without its problems. Dismissals for drunkenness and other offences were high in the early years of the New Police. Complaints were made against police officials, in the press and in person to the Commissioners, who dealt with each complaint individually, as a scrapbook held at the Metropolitan Police Museum shows. All complaints received a written response that explained the steps taken to rectify the problem which had led to the complaint and the treatment meted out to the constable involved. The openness to public scrutiny and willingness to account for its behaviour that the New Police displayed were major factors in their eventual acceptance by the public. The discipline which ensured the regular and regulated appearance of the police on the streets also enabled their insertion into ideology: they became a part of the London culture, as demonstrated in Dickens's *Sketches*. Public acceptance of the police was assisted by their proven efficacy in the prevention of crime and the diminution of disorder in the Metropolis. Radzinowicz offers statistics which suggest that the increase of recorded cases of assaults and larceny demonstrated the improved arrest rate, while the decrease in more serious offences such as burglary or larceny within a dwelling indicated the deterrent effect of the police presence.[74] The advent of the New Police in a district invariably led to an increase in arrests for petty offences and misdemeanours, and the streets would be cleared of loiterers, street traders, prostitutes, and vagrants. The traffic was better controlled under police supervision; dangerous and drunk driving are not offences restricted to the twenty-first century, but problems that were familiar, if horse-driven, to the nineteenth-century Londoner. While the prevention of crime was a laudable aim, and the police presence must have dissuaded some potential criminals, crime in London did not cease with the inauguration of the New Metropolitan Police. And when a crime had been committed, the police had no official body to deal with the consequences. In the *General Instruction Book*, emphasising the necessity for the prevention of crime, the Commissioners had stated that '[t]he security of person and property, the preservation of public tranquillity, and all the other objects of a Police establishment, will thus be better effected than by the detection and punishment of the offender, after he has succeeded in committing the crime'.[75] But prevention, it seemed, was not enough. A crime that had been successfully committed required a specialist to seek out the offender: a detecting agent.

In practice, the average constable on the beat had little opportunity or enthusiasm for detective work, but, of necessity, some detection was carried out in the first years of the force. In the aftermath of serious crimes, what might loosely be termed 'detective work' was done, most commonly by uniformed police sergeants or inspectors. Belton Cobb has made a good, if hypothetical, argument for Richard Mayne being aware of the necessity for, and subsequently being responsible for the creation of, a detective police.[76] Cobb's text is not an academic study, and lacks sufficient references or a bibliography that would provide sources with which to substantiate all his claims, but the cases he describes are a matter of public record, reported variously in the newspapers and broadsides of the time. Detective work was certainly carried out by the police involved in these cases, but it was work done in uniform and in the eye of the public. What that public feared was something which is commonplace in the twenty-first century, that is, the plain-clothes detective. Such an officer, unidentifiable as a member of the police, conformed to the concept of spy that was anathema to the English. That plain-clothes policing was effective in the fight against crime was evident in the work of the Bow Street Runners, who continued to operate in parallel, if not in accord, with the New Police. And until 1839, when the institution of the Runners was terminated, to some extent this continued. Unfortunately, the two systems worked in isolation, without the exchange of information that would have facilitated both crime prevention and its detection.

From 1829 to 1839 the New Police concentrated on crime prevention, leaving detection largely to their 'rivals', the Bow Street Runners, and this state of affairs may have carried on indefinitely, with the police undertaking a minimal amount of detective work and having no specialists in the field. But in 1839, after another select committee had conducted an investigation into the relationship between the parallel police systems, it was decided to disband the Bow Street Runners. This left the metropolis without any official detecting force; although the Runners were offered the opportunity to join the New Police, their detecting abilities would not be utilised fully in what was still a preventive police. As Patrick Pringle notes in his Introduction to Henry Goddard's *Memoirs of a Bow Street Runner*, the demise of the Bow Street Runners on Saturday 24 August 1839 attracted no public attention: 'I have not seen this date recorded in any history of the police, and the event passed unnoticed at the time. The *Annual Register* ignored it completely; so did the daily Press.'[77] And the lack of an official detective agency also went unnoticed until 1842. A series of cases in this year highlighted the inefficiency and incompetence of the police when it came to detective work. The first was that of the murderer Daniel Good, who in spite of being practically in police hands, made good his escape and eluded capture for nine days after the discovery of the dismembered body of his common-law wife Jane Good. His eventual arrest was at the hands of the Railway Police, and the incompetence of the Metropolitan Police in the case attracted much attention from the press. A second display of incompetence was the case of Thomas Cooper, a known violent criminal who killed a policeman involved in his pursuit. And finally, the police, even with forewarning, failed to prevent the attempted assassination of Queen Victoria by one John Francis. The attempt was unsuccessful, but could have been prevented had the police been more efficient in their actions.

The press was always quick to criticise the police, and their criticism here, as it had in the early days of the police, had an effect on their subsequent actions. As R. F. Stewart observes:

> When papers such as the *Weekly Dispatch*, a regular police critic, and *The Times*, a staunch defender, joined in condemnation of this run of ineptitude and in demands for a detective department, it is not surprising that a move was made in this direction and unopposed when it materialised.[78]

On 20 June 1842, a scant three weeks after the assassination attempt on the Queen, the then Home Secretary, Sir James Graham, authorised the appointment of two inspectors and six sergeants for detective work. There was finally, and with public approval, an official detective force within the police. To alleviate any remaining fears of a spy police, the new detective force was tiny in relation to the size of the Metropolitan

Police as a whole; its members, based at Scotland Yard, were directly answerable to the Commissioners, and circumscribed in their actions, especially the association with the criminal class that their work made necessary. And while they were not in uniform, they carried at all times a warrant card that proved their identity and status for the literate, and a brass tipstaff that performed the same function for those who could not read. The tipstaff had historically been associated with the office of watchmen, parish constables, and the Bow Street Runners, and thus provided a readily recognised badge of office for the new detectives. These men were recruited from the existing preventive force: Inspector Nicholas Pearce became Senior Detective Inspector, Inspector John Haynes was his junior officer, and the six sergeants were Thornton, Gerrett, Shaw, Braddick, Goff, and Whicher. They were later joined by Shackell and Field. These sergeants would latterly become the heroes of Charles Dickens's Detective Police anecdotes, but in the early days of the detective force, they kept a low profile and avoided public attention. The detective department had come into existence, but it would take some years before its officers were fully accepted by the public they served.

As part of the institution of the Metropolitan Police, the newly formed detective department was subject to the same discipline and subscribed to the same ethos of public service as their preventive fellow officers, but the nature of detective work required that they be less visible, and accountable to their superior officers rather than to the public. The overt surveillance of the preventive police was predicated on their visibility, which in turn rendered them open to the inspecting gaze of the public. A detective police requires surveillance to be covert in order to fulfil the detective function, and a detective sergeant working in plain clothes is invisible to the public gaze. Serious crimes had allowed the inception of the detective police, and it was in the crime reports of the newspapers that an account of their work was given. Serious crimes and major trials in which the police detectives appeared as witnesses were covered by the press, and most newspapers, from *The Times* down to small local papers, carried brief details of more commonplace crime and the police activities consequent upon such crime. This had a twofold effect. First, the reports showed that the detectives were concerned mainly with the activities of the criminal underworld, alleviating fears of an erosion of the civil liberties of the respectable middle classes, and secondly, the inspectorial aspect of newspaper reportage not only made the detectives accountable at second hand but also had a normalising function. Frequent reports in the newspapers and broadsides that related the details of crimes and the steps taken by the police to apprehend criminals brought the otherwise invisible detective to the attention of the public and made the detective a familiar figure. Simultaneously, the textualisation of the detective inherent in these reports opened a discursive space for the detective figure that had, like the detecting agent itself, been lacking.

The process of familiarisation and normalisation was slow. In the 1840s there was still resistance to the detective force, articulated in the same papers that reported on their activities. And for most of this period, detectives remained in the factual discursive space of the newspapers. But by 1849, the police, including the detective component, were sufficiently assimilated into the metropolitan culture to appear in fictional form. The emergent status of policing as a profession made the policeman, and implicitly the detective, suitable material for the anecdotes of professional men that proliferated in the periodicals of the 1830s and 1840s. In July 1849, the first of William Russell's 'Recollections of a Police Officer' appeared in *Chambers's Edinburgh Journal*.

3.7 The profession of policing

In 1849 a fictional account of crime and detection was to achieve the popularity that in 1827 had eluded *Richmond: Scenes in the Life of a Bow Street Runner*. Where *Richmond*, as I have argued, was transitional, juvenile, and delinquent in form, content and protagonist, lacking both internal discipline and disciplinary effect, 'Recollections of a Police Officer' benefited from the intervening years between the two narratives. By the time that the pseudonymous 'Waters' penned his anecdotes, the textualisation of the Metropolitan Police and its small detective contingent had created the discursive space denied to the earlier text. The established and accepted institution of the police is the culmination of the process that had rendered *Richmond* a transitional text in a historical and social sense, and provides a disciplined and disciplinary framework for the work of the detective protagonist. The delinquency of Richmond's 'Early Life', with its connotations of a criminality which can subsequently be employed in the service of the law, is absent from the 'Recollections'. The hero of the 'Recollections' is, in contrast, a respectable man of good birth who in his youth is the victim, not the perpetrator, of crime, and it is as a result of this that he enters the police. I do not suggest that Waters acts from vengeful or vigilante motives. He becomes a policeman because, as he states in his first case, 'adverse circumstances [...] compelled me to enter the ranks of the Metropolitan Police, as the sole means left me of procuring food and raiment'.[79] Waters is from the first an agent of the law, whose knowledge of, and association with, crime and criminality comes from his roles as victim and later as policeman. In contrast to the delinquency of form seen in *Richmond*, with its *mélange* of genres and its nascent—but still juvenile—case structure, the 'Recollections' are located in, and conform to, an established sub-genre of professional anecdotes, and adhere rigidly to a formula of retrospective, coherent and complete individual case-histories. The discipline of form and content in the 'Recollections' enables their function as part of disciplinary power. Crime is contained and the criminal punished: order is reinstated. And the reader internalises the values and ideology implicit in the narratives. The fictional representation of the police polices its audience.

The institutional, textual, discursive, and generic frameworks in place when the 'Recollections' first appeared enabled the creation of a policeman who could also be a hero in spite of the methodologies he employs in his detective work. The fictional account exploits existing textual representations of the real police institution, but the protagonist of the narratives is constructed as a figure with which the intended readership could identify and whom they could admire. This is in contrast to the eponymous protagonist of *Richmond*, whose unstable social status, potentially corrupt employment, and dubious actions may have contributed to the unpopularity of his text. The comparison of *Richmond* and the 'Recollections' reveals not only the gaps between the texts, but also the similarities. Both Ian Ousby and Martin Kayman note these similarities, Kayman suggesting that Waters is closest to Tom Richmond in his independence of action and detective methods.[80] Ousby goes further, arguing that Waters is a continuation of and development from Richmond, and speculating that 'Waters' first adventure [. . .] may even be directly indebted to Gaspey's novel, which was republished in 1845' (Ousby attributes *Richmond* to Thomas Gaspey).[81] While broadly in agreement with both critics, I want to consider why what had been unacceptable and unpopular in 1827 is, by 1849, both accepted and popular. An analysis of the textual location of the 'Recollections' and of their structure and contents offers an answer to this question.

As with much of the material that appeared in the periodicals of the nineteenth century, the series of anecdotes that comprised the 'Recollections of a Police Officer' were published anonymously. When the collected edition was issued in 1856, under the title *Recollections of a Detective Police Officer* (my emphasis), the author was given as 'Waters', the subject and narrator of the pseudoautobiographical account.[82] 'Waters' was the pseudonym of William Russell, a hack journalist who, as R. F. Stewart suggests, 'seems to have been the first [. . .] [and] to have written more than anyone else' on, among other subjects, detection in fictional form.[83] Russell's initial foray into the topic was on 28 July 1849, when the introductory 'Recollection' appeared in *Chambers's Edinburgh Journal*, and he continued to produce further 'Recollections' until 3 September 1853, when the twelfth and, in periodical format, final story appeared.

Thematically, the 'Recollections' fall within the sub-genre of anecdotes of professional men which proliferated in the periodicals of the 1830s, 1840s, and early 1850s. This suggests that by the time Russell was writing, policing had come to be regarded as a profession, and, simultaneously, demonstrates the general acceptance of, and interest in, the activities of the police. The textualisation of the police had, until this point, largely been confined to the factual reports of the newspapers and articles and essays in the periodical press. The location of the fictional 'Recollections' in the popular and populist *Chambers's Edinburgh Journal* is evidence for the successful insertion of the police into the general contemporary culture. Founded in 1832 in Edinburgh by the Chambers brothers, and priced at three-halfpence, the weekly publication was aimed at a wide audience in terms of class. According to Louis James, *Chambers's* declared intention was 'to supply "a meal of healthful, useful, and agreeable mental instruction" for readers of every age and profession, and in particular for the working-class man or woman who was beginning to discover literary culture'.[84] While this may have been true in the early years of the journal, James goes on to note that 'the nature of the magazine became increasingly middle class'.[85] And as I have suggested, it is this sector of society that stood to benefit most from a police force and the class with which the police first found favour.

Publication of the 'Recollections' by Waters in *Chambers's Edinburgh Journal* was, in 1849, seven years after the establishment of the official police detective department. This poses the question of why Waters was constructed as a policeman rather than a detective. In creating Waters, Russell was buying into an established sub-genre of literature that claimed authenticity in its appearance as memoirs taken from the diaries or notes of the professionals who were their subjects. In the first half of 1849 the 'Experiences of a Barrister', which was another example of the retrospective professional anecdotes of the time, was running in *Chambers's*, and it is difficult to believe that Russell was unaware of its format when creating his own contribution to the genre. Locating his narratives in the decades preceding that of publication distanced Russell's police protagonist from the real detectives, who were known to the public from their appearances in the press. Equally, the use of a retrospective format implicitly based on the diaries or case-histories of the protagonist in the professional anecdotes required that the narrative be set in a past recent enough to be recognisable but distanced from the present of its publication. Russell makes clear the temporal location of the narratives by including dates in four of the twelve stories, dates which construct a chronological framework to the anecdotes, as do their contents. The first has a brief account of the protagonist's entry into the police, while the final tale speaks of his semi-retirement from the force. Waters moves to London in 1831, as his penultimate case, 'The Monomaniac' (*Chambers's* n.s., 17:434 [24 April 1852], pp. 259–263), relates, 11 years before the formation of the detective police, which means that he must necessarily be depicted as a police constable in the newly formed Metropolitan Police, but he functions in a detective mode.

This conflation of policing with detection in the early years of the police leads to anachronisms within the text. Waters frequently refers to his 'brother-detectives' at a time prior to their actual existence, and enlists the help of the Chief of Police in Birmingham when in reality Birmingham only instituted a police force modelled on the metropolitan example in 1839. Further, Waters consistently works in plain clothes where the real police officer of the 1830s was uniformed except in special circumstances and with express permission. This permission is specified in Waters's first case, when the commissioner instructs him to call on Lady Everton 'in plain clothes of course', but the instruction is not reiterated in subsequent cases. While plain-clothes policemen did operate in the New Police, it was without drawing the fact to the attention of the public, and in the 'Recollections' Waters frequently refers to the press reports of his adventures. By 1849, the concept of a non-uniformed detective force was commonplace and accepted, at least in London, and presumably the readers of the 'Recollections' either were unaware of the anachronisms in the narratives or chose to ignore them. That the 'Recollections', in spite of their inaccuracies, were popular with their readers is evident in their continued appearance in *Chambers's* over the four years from 1849 to 1853 and their reissue in collected form in 1856. This is largely because the depiction of Waters in both lifestyle and attitudes offered his middle-class readership a reflection of their own idealised behaviour and values. Waters is a professional man, but the adventures that comprise his work are contained and framed by his domestic life, and the necessary association with criminals implicit in his adventures is authorised and regulated by his superior police officers. The 'life, partly regular, partly adventurous' that the semi-delinquent hero yearned for in *Richmond* is fully realised in the 'Recollections' in a form acceptable to the middle-class Victorian reader. The discursive space for a detective that was lacking in *Richmond* is fully established in the media by 1849, when the textualisation of policing and detection has ensured their place in the contemporary, and in the case of Waters, popular culture.

In Waters, Russell created a character with which the middle-class reader and his family could identify themselves. This is apparent in the tone and register of the writing, which neither attempts to reproduce working-class dialogue or thieves' 'cant', nor does it aspire to the convoluted conversational style of the upper classes commonly depicted in fiction. Narrative and character speak to the audience in their own discourse. As a professional man, Waters goes about the daily business which forms the basis for his 'Recollections', but he often mentions his wife and family and offers details of his domestic arrangements that would have resonated with his audience. Waters weaves aspects of his past life into the texture of his narratives. The reader gradually learns that Waters's entrance into the police is the result of the loss of his money and property at the hands of professional gamblers and cheats. His origins lie in Yorkshire, and his education has been that appropriate to a gentleman. This is apparent in his reaction to Lady Everton's attitude towards him in his first case: 'I was silly enough to feel somewhat nettled at the noble lady's haughtiness of manner [...] but fortunately the remembrance of my actual position, spite of my gentleman's attire, flashed vividly upon my mind.'[86] The 'best part of my wardrobe [which] had been fortunately saved by Emily from the wreck of my fortunes' is not only evidence for his gentlemanly background, but in conjunction with his original social status it acts as a 'disguise' that renders him the perfect choice for cases which require him to move in elevated social circles.[87] His ability to speak French, a skill more often found in the upper and upper-middle classes, is cited as the reason for his superiors selecting him to work on a case in which the apparent victims of the crime are French: 'You know French too, which is fortunate; for the gentleman who has been plundered understands little or no English' ('Legal Metamorphoses', *Chambers's* n.s., 14:352 [28 September 1850], pp. 195–199).[88]

Reduced to modest circumstances, Waters makes no complaint, but readjusts to his new position in society, regretting only that his loss of fortune has reduced the social standing of his wife. 'A young and gentle wife [...] cast down from opulence to sordid penury' is a strong motive for Waters to solve his first case, enabling him to revenge himself under the auspices of the law against the very man who had caused his ruin.[89] The small personal and domestic touches woven into the narratives construct Waters as a family man with responsibilities, fallen on hard times but using his skills to follow a profession in the hopes of bettering himself, a pattern and a goal shared by a middle-class Victorian audience for whom social ambition was inextricably linked to social progression. Domesticity is an integral part of the 'Recollections'. And this domestic setting, familiar to, and respected by, the contemporary reader, has a secondary, disciplinary function. It offers a desirable, orderly, and normative familial model to its audience, an ideological construct which is contrasted against the disorder and deviance of the criminality represented in the narratives.

Central to Waters's domestic life is his wife, Emily, whose social status has been reduced concomitantly with Waters's loss of fortune. But her moral character is above reproach: she is the perfect wife and mother. Emily on occasion advises or even assists Waters in his work. In 'Mary Kingsford' (*Chambers's* n.s., 15:383 [3 May 1851], pp. 274–279), it is Emily's identification of the stolen diamond brooch as a fake which facilitates Waters's eventual resolution of the case. Her ability to discern between fake and real jewellery suggests a familiarity with gemstones that hints at her elevated social origins.[90] Her physical and moral support for Waters in cases which involve other women is apparent in 'The Widow' (*Chambers's* n.s., 13:333 [18 May 1850], pp. 313–318) and 'The Monomaniac'. But, in true Victorian patriarchal and protective mode, Waters keeps the more dangerous aspects of his work hidden from his wife. An attempt on his life in 'The Revenge' (*Chambers's* n.s., 14:358 [9 November 1850], pp. 294–298) renders him 'anxious to conceal the peril [. . .] from my wife; and it was not until I had left the police force that she was informed of it'.[91] The chivalry with which Waters treats the majority of the women in the 'Recollections' is an important factor in his construction as a hero: equally, that chivalry serves to conceal the construction of women as property which, like any other valuable or commodity, must be protected.

The 'Recollections' offer the reader idealised and ideologically correct feminine images, and women feature most frequently in appropriate and proper female roles such as mother, sister, wife, or potential wife. Their presence and frequent involvement in the criminal case-histories illustrates the threat to the stability of the family posed by crime, and Waters works to restore order and reinstate the familial and social *status quo*. The centrality of the patriarchal family in Victorian middle-class society is affirmed in the 'Recollections', of which four are concerned with the perils that confront the unprotected single woman. In 'The Widow', 'The Twins' (*Chambers's* n.s., 13:338 [22 June 1850], pp. 387–390), and 'The Monomaniac', recently widowed women are threatened by men. The crime in the first two cases is concerned with inheritance, and

Waters's intervention ensures that the money and property at risk are safely restored to their rightful owners, that is, the sons of the widowed women. Although Waters appears to be responding to chivalric impulse in these cases concerned with women, the rescue and protection of the women from the men who seek to defraud them are in fact secondary to the cause of rightful restitution of property to the male line.

'The Monomaniac' features a madman who imagines the recently widowed Mrs Irwin, lodging in the same house, to be his long-dead love returned, and as Waters states, the 'narrative relates more to medical than to criminal history'.[92] Nonetheless, he is motivated by the desire to protect a young and defenceless woman and her child, temporarily substituting his masculine protection for that of her dead husband. 'Mary Kingsford' is the most overt declaration of the necessity for women to be under the protection of men. Young, innocent, fatherless Mary comes to London to seek her fortune, and falls victim to professional thieves who use her in their crime as an unknowing repository for a stolen diamond brooch. It is only the intervention of Waters that saves Mary, from both her attempted suicide and her certain conviction for theft. He finds the real criminals, exculpates Mary, returns her to her family and subsequently delivers her into the safe hands of a husband. At Mary's wedding, his role is made clear: he officiates 'as bride's father'.[93] The message is plain: single women require men to order and regulate their lives and protect them from crime. The audience of *Chambers's* included women, and the portrayal of femininity in the 'Recollections' served to instruct female readers in their proper roles. Young women and marriage are also portrayed as having a recuperative or reformative function: love and/or marriage have a normative effect on those masculine characters somehow touched by crime. In 'The Pursuit' (*Chambers's* n.s., 14:341 [13 July 1850], pp. 23–26), incidentally the only case in the 'Recollections' where Waters fails as a detective, the criminal's wife deceives Waters to facilitate her husband's escape, but once safely in America, she ensures that the erstwhile criminal reforms.

There are female criminals in the 'Recollections', but these women are shown to have been driven into criminality, and are further shown to be open to reform with, of course, the aid of Waters. 'The Revenge' relates the story of the attempted murder of Waters by a criminal whose apprehension had been at Waters's hands. There is a second narrative woven into the main story, which is the tale of a Frenchwoman driven mad by the loss of her child and thrown into the haunts of criminals by her post-bedlam destitution. Waters uses Mme Jaubert as an informant in the case he is conducting, and when she turns double agent and delivers him into the hands of a potential murderer, he tells her he knows the whereabouts of her lost child. She helps him to escape, but when Waters reveals his deception and confesses that he has no knowledge of the child's fate, she sinks once more into insanity. On her recovery, Waters, perhaps partly through guilt, contributes financially to a fund set up to enable her return to respectability. Her brush with crime is the result of special and unique circumstances rather than greed or innate criminality. This is also true of the woman in Waters's tenth case, 'Flint Jackson' (*Chambers's* n.s., 16:411 [15 November 1851], pp. 306–311). Sarah Purday, imprisoned for a proven theft, is persuaded by Waters to offer him assistance in proving the innocence of a woman charged with attempted murder. He solves the case and finds the real perpetrator, and rewards Sarah by obtaining a pardon for her. An investigation into her past reveals 'painful circumstances in her history' which presumably led her into crime, and, pardoned, she starts a new and respectable life in Canada.[94] These women who are either criminal or associated with crime are recuperated into society, but sent outside England, to France, America, and Canada. As single women, they are a potential threat to a patriarchal society, a threat that is displaced onto foreign soil.

The ideology of the narratives locates Waters not only as a policeman concerned with crime, but also as a figure who polices moral and social values. The peritext surrounding the crimes in the 'Recollections' reinforces and propagates the contemporary social mores. The narratives function both to discipline readers against committing crime, as the monitory effect of crime detected and punished is internalised by the reader, and further, to encourage the internalisation of the ideology and values in the text to produce a docile subject. The resemblance of the 'Recollections' to reality is an important part of this process. The fiction purports to be fact, and employs a number of techniques to achieve this aim. It advertises itself as the memoirs of a policeman, taken from his case-notes, as the references made to these notes show: 'have you your memorandum book ready?' and 'opening the note-book from which I am now transcribing'.[95] There is a temporal progression in the narratives, marked by dates given in the text and by Waters's own career path from first joining the police to the verge of retirement. Domestic settings and arrangements, food, and clothing, all serve to create an air of authenticity. The press is recruited into the process, to provide a backdrop to Waters's actions, to report his cases, and occasionally as an aid to his work when he inserts notices into the daily papers to obtain information or inveigle suspects into meeting him, a method frequently employed by Doyle's later detective, Sherlock Holmes. In a pre-electronic culture, the press was not only the major source of information on current events, but acted as a medium for the transmission of messages between individuals. The newspapers mentioned are actual contemporary publications: *The Times*, the *Police Gazette* (an in-house police journal), the *Morning Post*, the *Herald*, and the *Chronicle*, titles known to the readers of *Chambers's*. A footnote to the first 'Recollection', present in both the periodical and the collected edition, implies authenticity in its declaration that '[t]he names mentioned in these narratives are, for obvious reasons, fictitious'.[96] The representation of reality thus constructed is more effective in the 'Recollections' than it had been in *Richmond*, where such details were sparse. But both texts utilise geographical and topographical information to authorise and authenticate their narratives.

Waters's work often starts or is based in the metropolis, but his cases take him to less familiar locations such as Liverpool, Birmingham, or Plymouth. The inclusion of these other cities perhaps reflects the country-wide circulation of *Chambers's*, and allowed readers outside London to feel more involved with Waters's narratives. It is not only cities which feature in the 'Recollections'. Small towns and villages are not without crime, and Waters ventures into the countryside when, as in 'Flint Jackson', he is ordered to Farnham 'to investigate a case of burglary [...] which had completely nonplussed the unpractised Dogberrys of the place'.[97] Crimes which originate in London sometimes involve travel outside the city, and Waters has a case which takes him to the New Forest and which involves a criminal named Jones. In *Richmond*, Tom's pursuit of the arch-criminal Jones takes him to the New Forest, a point of similarity between the texts which supports the proposition that Russell knew the *Richmond* text. The use of real locations as a backdrop to Waters's cases lends the narratives an element of authenticity enhanced by the fact that the real detective police, whose assistance was frequently sought by authorities outside London, also travelled all over the country. A further element of authenticity, which emphasises the chronological development of the 'Recollections', is given by the various modes of transport adopted by Waters. In the early stories he travels by coach, as 'the railway was just begun, I remember'.[98] This is in 'XYZ' (*Chambers's* n.s., 12:307 [17 November 1849], pp. 308–312), which is internally dated 1832. By 1836, the date allocated to 'Mary Kingsford', Waters meets Mary on a train travelling back from Liverpool. History as well as geography is incorporated into the fiction to support its status as fact.

Waters, then, is in terms of domesticity a recognisable figure who carries out his work in familiar and real locations, a creation that re-presented the Victorian middle-class reader of *Chambers's* to themselves. But detective work was not a profession with which such readers were overly familiar, nor was it something that they might encounter very often in normal daily life. Sensational crime was reported in the newspapers and broadsides, and accounts of ordinary crime appeared in the police reports of journals such as *Cleaves Weekly Police Gazette*. The gory murders and rapes that the broadsides and penny magazines delighted in and the heroisation of the criminal implicit in the so-called Newgate Novels of the 1830s and 1840s made much nineteenth-century criminography implicitly inappropriate for middle-class family consumption. That the police deal with criminals is self-evident; what Russell had to do was construct Waters in such a way that the criminality with which he must necessarily come into contact did not in any way taint his respectability. Equally, the crimes he solves, while arousing and maintaining the interest of the reader, must avoid sensationalism but eschew the tedium of the commonplace. For the middle class audience, the crimes must also be middle class, both in their felonious nature and in their location between the ordinary and the sensational. Russell's awareness of this is evident: in the Preface to the collected edition he, in the guise of Waters, assures the reader that 'nothing will be found in these brief memoranda of a varied experience to in the slightest degree aliment a "Jack Sheppard" vocation, nor one line that can raise a blush on the most sensitive cheek'.[99] The detective is firmly located as the hero of his narratives, and the crimes and criminals he investigates are neither violent nor overtly sexual in nature. In the only case where murder occurs, the victim is a servant-woman, killed in the course of a robbery in 'Guilty or Not Guilty' (*Chambers's* n.s., 12:55 [25 August 1849], pp. 115–120), and her death is glossed over, being more a function of the plot than the focus of the investigation.

Crime in the 'Recollections' is concerned wholly with the threat to that which is closest to the middle-class heart: property and money. Acceptance of the police came first from the propertied middle class, who stood to benefit most from a preventive police whose aim was the protection of property through the prevention of crime. Waters's role is to ensure the restoration of property when the first line of defence has failed. Implicitly he functions also to restore order. His actions ensure the capture of the criminal and his or her removal from society, and indirectly serve to maintain the social *status quo*. In contrast to Dickens's *Sketches*, crime is not an adjunct to social deprivation in the 'Recollections'. The majority of Russell's criminals conform to the contemporary middle-class conception of a criminal class motivated by idleness to prey on the property obtained by the hard work of others. The victims of crime in the 'Recollections' are of the same class as the intended audience: businessmen, men of property, and defenceless respectable women. Seven of Waters's twelve cases feature criminals who might loosely be termed professionals. These include the gang of 'blacklegs, swindlers, and forgers' whose gambling activities ruined Waters and who threaten to repeat their performance with young Merton in 'One Night in a Gaming-House' (the first 'Recollection', *Chambers's* n.s., 12:291 [28 July 1849], pp. 55–59); the 'detachment of the swell-mob' who commit murder in the course of a robbery and then try to frame an innocent man for the crime in 'Guilty or Not Guilty'; the young 'swells' who involve Mary Kingsford in theft; and the receiver of stolen goods, Flint Jackson, in the story of that name.[100] But if the 'Recollections' were simply straightforward accounts of criminality, the audience would quickly have lost interest. Russell attracts and retains the reader's attention by creating complications in the narratives.

These complications function through plot mechanisms, as in 'Guilty or Not Guilty', where Waters's detective work is made more complex by the criminals cleverly laying a trail of evidence that points to their victim's nephew as the guilty man. In a double twist, one of their number poses as a detective, suggesting that the criminals have a working knowledge of police detective methods and practices. In 'Flint Jackson', one crime is linked to a second, the connection being the receiver of stolen goods, Flint Jackson. Waters's attempts to trace the stolen property lead him to a case of attempted murder that is part of Jackson's plans to defraud his lodgers of a recent inheritance. Waters's final case in the periodical series is 'The Partner' (*Chambers's* n.s., 20:505 [3 September 1853], pp. 149–153). Undertaken when Waters is on the verge of retirement, this case concerns a young man wrongly accused of theft from his employer. In a convoluted plot, the crime is revealed to be blackmail, not theft, as Mr Hutton seeks to force his business partner, the young man's father, to cancel the debts that Hutton has incurred in return for clearing his son's name. Money and property as such are not the focus of this case. Rather, it illustrates the necessity of having 'a good name', an intangible property equally as open to theft as cash or tangible goods, and an invaluable part of middle-class self-esteem and peer-perception. Waters is at pains in the 'Recollections' to reassure his readers that his job is as much to protect the innocent, as in 'The Partner', as to prosecute the guilty. As he states in 'Guilty or Not Guilty', '[m]y duty, I knew, was quite as much the vindication of innocence as the detection of guilt', a statement that suggests his role as protector of, rather than threat to, civil liberties.[101] It further marks the beginning of an important shift in criminography from the emphasis placed on confession of guilt seen in the early criminographic material of the *Newgate Calendars* to what will become a common theme in later crime fiction, that is, the protection of the wrongly accused.

The protection of the innocent often involves a woman in the 'Recollections', either as a victim or as an added twist in the plot. Romance has a dual function in the 'Recollections'. It both allows for complications of plot, and provides a love interest for the female readers of the narratives. In 'XYZ' the plot turns on a father's desire to prevent what he considers an unsuitable marriage for his son. This motivates him to set Waters on the case as much as the desire to regain his stolen property, but the clue that leads Waters to the criminal is found in a love letter. If love here facilitates detection, in 'The Partner', it is the desire to contract a parentally forbidden marriage that facilitates the crime when Edmund Webster borrows money to enable him to marry Ellen Bramston. The problems of contracting suitable marriages reveals an element of class conflict in the narratives. This is apparent in 'The Partner', where the love object, Ellen, is the daughter of an East India Company Captain whose distant family connection to an Earl gives him pretensions to the nobility. Her suitor, Edmund, has a father who is in trade and wealthy, and as Edmund states, 'like most of the successful City men [...] more heartily despises poverty with a laced coat on its back than in rags'.[102] The dichotomy is clear. Wealthy middle-class trade despises noble poverty: equally, fallen nobility despises trade. Ellen's father 'would rather see his daughter in a coffin than married to a trader'.[103] A resolution is effected in the interests of plot, but the terms of the reconciliation of both fathers is not made clear. What seems to be implied is that class boundaries can be and are being eroded as wealth becomes equated with and marries into rank. The external threat to society presented by crime enables a re-evaluation of social values in which the stability of the family is seen to be pre-eminent. The deviant other of criminality promotes the coherence of the normative centre, and these narratives use crime and detection to consolidate the prevailing, contemporary social ideology. They also function to reveal social perceptions not only of the police and policing, but of the structure of society itself.

In the 'Recollections' crime is most often perpetrated by criminals who belong to a recognisable criminal class. The victims are generally middle class, and the object of the crime is property. Although Waters is a police officer, his detective work, undertaken in plain clothes, is reminiscent of that of a private detective. His cases are instituted and authorised by his superior officers, but he works on his own initiative. The construction of Waters as a middle-class figure, investigating the private affairs of the middle classes, requires that he is unobtrusive and unrecognisable as a police officer, but still someone whose actions are authorised by the law. Acceptance of the police by the middle class was premised on the concept that the police policed criminals to protect, not police, the middle class. Waters's quasi-private detecting begins to make acceptable to the middle class the fact that the law worked in and on as well as for them. This is not yet fully realised in the 'Recollections'. Where the criminals are of the lower orders, detection is followed by prosecution and punishment within the law. When the perpetrator is of the middle class, detection reveals his or her criminality, but does not always lead to public prosecution or punishment by the state. To suggest that the middle-class criminal must share the ignoble fate of his or her lower-class equivalent would be to alienate the audience that the 'Recollections' strove to entertain. The narratives do not attempt to deny the possibility of the middle-class criminal, but they resist inflicting the legal process on such a perpetrator. This is apparent in 'The Partner', where the criminal is the businessman Hutton. He is not subjected to secular law, rather 'the unhappy man chose to appear before a higher tribunal than that of the Old Bailey. He was found dead in his bedroom.'[104] Waters's detecting skills are applied to the middle classes, but the process of judgement and retribution remains within a personal and religious framework. Nonetheless, Waters's activities in this and other cases in the 'Recollections' take policing into the middle sector of society, albeit in an unthreatening way.

Importantly for his middle-class audience, Waters also takes policing into the higher echelons of society, as in 'One Night in a Gaming-House', where the miscreants are of the criminal class and their victim is related to the nobility. As in *Richmond*, the portrayal of the upper classes is not entirely favourable. In 'One Night in a Gaming-House', Lady Everton subjects Waters to a 'haughty and incredulous stare', which, on realising his police status, is mitigated to 'a glance of lofty condescendent civility'.[105] Her son, Charles Merton, is depicted as a gullible and foolish young man, spoiled by his over-indulgent mother, and Waters is motivated less by a desire to save him than by the opportunity to wreak revenge for his own satisfaction—and to improve the prospects for his promotion. There is a later case, 'The Twins', which is located entirely within high society, and which reveals the middle-class suspicion that the law, embodied in the police, does not apply to the upper class in the same way that they have reluctantly accepted that it does to themselves. This case is significant not only for that reason, but because in it, Waters, although initially given the case by 'the superintendent', thereafter is instructed by a solicitor in the employ of the estate in question. Although the police are involved, they are directed by a private individual in a case that the family involved wish to keep as far as possible in the private domain. The ostensible reason given for including the account in the 'Recollections' is as an example of the 'flagrant violations of natural justice [that] are, from various motives, corrupt and otherwise, withdrawn not only from the cognisance of judicial authority, but from the reprobation of public opinion'.[106] In 1849, prosecutions were still brought by private individuals, except 'in cases of flagrant and startling crimes, which are of course earnestly prosecuted by the Crown lawyers'.[107] There must have been many other examples of non-prosecution of cases that Russell could have fictionalised, and I suggest that the selection of a case involving the upper class was intentional, playing as it does on the susceptibilities and social insecurities of the middle class.

'The Twins' (*Chambers's* n.s., 13:338 [22 June 1850], pp. 387–390) is the story of a stolen inheritance, in which a distant relative ensures his succession to the title and accompanying estates and income by stealing the newborn male twin who should have inherited. The plot necessitates the death of the holder of the title and his heir in a riding accident, and the subsequent grief-induced confinement of the heir's wife. Waters recovers the stolen child and order is restored, but the perpetrator of the scheme, Sir Charles Malvern, and his accomplices, escape prosecution: 'no inducement, no threats, could induce the institutors of the inquiry to appear against the detected criminals'.[108] Waters's tone at the conclusion of the narrative is indignant and revelatory. He observes that in this case, 'a concealing gloss [is placed] over deeds which, in other circumstances, would have infallibly consigned the perpetrators to a prison, or perhaps the hulks'.[109] 'Other circumstances' can only be a veiled reference to social status, and the implication is clear. Policing is limited in its power over those who believe that their class places them above the law. A simplistic reading of the case might suggest a critique of the prosecution system, but the other 'Recollections' are not overtly political or concerned with legal reformation, and the content of 'The Twins' in fact panders to middle-class perceptions of their social superiors. But the popular, if incorrect, perception of the upper classes as somehow above the law is becoming eroded by the mid-century, as Waters's admittedly unsuccessful case suggests. Unsuccessful possibly, but the very fact of his attempt suggests the possibility of the upper classes eventually being subject to the same law as everyone else. Further, this case shows how the detective methods employed by Tom Richmond, which were anathema to the public, ranging as they did across society and prying into private lives, were, in the hands of Waters, seen to be reasonable and effective, not to say entertaining.

For the methods had not significantly changed. The tactics used by Tom Richmond in fiction and the Bow Street Runners in fact were, if anything, more minutely described in and important to the 'Recollections'. Waters uses precisely those activities which the public feared at the inception of the police: disguise, infiltration, entrapment, threatening witnesses, illegal searches, and spying. And of course, Waters relies on his observation and surveillance skills. He prides himself on his keen eye and sharp memory, which allow him to recognise members of the 'swell mob'. As he notes of a party of seemingly fashionable gentlemen, '[t]o an eye less experienced than mine in the artifices and expedients of a certain class of "swells" they might have passed muster for they assumed to be', but Waters can see through their disguise.[110] He himself is a master of disguise, seeming to take a pleasure in donning identities other than his own. In six of the twelve cases in the 'Recollections', Waters pretends to be something he is not to obtain information about the crime. Usually, his disguise is a verbal construction, as he names himself a businessman, potential property purchaser, or even poses as a criminal, but he also resorts to dressing up in a quite theatrical manner. This is most apparent in his second case, 'Guilty or Not Guilty', where he is '[t]ransformed, by the aid of a flaxen wig, broad-brimmed hat, green spectacles, and a multiplicity of waistcoats and shawls, into a heavy and elderly, well-to-do personage'.[111] Hiding his keen eye behind green spectacles is reminiscent of M. Dupin in Poe's 'The Purloined Letter', and it is reasonable to assume that Russell had read Poe's story, which had appeared in abbreviated form in *Chambers's* in 1844.[112] Poe's putative influence can perhaps also be seen in Waters's self-declared attempts at 'deductive' analysis, which he calls 'my professional habits of thinking' and 'police philosophy'.[113] There is very little of what Poe called 'ratiocination' in the Waters stories, but the protagonist tries at times to shroud his empirical methods in a cloak of undisclosed analytic thought. In practice, this usually amounts to no more than inventing a new scheme for obtaining the truth, but the pretence of intellectualism makes more acceptable his actual practices.

Despite his self-proclaimed intellectual approach to detection and his frankly underhand methodologies, to a great extent Waters relies on luck and coincidence to solve his cases. The words 'lucky', 'fortune', 'fortunate', and 'Providence' recur frequently in the narratives, and Waters regularly 'happens' to be in the right place at the right time or 'happens to meet' brother officers who have just the information he requires. This allies the work of the detective not only with secular justice, but also with a higher justice or Providence that endorses and justifies the existence and actions of the police. Their role is seen not as repressive, but protective, and the Providential endorsement apparent in the 'Recollections' seems to erase the possibility of error in police work. The preventive role of the ordinary police constable served to protect property in the first instance. The role of the detective extends into the protection of the individual and his or her interests, and Waters's emphasis on his perceived duty to vindicate innocence as much as detect guilt marks a significant moment in the development of the detective in fiction as well as fact. Increasingly, crime fiction from the 1840s onwards is concerned with righting the wrongs of false accusations or unreliable evidence. There was a growing anxiety about the reliability of the circumstantial evidence on which a pre-forensic-age police had to depend in their fight against crime. This was an important factor in the recognition of the necessity for and acceptance of a detective police, and goes some way to explaining Waters's penchant for concealing himself in cupboards or under beds in order to witness criminal acts rather than relying on the evidence of a chain of circumstances.

The sense of duty that Waters feels in respect of his work contributes to his construction as a professional, and implicitly middle-class, Victorian man. He not only sees his duty as the protection of the innocent and the detection of the guilty, but also as a question of integrity. When Mr Smith in 'XYZ' hopes that 'no sentimental crotchet will prevent you doing your duty', Waters makes clear his recognition of the difference between personal feelings and professional obligations in his response: '[m]y manner but interpreted my thoughts: still, sir, I know what belongs to my duty, and shall perform it'.[114] The personal inclination that motivated much of Tom Richmond's detecting is, in the 'Recollections', overridden by duty. The separation of the personal from the professional is articulated in the Police Orders of 3 June 1835: the police officer should make it apparent that he enforced the law without personal motives, but rather 'as a public servant performing a necessary and unpleasant duty'.[115] And duty, defined in the dictionary, is both 'a task or action that a person is bound to perform for moral or legal reasons' and also 'a job or service allocated'.[116] Waters, with the aid of Providence, is able to bring morality and legality together in his cases, while his status as an employee of the state carries with it certain duties, or services, that he must perform. He is as much a public servant as the police constable on the beat, and his detective and protective roles in the 'Recollections' are carried out in the interests and the service of the public. This is acknowledged in the first 'Recollection', 'One Night in a Gaming-House', where Waters refers to his success in the case as 'the first step in the promotion which ultimately led to my present position in another branch of the public service'.[117] This affirmation of the factual police role in the fiction demonstrates how effectively the police had been ideologically constructed as a protective servant of the public rather than an oppressive agent of the state.

Waters, then, exploits and exemplifies the ideologically inculcated public perception of the police. He represents to his audience a reflection of themselves in terms of domesticity and social status, and the criminography offers a safe, professional, unthreatening, and protective figure that restores order to a middle-class world disordered by crime. He is part of the orderly body of men that Rowan and Mayne envisaged in their plan for the New Police, but he combines the constraint of the corporate structure with independent action in the interests of the individual. His independence of action is, nonetheless, firmly embedded in authority, and this is evident in the narrative format and in the content of the 'Recollections'. The text is itself subject to regulation, and the nascent case structure of *Richmond* is here fully realised. Each criminal account in the 'Recollections' stands by itself as a complete entity, with Waters acting as the link that connects them one to another. On occasion, Waters will refer back to his last case, or cases are related to each other, as in 'Legal Metamorphoses' and 'The Revenge', where the criminal featured in the former returns to seek vengeance upon Waters in the latter, but each narrative works from a problem (the crime) to a solution. This is most usually framed by the law and the state in the capture, trial, and sentence of the criminal, or the death of the antagonist, as in 'The Partner' and 'The Monomaniac'. The exceptions are 'The Pursuit', where the culprit escapes, but is shown to have reformed in America, and 'The Twins', where the client's refusal to prosecute prevents the law following its course, and even then there is an element of punishment in Sir Charles Malvern's self-imposed exile abroad. In the majority of the 'Recollections', the sub-plot of romantic interest culminates in marriage or the promise of marriage, reiterating and restoring social order in the form of the middle-class family that was the centre of Victorian society.

The framework of the law not only contains the crime, but also contains and constrains the actions of Waters, and further, his work is endorsed and authorised by the state. Even in cases where he is not instructed personally by a superior police officer, he makes recourse to the institution of the police, either by reference to his fellow officers or by the use of police facilities. Waters admires and respects his superior officers, conforming to and confirming an idealised representation of the master/servant relationship, while retaining the independence of thought and action that, unfettered by authority in *Richmond*, gave rise to anxiety in the contemporary reader. The containment of crime and the constraints on the detective remove the fear of policing, while imagining effective crime control. The fear of uncontrolled intrusion by the detective into the private lives of the respectable middle class is negated. The 'Recollections' simultaneously reassure and discipline the reader. Crime and criminality are represented as subject to detection and ineluctably to result in punishment, and the monitory effect is internalised by the audience. Waters's independence of action contributes to his construction as a professional and a gentleman, but the authority in which it is contained ensures a measure of state control. A public servant, Waters is also an employee of the state, which in turn presents itself as in the service of the public: both the state in fact and society in ideological terms control and condone the policeman's work. State and social endorsement of covert activities in the interests of crime containment mean that the nineteenth-century Waters is, effectively, licensed to detect.

The Waters narratives are the fictional culmination of the process seen in transitional form in *Richmond*. The delinquency of text and protagonist apparent in the earlier work is, in the 'Recollections', reformed into an orderly structure with a hero who works entirely within the law. The development of the police in the 22 years that separate the texts provided the discursive space for a detective hero and made such a figure acceptable to the public. The 'Recollections' built upon that base in the creation of Waters, who, as gentleman and professional, could lay claim to heroic status, while his anecdotal narratives took crime into the middle class. In contrast to *Richmond*, which advertised itself as a text 'to beguile an idle hour', with a secondary function of demonstrating 'to those, who are inexperienced, the innumerable snares which beset the path of life', the Preface to the *Recollections* suggests a more serious motive.[118] It designates these narratives as both explanation and legitimation of policing and detection:

> I, therefore, offer no apology for placing these rough sketches of police-experience before the reader. They describe incidents more or less interesting and instructive of the domestic warfare constantly waging between the agents and breakers of the law, in which the stratagems and disguises resorted to, by detective officers, are, in my opinion, and in the opinion of thousands of others, as legitimate, ay, and *quite* as honorable [as] *ruses de guerre*.[119]

The Preface is retrospective, being written in 1856, seven years after the first 'Recollection' was published, and takes advantage of the popularity conferred on the police detectives by Dickens's eulogistic articles on the subject in the early 1850s. But just as the fact of the police had made possible the fiction of Waters, Waters brought police detectives to the attention of the public before Dickens wrote his factual accounts of police-work.

The 'rough sketches' of the 'Recollections' are described as 'interesting and instructive'. Their interest lay in the unfamiliar subject matter. The 'Recollections' offered their audience adventure and the excitement of a distanced contact with crime framed in social conformity and recognisable normality, but their function and effect was not limited to entertainment. While the broadsides relied on sensationalism to broadcast their monitory message to a mass public, the certainty of punishment following crime is more subtly inserted into the psyche of the reader by a narrative which itself centres on individuals and which closely traces their motives and actions. But the 'instruction' of the 'Recollections' goes beyond the merely monitory. In representing the middle class to themselves in a hero with whom they could identify and in settings and events recognisable to them, the 'Recollections' reproduce and reiterate contemporary cultural and ideological values. They make policing and detection acceptable, even valued and necessary, via the medium of entertainment. The role of women is definitive and didactic, the correct behaviour of men scarcely less so. A whole social system is apparent in the 'Recollections', and as the police detective polices the fictional world, the fiction polices the reality. The narratives discipline the reader as the obedient subject of both text and state, encouraging conformity and compliance.

Central to the acceptance and disciplinary function of the 'Recollections' is the construction of Waters as a gentleman fallen on hard times who enters the police and raises police detection to the status of a profession. In narrating his 'Recollections', he professes his expertise in his chosen career, describing the details of a detective's work, which although imaginary, bear a strong resemblance to the reality in their methodology. This first fictional account of the profession of police detection realises the heroisation of the detective figure impossible in and absent from *Richmond*, and in so doing, expands the discursive space created by the media coverage of the Metropolitan Police from their inauguration in 1829. But Waters was not a real policeman. He is a fictional construct, and fiction allows for a certain latitude in its representation of reality, an element of romance. And the central romance in the 'Recollections' is Waters's social status. This was a factor in the popularity of his narratives, and played a significant part in making police detection acceptable to the middle class. The fact remains that Rowan and Mayne, on Peel's explicit instructions, recruited their policemen from the ranks of the lower orders, from the class which was perceived to be the main source of crime. In addition, the pay was very low: in 1829 the rate was set at £200 p.a. for a superintendent, £100 p.a. for an inspector, and a mere 21 s. per week for a constable. The ban against recruiting 'gentlemen' into the police, in conjunction with the low pay, make implausible Waters's assertion that he entered 'the ranks of the Metropolitan Police as the sole means left me of procuring food and raiment'.[120] In 1831, the approximate date of Waters's entry into the police, it is unlikely that the wages had risen, or that the ban had been lifted.

The crimes in the 'Recollections' also have an air of fantasy about them. While property is the focus of criminal depredation in the narratives, the plot complications which make the stories interesting to their readers stray away from the reality of crime in the mid-nineteenth century. Real crime was more prosaic and sometimes more violent than the fiction suggests, but there is no reason to suppose that the people who read the 'Recollections' did not assume them to be true. The editors of *Chambers's* stopped short of advertising them as such: in the index to the periodical, the 'Recollections' were listed in the Index under 'Tales and Other Narratives' rather than 'Miscellaneous Articles of Instruction and Entertainment'. Equally, 'other narratives' does not rule out the inclusion of factual accounts under that broad heading. It is not known whether or not William Russell studied the work of the real police, but there are striking similarities between Waters's methods and those of the police, as my analysis of Dickens's 'Detective Police Anecdotes' will demonstrate.

But there are also striking differences between Waters's 'Recollections' and Dickens's journalistic accounts of the real workings of the police detectives. His detectives were not of the same social class as the gentlemanly Waters, although their detection was carried out in the same fashion. There, the resemblance ends. Dickens's accounts of real police detectives popularised their subject and praised and admired the profession of detection, but the individual detective officers were not heroic protagonists in the literary sense, nor did they fulfil the same disciplinary and ideological functions as had the 'Recollections'.

3.8 Dickens's 'Detective' Police

The 'Recollections' of 'Waters' were grounded firmly in middle-class culture. Characters, hero, plot, and crime were all located in the same social sector as the intended readers of the narratives. By the mid-century, *Chambers's* audience was essentially drawn from the middle class, and Dickens's periodical, *Household Words*, first published in 1850, was aimed at that same audience. Altick observes that it was '[o]n a higher level of literary interest [...] though sometimes banal and oversentimental' and goes on to state that it 'was primarily a middle-class paper with little appeal to the average working-class reader'.[121] There was a halfpenny difference in cost, with *Chambers's* at a penny-halfpenny, and *Household Words* at two pence, which perhaps limited the latter's audience slightly but not significantly, and the content was not dissimilar, although Altick suggests that *Household Words* employed 'competent professionals' as writers and editors, which presumably accounts for its literary superiority.[122] Dickens's own literary prestige and the quality of the writing in the periodical not only ensured its popularity with the literary middle class, but made it acceptable to, and equally popular with, the upper classes. Dickens's portrayal of the police reassured this socially broad audience that the function of the police detective was directed wholly against the criminal element in society rather than at society as a whole.

Dickens's depiction of the police detectives of the metropolis reinforces the concept of the police, and implicitly the detectives, as public servants, working for the social groups that comprised the audience of *Household Words* against what had come to be regarded as the criminal class. The 'Detective' anecdotes are less concerned with offering a hero with whom the reader could identify, or a *milieu* which reflected his or her social and domestic circumstances, than with reiterating and reinforcing the police role as protectors and servants of the public. Dickens's detective subjects are not the social equals of the reader, but their inferiors in matters of class. Indeed, Philip Collins has surmised that much of Dickens's affection and admiration for the police was because of the social divide: 'Always, along with his admiration for the police, there is the sure reminder that they are not his social equals. Important among his reasons for praising them [...] was his being able also to patronise them.'[123] Where in the 'Recollections' Waters as detective was the focus of interest, in Dickens's 'Detective Police' stories it is the detection as much as the detective that is central to the narratives. Dickens's readers are not the objects of detection nor the subjects of surveillance in the detective 'Anecdotes'. Waters's 'Recollections' function as a form of moral policing, following the example of Warren's *Passages from the Diary of a Late Physician* and the *Experiences of a Barrister*, and disciplining the individual reader. Dickens's police narratives serve rather to reassure their audience that the threat of crime is contained and the criminals are disciplined by the omnipresent, omniscient detectives they describe. But a mere account of detective work would not in itself have held sufficient interest. Dickens needed to make detection and its practitioners into something more mysterious and exciting than the often prosaic and tedious reality, while adhering to the facts. And to this end, he created a mythology of police detection, endowing his detectives with an aura of supranatural power, centred on their acutely observant eyes, that disguised the mundane methodologies they in reality used.

It is not known whether or not Dickens was aware of the 'Recollections' prior to writing his 'Detective Police' anecdotes for *Household Words*, but his factual accounts have elements in common with their fictional predecessor, most notably in the use of the case-history format and the methods of detection. Dickens's reading ranged across a wide spectrum of literature: fiction and fact in book form and in the periodicals and newspapers of the time.[124] It included Wight's police reports in the *Morning Herald*, later issued in collected form as *Mornings at Bow Street* (1824), *More Mornings at Bow Street* (1827), and *The Newgate Calendar*, texts that are indicative of Dickens's burgeoning interest in matters criminal. He must also have been aware of, and undoubtedly read, the criminal and execution broadsides. It seems reasonable to suppose that Dickens would also have come across *Chambers's* in his voracious reading, and that the 'Recollections' may in part have inspired him to write his own detective narratives. It appears more than coincidental that the first 'Recollections' came out in 1849, and Dickens's articles on the police in the following year. The Waters stories are, of course, works of fiction, and Dickens chose to examine the facts of police detection in what was an early, if not the first, example of a factual journalistic inquiry into the lives of individual professionals and their work. And Dickens's method of making the police detectives interesting to the public was to share what Collins calls his 'boyish hero-worship' with the reader.[125] Dickens's own enthusiasm for the detectives led him to portray them as almost superhuman 'paragons of virtue and sagacity', with all-seeing eyes and a profound knowledge of the criminal world.[126]

The police detectives, as represented by Dickens, raised what are in fact prosaic skills and methods to the level of a science. In his hands they became professionals whose entire purpose in life was the detection and apprehension of the criminals that threatened an orderly society with disorder. Collins speculates that Dickens's own 'instinctive reaction against disorder' and his 'mania for tidiness, punctuality, routine and efficiency' was instrumental in his passion for the police, which he perceived to be 'a superbly efficient organisation' dedicated to the maintenance of order in society.[127] Despite this, the covert contribution to the ordering, the disciplining, of the social body that is inherent in the 'Recollections' is absent from Dickens's detective anecdotes. Russell's narratives depict a world familiar to the reader, providing role models of orderly behaviour and warning against the consequences of crime. Waters's cases are the conduit that brings crime into the middle class, and Waters is the agent who then illustrates and suggests the certainty of its consequences, inherently disciplining the potentially disruptive individual. Dickens's anecdotes work rather to reiterate and reinforce the perception of the police detectives as servants of the public dealing with a criminal class other, and largely unknown, to the reader. The 'Recollections', in contrast, brought admittedly fictional crime and criminals into direct contact with the middle class that comprised the audience of *Chambers's*. Dickens's factual account of police detection and its practitioners is, I suggest, as much an illusory construct of the reality as Russell's pseudoautobiographical 'Recollections'. In eulogising the detective department and its officers, Dickens did much to ensure its popularity with, and demand the respect of, the public they served. But his hero-worship of the police notwithstanding, Dickens's detectives were not the heroes of his narratives. Rather, the hero was Dickens himself. It was he who brought to the attention of that public the 'Detective Force [...] so well-chosen and trained, [that] proceeds so systematically and quietly, does its business in such a workman-like manner, and is always so calmly and steadily engaged in the service of the public.'[128] We see the police detectives through Dickens's eyes and from his perspective: their own accounts of their work are re-presented in Dickens's words. The bare factual outline of the detective police is framed and coloured by the writer/narrator.

These representations of reality commenced with an article by W. H. Wills, Dickens's deputy editor at *Household Words*. His contribution was 'The Modern Science of Thief-Taking' (*Household Words* 1:16 [13 July 1850], pp. 368–372). Wills appears to have shared Dickens's admiration for the police detectives, calling them 'a superior order of police'.[129] Wills's article, while as laudatory as those of Dickens, is different in tone. It focuses on the methodologies of the detectives, raising these practices—and practicalities—to the level of a science, but it is a science based on surveillance. As Dickens's police detective informant states: 'The eye [...] is the great detector.'[130] Wills also makes much of the parallel, if oppositional, attributes of the police and the thieves:

If thieving be an Art [...], thief-taking is a Science. All the thief's ingenuity; all his knowledge of human nature; all his courage; all his coolness; all his imperturbable powers of face; all his nice discrimination in reading the countenances of other people; all his manual and digital dexterity; all his fertility in expedients, and promptitude in acting upon them; all his Protean cleverness of disguise and capability of counterfeiting every sort and condition of distress; together with a great deal more patience, and the additional qualification, integrity, are demanded for the higher branches of thief-taking.[131]

The detective is shown to utilise the same methods as the thief, and to require the same skills. This constructs the detective figure as 'other' to the respectable middle-class reader by dint of his association with, and similarity to, the criminal. The detective is placed as a buffer between criminality and respectability, a liminal figure who can detect the criminal by appropriating his or her methodologies, functioning to protect the ordinary respectable citizen from future criminal depredations.

Wills's exposition on the detective police is paradigmatic for the later articles by Dickens. In these, as in Wills's narrative, there is no question of the vindication of innocence or the protection of the wrongly accused as seen in the fictional 'Recollections'. The 'real' detectives deal solely with real criminals. Wills illustrates his article with case-histories that demonstrate the deficiencies of the ordinary policeman, and reveal the necessity for the specialist detective. In these cases, the professionalism of the detective is paralleled by that of the criminals, who are themselves professionals. The detectives in Wills's account describe the practices of a 'Dancing School', that is, thieves who break in through conjoined roof-spaces in terraced houses and 'dance' away with the goods, and the work of members of the 'Swell Mob', who 'hold first place in the "profession"'.[132] Detection in all these cases is contingent on the detective's knowledge of criminal practice. And the visibility of the *Household Words* detectives to those they police is at times an essential part of that policing. In getting to know the members and practices of the professional criminal class, the face of the detective becomes known to, and feared by, the individual criminal. The potential perpetrator of crime is effectively disempowered by that recognition of the detective. To work effectively, the criminal's power lies in his anonymity and the secrecy of his methods. To be known to the police is to be circumvented in his or her actions. The appearance, and recognition, of a detective at the scene of a proposed crime prevents the commission of that crime.

Wills gives an example of this in his article, when a group of the swell mob, enjoying a pre-crime dinner, are 'dumbfounded' and intimidated by the appearance of 'Sergeant Witchem' into giving up their nefarious plans and returning empty-handed to London.[133] The detective, when known to the criminal, is both a preventive and a detective officer. That Wills recognises the preventive role of the detective force is evident in his statement that:

> In order to counteract the plans of the swell mob, two of the ser-
> geants of the Detective Police make it their business to know every
> one of them personally. The consequence is, that the appearance of
> either of these officers upon any scene of operations is a bar to anything
> or anybody being 'done'. This is an excellent characteristic of the
> Detectives, for they thus become as well a Preventive Police.[134]

Wills makes no attempt to personalise the detectives he is discussing. Only one is named, 'Sergeant Witchem', in reality Sergeant Whicher, who would appear under the same pseudonym in Dickens's articles and in fictional form as Sergeant Cuff in Wilkie Collins's *The Moonstone*. The focus of Wills's piece is on the methods of the detectives and the knowledge they possess. When Dickens produced his anecdotes, the focus is initially on the detectives, then latterly in their transcribed accounts, on their methods.

Dickens wrote five articles on the police between 1850 and 1853. These were 'A "Detective" Police Party', published in two parts (Part I, *Household Words* 1:18 [27 July 1850], pp. 409–414; Part II, *Household Words* 1:20 [10 August 1850], pp. 457–460); 'Three "Detective" Anecdotes' (*Household Words* 1:25 [14 September 1850], pp. 557–580); in collabor-ation with Wills, 'The Metropolitan Protectives' (*Household Words* 3:57 [26 April 1851], pp. 97–105); 'On Duty with Inspector Field' (*Household Words* 3:64 [14 June 1851], pp. 265–270); and 'Down with the Tide' (*Household Words* 6:150 [5 February 1853], pp. 481–485). 'The Metro-politan Protectives' follows the events over a single night in a police station, and focuses on the ordinary police. 'Down with the Tide' relates the business of the Thames River Police, and 'On Duty with Inspector Field' is an account of Inspector Field's night-time progress through the rookeries of St Giles in company with Dickens. These articles are not specifically about detection, and I do not propose to analyse them here. Rather, I will concentrate on the two articles which introduced the police detectives to the public and in which their methods are most fully described. These are 'A "Detective" Police Party' and 'Three "Detective"

Anecdotes'. It is in these narratives that Dickens set the parameters for his depiction of detection and in which he created the myth of the quasi-mystical powers of the detectives.

He begins, in 'A "Detective" Police Party', by introducing the idea of the police detectives as possessing 'extraordinary dexterity, patience, and ingenuity' and makes clear his claim to the truth of his narrative: 'That our description may be as graphic as we can render it, and may be perfectly reliable, we will make it, so far as in us lies, a piece of plain truth.'[135] To consolidate his construction of the detective police as superior beings, he goes on to make a disparaging reference to their predecessors, the Bow Street Runners: 'as a Preventive Police, they were utterly ineffective, and as a Detective Police were very loose and uncertain in their operations'.[136] There is, though, a contradiction in his assertion that the Runners were 'puffed', that is, extravagantly praised, by the 'penny-a-liners of that time', when he is effectively performing the same function for the detective police.[137] What follows this brief authenticating introduction is an account of 'a social conference between ourselves and the Detectives, at our Office', carried out with the blessing of the authorities at Scotland Yard.[138]

The opening of the narrative creates a sense of reality, with factual details of the steps taken to arrange the meeting, the venue, with full address, the setting, in the 'Sanctum Sanctorum' of the Editor's office, the time of day (dusk), the weather (sultry), and the scene outside the office, with 'watermen and hackney-coachmen at the Theatre opposite'.[139] The detectives are introduced by their ranks and by their names, which Dickens makes clear are pseudonyms, but which are remarkably close to actuality: Inspector Field becomes 'Wield', and Sergeant Whicher is 'Witchem'. The magical connotations of the name 'Witchem' reflect the quasi-supernatural skills of the detective in detecting and/or preventing crime, and the name 'Wield' signifies, surely, the power that Inspector Field wielded over the criminal fraternity. They are brought to life on the page with small personal details: Wield's 'large, moist, knowing eye', Sergeant Dornton's 'air of one who has been a Sergeant in the army', Witchem's 'reserved and thoughtful air, as if he were engaged in deep arithmetical calculations'.[140] Each is allocated a specific skill in detection: Dornton is 'famous for steadily pursuing the inductive process'; Witchem is 'renowned for his acquaintance with the swell mob'; Straw is a master of disguise, able to 'knock at a door and ask a series of questions in any mild character you chose'.[141] What they have in common is an air of respectability, 'unusual intelligence [...] keen observation and quick perception', while their faces bear 'traces [...] of habitually leading lives of strong mental excitement'. Above all, they possess 'good eyes'.[142] The observant, inspecting eye is the key to the detectives' success, and Dickens constantly refers to the detectives' gaze in his narratives. The conversation reported is at first general, discussing the different types of crime and criminal, moving gradually to the more specific and attributable with a reference to the notorious Manning case of 1849, where Mr and Mrs Manning murdered their lodger. The mention of the Manning murder coincidentally adds a *frisson* of sensationalism to the account and implies that detective work is not merely concerned with theft, but encompasses violence and sudden death.

Having set up the detectives as superior beings, with specific skills and intellectual attributes, Dickens's text then subverts their mythical status, firmly locating the detectives as members of the lower classes, and, in describing their detective practices, deconstructing the myth of their methodological excellence. The detectives' social status is apparent in the transcription of their verbal accounts of detection. These are written in a colloquial idiom that identifies the detectives' lowly social origins, and which contrasts sharply against the modulated tones of the editorial voice. And the detectives' own narratives reveal their methods of detection to be no different to those of Tom Richmond or Waters. Despite the claims of following inductive processes, or of making intelligent analyses of the facts in order to reach a correct conclusion, in practice, the detectives follow suspects, resort to disguise and trickery, rely on overheard conversations, and deceive the innocent as to their police identity to obtain information. The cases range from tracing a known thief to tricking a suspected forger into custody; from infiltrating a gang of criminals and discovering their plans to the role played by a carpet bag in following the trail of a 'bill-stealer'. As in the 'Recollections', coincidence and luck play a major role in the detectives' work. In the second of Dickens's articles, 'Three "Detective" Anecdotes', it is the accidental and Providential discovery of a pair of gloves that leads Wield to the criminal. The second 'Anecdote' illustrates Witchem's criminal knowledge when he uses a thief's hand-signal to deceive him into passing on the stolen diamond pin he carries. The final narrative bears a strong resemblance to a Waters case, 'The Partner', in which Waters conceals himself under a bed in order to overhear the criminal threaten his victim. In the ' "Detective" Police Anecdote', Sergeant Dornton similarly conceals himself under a sofa to catch the thief who has been stealing money from coats left hanging in a hospital cloakroom.

In these narratives, as in the 'Recollections', there is nothing of the ratiocination of a Dupin, or the illusory self-proclaimed intellectual excellence of Holmes. Dickens's detectives are ordinary men who employ ordinary methods in their pursuit of criminals. The quasi-mythical status conferred upon them by Dickens is revealed in their actions to be an illusion. What contains and to some extent conceals the illusion is Dickens's framing narrative. In the closing paragraphs of 'A "Detective" Police Party' (part 2), he likens detective work to 'games of chess, played with live pieces', perhaps unconsciously invoking Edgar Allan Poe's detective, Dupin. But the first of what have come to be known as Poe's detective stories denigrates chess as being too rigorously bound by rules which reject the intuitive processes that are essential to analysis, and by inference, detection.[143] In 'The Murders in the Rue Morgue', the narrator observes of chess that 'to have a retentive memory, and to proceed by "the book," are points commonly regarded as the sum total of good playing. But it is in matters beyond the limits of mere rule that the skill of the analyst is evinced.'[144] Dickens's detectives are bound by their practical methodologies and by the rules of policing. The air of adventure and excitement, of intellectual powers beyond the norm given to the detectives by Dickens's eulogistic anecdotes, proves, on close examination, to be as illusory in fact as it was in fiction. Yet it was to be Dickens's portrayal of the lower-class, public-servant police detective which persisted, as the reality overlaid the fiction created by Russell in the 'Recollections'. Public recognition and acceptance of the police detective, encouraged by Dickens, made unnecessary the gentlemanly status of Waters which had made him palatable to his middle-class audience, and detectives of and for the middle class re-emerge as the amateur sleuths driven by circumstance in the sensation fiction of the 1860s. The apotheosis of the fictional police detective can be seen in Dickens's Inspector Bucket, who was loosely based on the real Inspector Field, the subject of 'On Duty with Inspector Field'.[145] Although Dickens relates the activities of various Metropolitan Police detectives in his articles for *Household Words*, it is the figure of Field, or 'Wield' in the early anecdotes, which comes to dominate them and which is transmogrified into Inspector Bucket.

Bucket featured in *Bleak House* (1853) as the infallible, omniscient, and omnipresent police detective, who appears, apparently from nowhere, in Mr Tulkinghorn's chambers. Bucket's entry into the novel is relatively late, not occurring until a third of the way into the text. He is described as 'a stoutly-built, steady-looking, sharp-eyed man', with the emphasis on his powers of observation.[146] His methods, although cloaked in a quasi-supernatural aura, are those of his predecessors, and he does discover the solution to the crime. In a sense, Bucket is the figure that incorporates and contains the material of Waters and his factual counterparts, serving as a repository for later writers to draw upon in their depiction of police detectives. But his representation as an infallible detecting figure is not perfect, and his exemplarity is eroded over time. In *Bleak House*, Bucket is knowledgeable of and at ease with lower and middle-class characters, criminal and otherwise. Where he fails is in his dealings with the aristocracy, Lord and Lady Dedlock. Described by ex-trooper Mr George as 'a rum gent', Bucket admits to his own lowly origins in a conversation with 'Mercury', the generic name Dickens confers on the footmen of the Dedlock household.[147] Perhaps disingenuously, Bucket tells the footman that '[my] father was first a page, then a footman, then a butler, then a steward, then an innkeeper' who 'considered service the most honourable part of his career'.[148] When speaking to his upper-class client, Sir Leicester Dedlock, Bucket reveals his ignorance of correct social custom by addressing Sir Leicester by his full title, that is, as 'Sir Leicester Dedlock, Baronet'. Here he lacks the social mobility of the gentlemanly Waters, whose background served to make him at ease in the higher echelons of society. Bucket is fixed as a member of the lower class, and for the detective to succeed across society, he—or increasingly she—requires social skills that Bucket lacks. His detective skills ensure the capture of Mademoiselle Hortense, the murderer of Tulkinghorn, but they fail him in his pursuit of Lady Dedlock, who is dead before he, in the company of Esther Summerson, finally traces her whereabouts.

Dickens's police detectives represent a reality which associates them with the criminal class that is seen as their primary target. When crime occurs in higher social groups, the police detective is disadvantaged, literally and literarily. What is required here is the socially mobile Waters or the legal professional Mr Ferret. Failing these models, the amateur 'detective' pioneered by Poe, and the bourgeois protagonists of sensation fiction exemplified in Collins's quasi-detective novels *The Woman in White* and *The Moonstone* come to dominate later detective fiction. Certainly, there is a police detective in *The Moonstone*, but Sergeant Cuff shares the lowly origins of Bucket, and similarly fails in his dealings with the upper class when his detective activities lead him to suppose that Rachel Verinder is guilty of the theft of the moonstone, thereby alienating him from the Verinder household. The middle-class intellectual private but professional detective that replaces the amateur is later epitomised by Doyle's Sherlock Holmes, the first 'consulting detective'.[149] Nevertheless, the police detective does not die out. He continues to appear throughout the latter part of the nineteenth and into the twentieth century, but is increasingly of middle-class status and of superior police rank. Further, his appearances tend to be contained within the pages of the periodicals or are found in texts that follow the casebook format made familiar by Russell's collected *Recollections* rather than in the serialised or three-decker novel.

The 'Recollections' of Waters, while at least as popular as Dickens's 'Anecdotes', were influential in their time, spawning a host of fictional detective stories written in a similar fashion in the 1860s and 1870s. But they are no longer in circulation, where Dickens's literary fame and prestige has ensured the survival of his representation of police detection. In bringing the police detectives to the attention of the public, Dickens in fact began the process of destroying the very mystique he strove to create. Familiarity bred contempt, and Dickens's model of the detective slowly acquired feet of clay, becoming an object of derision rather than admiration in the Victorian novel. In firmly locating his detectives in the lower classes, Dickens effectively prevented them from being seen as heroes in literary terms. They are public servants, with the emphasis on servant, in spite of their professional skills. Dickens's anecdotes work to popularise the police detective, and to suggest the containment of crime in the manner of the *Newgate Calendar*. The police voice has entirely replaced that of the criminal in these narratives, as it had in the 'Recollections'. But Dickens's detective stories, even though factual, fail to have a monitory or disciplinary effect on the reader. They reassure rather than regulate. The 'Recollections' in their time played a more significant role in the development of detective fiction and in the literary policing of society than did Dickens's accounts of the reality of police detection. The fictional narratives introduced the disciplinary detective into literature. The construction of Waters as a gentleman and the relatively genteel crimes he detected took crime and detection into the middle classes. But the ephemeral nature of periodical publication, and the transience of the 'yellow-back' format in which the collected stories were published, in conjunction with Dickens's literary fame, has ensured that Dickens's early representation of the detective, factual and fictional, outlasted that of his contemporary fictional rivals. The disciplinary detective will work in the private sphere rather than the public domain, and largely remain there until the advent of police procedurals in the twentieth century. And even there, the successful police detective will be marked as other to his or her police colleagues by quirky elements of character which can be directly related back to the initiatory, and in many ways prophetic, figures of Richmond and Waters.

Conclusion

A rich inheritance

It seems that by the mid-nineteenth century a criminographical floodgate had been opened. The popularity of the Waters stories and Dickens's 'Detective' Anecdotes of 1850–1853 led to a flourishing sub-literary culture of fictional detective reminiscences. There was a proliferation of texts concerned with detection which continued into the 1860s, and which appeared in the periodicals and increasingly in the form of the cheaply produced and priced books that came to be called 'yellow-backs' because of their distinctive covers. The relatively low cost (sixpence) of what might be termed the Victorian equivalent of the modern paperback was calculated to appeal to the readers of the periodicals that had first brought the sub-genre to the reading public, that is, to the literate middle class. Waters's successors included Russell's later creation, Inspector F, in *Experiences of a Real Detective* (1862) and his *Autobiography of an English Detective* (1863); the *Diary of an Ex-Detective* (1859), supposedly edited by Charles Martel (the pseudonym of the author, Thomas Delf), and its sequel, *The Detective's Notebook* (1860); and Robert Curtis's *The Irish Police Officer* (1861). There was also the pseudonymous Andrew Forrester Jnr, whose contributions included *Revelations of a Private Detective* (1863), and *Secret Service, or Recollections of a City Detective* (1864). Rather more innovative than his—or, as Stephen Knight has suggested, her—rivals, in 1864 Forrester created the first professional woman detective in *The Female Detective*.[1] The protagonist works for the police but is not officially a member of the police force: it would take another 50 years and a world war before there would be a Women's Police Service, and longer still before they were permitted to perform a detective function. Later the same year, *The Experiences of a Lady Detective* (1864), attributed to W. S. Hayward, followed Forrester's example. This was a detective story featuring a Mrs Paschal, who again worked for the police, but in an unofficial capacity. There are undoubtedly many other fictional detective narratives in this period, but the cheap and consequently fragile physical construction of the texts has resulted in their rarity in the twenty-first century.

The depiction of the detective figures may vary according to the demands of the market and the target audience, but their practices remain remarkably constant and parallel the methods of the Metropolitan Police detectives portrayed by Dickens. A second, and later, confirmation of the similarities between fictional and factual detection can be seen in the memoirs of the real-life Edinburgh detective James McLevy. *Curiosities of Crime in Edinburgh* and *The Sliding Scale of Life: or, Thirty Years' Observations of Falling Men and Women in Edinburgh* both appeared in 1861.[2] They purported to be accounts of the cases undertaken by McLevy in his 30-year career with the Edinburgh police from 1830 until his retirement in 1860. That there was such a person is confirmed in the minutes of the Watching Committee of Edinburgh Town Council, which records McLevy's petition for retirement: 'Read report by the Lord Provost's Committee to whom was remitted Petition of James McLevie, Principal Criminal Officer, praying to be relieved from ordinary duty.'[3] McLevy, writing from experience, at a time when the police detective had been popularised by Dickens, and with less concern than Dickens for the sensibilities of his audience, was criticised in a contemporary review of *The Sliding Scale of Life* in the *Athenaeum*: 'Some of his stories are very painful, and some so coarse that they are unfit for the drawing-room table.'[4] The facts of police detection presented at first-hand were more sensational—and possibly distasteful—than the fictional equivalent. But the methodologies of police detection and the criminality they seek to contain remain constant, both in fiction and in its factual counterpart.

And it was not only the police detective who appeared in the contemporary literature. Novels, particularly those of the sensation genre, in which crime featured as part of the plot had, necessarily, to provide a detecting figure also. Sometimes, as in Mary Braddon's *Lady Audley's Secret* (1862), this role would be undertaken by a gentleman of private means or with an appropriate profession, here, the barrister Robert Audley. In Wilkie Collins's *The Woman in White* (1860), detective agency is initially conferred on plain, single Marian Halcombe, although in the event her innate feminine frailty prevails: she falls conveniently ill, allowing the aptly named Walter Hartright to take over the investigative role. Where in Dickens's *Bleak House* (1853) a police detective pursued the case, in these later novels the police are at best marginal to the narrative and, more often, are actually absent. The middle class, it seemed, was still resistant to the intrusion of the police into the domestic sphere. Collins's *The Moonstone* (1868) perhaps demonstrates this most clearly in Sergeant Cuff's failure to read the clues correctly and reach the right conclusion while in the Verinder household: once the case moves beyond the bounds of domesticity, Cuff is shown to be able to function efficiently once again.

This separation of public and private detection continues for much of the latter part of the nineteenth century, although fictional police detectives were depicted as being of increasingly higher social status and therefore more acceptable to the reader. The corruption within the real police force revealed in the arrest of four divisional detectives in 1878 for their involvement in an international swindling racket cannot have endeared the police detective to the reading public. Equally, the increasing numbers of police detectives—800 men by the mid-1880s—and their professionalisation within the newly created Criminal Investigation Department further distanced the detective from the public. It was not until late in the century that a fictional figure appeared that combined the skills and methods of the police detective with the attributes and social status of the amateur detective to create and popularise the fully fashioned private detective. This was, of course, Arthur Conan Doyle's Sherlock Holmes, who, like his predecessors, made most of his appearances in the pages of a periodical. The first Holmes adventure, *A Study in Scarlet*, was published in *Beeton's Christmas Annual* of 1887, and later adventures appeared in *The Strand Magazine*. In these stories, while Holmes is the unchallenged hero and expert detective, the police also feature, offering a pleasing contrast to the effective detection of Holmes in their bumbling and largely ineffectual attempts at tracking down the criminal. What remains unspoken and under-investigated, but which is a clear factor in Holmes's successes, is the access to police information and infrastructure that his contact with the police permits. That Doyle was aware of Holmes's literary predecessors, factual and fictional, is apparent in his own references to Poe's Dupin stories, to Gaboriau's detective fictions, and also to 'Mr Sharpes or Mr Ferrets'.[5]

Holmes, then, is in a sense the conclusion to the development of crime fiction as a genre, a development that has come to focus on the detective rather than, as I suggested in the early pages of this book, on the criminal. But how the pattern mutated from the 'Experiences of a Barrister' and Russell's 'Recollections of a Detective Police Officer' into the polished and popular figure of Holmes is material for another time and place. Here, I have attempted to fill in the gaps left by traditional accounts of the narrative of crime fiction, and in so doing, I have established a new narrative that, in its focus on ephemeral and periodical material, leads more directly and logically to that apotheosis of the detective, Sherlock Holmes.

Notes

1 Criminal narratives: Textualising crime

1. Henry Mayhew, *London Labour and the London Poor Vol. 1: The London Street Folk* (London: Frank Cass, 1967 [1851]), pp. 308–309.
2. Ibid., p. 223.
3. Ibid., p. 230.
4. Michael Hughes, 'Foreword' to Charles Hindley's *Curiosities of Street Literature* (London: Seven Dials Press, 1969), p. 11. The original text by Hindley was published by Reeves and Turner of London in 1871.
5. Thomas W. Laqueur, 'Crowds, Carnival and the State in English Executions, 1604–1868', in *The First Modern Society: Essays in English History in Honour of Lawrence Stone*, eds, A. L. Beier, D. Cannadine and James M. Rosenheim (Cambridge: Cambridge University Press, 1989), pp. 305–355, p. 309.
6. V. A. C. Gatrell, *The Hanging Tree: Execution and the English People* (Oxford: Oxford University Press, 1994), p. 94.
7. October 1861, p. 399. Cited in Victor Neuberg, *Popular Literature: A History and Guide* (Harmondsworth: Penguin, 1997), p. 142.
8. Richard Altick, *Victorian Studies in Scarlet* (London: Dent, 1972), p. 42.
9. Mayhew, *London Labour*, p. 234.
10. Ibid.
11. Leslie Shepard, *The History of Street Literature* (Newton Abbot: David and Charles, 1973), p. 193.
12. Laqueur, 'Crowds, Carnival and the State', p. 309.
13. Charles Hindley, *Curiosities of Street Literature*, p. d.
14. Ibid., p. 2.
15. Mayhew, *London Labour*, p. 222.
16. Hindley, *Curiosities*, p. 197.
17. Ibid.
18. Gatrell, *The Hanging Tree*, p. 70.
19. Altick, *Victorian Studies in Scarlet*, p. 39.
20. 'A collection of miscellaneous broadsides, consisting chiefly of Almanacks and accounts of criminal trials 1801–58', British Library. No publisher or specific date is given to this collection. It appears to be the work of a private individual.
21. Hindley, *Curiosities*, p. 192.
22. Laqueur, 'Crowds, Carnival', p. 309.
23. Ibid., p. 315.
24. Hindley, *Curiosities*, p. 188.
25. Ibid.
26. Ibid.
27. Gatrell, *The Hanging Tree*, p. 75.
28. Hindley, *Curiosities*, p. 188.

29. Martin J. Wiener, *Reconstructing the Criminal: Culture, Law and Policy in England, 1830–1914* (Cambridge: Cambridge University Press, 1994 [1990]), p. 96.
30. Mayhew, *London Labour*, p. 234.
31. For an acount of the Newgate novel see Keith Hollingsworth, *The Newgate Novel 1830–47: Bulwer, Ainsworth, Dickens and Thackeray* (Detroit: Wayne State University Press, 1963).
32. This apologia appeared in the *Gazette* of 8 August 1818, and is cited in Charles Pollit, *De Quincey's Editorship of the Westmorland Gazette* (Kendal and London: n.p., 1890), pp. 12–13.
33. De Quincey, in the *Gazette* of 18 September 1818, cited in Pollit, *De Quincey's Editorship*, pp. 5 and 15.
34. Ibid., p. 8.
35. De Quincey, 'On Murder Considered as One of the Fine Arts', *Blackwood's Edinburgh Magazine* 21:122 (February 1827), pp. 199–213.
36. The murders were committed in December 1811, but De Quincey consistently, in all his work on the subject, gives the date as 1812.
37. This essay was first published in the *London Magazine* (October 1823) under the series title of 'Notes from the Pocket-Book of a Late Opium-Eater'. See also David Masson, ed., *The Collected Writings of Thomas De Quincey Vol. X: Literary Theory and Criticism* (Edinburgh: Adam and Charles Black, 1890), pp. 389–394.
38. Masson, *The Collected Works Vol. X*, p. 390.
39. Ibid., p. 391.
40. De Quincey, 'On Murder Considered as One of the Fine Arts', in *The Collected Works of Thomas De Quincey Vol. XIII: Tales and Prose Phantasies*, ed., David Masson (Edinburgh: Adam and Charles Black, 1890), p. 9.
41. Ibid., p. 10.
42. Ibid., p. 11, cited by Masson in footnote 1.
43. Ibid., p. 71.
44. Ibid., p. 11.
45. Ibid., p. 46.
46. Ibid., p. 12.
47. Ibid., p. 13.
48. Ibid., p. 12.
49. Ibid., pp. 14–15.
50. Ibid., p. 35.
51. Ibid.
52. Ibid., p. 47.
53. A. S. Plumtree, 'The Artist as Murderer', in *Thomas De Quincey Bicentenary Studies*, ed., Robert Lance Snyder (Norman and London: University of Oklahoma Press, 1985), pp. 140–163, p. 155.
54. De Quincey, 'Murder Considered as One of the Fine Arts', *Blackwood's Edinburgh Magazine* 46:289 (November 1839), pp. 661–668.
55. Masson, *The Collected Works Vol. XIII*, p. 53.
56. Ibid., p. 70, footnote 2.
57. Ibid., p. 74.
58. Grevel Lindop, *The Opium-Eater: A Life of Thomas De Quincey* (London: Dent, 1981), pp. 378–379.
59. Lennard Davis, *Factual Fictions: The Origins of the English Novel* (Philadelphia: University of Pennsylvania Press, 1996 [1983]), p. 48.

60. 'Introduction', Robert Morrison and Chris Baldick, eds, *Tales of Terror from Blackwood's Magazine* (Oxford and New York: Oxford University Press, 1995), pp. vii–xxi, p. xv.
61. Hindley, *Curiosities*, p. 4.
62. Alvin Sullivan, ed., *British Literary Magazines, Vol. II: The Romantic Age 1789–1836* (Westport, Conn. and London: Greenwood Press, 1983), p. 45.
63. *Blackwood's Edinburgh Magazine* was 'a 2s. 6d monthly' publication, a price which placed it beyond the reach of much of the population. See Scott Bennett, 'Revolutions in Thought: Serial Publication and the Mass Market for Reading', in *The Victorian Press: Samples and Soundings*, eds, Joanne Shattock and Michael Wolff (Leicester: Leicester University Press, 1982), pp. 225–260, pp. 235–236.
64. Robert D. Mayo, 'Gothic Romance in the Magazines', *Publications of the Modern Language Association* 65 (1950), pp. 762–789, p. 764.
65. Daniel Keyte Sandford, 'A Night in the Catacombs', *Blackwood's Edinburgh Magazine* 4:19 (October 1818), pp. 19–23; William Maginn, 'The Man in the Bell', *Blackwood's Edinburgh Magazine* 10:57 (November 1821), pp. 373–375; Anon., 'The Last Man', *Blackwood's Edinburgh Magazine* 19:110 (March 1826), pp. 284–286.
66. 'Cautionary Hints to Speculators on the Increase of Crimes', *Blackwood's Edinburgh Magazine* 3:14 (May 1818), pp. 176–178, p. 176.
67. Ibid., p. 176.
68. Ibid., pp. 177–178.
69. Ibid., p. 177.
70. 'Hints for Jurymen', *Blackwood's Edinburgh Magazine* 13:78 (June 1823), pp. 673–685.
71. Ibid., p. 674.
72. Ibid.
73. Ibid., pp. 679ff. and p. 681.
74. John Galt, 'The Buried Alive', *Blackwood's Edinburgh Magazine* 10:56 (October 1821), pp. 262–264, and Henry Thomson, 'Le Revenant', *Blackwood's Edinburgh Magazine* 23:124 (April 1827), pp. 409–416.
75. 'Hints for Jurymen', p. 684.
76. Ibid.
77. Ibid., pp. 684–685.
78. Robert MacNish, 'An Execution in Paris', *Blackwood's Edinburgh Magazine* 24:146 (December 1828), pp. 785–788.
79. Ibid., 'An Execution in Paris', p. 785.
80. Ibid., p. 788.
81. Ibid.
82. Ibid., p. 787.
83. 'Beck and Dunlop on Medical Jurisprudence', *Blackwood's Edinburgh Magazine* 17:98 (March 1825), pp. 351–352, p. 352.
84. John Wilson, 'Extracts from Gosschen's Diary', *Blackwood's Edinburgh Magazine* 3:17 (August 1818), pp. 596–598.
85. Ibid., p. 597.
86. Ibid.
87. Thomson, 'Le Revenant', p. 409.
88. Ibid.

89. Ibid.
90. Letter from Lamb to William Hone. See Charles and Mary Lamb, *Letters*, ed., E. V. Lucas (London, 1912), II, p. 773. Cited in Hollingsworth, *The Newgate Novel*, p. 59.
91. Thomson, 'Le Revenant', p. 416.
92. Anon., 'The Forgers', *Blackwood's Edinburgh Magazine* 9:53 (August 1821), pp. 572–577, pp. 572 and 573.
93. Stephen Knight, *Form and Ideology in Crime Fiction* (Bloomington: Indiana University Press, 1980), p. 11.
94. 'The Forgers', p. 574.
95. Ibid.
96. 'The Forgers', p. 575.
97. Ibid., p. 577.
98. Ibid., p. 573.
99. Ibid., p. 574.
100. John Wilson, 'Expiation', *Blackwood's Edinburgh Magazine* 28:172 (October 1830), pp. 628–643.
101. Ibid., p. 629.
102. Ibid.
103. Ibid., p. 630.
104. Ibid., pp. 631 and 633.
105. Ibid., p. 639.
106. Ibid., p. 632.
107. Ibid.
108. Ibid., p. 636.
109. Ibid.
110. Ibid., p. 637.
111. Ibid., p. 638.
112. Ibid., p. 643.

2 Making the case for the professionals

1. C. R. B. Dunlop, 'Samuel Warren: A Victorian Law and Literature Practitioner', *Cardozo Studies in Law and Literature*, New York 12:2 (Fall–Winter 2000), pp. 265–291, p. 284.
2. *A Popular Introduction to Law Studies* (1835), *The Moral, Social, and Professional Duties of Attorneys and Solicitors* (1848), *Blackstone's Commentaries Systematically Abridged and Adapted to the Existing State of the Law and Constitution With Great Additions* (1855–1856).
3. Samuel Warren, *Miscellanies Critical, Imaginative, and Juridical*, 2 Vols (Edinburgh and London: William Blackwood, 1855).
4. The 'Passages' were later published in collected form as *Passages from the Diary of a Late Physician* (Edinburgh and London: William Blackwood, 1842 [1838]), p. vi. All further references will be to the collected edition, with details of original publication in *Chambers's* given in the text.
5. Arthur Conan Doyle, *A Study in Scarlet* (London: Penguin, 1981 [1887]), p. 23.
6. Samuel Warren, Preface, *Passages from the Diary of a Late Physician*.

7. *Ten-Thousand a Year*, serialised in *Blackwood's* (1839–1841), published in book form in 1841 by William Blackwood, and *Now and Then* (Edinburgh and London: William Blackwood, 1847).
8. Peter Drexler, *Literatur, Recht, Kriminalität: Untersuchungen zur Vorgeschichte des englischen Detectivromans 1830–1890* (Frankfurt: Peter Lang, 1991), p. 94. Translation approved by author.
9. Warren, Preface to *Passages* (1842), p. vi.
10. Warren, 'The Bracelets', *Blackwood's Edinburgh Magazine* 31:1 (January 1832), pp. 39–53.
11. Warren, Preface to *Passages* (1842), p. vii.
12. Robert Morrison and Chris Baldick, eds, 'Introduction', *Tales of Terror from Blackwood's Magazine* (Oxford and New York: Oxford University Press, 1995), p. xvii.
13. Edgar Allan Poe, 'Ten Thousand a Year. By the Author of "The Diary of a London Physician." Carey and Hart, Philadelphia', in *Graham's Magazine* November (1841), reprinted in *The Complete Works of Edgar Allan Poe, Vol. X: Literary Criticism Vol. III*, ed., James A. Harrison (New York: AMS Press Inc., 1965), pp. 210–212, p. 210.
14. Warren, 'Introduction' to *Passages*, p. xvii.
15. 'Introduction' to 'Passages from the Diary of a Late Physician', *Blackwood's* 28:170, Pt 2 (August 1830), p. 322.
16. Ibid.
17. Ibid.
18. Ibid.
19. Cited in the Preface to the 1838 edition of *Passages*, written by Warren himself. Preface, *Passages from the Diary of a Late Physician* (London: William Blackwood and Sons, 1842 [1838]), pp. v–xi, p. ix.
20. Ibid., p. viii.
21. Ibid., p. x.
22. 'Cancer', in Warren, *Passages*, Vol. 1 (1842), pp. 33–37, p. 33. For convenience, while original dates of publication in *Blackwood's* will be given in the text, references will be to this edition of *Passages*.
23. Warren, 'Consumption', *Passages*, Vol. I, pp. 105–130, p. 107.
24. Warren, 'Grave Doings', *Passages*, Vol. I, pp. 236–249, p. 236.
25. Warren, 'Death at the Toilet', *Passages*, Vol. 1 (1842), pp. 187–191, p. 187.
26. Ibid., pp. 187–188.
27. Ibid., p. 188.
28. Ibid., p. 190.
29. Ibid.
30. Warren, 'The Magdalen', *Passages*, Vol. 2 (1842), pp. 105–169, p. 105.
31. Ibid., p. 107.
32. Ibid., p. 120.
33. Warren, 'Mother and Son', *Passages*, Vol. 2, pp. 1–66, p. 1.
34. Ibid., p. 2.
35. Ibid., p. 66.
36. Warren, 'A "Man About Town" ', *Passages*, pp. 151–185, p. 152.
37. Ibid., p. 152.
38. Ibid., pp. 163–164.
39. Warren, 'The Forger', *Passages*, pp. 138–159, p. 138.

40. Ibid.
41. Ibid., p. 139.
42. Ibid.
43. Ibid., p. 140.
44. Ibid., p. 141.
45. Ibid., p. 142.
46. Ibid., p. 146.
47. The death penalty for forgery was not abolished until 1832.
48. Ibid., pp. 149–150.
49. Samuel Warren, 'My First Circuit: Law and Facts from the North', *Blackwood's Edinburgh Magazine* 44:273 (July 1838), pp. 57–93. The article itself is dated 10 June 1838, and must have been written shortly after Warren had completed his first Circuit. It was reprinted in abbreviated form in Warren's *Miscellanies*, Vol. I, pp. 33–79.
50. Ibid., p. 73.
51. Ibid., pp. 77 and 81.
52. Ibid., p. 83.
53. Samuel Warren, 'Who is the Murderer? A Problem in the Law of Circumstantial Evidence', *Blackwood's Edinburgh Magazine* 51:319 (May 1842), pp. 553–578; 'The Mystery of Murder and its Defence', *Miscellanies*, Vol. 2, pp. 1–68.
54. 'The Mystery of Marie Rogêt' was published in America in the *Southern Literary Messenger* 1842–1843. Poe based his story on the actual case of the unsolved murder of Mary Cecilia Rogers in New York. He transposed the action to Paris, but used extensive quotations from the American press reports of the real case, attributed in the fiction to Parisian newspapers, but with footnotes giving the true origin.
55. Warren, 'Who is the Murderer? A Problem in the Law of Circumstantial Evidence', *Miscellanies*, Vol. I, pp. 185–242, p. 185.
56. Ibid., p. 185.
57. Ibid., pp. 192–193 and 187.
58. Aram's case was notorious in its time, and found its place in literature in both factual and fictional accounts, perhaps the best known of which was Edward Bulwer-Lytton's fictional reworking of the crime in his 1832 novel *Eugene Aram*.
59. Warren, 'Who is the Murderer?', p. 186.
60. Ibid., p. 242.
61. Richard Altick, *The English Common Reader: A Social History of the Mass Reading Public 1800–1900* (Columbus: Ohio State University Press, 1998 [1957]), p. 332.
62. Publisher's Preface to *The Experiences of a Barrister*, by S_____, DCL (London: J & C Brown, 1856), p. 5. The British Library attributes this title to Samuel Warren in the catalogue.
63. Drexler, *Literatur, Recht, Kriminalität*, p. 106.
64. Ibid.
65. Ibid., p. 107.
66. Ibid., p. 110.
67. 'The March Assize', *The Experiences of a Barrister and The Confessions of an Attorney*, attrib. to Samuel Warren (New York: Arno Press, 1976), p. 13. This is a facsimile edition of that originally published by Wentworth Hughes and

Co. of Boston in 1859. All references are to the 1976 facsimile, but the dates of the original publication of the 'Experiences' in *Chambers's* will be given parenthetically in the text.

68. *The Experiences of a Barrister* (1979 [1859]), p. 15.
69. Ibid.
70. Ibid.
71. Ibid., p. 19.
72. Ibid., pp. 18–19.
73. Ibid., pp. 21–22.
74. 'The Northern Circuit', *The Experiences of a Barrister* (1976 [1859]), p. 30.
75. Ibid., p. 31.
76. Ibid.
77. Ibid., p. 35.
78. Ibid., p. 36.
79. In fact, he has been press-ganged and is unable to inform his wife of his whereabouts until it is too late.
80. Ibid., p. 98.
81. Ibid.
82. 'Esther Mason', *The Experiences of a Barrister* (1976 [1859]), p. 99.
83. Ibid., p. 102.
84. 'Circumstantial Evidence', *The Experiences of a Barrister* (1976 [1859]), p. 147.
85. Ibid.
86. Ibid., p. 148.
87. Ibid., p. 149.
88. Ibid., p. 152.
89. Ibid.
90. Ibid., pp. 155–156.
91. Ibid., pp. 151–152.
92. Ibid., p. 164.
93. Ibid., p. 147.
94. 'The Contested Marriage', *The Experiences of a Barrister* (1976 [1859]), pp. 39–40.
95. Ibid., p. 40.
96. Ibid., p. 45.
97. Ibid., p. 47.
98. ' "The Writ of Habeas Corpus" ', *The Experiences of a Barrister* (1976 [1859]), p. 94.
99. Ibid., p. 76.
100. Ibid., p. 80.
101. Ibid., p. 85.
102. Ibid., p. 87.
103. Ibid., p. 88.
104. 'The Marriage Settlement', *The Experiences of a Barrister* (1976 [1859]), p. 109.
105. Ibid., p. 110.
106. Ibid., p. 124.
107. The word 'Reminiscences' is substituted for 'Confessions' in the later numbers of this series, and the index to *Chambers's* varies between the two, sometimes listing the stories under both titles, sometimes using one in the index and the other in the story-heading. The collected edition was

published with the 'Experiences' as 'Confessions', and the narratives were also included in *Leaves from the Diary of a Law Clerk* (London: J & C Brown, 1857), which was written by William Russell. The 'Confessions' are appended to the *Leaves* and distinguished from them, but the title is not used. It is unclear whether or not they were written by Russell, or just incorporated to fulfil the demands of publication.

108. *The Experiences of a Barrister, and Confessions of an Attorney* (1976 [1859]), p. 207. Hereafter referred to as *Confessions*.
109. *Confessions* (1979 [1859]), p. 206.
110. Cited in Hutter, Albert D. and Miller, Mary W., eds, ' "Who Can Be Trusted?": *The Detective*, An Early Journal of Detection', *Mystery and Detection Annual* 23 (1973), pp. 167–192, p. 167. *The Detective* ran from 10 December 1859 to 3 March 1860.
111. Ibid., p. 206.
112. In the American edition (1979 [1859]), this title is altered to 'The Life Policy'.
113. *The Confessions* (1979 [1859]), p. 219.
114. Ibid., p. 236.
115. *The Confessions* (1979 [1859]), p. 254.
116. In *Chambers's*, this narrative came under the heading of 'Reminiscences of an Attorney' in the body of the text, but was listed under 'Confessions' in the index.
117. Ibid., p. 268.

3 A conspicuous constabulary: or, why policemen wear tall helmets

1. Henry Goddard, *Memoirs of a Bow Street Runner*, ed. and intro. by Patrick Pringle (London: Museum Press Ltd, 1956), Introduction, p. ix.
2. John Wight, 'Advertisement to the First Edition', *Mornings at Bow Street: A Selection of the Most Entertaining Reports Which Have Appeared in the Morning Herald* (London: George Routledge and Sons, 1875 [1824]), p. iv.
3. George Sala, 'Introduction', *Mornings at Bow Street*, p. xxvi.
4. Anon., *Richmond: Scenes in the Life of a Bow Street Runner, Drawn Up From His Private Memoranda*, ed. and intro. by E. F. Bleiler (New York: Dover Publications, 1976 [1827]), all references are to this edition and are given parenthetically in the text.
5. Anon., 'Recent Novels and Tales', *Monthly Review* n.s., 5 (June 1827), p. 271.
6. Ibid.
7. *Literary Gazette* 531 (24 March 1827), p. 181.
8. This is evident in Goddard's *Memoirs*, which offer a verifiable but retrospective authentic account of the activities and duties of a Runner.
9. Anon., 'Recent Novels', *Monthly Review* n.s., 5 (June 1827), p. 271.
10. Clive Emsley, *The English Police: A Social and Political History* (London: Addison, Wesley, Longman, 1996 [1991]), p. 20.
11. Tom's partnerships with these two men in various cases prefigure the detective companion that will become a standard feature of later detective fiction, realised most famously in Conan Doyle's Watson, companion to Holmes, and Christie's Hastings, assistant to Poirot.

12. Belton Cobb, *The First Detectives and the Early Career of Richard Mayne* (London: Faber & Faber, 1962), p. 40.
13. This extract is from the *Morning Herald* of 15 October 1829. It is taken from a collection of newspaper cuttings held at the Metropolitan Police Museum, Charlton, London. While the cuttings are arranged in temporal order, the page numbers from the originals are largely absent.
14. Peter Drexler, *Literatur, Recht, Kriminalität: Untersuchungen zur Vorgeschichte des englsischen Detektivromans 1830–1890* (Frankfurt: Peter Lang, 1991), p. 109. Drexler is citing Christopher Pulling, *Mr. Punch and the Police* (London: Butterworth, 1964).
15. Patrick Colquhoun, *A Treatise on the Police of the Metropolis, etc.*, 7th edition (London, 1806 [1796]), p. 10.
16. Cited in Clive Emsley, *Crime and Society in England 1750–1900* (London: Longman, 1996 [1978]), p. 56.
17. Colquhoun notes that 'depredations on ships in the River Thames [...] were estimated at half a million [pounds] (*Treatise*, p. 10).
18. Stanley French, *River Court: The Early History of Thames Magistrates' Court*, a pamphlet held in the River Police Museum, Wapping. The pamphlet is undated, but was written in the late twentieth century. The pages are not numbered.
19. This combined approach is well documented. My direct sources here are various accounts held at the Thames River Police Museum, for which I am deeply grateful to Curator Bob Jefferies.
20. Patrick Colquhoun, 'Preface', *Treatise on the Commerce and Police of the River Thames* (London, 1806 [1800]), n.p.
21. Colquhoun, *Treatise on the Commerce and Police*, p. 205.
22. Ibid., p. 207.
23. Ibid., p. 258.
24. Colquhoun, 'Preface', *Treatise on the Police*, n.p.
25. Rowan and Mayne, *General Instruction Book* (1829), p. 1. A copy of this book, with detailed instructions for the activities of the different ranks of policemen, was issued to each recruit on joining the force. It was in print by September 1829, but required amendment and was reissued with corrections in October 1829. See David Ascoli, *The Queen's Peace: The Origin and Development of the Metropolitan Police 1829–1979* (London: Hamish Hamilton, 1979), p. 85, n. 1.
26. David Robinson, 'The Local Government of the Metropolis, and Other Populous Places', *Blackwood's Edinburgh Magazine* 29:175 (January 1831), pp. 82–104. Originally published anonymously, this article has been ascribed to David Robinson by the *Wellesley Index to Periodicals 1824–1900*.
27. Ibid., p. 82.
28. Ibid.
29. Ibid., p. 83.
30. Ibid.
31. Ibid.
32. Ibid., p. 84.
33. Ibid., pp. 86–87.
34. Ibid., p. 86.
35. Ibid., p. 84.
36. Ibid., p. 86.
37. Ibid.

38. Ibid., p. 101.
39. Edwin Chadwick, 'Preventive Police', *London Review* 1:1 (30 January 1829), pp. 252–308, p. 290.
40. Robinson, 'Local Government of the Metropolis', p. 95.
41. Ibid.
42. Metropolitan Police Museum cuttings collection.
43. Ibid.
44. Anon., 'The New Police', *New Monthly Magazine* 26:108 (November 1829), pp. 426–432, p. 426.
45. Ibid., p. 428.
46. Ibid.
47. Ibid., p. 429.
48. Ibid., p. 427.
49. Ibid., p. 432.
50. Ibid., p. 430.
51. Editorial, *The Times* (4 November 1830). From the Metropolitan Police Museum cuttings collection.
52. Editorial, *John Bull* (7 November 1830). From the Metropolitan Police Museum cuttings collection.
53. Publisher's note, Microfilm held in Cardiff University Arts and Social Studies Library.
54. Editorial, *John Bull* (7 November 1830).
55. Duane DeVries, *Dickens's Apprentice Years: The Making of a Novelist* (New York: Harvester Press, 1976), p. 18.
56. Charles Dickens, *Sketches by Boz, Illustrative of Every-Day Life and Every-Day People* (London: Oxford University Press, 1957 [1836–1837]), p. 47.
57. Ibid., p. 54.
58. Ibid., p. 59.
59. Ibid., p. 66.
60. Ibid., p. 69.
61. Ibid., pp. 72 and 73.
62. Ibid., p. 75.
63. Ibid.
64. Ibid., p. 135.
65. Ibid., p. 146.
66. Ibid., p. 150.
67. Ibid., p. 170.
68. Ibid., p. 186.
69. Ibid., p. 187.
70. Philip Collins, *Dickens and Crime* (London: Macmillan, 1965 [1962]), p. 2.
71. 'A Visit to Newgate' was one of the longer tales written specifically for the collected *Sketches* and was completed in November 1835. See Collins, *Dickens and Crime*, 'Newgate', pp. 27–51, pp. 40–41; and Harvey Peter Sucksmith, 'The Secret of Immediacy: Dickens's Debt to the "Tales of Terror" in *Blackwood's*', *Nineteenth-Century Fiction* 26 (1971–1972), pp. 145–157.
72. Dickens, *Sketches by Boz*, p. 199.
73. Stephen Inwood, 'Policing London's Morals: The Metropolitan Police and Popular Culture, 1829–1850', *London Journal* 15:2 (1990), pp. 129–146, p. 144.

74. Leon Radzinowicz, *A History of English Law and its Administration from 1750 Vol. IV: Grappling for Control* (London: Stevens and Sons, 1956), pp. 191–192.
75. *General Instruction Book,* pp. 1–2.
76. Cobb, *The First Detectives.*
77. Pringle, 'Introduction' in Goddard's *Memoirs of a Bow Street Runner,* p. xx.
78. R. F. Stewart, ... *And Always a Detective: Chapters on the History of Detective Fiction* (London: David and Charles, 1980), p. 126.
79. Waters, 'One Night in a Gaming-House', *Recollections of a Detective Police-Officer* (London: W. Clover, 1856), pp. 9–28, p. 9. The story originally appeared as the first 'Recollections of a Police-Officer', without the sub-title. *Chambers's Edinburgh Journal* n.s., 12:291 (28 July 1849), pp. 55–59. The collected edition of 1856 prints the 'Recollections' in the same order as and without alteration from the original serial format, and for convenience all further references will be to the collected edition. Details of original publication will be given parenthetically in the text.
80. Martin Kayman, *From Bow Street to Baker Street: Mystery, Detection, and Narrative* (London: Macmillan, 1992), p. 119.
81. Ian Ousby, *The Bloodhounds of Heaven: The Detective in English Fiction from Godwin to Doyle* (Cambridge, Mass., and London: Harvard University Press, 1976), p. 70.
82. The word 'detective' was added to the title of the collected edition, perhaps influenced by the success of Dickens's Detective Police anecdotes of 1850–1853.
83. Stewart, ... *And Always a Detective,* p. 153.
84. Louis James, *Fiction for the Working Man, 1830–1850* (Harmondsworth: Penguin University Books, 1974 [1963]), p. 17.
85. Ibid.
86. *Recollections,* p. 13.
87. Ibid., p. 12.
88. Ibid., p. 148.
89. Ibid., p. 15.
90. In 'Mary Kingsford', the brooch in question is initially described as 'diamond', but has somehow become 'a splendid emerald, encircled by large brilliants' by the time that Emily identifies it as a fake. See *Recollections of a Detective Police-Officer,* pp. 204, 208 and 210.
91. 'The Revenge', *Recollections,* p. 188.
92. *Recollections,* p. 242.
93. Ibid., p. 214.
94. Ibid., p. 241.
95. Ibid., pp. 60 and 261.
96. Ibid., note, p. 11.
97. Ibid., pp. 216–217.
98. Ibid., p. 70.
99. Russell, Preface, *Recollections,* p. v.
100. *Recollections,* pp. 11 and 34.
101. Ibid., p. 36.
102. Ibid., p. 263.
103. Ibid.

104. Ibid., p. 282.
105. Ibid., p. 12.
106. Ibid., p. 108.
107. Ibid., p. 109.
108. Ibid., p. 124.
109. Ibid., p. 125.
110. Ibid., p. 192.
111. Ibid., pp. 87–89.
112. 'The Purloined Letter', abridged, *Chambers's Edinburgh Journal* n.s., 2:48 (30 November 1844), pp. 343–347. A collection of Poe's stories, *Tales by Edgar A. Poe*, selected by Evert E. Duyckinck, which included Poe's three 'tales of ratiocination', 'The Murders in the Rue Morgue', 'The Mystery of Marie Rôget', and 'The Purloined Letter', was published in England in July 1845.
113. *Recollections*, pp. 35 and 57.
114. Ibid., p. 69.
115. Cited in Radzinowicz, *A History of English Criminal Law*, Vol. IV, p. 166.
116. *Collins' English Dictionary*.
117. *Recollections*, p. 28.
118. Anon., *Richmond*, p. 266.
119. Preface, *Recollections*, pp. vi–vii.
120. *Recollections*, p. 9.
121. Richard Altick, *The English Common Reader: A Social History of the Mass Reading Public, 1800–1900* (Columbus: Ohio State University Press, 1998 [1957]), p. 347.
122. Ibid.
123. Collins, *Dickens and Crime*, p. 219.
124. See Philip Collins, 'Dickens's Reading', *Dickensian* 60 (1964), pp. 136–151.
125. Collins, *Dickens and Crime*, p. 206.
126. Ibid., p. 206.
127. Ibid., p. 216.
128. Charles Dickens, 'A "Detective" Police Party', reprinted in *Hunted Down: The Detective Stories of Charles Dickens*, ed. by Peter Haining (London: Peter Owen, 1996), pp. 71–90, p. 73. The original was published in *Household Words* 1:18 (27 July 1850). As the articles are reprinted in Haining's text without alteration, for convenience all references will be to that edition. Dates of the originals are given parenthetically in the text.
129. W. H. Wills, 'The Modern Science of Thief-Taking', *Hunted Down*, pp. 61–70, p. 61.
130. Ibid., p. 70.
131. Ibid., p. 61.
132. Ibid., p. 66.
133. Ibid., pp. 68–69.
134. Ibid., p. 67.
135. Dickens, 'A "Detective" Police Party', *Hunted Down*, p. 71.
136. Ibid.
137. Ibid. The term 'penny-a-liners' refers to the hack journalists of the time.
138. Ibid., p. 73.
139. Ibid.
140. Ibid., pp. 73–74.

141. Ibid., p. 74.
142. Ibid.
143. See the introductory preamble to 'The Murders in the Rue Morgue', in *Poe's Tales of Mystery and Imagination* (London: Dent, 1968), pp. 378–381.
144. Poe, 'The Murders in the Rue Morgue', p. 380.
145. Charles Martel acknowledged his debt to Dickens's depiction of Field when he dedicated *The Detective's Notebook* (1860) to the then recently retired Inspector Field. William Russell's *Experiences of a Real Detective* (1862) implicitly pays homage to Field in naming its detective 'Inspector F'.
146. Dickens, *Bleak House* (Harmondsworth: Penguin, 1996 [1853]), p. 355.
147. Ibid., p. 722.
148. Ibid., p. 813.
149. Doyle, *A Study in Scarlet*, p. 23.

Conclusion

1. Stephen Knight, *Crime Fiction 1800–2000: Detection, Death, Diversity* (Basingstoke: Palgrave Macmillan, 2004), p. 36.
2. James McLevy, *Curiosities of Crime in Edinburgh* (Edinburgh: William P. Nimmo, 1861), and *The Sliding Scale of Life: or, Thirty Years' Observations of Falling Men and Women in Edinburgh* (Edinburgh: William P. Nimmo, 1861) and simultaneously (London: Houlston and Wright, 1861).
3. Cited in R. F. Stewart, ... *And Always a Detective: Chapters on the History of Detective Fiction* (Newton Abbot: David and Charles, 1980), p. 159.
4. Review of *The Sliding Scale of Life* in the *Athenaeum*, 24 August 1861.
5. Arthur Conan Doyle, *Memories and Adventures* (Oxford: Oxford University Press, 1989 [1924]), pp. 74–75.

Bibliography

Primary sources

Where texts have appeared in periodicals prior to publication in collected editions, I have given the collected volume details in the bibliography. Details of periodical publication are given in the body of the text. These collected editions are indicated in the bibliography with *.

Anon., 'Cautionary Hints to Speculators on the Increase of Crime', *Blackwood's Edinburgh Magazine* 3:14 (May 1818), pp. 176–178.

——, 'The Forgers', *Blackwood's Edinburgh Magazine* 9:53 (August 1821), pp. 572–577.

——, 'Hints for Jurymen', *Blackwood's Edinburgh Magazine* 13:78 (June 1823), pp. 673–685.

——, 'Beck and Dunlop on Medical Jurisprudence', *Blackwood's Edinburgh Magazine* 17:98 (March 1825), pp. 351–352.

——, *Richmond: Scenes in the Life of a Bow Street Runner, Drawn Up From His Private Memoranda*, ed. and intro. E. F. Bleiler (New York: Dover, 1976 [1827]).

——, 'The New Police', *New Monthly Magazine* 26:108 (November 1829), pp. 426–432.

——, 'The Incendiary', *Chambers's Edinburgh Journal* 17:446 (5 June 1852), pp. 355–360.

——, 'Criminal Returns', 'Metropolitan Police 1850', 'Metropolitan Police and Police Courts' Accounts 1850', *Edinburgh Review* 95:195 (July–October 1852), pp. 1–33.

——, *The Experiences of a Barrister, and Confessions of an Attorney*, attrib. to Samuel Warren (New York: Arno Press, 1976 [1859])*.

——, *A Collection of Miscellaneous Broadsides, Consisting Chiefly of Almanacks and Accounts of Criminal Trials 1801–1858*, held in the British Library.

Braddon, Mary Elizabeth, *Lady Audley's Secret*, ed. and intro. David Skilton (Oxford: Oxford University Press, 1987).

Bulwer-Lytton, Edward, *Pelham: or, The Adventures of a Gentleman* (London: Henry Colburn, 1833 [1828]).

——, Edward, *Paul Clifford* (London: Waverley Book Co., 1848 [1830]).

——, Edward, *Eugene Aram* (London: George Routledge and Sons, 1849 [1832]).

Chadwick, Edwin, 'Preventive Police', *The London Review* 1:1 (30 January 1829), pp. 252–308.

Cleaves Weekly Police Gazette 1834–36. Incomplete set held on microfiche, Arts and Social Studies Library, Cardiff University.

Collins, Wilkie, *The Woman in White*, ed. and intro. Julian Symons (Harmondsworth: Penguin, 1985 [1859–1860]).

——, *The Moonstone*, ed. and intro. J. I. M. Stewart (Harmondsworth: Penguin, 1986 [1868]).

——, *Mad Monkton and Other Stories*, ed. and intro. Norman Page (Oxford: Oxford University Press, 1994).

Crowe, Catherine, *Susan Hopley; or, The Adventures of a Maid-Servant* (Edinburgh: William Tate, 1842).

Cult Criminals: The Newgate Novels 1830–47, ed. Juliet John (London: Routledge, 1998).

Defoe, Daniel, *The True and Genuine Account of the Life and Actions of the Late Jonathan Wild* (1725), in Henry Fielding, *Jonathan Wild*, ed. David Nokes (London: Penguin, 1986), pp. 225–227.

De Quincey, Thomas, 'On Murder Considered as One of the Fine Arts', *Blackwood's Edinburgh Magazine* 21:122 (February 1827), pp. 140–163.

——, 'Murder Considered as One of the Fine Arts', *Blackwood's Edinburgh Magazine* 45:289 (November 1839), pp. 661–668.

——, 'Postscript', in *The Collected Writings of Thomas De Quincey, Vol. 13, Tales and Phantasies*, ed. David Masson (London: Adam and Charles Black, 1897), pp. 70–124.

Dickens, Charles, 'A "Detective" Police Party' Pt I, *Household Words* 1:18 (27 July 1850), pp. 409–414.

——, 'A "Detective" Police Party' Pt II, *Household Words* 1:20 (10 August 1850), pp. 457–460.

——, 'Three "Detective" Anecdotes', *Household Words* 1:25 (14 September 1850), pp. 557–580.

——, 'On Duty with Inspector Field', *Household Words* 3:64 (14 June 1851), pp. 265–270.

——, 'Down with the Tide', *Household Words* 6:150 (5 February 1853), pp. 481–485.

——, *Sketches by Boz, Illustrative of Every-Day Life and Every-Day People* (London: Oxford University Press, 1957 [1836–1837]).

——, *Bleak House* (Harmondsworth: Penguin, 1996 [1853]).

——, *Hunted Down: The Detective Stories of Charles Dickens*, ed. Peter Haining (London: Peter Owen, 1996)*.

Dickens, Charles and W. H. Wills, 'The Metropolitan Protectives', *Household Words* 3:57 (26 April 1851), pp. 97–105.

Doyle, Arthur Conan, *A Study in Scarlet* (Harmondsworth: Penguin, 1981 [1887]).

Forrester, Andrew, *Revelations of a Detective* (London: Ward Lock, 1863).

——, *The Female Detective* (London: Ward Lock, 1864).

Galt, John, 'The Buried Alive', *Blackwood's Edinburgh Magazine* 10:56 (October 1821), pp. 262–264.

Hayward, W. S., *The Experiences of a Lady Detective* (London: Charles Henry Clarke, 1864).

Hindley, Charles (ed.), *Curiosities of Street Literature* (London: Seven Dials Press, 1969 [1871]).

MacNish, Robert, 'The Metempsychosis', *Blackwood's Edinburgh Magazine* 19:112 (May 1826), pp. 511–529.

——, 'An Execution in Paris', *Blackwood's Edinburgh Magazine* 24:146 (December 1828), pp. 785–788.

Maginn, William, 'The Man in the Bell', *Blackwood's Edinburgh Magazine* 10:57 (November 1821), pp. 373–375.

McLevy, James, *Curiosities of Crime in Edinburgh* (Edinburgh: William P. Nimmo, 1861).

——, *The Sliding Scale of Life; or, Thirty Years' Observations of Falling Men and Women in Edinburgh* (Edinburgh: William P. Nimmo, 1861).

——, *The Casebook of a Victorian Detective*, ed. and intro. George Scott-Moncrieff (Edinburgh: Canongate, 1975).

Poe, Edgar Allan, *Tales of Mystery and Imagination* (London: Dent, 1968).

Post, Melville D., 'The Corpus Delicti', *The Strange Schemes of Randolph Mason* (Westport, Conn.: Hyperion Press, 1975 [1896]), pp. 13–67.

Robinson, David, 'The Local Government of the Metropolis, and Other Populous Places', *Blackwood's Edinburgh Magazine* 29:175 (January 1831), pp. 82–104.

Russell, William ('Waters'), *Recollections of a Detective Police-Officer* (London: W. Clover and Sons, 1856)*.

—— ('Waters'), *Leaves from the Diary of a Law Clerk* (London: J & C Brown, 1857).

Sandford, David Keyte, 'A Night in the Catacombs', *Blackwood's Edinburgh Magazine* 4:19 (October 1818), pp. 19–23.

Stephen, Sir George, *Adventures of an Attorney in Search of Practice* (London: Saunders and Otley, 1839 [1835]).

Thomson, Henry, 'Le Revenant', *Blackwood's Edinburgh Magazine* 23:124 (April 1827), pp. 409–416.

Warren, Samuel, 'The Bracelets', *Blackwood's Edinburgh Magazine* 31:1 (January 1832), pp. 39–53.

——, *A Popular and Practical Introduction to Law Studies* (London: William Blackwood, 1835).

——, 'My First Circuit: Law and Facts from the North', *Blackwood's Edinburgh Magazine* 44:273 (July 1838), pp. 57–93.

——, *Passages from the Diary of a Late Physician* (Edinburgh and London: William Blackwood, 1842 [1838])*.

——, 'Who is the Murderer? A Problem in the Law of Circumstantial Evidence', *Blackwood's Edinburgh Magazine* 51:319 (May 1842), pp. 553–578.

——, *Miscellanies Critical, Imaginative, and Juridical*, 2 Vols (Edinburgh: William Blackwood and Sons, 1855).

——, 'The Mystery of Murder, and its Defence', in *Miscellanies Critical, Imaginative, and Juridical*, Vol. 2 (Edinburgh: William Blackwood and Sons, 1855), pp. 1–68.

Wight, John, *Mornings at Bow Street: A Selection of the Most Entertaining Reports Which Have Appeared in the Morning Herald* (London: George Routledge and Sons, 1875 [1824]).

Wills, W. H., 'The Modern Science of Thief-Taking', *Household Words* 1:16 (13 July 1850).

Wilson, John, 'Extracts from Gosschen's Diary', *Blackwood's Edinburgh Magazine* 3:17 (August 1818), pp. 596–598.

——, 'Expiation', *Blackwood's Edinburgh Magazine* 28:172 (October 1830), pp. 628–643.

Secondary sources

Anon., 'Recent Novels and Tales', *Monthly Review* n.s., 2 (June 1827), pp. 271–279.

——, 'The Young Surgeon', *New Monthly Magazine* 25 (1829), pp. 345–352 and pp. 458–465; 26 (1829), pp. 11–26.

——, 'Some Passages from the Diary of a Late Fashionable Apothecary', *New Monthly Magazine* 31 (September 1831), pp. 233–241.

——, 'Review of *A Popular and Practical Introduction to Law Studies* by Samuel Warren', *Quarterly Review* 56:112 (July 1836), pp. 521–530.

——, 'The Increase of Crime', *Blackwood's Edinburgh Magazine* 55:343 (May 1844), pp. 533–545.

——, *Tales by a Barrister* (London: Chapman & Hall, 1844).

Adburgham, Alison, *Silver Fork Society: Fashionable Life and Literature from 1814 to 1840* (London: Constable, 1983).

Alexander, J. H., '*Blackwood's Magazine* as a Romantic Form', *Wordsworth Circle* 15 (1984), pp. 51–68.

Allen, Michael, *Poe and the British Magazine Tradition* (New York and Oxford: Oxford University Press, 1969).

Althusser, Louis, 'Ideology and Ideological State Apparatuses (Notes Towards an Investigation)', in *Lenin and Philosophy and Other Essays*, trans. Ben Brewster (New York: Monthly Review Press, 1971), pp. 121–173.

Altick, Richard, *The English Common Reader: A Social History of the Mass Reading Public, 1800–1900* (Columbus: Ohio State University Press, 1998 [1957]).

——, *Victorian Studies in Scarlet* (London: Dent, 1972).

Ascari, Maurizio (ed.), *Two Centuries of Detective Fiction: A New Comparative Approach* (COTEPRA: University of Bologna, 2000).

Ascoli, David, *The Queen's Peace: The Origin and Development of the Metropolitan Police 1829–1979* (London: Hamish Hamilton, 1979).

Barker, Hannah, *Newspapers, Politics, and English Society 1689–1855* (Harlow: Longman, 2000).

Bell, Ian A., *Literature and Crime in Augustan England* (New York and London: Routledge, 1991).

Bentham, Jeremy, *Works*, Vol. IV (Edinburgh: William Tate, 1843).

Black, Joel, *The Aesthetics of Murder: A Study in Romantic Literature and Contemporary Culture* (Baltimore and London: Johns Hopkins University Press, 1991).

Bloom, Clive (ed.), *Nineteenth-Century Suspense: From Poe to Conan Doyle* (New York: St Martin's Press, 1988).

Botting, Fred, *Gothic* (London and New York: Routledge, 1996).

Brake, Laurel, 'Criticism and the Victorian Periodical Press', in *Subjugated Knowledges: Journalism, Gender and Literature in the Nineteenth Century* (Basingstoke: Macmillan, 1994), pp. 1–35.

Brake, Laurel, Aled Jones and Lionel Madden (eds), *Investigating Victorian Journalism* (Basingstoke: Macmillan, 1990).

Brantlinger, Patrick, *The Spirit of Reform: British Literature and Politics 1832–1867* (Cambridge, Mass., and London: Harvard University Press, 1977).

——, 'What is Sensational about the "Sensation Novel"?', *Nineteenth-Century Fiction* 37:2 (1982), pp. 1–28.

——, 'The Case of the Poisonous Book: Mass Literacy as Threat in Nineteenth-Century British Fiction', *Victorian Review* 20:2 (Winter 1994), pp. 117–133.

Briggs, John, Christopher Harrison, Angus McInnes and David Vincent (eds), *Crime and Punishment in England: An Introductory History* (London: University College London Press, 1996).

Brown, Lucy, *Victorian Novels and Newspapers* (Oxford: Clarendon Press, 1985).

Burke, Thomas, 'The Obsequies of Mr. Williams: New Light on De Quincey's Famous Tale of Murder', *The Bookman* 68:3 (November 1928), pp. 257–263.

Campbell, Duncan, 'The Murd'rous Sublime: De Quincey and the Ratcliffe Highway Killings', in *The Art of Murder: New Essays on Detective Fiction*, eds H. Gustav Klaus and Stephen Knight (Tübingen: Stauffenburg, 1998), pp. 26–37.

Carter, John (ed.), *New Paths in Book Collecting: Essays by Various Hands* (London: Constable, 1943).

Cobb, Belton, *The First Detectives and the Early Career of Richard Mayne, Commissioner* (London: Faber & Faber, 1962).

Cockburn, J. S. (ed.), *Crime in England 1550–1800* (London: Methuen, 1977).

Collins, Philip, *Dickens and Crime* (London: Macmillan, 1965 [1962]).

——, 'Dickens's Reading', *The Dickensian* 60 (1964), pp. 136–151.

Colquhoun, Patrick, *A Treatise on the Police of the Metropolis* (London: n.p., 1806 [1796]).

——, *A Treatise on the Commerce and Police of the River Thames* (London: n.p., 1806 [1800]).

Critchley, T. A. and P. D. James, *The Maul and the Pear Tree: The Ratcliffe Highway Murders 1811* (Harmondsworth: Penguin, 1990 [1971]).

Dalziel, Margaret, *Popular Fiction 100 Years Ago: An Unexplored Tract of Literary History* (London: Cohen and West, 1957).

Davis, Lennard, *Factual Fictions: The Origins of the English Novel* (Philadelphia: University of Pennsylvania Press, 1996 [1983]).

——, *Resisting Novels: Ideology and Fiction* (London and New York: Methuen, 1987).

Davis, Sandra, *Law Breaking and Law Enforcement: The Creation of a Criminal Class in Mid-Victorian London* (Unpublished doctoral dissertation, Boston College, 1985).

Delamater, Jerome H. and Ruth Prigozy (eds), *Theory and Practice of Classic Detective Fiction* (Westport, Conn. and London: Greenwood Press, 1997).

DeVries, Duane, *Dickens's Apprentice Years: The Making of a Novelist* (New York: Harvester Press, 1976).

Dove, George N., *The Reader and the Detective Story* (Bowling Green, Ohio: Bowling Green State University Popular Press, 1997).

Drexler, Peter, 'Von der Kriminalerzälung zur *Detective Story*: Medialer Kontext und politische Tendenz', *Literatur, Recht, Kriminalität: Untersuchungen zur Vorgeschichte des englischen Detektivromans 1830–1890* (Frankfurt: Peter Lang, 1991), pp. 91–136 (trans. B. Hubbard, ed. H. Worthington; trans. approved by author).

Dunlop, C. R. B., 'Samuel Warren: A Victorian Law and Literature Practitioner', *Cardozo Studies in Law and Literature* 12:2 (Fall–Winter 2000), pp. 265–291.

During, Simon, *Foucault and Literature: Towards a Genealogy of Writing* (London and New York: Routledge, 1992).

Ellegard, Alvar, *The Readership of the Periodical Press in Mid-Victorian Britain* (Göteborg: n.p., 1957).

Emsley, Clive, *Policing and its Context 1750–1870* (London: Macmillan, 1985).

——, *Crime and Society in England 1750–1900* (London: Longman, 1996 [1987]).

——, *The English Police: A Social and Political History* (London: Addison, Wesley, Longman, 1996 [1991]).

Emsley, Clive and Louis A. Knafla, *Crime Histories and Histories of Crime: Studies in the Historiography of Crime and Criminal Justice in Modern History* (Westport, Conn. and London: Greenwood Press, 1996).

Finkelstein, David, *The House of Blackwood: Author–Publisher Relations in the Victorian Era* (Pennsylvania: Pennsylvania State University Press, 2002).

Fisher, Benjamin F., 'Poe in Great Britain', in *Poe Abroad: Influence, Reputation, Affinities*, ed. Lois Davis Vines (Iowa City: University of Iowa Press, 1999), pp. 52–61.

Fitzgerald, P., *Chronicles of Bow Street Police Station*, 2 Vols (London: Chapman & Hall, 1888).

Foucault, Michel, *Madness and Civilization: A History of Insanity in the Age of Reason*, trans. Richard Howard (London: Routledge, 1971 [1967]).

——, *The Birth of the Clinic: An Archaeology of Medical Perception*, trans. A. M. Sheridan Smith (London: Tavistock, 1973 [1963]).

——, *Power/Knowledge: Selected Interviews and Other Writings 1972–1977*, trans. Colin Gordon *et al.*, ed. Colin Gordon (London: Longman, 1980).

——, *Politics, Philosophy, Culture: Interviews and Other Writings 1977–1984*, trans. Alan Sheridan *et al.*, ed. and intro. Lawrence D. Kritzman (London: Routledge, 1988).

——, *Discipline and Punish: The Birth of the Prison*, trans. Alan Sheridan (Harmondsworth: Penguin, 1991 [1997]).

French, Stanley, *River Court: An Early History of Thames Magistrates' Court* (Pamphlet, undated, held at the Thames River Police Museum, Wapping, London).

Freud, Sigmund, 'Psychoanalysis and the Establishment of Facts in Legal Proceedings', in *The Complete Psychological Works of Sigmund Freud*, Vol. IX, trans. James Strachey (London: Hogarth Press, 1959).

Gatrell, V. A. C., Bruce Lenman and Geoffrey Parker (eds), *Crime and the Law: The Social History of Crime in Western Europe since 1500* (London: Europa, 1980).

Gatrell, V. A. C., *The Hanging Tree: Execution and the English People 1170–1868* (Oxford: Oxford University Press, 1994).

Gilbert, Elliot L., 'The Detective as Metaphor in the Nineteenth Century', *Journal of Popular Culture* 3 (Winter 1967), pp. 256–262.

Goddard, Henry, *Memoirs of a Bow Street Runner*, ed. and intro. Patrick Pringle (London: Museum Press, 1956).

Goldman, Albert, *The Mine and the Mint: Sources for the Writings of Thomas De Quincey* (Carbondale and Edwardsville: Southern Illinois University Press, 1965).

Gretton, Thomas (ed.), *Murders and Moralities: English Catchpenny Prints 1800–1860* (London: British Museum Press, 1980).

Groom, Nick (ed.), *The Bloody Register: Crime and Misdemeanours in the Eighteenth Century* (London: Routledge, 1999).

Harris, Wendell V., 'English Short Fiction in the Nineteenth Century', *Studies in Short Fiction* 6 (1968–1969), pp. 1–93.

——, *British Short Fiction in the Nineteenth Century: A Literary and Bibliographic Guide* (Detroit: Wayne State University Press, 1979).

Harrison, James A. (ed.), *The Complete Works of Edgar Allan Poe, Vol. X: Literary Criticism Vol. III* (New York: AMS Press, 1965).

Haycraft, Howard (ed.), Intro. Robin W. Winks, *The Art of the Mystery Story: A Collection of Critical Essays* (New York: Carroll and Graf, 1992 [1948]).

Hilfer, Tony, *The Crime Novel: A Deviant Genre* (Austin: University of Texas Press, 1990).

Hollingsworth, Keith, *The Newgate Novel 1830–47: Bulwer, Ainsworth, Dickens and Thackeray* (Detroit: Wayne State University Press, 1963).

Houghton, Walter, *The Victorian State of Mind, 1830–1870* (New Haven and London: Yale University Press, 1957).

—— (ed.), *The Wellesley Index to Victorian Periodicals 1824–1900* (Toronto: University of Toronto Press, 1966).

Hühn, Peter, 'The Detective as Reader: Narrativity and Reading Concepts in Detective Fiction', *Modern Fiction Studies* 33 (1987), pp. 451–466.

Hutter, Albert D., 'Dreams, Transformations, and Literature: The Implications of Detective Fiction', *Victorian Studies* 19:2 (December 1975), pp. 180–209.

Hutter, Albert D. and Mary W. Miller, ' "Who Can Be Trusted?": *The Detective*, An Early Journal of Detection', *Mystery and Detection Annual* 23 (1973), pp. 167–192.

Inwood, Stephen, 'Policing London's Morals: The Metropolitan Police and Popular Culture 1829–1850, *The London Journal* 15:2 (1990), pp. 129–146.

Jack, Ian, *English Literature 1815–1832* (Oxford: Oxford University Press, 1963).

Jacobs, Edward, 'Bloods in the Street: London Street Culture, "Industrial Literacy", and the Emergence of Mass Culture in Victorian England', *Nineteenth-Century Contexts* 18 (1995), pp. 321–347.

James, Louis, *Fiction for the Working Man 1830–1850* (Harmondsworth: Penguin University Books, 1974 [1963]).

——, 'The View from Brick Lane: Perspectives in Working-Class and Middle-Class Fiction of the Early Victorian Period', in *The Social Context of Early Victorian Britain*, ed. Louis James (Columbia: Columbia University Press, 1976), pp. 87–101.

Jenkins, Alice and Juliet John (eds), *Rereading Victorian Fiction* (London: Macmillan, 2000).

John, Juliet and Alice Jenkins (eds), *Rethinking Victorian Culture* (London: Macmillan, 2000).

Jones, D. V. D., 'The New Police, Crime and People in England and Wales, 1829–1888', *Transactions of the Royal Historical Society* 5:33 (1983), pp. 151–168.

Jordan, John O. and Robert L. Patten (eds), *Literature in the Marketplace: Nineteenth-Century British Publishing and Reading Practices* (Cambridge: Cambridge University Press, 1995).

Joyce, Simon Paul, *The Closed Text Mystery: The Police, Crime Fiction, and Popular Culture Between 1790–1848* (Unpublished doctoral thesis, New York State University, 1993).

Kalikoff, Beth, *Murder and Moral Decay in Victorian Popular Literature* (Michigan: University of Michigan Press, 1986).

Kayman, Martin, *From Bow Street to Baker Street: Mystery, Detection, and Narrative* (London: Macmillan, 1992).

Kirk, Harry, *Portrait of a Profession: A History of the Solicitor's Profession, 1100 to the Present Day* (London: Oyez, 1976).

Knight, Stephen, *Form and Ideology in Crime Fiction* (Bloomington: Indiana University Press, 1980).

——, 'Enter the Detective', in *The Art of Murder: New Essays on Detective Fiction*, eds H. Gustav Klaus and Stephen Knight (Tübingen: Stauffenburg, 1998), pp. 10–26.

——, *Crime Fiction 1800–2000: Detection, Death, Diversity* (Basingstoke: Palgrave Macmillan, 2004).

Landrum, Larry, Pat Browne and Ray B. Browne (eds), *Dimensions of Detective Fiction* (New York: Popular Press, 1976).

Langland, Elizabeth, *Nobody's Angels: Middle-class Women and Domestic Ideology in Victorian Culture* (Ithaca and London: Cornell University Press, 1995).

Laqueur, Thomas W., 'Crowds, Carnival and the State in English Executions', in *The First Modern Society: Essays in English History in Honour of Lawrence Stone*, eds A. L. Beier, D. Cannadine and J. Rosenheim (Cambridge: Cambridge University Press, 1989).

Lehman, David, *The Perfect Murder: A Study in Detection* (Michigan: University of Michigan Press, 2000).

Liddle, Dallas, 'Salesmen, Sportsmen, Mentors: Anonymity and Mid-Victorian Theories of Journalism', *Victorian Studies* 41:1 (Autumn 1997), pp. 53–90.

Lindop, Grevel, *The Opium-Eater: A Life of Thomas De Quincey* (London: Dent, 1981).

Linebaugh, Peter, *The London Hanged: Crime and Civil Society in the Eighteenth Century* (Harmondsworth: Penguin, 1991).

Lohrli, Anne (comp.), *Household Words: A Weekly Journal 1850–1854 Conducted by Charles Dickens: Contents, Contributors, Contributions* (Toronto: University of Toronto Press, 1973).

Macherey, Pierre, *A Theory of Literary Production*, trans. Geoffrey Wall (London: Routledge, 1978).

MacKenzie, William, 'An Appeal to the Public and the Legislature, on the Necessity of Affording Dead Bodies to the Schools of Anatomy by Legislative Enactment', *Westminster Review* 2 (July–October 1824), pp. 59–97.

Magistrale, Tony and Sidney Poger (eds), *Poe's Children: Connections Between Tales of Terror and Detection* (New York: Peter Lang, 1999).

Maidment, Brian E., 'Magazines of Popular Progress and the Artisans', *Victorian Periodicals Review* 17 (1983), pp. 83–94.

Mandel, Ernest, *Delightful Murder: A Social History of the Crime Story* (Minneapolis: University of Minnesota Press, 1986).

Mansel, H. L., 'Sensation Novels', *Quarterly Review* (April 1863), pp. 480–513.

Masson, David (ed.), *The Collected Writings of Thomas De Quincey, Vol. X: Literary Theory and Criticism* (Edinburgh: Adam and Charles Black, 1890).

Maxwell, Richard C., 'G. M. Reynolds, Dickens, and the Mysteries of London', *Nineteenth-Century Fiction* 32:2 (1977), pp. 188–213.

Mayhew, Henry, *London Labour and the London Poor Vol. I: The London Street Folk* (London: Frank Cass, 1967 [1851]).

Mayo, Robert D., 'Gothic Romance in the Magazines', *Publications of the Modern Languages Association* 65 (1950), pp. 762–789.

McGowan, Randall, 'Getting to Know the Criminal Class in Nineteenth-Century England', *Nineteenth-Century Contexts* 14:1 (January 1990), pp. 33–54.

McLellan, M. Faith, 'Images of Physicians in Literature: From Quacks to Heroes', *The Lancet* 348:9025 (17 August 1996), pp. 1–5.

Mercer, Colin, 'Entertainment, or the Policing of Virtue', *New Formations* 4 (Spring 1988), pp. 51–71.

Miller, D. A., *The Novel and the Police* (Berkeley: University of California Press, 1988).

Moretti, Franco, 'Clues', in *Signs Taken for Wonders: Essays in the Sociology of Literary Forms*, trans. Susan Fischer (London: Verso, 1983), pp. 130–156.

Morrison, Robert and Chris Baldick (eds), *Tales of Terror from Blackwood's Magazine* (Oxford and New York: Oxford University Press, 1995).

Mort, Frank, *Dangerous Sexualities: Medico-Moral Politics in England Since 1830* (London and New York: Routledge, 2000 [1987]).

Most, Glenn W. and William W. Stowe (eds), *The Poetics of Murder: Detective Fiction and Literary Theory* (San Diego, New York and London: Harcourt Brace Jovanovich, 1983).

Murch, A. E., *The Development of the Detective Novel* (London: Peter Owen, 1968 [1958]).

Murphy, Paul T., *Toward a Working-Class Canon: Literary Criticism in British Working-Class Periodicals 1816–1858* (Columbus: Ohio State University Press, 1994).

Neocleus, Mark, *The Fabrication of Social Order: A Critical Theory of Police Power* (London: Pluto Press, 2000).

Neuberg, Victor, *Popular Literature: A History and Guide* (Harmondsworth: Penguin, 1977).

Novak, Maximillian, 'Appearance of Truth: The Literature of Crime as a Narrative System (1660–1841)', *Yearbook of English Studies* 11 (1981), pp. 29–48.

Ousby, Ian, *Bloodhounds of Heaven: The Detective in English Fiction from Godwin to Doyle* (Cambridge, Mass., and London: Harvard University Press, 1976).

Parry, Noel and José Parry, *The Rise of the Medical Profession: A Study of Collective Social Mobility* (London: Croom Helm, 1976).

Peterson, Ted, 'British Crime Pamphleteers: Forgotten Journalists', *Journalism Quarterly* 4:22 (December 1945), pp. 305–316.

Philips, David, *Crime and Authority in Victorian England: The Black Country 1835–1860* (London: Croom Helm, 1977).

Phillips, Walter C., *Dickens, Reade and Collins, Sensation Novelists: A Study in the Condition and Theories of Novel Writing in Victorian England* (New York: Columbia University Press, 1919).

Plotz, Judith, 'On Guilt Considered as One of the Fine Arts: De Quincey's Criminal Imagination', *Wordsworth Circle* 19:2 (1988), pp. 83–88.

Pollit, Charles, *De Quincey's Editorship of the Westmorland Gazette* (Kendal and London: n.p., 1890).

Poole, William F., *Poole's Index to Periodical Literature 1802–1881* (Gloucester, Mass.: Peter Smith, 1963 [1882]).

Poovey, Mary, *Making a Social Body: British Cultural Formation 1830–64* (Chicago and London: Chicago University Press, 1995).

Porter, Dennis, *The Pursuit of Crime: Art and Ideology in Detective Fiction* (New Haven and London: Yale University Press, 1981).

Porter, Roy, *Bodies Politic: Disease, Death, and Doctors in Britain, 1650–1900* (London: Reaktion Books, 2001).

Priestman, Martin, *Detective Fiction and Literature: The Figure in the Carpet* (London: Macmillan, 1990).

Punter, David, *Gothic Pathologies: The Text, the Body, and the Law* (Basingstoke: Macmillan, 1998).

Pykett, Lyn (ed.), *The Sensation Novel: From* The Woman in White *to* The Moonstone (Plymouth: Northcote House, 1994).

Radzinowicz, Leon, *A History of English Criminal Law and its Administration from 1750 Vol. II: The Clash Between Private Initiative and Public Interest in the Enforcement of the Law* (London: Stevens and Sons, 1956).

——, *A History of English Criminal Law and its Administration from 1750 Vol. IV: Grappling for Control* (London: Stevens and Sons, 1968).

Rawlings, Philip (ed.), *Drunks, Whores and Idle Apprentices: Criminal Biographies of the Eighteenth Century* (London: Routledge, 1992).

Rowan, Charles and Richard Mayne, *General Instruction Book* (London, 1829).

Rudé, George, *Criminal and Victim: Crime and Society in Nineteenth-Century England* (Oxford: Clarendon Press, 1985).

Sadleir, Michael, *XIX Century Fiction: A Bibliographical Record Based on His Own Collection*, 2 Vols (London: Constable, 1951).

——, *Things Past* (London: Constable, 1944).

Samet, Elizabeth Dale, ' "When Constabulary Duty's To Be Done": Dickens and the Metropolitan Police', *Dickens Studies Annual* 27 (1998), pp. 131–143.

Sayers, Dorothy L., 'Introduction', in *Great Short Stories of Detection, Mystery and Horror*, 1st Series, ed. Dorothy L. Sayers (London: Victor Gollancz, 1928).

Shattock, Joanne and Michael Wolff, *The Victorian Press: Samples and Soundings* (Leicester: Leicester University Press, 1982).

Shepard, Leslie, *The History of Street Literature* (Newton Abbot: David and Charles, 1973).

Sinclair, Struan, *The Attribution of Blame in Detective Fiction from the Newgate Calendar to the Whodunit* (Unpublished doctoral thesis, Cardiff University, 2000).

Smith, Philip Thurmond, *Policing Victorian London: Political Policing, Public Order, and the London Metropolitan Police* (Westport, Conn. and London: Greenwood Press, 1985).

Snyder, Robert Lance (ed.), *Thomas De Quincey: Bicentenary Studies* (Norman and London: University of Oklahoma Press, 1985).

Stephen, Sir Leslie and Sir Sidney Lee (eds), *Dictionary of National Biography*, Vol. XX (Oxford: Oxford University Press, 1917).

Stewart, R. F., . . . *And Always a Detective: Chapters in the History of Detective Fiction* (Newton Abbot: David and Charles, 1980).

Storch, Robert D., 'The Plague of Blue Locusts: Police Reform and Popular Resistance in Northern England, 1840–57', in *Crime and Society: Readings in History and Theory*, comp. Mike Fitzgerald, Gregor McLennan and Jennie Pawson (London: Routledge, 1981), pp. 86–115.

Sucksmith, H. P., 'The Secret of Immediacy: Dickens's Debt to the Tale of Terror in Blackwood's', *Nineteenth-Century Fiction* 26 (1971–1972), pp. 145–157.

Sullivan, Alvin (ed.), *British Literary Magazines, Vol. II: The Romantic Age 1789–1836* (Westport, Conn. and London: Greenwood Press, 1983).

Sullivan, Margot Ann, *Murder and Art: Thomas De Quincey and the Ratcliffe Highway Murders* (New York and London: Garland Pubns, 1987).

Sutherland, John, 'Publishing History', *Critical Inquiry* 14 (1988), pp. 574–589.

——, *Victorian Fiction: Writers, Publishers, Readers* (Basingstoke: Macmillan, 1995).

Symons, Jelinger, *Tactics for the Times: As Regards the Condition and Treatment of the Dangerous Classes*, ed. Martin J. Wiener (New York and London: Garland Press, 1984 [1849]).

Symons, Julian, *Bloody Murder: From the Detective Story to the Crime Novel—a History* (Harmondsworth: Penguin, 1974 [1972]).

Taylor, David, *The New Police in Nineteenth-Century England: Crime, Conflict and Control* (Manchester and New York: Manchester University Press, 1997).

Thackeray, William M., 'Going to See a Man Hanged', *Fraser's Magazine* 22 (August 1840), pp. 150–158.

Thomas, Donald, *The Victorian Underworld* (London: John Murray, 1999 [1998]).

Thomas, Ronald R., *Detective Fiction and the Rise of Forensic Science* (Cambridge: Cambridge University Press, 1999).

Tobias, J. J., *Crime and Police in England 1700–1900* (Dublin: Gill and Macmillan, 1979).

——, *Nineteenth-Century Crime: Prevention and Punishment* (Newton Abbot: David and Charles, 1972).

——, 'Police and Public in the United Kingdom', *Journal of Contemporary History* 7:1–2 (January–April 1972), pp. 201–220.

Todorov, Tzvetan, *The Poetics of Prose*, trans. Richard Howard (Oxford: Blackwell's, 1977).

Topp, Chester W., *Victorian Yellowbacks and Paperbacks, 1849–1905*, 3 Vols (Denver: Hermitage Antiquarian Bookshop, 1993–1999).

Vann, J. Don and Rosemary T. Van Arsdel (eds), *Victorian Periodicals: A Guide to Research* (New York: Modern Languages Association, 1978).

—— (eds), *Victorian Periodicals and Victorian Society* (Toronto: University of Toronto Press, 1995).

Vicinus, Martha, *The Industrial Muse: A Study of Nineteenth-Century British Working-Class Literature* (London: Croom Helm, 1974).

Victorian Detective Fiction: A Catalogue of the Collection Made by Dorothy Glover and Graham Greene, ed. Eric Osborne and intro. John Carter (London: Bodley Head, 1966).

Walsh, John, *Poe The Detective: The Curious Circumstances Behind The Mystery of Marie Rogêt* (New Brunswick: Rutgers University Press, 1986).

Webb, R. K., *The Working-Class Reader 1790–1848: Literary and Social Tension* (New York: Augustus M. Kelly, 1971 [1955]).

——, 'The Victorian Reading Public', *Universities Quarterly* 12 (1957), pp. 24–44.

Welsh, Alexander, *Strong Representations: Narrative and Circumstantial Evidence in England* (Baltimore: Johns Hopkins University Press, 1992).

Wiener, Martin, *Reconstructing the Criminal: Culture, Law, and Policy in England 1830–1914* (Cambridge: Cambridge University Press, 1994 [1990]).

Winks, Robin (ed.), *Detective Fiction: A Collection of Critical Essays* (Vermont: Countryman Press, 1988).

Winks, Robin and Maureen Corrigan (eds), *Mystery and Suspense Writers: The Literature of Crime, Detection, and Espionage* (New York: Scribner, 1998).

Wynter, Andrew, 'The Police and the Thieves', *Quarterly Review* 99 (1856), pp. 160–200.

York, Samuel, *Samuel Warren: An Early Contributor to Victorian Literature* (Unpublished doctoral thesis, University of Washington, 1956).

Index

Ainsworth, William Harrison   29
Altick, Richard   8, 74, 160
'An Account of a Family Predisposition
   to Haemorrhage'   22
Angel in the House   56
Annual Register   138
Aram, Eugene   73
Aristotle   26, 27
'Asiatic Superstitions'   22
Athenaeum   171

Baldick, Chris   30, 50
   ed. with Robert Morrison, *Tales of*
      Terror from Blackwood's
      Edinburgh Magazine   2, 19, 29,
      30, 34, 49, 50, 81
Barrow, John   130
Bell's Life in London   130, 131
Blackwood, William   31, 32, 49, 50
Blackwood's Edinburgh Magazine   2, 3,
      19, 21, 23–41, 44–64, 68, 70–1, 74,
      77–8, 81, 122–3
Bleiler, E. F.   104–5, 107
Bow Street   25, 107
   Foot Patrol   118
   Horse Patrol   118
Bow Street Runners   4, 22, 103–8,
      110, 117–18, 122, 137–9,
      154, 165
Braddon, M. E.   102, 171
   Lady Audley's Secret   102, 171
broadside illustrations   10
broadside verses   10–11
broadsides   2, 3, 6–24, 29, 31–2,
      35–43, 51, 66, 83, 103, 105, 127,
      131, 137, 139, 149, 158, 161
Bulwer-Lytton, Edward   29,
      32, 111
   Paul Clifford   29

capital punishment, criticism of   66,
      79–83, 85, 100
Carlton Chronicle   133

case structure, development of   3, 46,
      48–9, 60, 76, 97, 101, 106, 115,
      141, 156
Catnach, 'Jemmy'   12, 16–17, 131–2
'Cautionary Hints to Speculators on
      the Increase of Crimes'   33, 44
Chadwick, Edwin   124
Chambers, William   74
Chambers's Edinburgh Journal   4, 47,
      68, 74, 76–8, 80, 82, 84, 86–7, 90,
      97–8, 100–1, 129, 140, 142–6,
      148–50, 153–4, 159–62
Chartism   78
Chartist petitions   78
Chartist riots   98
Christie, Agatha   43, 82
circumstantial evidence   19, 42–4,
      71–4, 75–6, 78, 79–89, 101, 155
Cleave, John   127
Cleave's Weekly Police Gazette   127–8,
      149
Cobb, Belton   115, 137
cocks   12–15, 31
Collins, Philip   134, 160–1
Collins, Wilkie   32, 102, 105, 164,
      168, 171–2
   The Moonstone   164, 168, 172
   The Woman in White   168, 171
Colquhoun, Patrick   119–21
   Treatise on the Commerce and Police of
      the River Thames   121
   Treatise on the Police of the Metropolis
      119
'Committal of Thompson, William,
      for the Murder of His Wife and
      Three Children'   13
'Confessions/Reminiscences of an
      Attorney'   47, 53, 67, 70, 78,
      97–102
   'Bigamy or No Bigamy'   100
   'The Chest of Drawers'   101
   'Every Man His Own Lawyer'
      100–1

'The Incendiary' 101
'Jane Eccles' 100
'The Life Policy' 98–100
'The Puzzle' 101
Conrad, Joseph 32
Cooper, Thomas 138
Courvoisier, François 72
Criminal Investigation Department 172
Crowe, Catherine 93
  Susan Hopley; or, Circumstantial Evidence 93
Curtis, Robert 170
  The Irish Police Officer 170

De Quincey, Thomas 3, 21–8, 34, 49
  'The Avenger' 24
  Collected Works of 28
  'The Household Wreck' 24
  'Murder as One of the Fine Arts' 27
  'On Murder Considered as One of the Fine Arts' 3, 24–7
  'On the Knocking on the Gate in Macbeth' 24
  'Postscript' 28
Delf, Thomas 170
  Diary of an Ex-Detective 170
  The Detective's Notebook 170
The Detective: A Journal of Social Evils 98
detective police, establishment of 137–40
The Detective's Notebook, see under Delf, Thomas; Martel, Charles
DeVries, Duane 130
Dickens, Charles 4, 20, 29, 40, 46, 102–3, 106, 130–6, 139, 149, 158–71
  Bleak House 102, 167–8, 171
  'A "Detective" Police Party' (Parts I and II) 164–5, 167
  'Down with the Tide' 164
  'Metropolitan Protectives' 164
  Oliver Twist 134
  'On Duty with Inspector Field' 164, 167
  Pickwick Papers 130
  Sketches by Boz, Illustrative of Every-Day Life and Every-Day

People – incorporating 'Scenes', 'Street Scenes', 'Sketches', 'Street Sketches', 'Sketches of London' 4, 130–6; 'Criminal Courts' (or The Old Bailey) 134–5; 'Early Coaches' 133; 'The First of May' 133; 'Gin Shops' 134; 'The Last Cab-Driver and the First Omnibus Cad' 133; 'Meditation in Monmouth Street' 132; 'Scotland Yard' 131; 'Seven Dials' 131; 'Shops and Their Tenants' 131; 'The Streets—Morning' 131; 'The Streets—Night' 131; 'A Visit to Newgate' 134
'Three "Detective" Anecdotes' 164, 166
'Dissection and Exposure of the Criminals, Chennel and Calcraft' 22
Doyle, Arthur Conan 1, 47, 105, 114–15, 147, 168, 172
  A Study in Scarlet 47, 172
'Dreadful Murder at Newington' 22
Drexler, Peter 50, 78, 117
Dunlop, C. R. B. 46

Edinburgh Review 32
Eliot, George 32
Emsley, Clive 110
Evening Chronicle 130–4
'The Experiences of a Barrister' 47, 53, 67, 70, 73–87, 89–90, 92–3, 95–102, 106, 142, 160, 172
  'The Accommodation Bill' 84
  'Circumstantial Evidence' 87, 89
  'The Contested Marriage' 90, 92–3, 98, 100
  'Esther Mason' 77, 82, 84, 85, 100
  'The March Assize' 70
  'The Marriage Settlement' 90, 95
  'The Northern Circuit' 70
  'The Refugee' 77, 86–7
  'The Second Marriage' 86
  'The Writ of Habeas Corpus' 90, 92–3, 95, 99

Ferret, Mr   89–99, 168, 172
Fielding, Henry   118
Fielding, John   118–19
    Plan for Preventing Robberies Within
        Twenty Miles of London   119
Flint, Mr   98, 100–2
Fonblanque, J. S. M.   34–5, 37, 44
    with Paris, J. A., *Medical*
        Jurisprudence   34
'The Forgers'   40–2
Forrester, Andrew Jnr   170–1
    The Female Detective   170
    Revelations of a Private Detective   170
    Secret Service, or Recollections of a City
        Detective   170
Foucault, Michel   4
Francis, John   138
Fraser's Magazine   21, 32

Gaboriau, Émile   105, 172
Gall, Dr Franz Joseph   36
gallows literature   14
Galt, John   34
    'The Buried Alive'   34
Gaspey, Thomas   107, 141
Gatrell, V. A. C.   8, 15, 18
'The Gendarmerie'   125
General Instruction Book   122, 137
Goddard, Henry   138
    Memoirs of a Bow Street Runner   138
Good, Daniel   138
Gordon Riots   118
Gouldsborough, Robert   72
Graham, Sir James   138
Greenacre, James   15–16

Harriott, John   120–1
Hayward, W. S.   171
    The Experiences of a Lady
        Detective   170–1
'Hints for Jurymen'   34–5
Household Words   160–4, 167
Hughes, Michael   7
Huntley, William   72

Inwood, Stephen   135

James, Louis   142
John Bull   127–8

Kayman, Martin   141
Knight, Stephen   1, 40, 170

Lamb, Charles   39
Laqueur, Thomas   8, 12, 16
'The Last Man'   33
Law Library   69
Law Review   72
Law Society   69
'The Life, Trial, Character and
    Confession: The Man that was
    Hanged in Front of Newgate, and
    Who is Now Alive!'   31
'The Life, Trial, Confession and
    Execution of James
    Greenacre'   16
Lindop, Grevel   28
    The Opium-Eater: A Life of Thomas
        De Quincey   28
Literary Gazette   107
'The Liverpool Tragedy'   13
London Magazine   21

McLevy, James   171
    Curiosities of Crime in Edinburgh   171
    The Sliding Scale of Life: or, Thirty
        Years' Observations of Falling Men
        and Women in Edinburgh   171
McNaughten rules   85
MacNish, Robert   36–7
    'An Execution in Paris'   36
Maginn, William   33
'The Man in the Bell'   33
Manning murder   166
Marine Police Institution/
    Establishment   120–1
Martel, Charles, *see under* Delf, Thomas
Masson, David   28
Mayhew, Henry   6–10, 13, 20
    London Labour and the London Poor   6
Mayne, Richard   115, 122, 128, 137,
    156, 159
Mayo, Robert D.   32
Medical Jurisprudence, see under Paris, J. A.,
    MD; Fonblanque, J. S. M.
men
    as negative role models   61–7
    as positive role models   56, 67,
        144–5, 158

Metropolitan Police, *see under*
New Metropolitan Police
Metropolitan Police Museum 136
The Mirror of Parliament 130
Monthly Magazine 130
Monthly Review 107
Morning Chronicle 130–2, 134, 148
Morning Herald 62, 104, 115,
125, 148
Morning Journal 125
Morning Post 148
Morrison, Robert, *see under* Baldick,
Chris
'Most Interesting Charges of Child
Murder' 22
'Mysterious Case: Murder of Margaret
Flood' 22

National Review 8
New Metropolitan Police 4, 67, 69,
97, 103–5, 115–17, 119, 121–31,
135–40, 143, 156, 158, 167
New Monthly Magazine 32, 125
'The New Police' 125–6
Newgate Calendar 2, 3, 9, 20–1, 40–1,
43, 103, 115, 151, 161, 169
Newgate Novels 21, 29, 40, 103, 149
Newgate Prison 10, 14, 16, 61, 66, 85
'Noctes Ambrosiae' 24
North, Christopher 25, 70

Old Bailey 10, 26, 39
Ordinary of Newgate 2, 3, 7
Accounts 2, 3, 7
Ousby, Ian 141
'Outrage & Murder on a Little Child at
Purfleet' 10

Paris, J. A., MD 34–5, 37, 44
see also under Fonblanque, J. S. M.
'Passages from the Diary of a Late
Physician', *see under* Warren,
Samuel
Peace Preservation Act (1814) 119
Peel, Robert 115, 118–19, 126, 159
Peelers 126
penny-a-liners 11, 165
Pitts, Johnny 131–2
Plumtree, A. S. 27

Poe, Edgar Allan 1, 3, 35, 51, 72, 93,
105, 154, 166–8, 172
'The Murders in the Rue
Morgue' 167
'The Mystery of Marie Rogêt' 72
'The Purloined Letter' 154
police complaints procedure 136
Police Gazette 148
'Police Orders' 155
Pollit, Charles 23
Poor Law Amendment Act
(1834) 127
Port of London 119–21
Pringle, Patrick 104, 138
Punch 117

Radzinowicz, Sir Leon 136
Railway Police 138
Ratcliffe Highway Murders 24, 27–8
Recollections of a Detective Police-Officer,
see under Russell, William
'Recollections of a Police Officer',
see under Russell, William
Resurrection Men 55
'Richmond, Tom' 106–17, 128, 141,
153–5, 166, 169
Richmond: Scenes in the Life of a Bow
Street Runner, Drawn Up from His
Private Memoranda 104–15, 128,
140–1, 143–4, 148, 152, 156–8
river police 120
Robinson, David 122–6
'The Local Government of the
Metropolis, and Other Populous
Places' 122–5, 126
Romilly, Sir Samuel 39, 77, 85
Rowan, Charles 115, 122, 128,
156, 159
Royal College of Physicians 48
Russell, William 4, 62, 129, 140–4,
148–50, 153–4, 159, 162, 167,
169, 170, 172
Autobiography of an English
Detective 170
Experiences of a Real Detective 170
as 'Waters', *Recollections of a*
Detective Police Officer 141, 172
as 'Waters', 'Recollections of a Police
Officer', serialised in *Chambers's*

Russell, William – *continued*
    Edinburgh Journal   4, 62, 78, 106,
      129; 'Flint Jackson'   147–8, 150;
      'Guilty or Not Guilty'   149–50,
      154; 'Legal Metamorphoses'
      144, 156; 'Mary Kingsford'
      145–6, 148, 150; 'The
      Monomaniac'   143, 145–6,
      156; 'One Night in a
      Gaming-House'   150, 152,
      156; 'The Partner'   150–2, 156,
      166; 'The Pursuit'   146, 156;
      'The Revenge'   145–6, 156;
      'The Twins'   145, 152–3, 156;
      'The Widow'   145; 'XYZ'   148,
      151, 155

St Sepulchre   10, 14, 16, 66
Sala, George   104
Sandford, Daniel Keyte   33
    'A Night in the Catacombs'   33
    'The Scarborough Tragedy'   13
Scotland Yard   131, 139, 165
Sharp, Mr   97–102, 172
Sherlock Holmes   1, 3, 35, 47, 93,
      113, 147, 167–8, 172–3
'Shocking Rape and Murder of Two
      Lovers'   13
social class, significance of   8–9,
      20–39, 48, 64–6, 68–9, 74–5,
      86, 109–13, 122–5, 142, 144–5,
      149–54, 158–60
Society of Friends   85
Stewart, R. F.   138, 141
The Strand Magazine   172
Surr, Thomas Skinner   107

Tait's Magazine   21
*Tales of Terror from Blackwood's
    Edinburgh Magazine*   3, 19, 28, 30,
      34, 48, 50, 81
    see also under Baldick, Chris
Thackeray, William M.   20
Thames River Police   164
Thomson, Henry   31, 34, 38–9, 64
    'Le Revenant'   31, 34, 38–40, 64
Thurtell, John   10
The Times   125–6, 130,
      138–9, 147

Trollope, Anthony   32
True Sun   130

Vidocq, Eugène François   1
    Memoirs of Vidocq   1

Warren, Samuel   3, 29, 42, 45–7,
      49–56, 61, 64, 67–74, 76–7, 79, 80,
      105–6, 160
    'The Bracelets'   50
    *Miscellanies Critical, Imaginative, and
      Juridical*, Vols I and II   46
    'My First Circuit: Law and Facts
      from the North'   70, 76, 80
    'The Mystery of Murder and its
      Defence'   72, 76
    Now and Then   178n7
    'Passages from the Diary of a Late
      Physician', published serially
      in *Blackwood's Edinburgh
      Magazine*   49–68; 'Cancer'
      54–5; 'Consumption'   54;
      'Death at the Toilet'   57–8;
      'The Dentist and the
      Comedian'   54; 'Duelling'   54;
      'Early Struggles'   50, 53;
      'The Forger'   64, 67;
      'Grave Doings'   55;
      'Introduction'   51–2;
      'The Magdalen'   58–60;
      'A Man about Town'   62–4;
      'The Merchant's Clerk'   60;
      'Mother and Son'   61–2, 86;
      'Preface by the Translator'
      (German edition)   52;
      'Preparing for the House'   54;
      'Resurrection Men'   55; 'Rich
      and Poor'   55; 'A Scholar's
      Deathbed'   54; 'A Slight
      Cold'   55; 'The Spectral
      Dog—An Illusion'   54;
      'The Turned Head'   54, 60;
      'The Wife'   54, 60
    *A Popular and Practical Introduction to
      Law Studies*   69
    Ten Thousand a Year   178n7
    'Who is the Murderer? A Problem in
      the Law of Circumstantial
      Evidence'   71–2, 74, 76, 80

'Waters', *see under* Russell, William
Weekly Dispatch 138
Welch, Saunders 119
  Observations on the Office of
    Constable 119
Westmorland Gazette 21–3,
  26, 34
White, Charles Thomas, execution
  of 17–18
Wiener, Martin J. 20
Wight, John 104, 161
  More Mornings at Bow Street 161
  Mornings at Bow Street 104, 161
Wild, Jonathan 105
Wills, W. H. 162–4

'The Modern Science of
  Thief-Taking' 162–4
Wilson, John 23, 25, 29, 37, 40, 42,
  49, 50
  'Expiation' 29, 40, 42–3, 78
  'Extracts from Gosschen's
    Diary' 29, 30, 37, 38, 43
Wilson, John Gleeson, execution
  of 14–15
women
  as negative role models 56–60
  as positive role models 55, 60–1,
    144–7, 158
Wordsworth, William 21
Wright, Sampson 118